continued . . .

A Gathering of Saints

"A baroque, delightfully gruesome serial-killer whodunit set in WWII London. . . . Hyde accomplishes a superb turn with his latest. . . . Well-researched, relentlessly grim, and remarkably evocative of its time and place."
—*Kirkus Reviews*

"Densely atmospheric. . . . Hyde's scrupulous research and deep knowledge of the political realities surrounding the Blitz make his story utterly convincing. . . . The procedural elements are perfect . . . with scenes of ghastly carnage rendered so crisply that one can almost smell the fear and death. . . . Readers who relish the raw truth of human, and inhuman, history will find here what they are looking for."
—*Publishers Weekly*

"What a read! . . . All the force of an exploding bomb."
—*The Herald-American* (Syracuse, NY)

"A gripping combination of history, spy story, and mystery. . . . Unrelentingly readable and vividly realistic. . . . Life outside this captivating book simply ceases."
—*Ottawa Citizen*

"Brilliantly realized and compulsively readable . . . [with] a jolt of malice and mayhem."
—*Maclean's*

"[Hyde] draws tension with the skill of a surgeon. A story that grips you with its characters, action and surprises, then won't let go, even after you turn out the light."
—*New York Times* bestselling author Michael Connelly

Wisdom of the Bones

"Extensive historical research. . . . Hyde manages to capture the essence of a changing world."
—*Publishers Weekly*

"Absorbing and atmospheric. . . . Author Hyde is a deft plotter who deserves considerably more attention than he receives."
—*January Magazine*

"A rich and entertaining police procedural . . . engrossing. . . . With a dark conclusion that resembles something from *Silence of the Lambs* . . . well worth the read."
—*I Love a Mystery*

Novels by Christopher Hyde

The Jane Todd Series

THE SECOND ASSASSIN

THE HOUSE OF SPECIAL PURPOSE

AN AMERICAN SPY

WISDOM OF THE BONES

Published by New American Library

AN
AMERICAN SPY

Christopher Hyde

A SIGNET BOOK

SIGNET
Published by New American Library, a division of
Penguin Group (USA) Inc., 375 Hudson Street,
New York, New York 10014, USA
Penguin Group (Canada), 10 Alcorn Avenue, Toronto,
Ontario M4V 3B2, Canada (a division of Pearson Penguin Canada Inc.)
Penguin Books Ltd., 80 Strand, London WC2R 0RL, England
Penguin Ireland, 25 St. Stephen's Green, Dublin 2,
Ireland (a division of Penguin Books Ltd.)
Penguin Group (Australia), 250 Camberwell Road, Camberwell, Victoria 3124,
Australia (a division of Pearson Australia Group Pty. Ltd.)
Penguin Books India Pvt. Ltd., 11 Community Centre, Panchsheel Park,
New Delhi - 110 017, India
Penguin Group (NZ), cnr Airborne and Rosedale Roads, Albany,
Auckland 1310, New Zealand (a division of Pearson New Zealand Ltd.)
Penguin Books (South Africa) (Pty.) Ltd., 24 Sturdee Avenue,
Rosebank, Johannesburg 2196, South Africa

Penguin Books Ltd., Registered Offices:
80 Strand, London WC2R 0RL, England

First published by Signet, an imprint of New American Library,
a division of Penguin Group (USA) Inc.

First Printing, May 2005
10 9 8 7 6 5 4 3 2 1

REGISTERED TRADEMARK—MARCA REGISTRADA

Printed in the United States of America

For Mariea, with all my love,
and to the memory of John Buchan,
whose writing started me on the long road
from Number 7, Rideau Gate

Every man, at the bottom of his heart, believes he is a born detective.

—John Buchan,
The Power House, chapter 2, 1916

Prologue

Newly minted War Correspondent Jane Todd sat in the cramped bombardier's seat of the B-17, munched on a very stale cheese-and-onion sandwich and stared out into the night. The four big Wright Cyclone engines thundered, shaking every rivet in the plane as well as her back teeth. The outside of the Plexiglas turret was crazed with frost. Jane was colder than she'd ever thought possible. She was wearing a heavily insulated flight suit, a borrowed leather flying jacket with the name *Daddy's Little Princess* on the back, three pairs of socks, two pairs of long johns, heated flight boots and two more pairs of socks stuffed in her bra. After finishing her sandwich, she shivered, popped an old stick of Beeman's in her mouth, and replaced the oxygen mask over her face, all the while wondering what the hell she was doing twenty thousand feet over Greenland in the middle of the night.

"Where the hell are we?" she bellowed.

Crabs Leslie, the copilot, bellowed back at her from a few feet above. "No idea! Ask Snake!"

Snake was Sidney "The Snake" Kerzner, the navigator. Sidney looked like an accountant and was heir to the Kerzner Junkyard fortune in Jamaica, New York, but now that he was in the Army Air Force he preferred to be called Snake for some reason. According to Crabs he'd also learned how to spit. Jane had no idea how Crabs had got his nickname and she didn't want to know.

"An hour out of Bluie West One," called out Snake in his reedy little voice. When they'd left Gander, Newfoundland, on the second leg of their ferry flight to England, Jane had been informed that Bluie West One was a single airstrip tucked in between two long, completely frozen fjords and flanked by a pair of spiky mountains that barely accommodated the wingspan of a B-17. It was the radio beacon that guided them toward Prestwick and the only civilization for a thousand miles in either direction. If they were an hour out of Bluie West One, that meant they were three hours shy of their refueling stop in Iceland. Since *Daddy's Little Princess* was on a ferry run she was flying with only pilot, copilot, radio operator and navigator. She carried no bombs, and in place of waist guns she carried extra gas tanks. Not only was the plane freezing, it also stank of kerosene and Crab's feet, the odor of which seemed to transcend every other malodorous thing in the world.

Suddenly there was a sound like tearing cloth and Jane saw a line of brilliant white light arcing toward them out of the darkness. In between the white there were faint traces of bright blue. Something hammered into the outer port-side engine and it turned instantly into a ball of flame.

"*Shit!*" screamed Crabs. The plane tilted nauseatingly onto its right side and dropped at least fifty feet like a plunging anchor. Directly in front of her

Jane had the brief impression of a massive, glistening hornet, nose gleaming in the pale moonlight. A flicker out of the corner of her eye resolved itself into the tail of another aircraft, this one bearing a large black swastika against a ghostly white-and-gray camouflage pattern.

"Fokker, Fokker Fokker!" screamed Kerzner, wailing out the name like some horrified expletive. Another rip of 20 mm cannon fire tore through the center of the aircraft and Kerzner exploded all over the radio room upstairs, a spraying gout of blood and tissue flushing down into the bombardier's station, covering Jane. All she could think about was that Kerzner had been wrong; it wasn't a Fokker at all, it was a Focke-Wulf 190, the ten of diamonds in the deck of Spotter cards she carried in her duffel bag.

"Shit shit shit!" said Crabs again, as though everything was said in terrified threes now, the port-side engine like a torch blown back by a hurricane wind, eating away the wing as Jane tried to blink Snake Kerzner's remains out of her eyes. She smashed herself back against the Plexiglas bubble, a quarter inch of freezing plastic between her and the frigid arctic darkness and the single, horrifying specter of a German Fw190 where it couldn't possibly be.

Jane reached out and grabbed the long red handle of the chin turret gun to drag herself back into her seat, letting out a howling spray of machine-gun and tracer fire from the twin fifties below her, marking their spinning path toward the barren, icy landscape far below. Jane dug the old Leica out from the depths of her flight suit and was now snapping away at the horror all around her.

Out of the corner of her eye, Jane spotted the

wraithlike shape of the German fighter bearing down on them again. She dropped her camera, grabbed the red firing lever and swung it around, punching the firing button as she did so, sending an arcing line of tracers across the sky, sweeping across the other aircraft like a paintbrush whitewashing a fence. The other plane jerked and pitched out of the way, vanishing as quickly as it had appeared. There was a deep, throaty cough from the left and Jane saw that both the left engines were out now. The two on the right didn't sound so hot either.

"Fuck!" said Crabs, back to single-word panic now. "Manifold pressure's falling!"

Jane grabbed her camera and crawled up behind the pilot's position. Snake was everywhere, not a piece of him bigger than the span of her hand. An eye connected to something else by some long, stringy, white things was swinging from the overhead hand supports like some insane voodoo doll. Jane knew that if she wasn't so scared she'd be throwing up about now. The back of Crabs's seat and his neck and shoulders were soaked with Snake's remains as well. Trying not to look, she swung around and into the empty navigator's seat.

"What, what what!?" yelled Crabs, back to three words again. Jane could see that the two starboard engines were struggling, sparks spitting into the night from both of them.

"Can we make it?" yelled Jane. The howling of the wind from the hole in the plane was enormously loud.

"Make what?! We're fucking going to crash, that's what we're going to make!" He dragged hard on the controls, desperately trying to level off the sluggish machine.

"Get on the fucking radio! Call Air-Sea Rescue!"

"The radio went with Snake I think."

"Shit, fuck, piss and corruption!" That was a new one. Jane figured it was a Midwestern thing since, as she recalled, Crabs came from Kansas. Toto territory, tornadoes and witches and yellow brick roads and Judy Garland with her tits strapped down. Jeez! That must have been painful; it was a wonder she could sing wrapped up in all that Ace bandage. Jane was crazy now, of course, and knew she was going to die in the next few seconds, but she put the viewfinder to her eye and took a couple of quick shots of Crabs in the deathly green light from the instruments. She spoke, just a split second before they struck: "Did you know that the Tin Woodsman's name was actually Hickory, and that the Cowardly Lion was Zeke?"

Crabs looked at her, then looked away, his teeth clenched, his flying helmet squashed down around his head, the ear flaps jumping up and down in the wind at his back, and then they tipped over on one wheel and the world filled with the sound of *Daddy's Little Princess* being torn apart in the ice and snow. Vaguely, Jane was aware that Crabs was no longer sitting beside her. In fact she wasn't sitting beside anybody. Things went black.

When she woke up a pleasant, smiling Eskimo was staring down at her in the morning light and saying something that sounded a little bit like *tupaksimayok, erkromayok ikkiertok inerkonartok.* At which point she knew she was alive, which was more than she could have expected.

Part One

SWAN HILL

One

The plain, three-storied country house looked very much out of place among the dripping pines around it; a bloody-minded statement in granite about man's inevitable triumph over nature, the arrogance of the heavy Norman towers on either side of the narrow doorway muted with an overgrowth of ivy. By English standards Charlton House was small, no more than twenty rooms, set on fifty acres or so of gently rolling woodland a mile or so to the east of Cheltenham in the Cotswolds.

The house stood at the top of a circular gravel driveway, the Stars and Stripes hanging limply from a flagpole on the front lawn, the red, white and blue a startling splash of bright color against the dull green of the trees and the ivy and the drizzling pewter of the lowering September sky.

Black on white, a freshly painted sign rammed into a dark, wet bed of earth to the right of the door announced that this was now the home of BOTJAG, Branch Office of the Judge Advocate General in the United Kingdom. From Charlton House, Brigadier General Lawrence H. Hedrick, acting under authority of the Visiting Forces Act, would prosecute crimes committed in the United Kingdom by members of the United States military and naval forces in the European Theater of Operations.

A black Vauxhall taxicab rolled slowly up the drive, tires crunching wetly on the gravel. It stopped opposite the front door of the house and a tall blond woman stepped out dressed in a perfectly cut "pinks and greens" uniform including one of the newly issued knee-length belted raincoats that most of the officers were wearing now. There was a U.S. War Correspondent woven badge on her forage cap and another one on the left breast pocket of her blouse. The entire uniform, including the trenchcoat, had been tailor-made for her at Luxenberg's in New York, a last indulgence before leaving the States. Her name was Jane Todd and she was a floater, working freelance for no particular newspaper or magazine and with the power to assign herself to almost any unit, a power often not appreciated by her fellow correspondents or the unit in which she was interested. Friends in high places was usually the rumor, but none of them guessed how high those places really were.

Jane ducked back into the taxi to retrieve her duffel bag, then paid off the driver in the unfamiliar currency she'd been issued after landing at Prestwick the previous day. Windshield wipers clacking, the taxi drove off and the woman hoisted the duffel. She went up the short flight of steps, banged the wrought-iron ring knocker on the darkly painted door, pushed the door open and stepped into the building.

The front hall was gloomy except for the small pool of light cast by a gooseneck lamp on the old

wooden desk directly in front of her. A clerk-corporal
sat at the desk, working the keys of a big office Un-
derwood. Behind the clerk, barely visible in the dim
light, the woman could see a long flight of stairs
leading up to the next floor. The hallway around her
and the wall of the staircase were paneled with dark
oak wainscoting, waist high. There was a candelabra
chandelier high over the clerk's head, but it was
unlit. The floor of the hall was a marble harlequin
pattern of diamonds in black and white, just like the
sign outside. There were file boxes piled everywhere.

"Jane Todd to see General Hedrick."

The clerk looked up from her typing. "Put your
duffel down over there and go right in, ma'am." She
gestured toward a heavy wooden bench to Jane's
right. Beside the bench there was a massive ele-
phant's foot umbrella stand and beside the umbrella
stand there was a high, darkly stained door. "You're
late," the clerk-corporal added dryly as Jane dropped
the heavy bag onto the bench. "You should have
been here two days ago."

"I was unavoidably detained," she explained. She
stripped off her trenchcoat, draped it over the duffel
bag and spent a few seconds doing what she could
to straighten out her rumpled uniform. When she
was done she poked at her hair a little, then knocked
on the door.

"Enter," said a voice. Jane did so. The room was a
half circle, occupying the base of one of the Norman
towers, wainscoted like the hall outside. At one end
of the room there was a desk flanked by the flags of
the United States and the Judge Advocate General's
Corps, a chair in front of the desk and a chair behind

it. The room was equipped with a glowing coal fire. The large triple windows looked out over the sign and the circular driveway. Between the windows and the desk there was a large, worn rug laid out across a glowing, cherry-hued hardwood floor.

The man seated behind the desk was wearing the uniform of a brigadier general but the round, pleasant face and the steel-rimmed glasses belonged to someone who looked more like a schoolteacher than an assistant judge advocate. Jane stepped up to the desk and came to attention. "Jane Todd, sir. I've been attached to your organization for the moment."

"You're late," said the general, his voice pleasant.

"Yes, sir. So I've been informed."

"Sit down," said the general. He pointed to the chair in front of the desk. Jane sat. "Presumably there is a reason for your tardiness."

"Yes, sir."

"And what would that reason be, Miss Todd?"

"We were shot down by a German fighter an hour out of Bluie West One."

"There are no German fighters that far out."

"This one was—two-tone gray paint job."

"Exciting."

"Not really, sir. Just cold."

"You were rescued relatively quickly?"

"Yes, sir. The next morning. Had to spend two more days in Reykjavik waiting for another B-17 to take us on to Prestwick. It'll make a good story eventually."

"Well, you're here now," said the general. "Fixed up with a room yet?"

"Yes, sir," Jane said. "The Lilley Brook I think it's

called." She was looking forward to the first good night's sleep since leaving Presque Isle, Maine, almost a week before.

"You have a tan," said the general, smiling lightly. "You didn't get that in Iceland." The smile broadened. "And certainly not in Scotland."

"No, sir. Los Angeles."

"You went to the provost marshal general's school at Fort Oglethorpe. Did one of your stories there as well."

"Yes, sir. I was interested in military law and criminal investigation."

"Purvis is teaching there, yes?"

"Yes, sir." Melvin Purvis, "The Man Who Got Dillinger," had gone from FBI agent to lieutenant colonel and teacher. Jane had quickly come to the conclusion that the man was a pompous fool who didn't know the first thing about criminal investigation. From her previous experiences she didn't have much respect for the Boss G-man himself, J. Edgar Hoover.

"Not the gung ho type, presumably."

"You mean Colonel Purvis, sir?" Jane asked blandly.

"I meant you."

"I'm not sure what you mean, sir."

"No interest in joining a combat unit. Writing under fire." He made the word writing sound like something only cowards did. Jane glanced at the campaign ribbons on the left chest of the general's tunic. Everything from the Army of Cuban Pacification to the 1918 Occupation of Germany ribbon, not to mention half a dozen silver Victory Medal clasps. Hedrick hadn't built his whole career behind a desk.

Jane kept her voice even. "When the times comes I'll join a combat unit. So far we haven't been doing much fighting over here."

"I see."

"I hope you do, sir. I didn't come over here to write about girls making do without silk stockings."

The general looked at Jane, a thoughtful expression on his plain, round face. "Is this your first time in England?"

"Yes, sir."

"What do you think so far?"

"It rains a lot, the trains are crowded, the sandwiches are terrible, and the cars and trucks drive on the wrong side of the road."

"My point exactly," said the general, leaning back in his chair.

"What point would that be, sir?" Jane asked.

"To them it's not the wrong side of the road, it's the right side."

"I don't quite understand."

"The British are sensitive, especially where we're concerned."

"We?"

"Americans. We think we're pulling their irons out of the fire, they think we're Johnny-come-latelies, just like the last war. We've been at war for less than a year. They've been at it for three. They think they've been bullied into letting us prosecute our own men under military law rather than in their civil courts."

"Have they?" Jane asked flatly.

"Have they what?"

"Been bullied."

The general's eyes flashed behind the schoolteacher

spectacles. "That would depend," he said quietly, "on how you looked at it."

"And how are we looking at it?" asked Jane.

"Sensitively," the general answered.

"Sensitively." Jane repeated the word, trying to figure out exactly what the general was getting at, and failing.

"Yes," said the general. "At the moment we are a very small group with a great deal to do. I only have seven officers on staff, all of whom are overworked already."

Jane nodded. "Yes, sir." In other words, she thought, "I want you as far away as I can get you."

"Within a few weeks I'll have a full complement of men, administrators, prosecutors and investigators from the Criminal Investigation Department. None of these people have the training necessary for dealing with problems that are of a . . . sensitive nature."

"What exactly do you mean by 'sensitive'?" asked Jane.

"Those problems which cannot be considered run-of-the-mill," said the general, still evading the question. "Most of the crimes we deal with will concern petty issues; pilfering, barroom battery, trading in cigarettes and the like. From time to time we will almost certainly face more serious crimes, just as we did in the last war: specifically, desertion, murder and rape." He paused. "We have prepared for this and so have the civil authorities. This office has already established a direct liaison with the British courts as well as Scotland Yard."

"But . . ." said Jane.

"But indeed," replied the general. He paused

again, pushing a small silver box across the desk toward Jane. "Smoke if you like."

"Thank you." Jane took a Lucky out of the silver box and lit it with the plain Zippo she'd picked up at Fort Oglethorpe.

"We have a small, special investigative unit here to look into such sensitive crimes." He looked down at her file. "Since you seem to have some experience in these matters, Colonel Donovan thought perhaps you might find Major Dundee's group of interest."

"Dundee?"

"Lucas Alexander Decimus Dundee." The general cleared his throat. "Comes from your neck of the woods actually. Los Angeles. Used to work for the district attorney's office there."

"Burton Fitts?" asked Jane. Fitts was one of the most corrupt municipal politicians who'd ever taken graft.

"Dundee quit the office," said the general. "From what I hear, that is a mark in his favor." He slid a large manila envelope across the desk. It had a string winder and a blob of sealing wax on it. Blue sealing wax. "This is his file. Normally I wouldn't hand it out to a . . . person such as yourself, but you seem to have some powerful friends." He made a waving gesture. "Read it when you have the time."

"So where do I find this Major Dundee?"

"A country property called Strathmere about fifty miles northwest of London. Not far from a little village called Swan Hill."

The man with the European accent smiled happily as he placed the object in its velvet-lined case. The small forge hissed, the open square of the brick-lined box sending out a flickering light across the gloomy length of the warehouse. As the man smiled, the hot light flickered off his thick glasses and the solid gold of his left incisor.

"It is done at last. You pay me now, yes?"

"You bet," said the man in the American colonel's uniform. "First we've got to get you and our little surprise here back to London."

"That is no problem. I catch one of the late trains. The station is quite close by."

"Don't be ridiculous," said The Colonel. "You did the United States Army a great service and we want to return the favor. Car's just outside."

"As you wish, Colonel. It is most kind."

The Colonel gestured to a junior officer who had been standing by. He was holding the uniform of a lieutenant in the Eighth Army Air Force.

"Would you mind putting this on?" asked The Colonel

"I do not understand," said the man.

"Just a little more cloak and dagger. We're under strict orders here—secrecy, loose lips sink ships, that kind of thing." The Colonel smiled pleasantly.

"I see," said the man, although it was perfectly obvious that he didn't. It took him a few minutes but he changed into the uniform. The junior officer picked up the man's civilian clothes and put them in a paper bag. The Colonel lowered the heat on the forge until the blue gas flame sputtered and went out. The interior of the hot box glowed cherry red. All three went out of the warehouse into the cool evening air, The Colonel carrying the velvet-lined box. The junior officer got behind the wheel of a drab Army-issue Chevrolet sedan. The Colonel and the man in the army air force uniform climbed into the back. The Colonel looked at the heavy gold watch on his wrist.

"Good," he said. "Almost time for the ten ten from Cambridge."

"I thought you said we were not taking the train?" said the man with the European accent.

"We're not," The Colonel answered and patted the man reassuringly on the knee. The car started up and they headed into the darkness.

TWO

The following morning brought overcast skies but no rain and, after a light breakfast and against the better judgment of everyone she talked to, the young woman chose to get herself to Swan Hill, appropriating a courier's olive drab jeep from the Charlton House motor pool. She'd never driven on the left-hand side of the road but, as far as she was concerned, anything was better than another interminable, somewhat smelly and claustrophobic train ride like the one she'd had coming down from Prestwick. With her duffel bag in the backseat, armed with a red cloth bound 3-to-1 Road Atlas and a saddlebag lunch packed for her by the hotel, she set off just after ten in the morning.

She managed to get lost within the first hour, which wasn't surprising when you considered that all road signs had been removed in case of invasion years ago, but she pressed on, astounded by the suicidal narrowness of the roads, which made the side you chose to drive on of no importance whatsoever, and equally surprised by how comfortable she felt in what was truly, at least to her, an utterly alien landscape.

Jane moved steadily east across Oxford, Buckingham and Bedford, thundering through towns and villages with names like Chipping, Tring and Leighton Buzzard, eventually striking slightly north through Buntingford, Baldock and Biggleswade, wondering if she'd somehow fallen into some child's wishing-dream; an ancient misty world of fairies and enchanters where dragons could be slain with swords fashioned on magic anvils in secret, glowing forges deep beneath the sleeping hills. She knew she was in a country in the throes of a terrible war, but it still felt as though she was in some fairy-tale land of her childhood where an elf could pop out from behind a tree at any moment and where the occasional troll lived under a bridge. This was the land of Arthur and Merlin and Robin Hood, and it was a hard feeling to forget.

Once, stopping to eat her lunch beside the road, she reached out and touched the stones of an old wall beside a stile that led out onto a small field and, just for a second, she thought she could faintly hear the past singing softly just underneath her hand. She smiled, cursing herself for a fool, then got back into the rattling jeep and continued on her way. She wasn't here to look for the arc of history, she was here to find a story. The job was the same as ever, only the scene of the crime was different.

By mid-afternoon, with the sky closing in again, Jane reached the small town of Royston in Cambridgeshire. Following her written instructions, she drove on for three miles until she reached the Bridgefoot Inn, a tumbledown old building with a large sign over its gloomy doorway advertising Reid's Ale. Just past the inn she swung the jeep left onto what the road atlas called a "B" road and headed north.

According to the instructions, her destination lay midway between the turn she'd just made and the village of Thriplow, four miles to the north. To left and right, beyond the trees and bramble hedges lining the road, she could see low hills and fields broken into odd shapes by ancient hedgerows, some planted with what appeared to be turnips, others left in grass for grazing sheep.

A minute or two after making the turn there was a shattering, deep-throated roar directly above her head and she ducked instinctively and squeezed the brake, nearly putting the jeep into the ditch. For a split second she caught sight of a flight of sharp-nosed Spitfires as they streamed up into the overcast, the brightly colored RAF roundels on their wings and fuselages like archer's targets. They were so low she could see the canvas patches over the machine-gun ports on the leading edges of the wings. Presumably there was a fighter squadron based nearby.

With the aircraft gone, Jane started up the jeep again and followed the road as it curved through a thick stand of beech trees, boughs bent so close over the road that in a larger car they'd be scratching against the side panels of the hood. "Bonnet," she said, correcting herself out loud, remembering the passage about language in *A Short Guide to Great Britain*, the pamphlet that had been her only reading material since leaving the U.S. The hood was a "bonnet," the trunk was a "boot," fenders were "wings" and a wrench was a "spanner." According to the guide book, gas was "petrol," a truck was a "lorry" and the sidewalk was really the "pavement." The money was even worse. Copper pennies the size of silver dollars, half crowns when there were no crowns—and mostly called two and six—and shillings called "bob" but never "bobs."

She came out of the small beech forest and brought the jeep to a halt again, this time intentionally. She got out and stretched her legs for a moment. In front of her, a long narrow valley opened up, the road dipping down with the trees still thick on her right, while to the left there were open, rolling fields, broken by a checkerboard of hedgerows, and low rises of land topped by lonely stands of trees.

At the bottom of the valley where the road dipped to its lowest point she could see a half-hidden village; red tile, thatch and dark slate roofs peeking out of trees and shrubbery, with the short, crenellated tower of an old Norman church the tallest building in sight. There was a brief flash of dark blue among the trees that had to be a river. Squinting, Jane thought she could see a narrower stream running at right angles to its larger brother. Just outside the village on the smaller stream Jane saw a large building set with a mill's undershot wheel, and she knew there'd be trout nearby, and probably pike as well.

All of this was lit with a burst of cool spring light that cut down through a ragged hole in the low-running clouds above, the light strongest on the ruins of an old abbey or castle that stood on a sharp rise above the village, bleak and cold like the broken stump of a dead and blackened tooth. Swan Hill. Jane shivered as a breeze brewed up from the valley, pushing at the grass in the fields and shimmering through the beech trees with the soft, ghostly sound her mother called Heaven's Breath.

Like everything else she'd seen so far in England, Swan Hill looked old and tired and down-at-heel, which was fair enough, all things considered.

The woman climbed into the jeep again and drove down into the village, the country road becoming the High Street. On the outskirts she saw a tall stone wall overgrown with ivy, and through a roofed linch-gate she spotted a large brick building surrounded by trees, almost surely a school. A few thatched cottages went by, left and right, and then she was into the village proper, cottages giving way to more substantial brick and stucco single- and two-story buildings, cheek by jowl, their signboards advertising Martin's Garage and Ironmonger, which looked as though it might once have been a blacksmith's forge, Granby Sweets and Leeming Bakery. There was a Boots Chemist, which Jane knew was really a drugstore, a Saddle Shop, a Fish Shop, a Butcher Shop and a Drapers. The street was deserted and the shops were all shuttered and closed.

Finally, at a crossroads there was the church she'd seen from the head of the valley, a large, faded sign identifying it as St. Magnus the Martyr. Kitty-corner to it on the far side of the dusty road there was a long, low, whitewashed building with a painted swinging sign above the door. The sign showed a medieval knight on a white horse, the cross on his shield identifying him as a crusader, the hacked-off heads of several dark-haired Saracens dangling from the pommel of his saddle. The name on the sign was THE JOURNEY TO JERUSALEM.

Jane slowed and pulled off the road, parking close to the side of the country pub. The people at Charlton House hadn't been exactly sure of where to go after reaching Swan Hill, but presumably someone in the pub could give her directions. According to the plain wooden board bolted to the wall beside the narrow door, the publican and proprietor was a man named Howard Blundel who was licensed to sell "Ale, Beer and Tobacco to be consumed on or off the premises." Bar, liquor store and smoke shop all in one. Jane got out of the car, straightened her uniform and prepared to meet her first real Brit, face-to-face.

She stepped through the door, ducking just in time to avoid smacking her head on a low beam just inside, and found herself in a long, narrow room with open doors at either end and a long, curving bar running its length. There were wooden stools at the bar and benches under a pair of half-curtained windows. The beams and woodwork in the room were dark painted oak, the ceiling was yellow plaster, and the floors were bare and made of enormous planks, each one at least eighteen inches wide.

Behind the bar, against the far wall, there were rows of casks, each one marked with its contents, port and sherry, with a bleak collection of dusty bottles on narrower shelves above. At the center of the bar the woman could see a trio of blue-and-white decorative porcelain beer pulls. Like the street outside, the bar was empty. The room smelled faintly of wood smoke and hops, and over all of it there were the dark scents of rotting plaster and mold.

Jane turned and went through the low door on the left, stumbling down an unexpected step into a low-ceilinged parlor. Two smaller windows were fully curtained in nicotine-stained cheesecloth, and on the plastered walls there was a row of framed game-fish prints. There was a massive fireplace around a hearth large enough to roast a side of beef, and several plain round tables together with comfortable-looking wooden armchairs. The wide-plank floors were partially covered by a scattering of thin rag rugs in stripes of muted color. On each of the tables there was a small vase filled with lilacs and an ashtray. To the right, against the wall, a narrow flight of stairs led steeply to the floor above. Like the bar, the parlor room was empty.

Taking a second look at the fireplace Jane noticed that above the mantel, set on wooden pegs, there were several long, tapered bamboo fly rods; and on the mantelpiece below them, a display of reels. Interested, she went over to examine them. After leaving New York it was the one thing she'd tried and found she loved—fly fishing in northern California and Colorado streams. She'd surprised herself by being good at it, and she'd done the best she could to learn as much about the sport as she could, even though she only considered herself a novice.

The top two rods were Hardy Brothers, one a J. J. Hardy Triumph, a three-piece trout rod, eight feet, nine inches long, the second an older Fairchild nine-footer. The bottom rod was a gigantic LRH Fairy Palakona, a two-handed salmon rod at least thirty years old and a good fourteen feet long. The reels on the mantel ranged from a J. W. Young Bedaux to an Ogden Smith Whitechurch with a sterling-silver drag adjuster. The rods and reels all appeared to be in perfect condition. An old, dark-varnished wicker creel with a leather strap hung from a peg on the side of the fireplace surround.

"Interested in fishing then, are you?"

Jane turned. A slight man with thinning gray hair

and a lean, lined and long-jawed face stood in the doorway that led back to the bar. In his mid-fifties, the man was wearing a dark shirt, open at the neck, a dark brown jacket with worn, shiny lapels, and trousers to match. His shoes were heavy and worn. The man's clothes had a dusty look, just like the bar. He took the step down into the parlor room, hands jammed into the pockets of his jacket, his dark eyes on Jane.

"Yes." Jane nodded back to the rods above the mantel. "They're beautiful."

"Not meant to be beautiful then, are they?" the man answered. "Meant to fish with."

There was nothing in her booklet about terse barkeeps. Jane smiled as pleasantly as she could. "Still, they are beautiful."

"In the eyes of the beholder that is, or so they say," the man answered. "Belonged to my son Arthur. He was the fisherman in the family. Died in Ypres he did, blown to bits. Not enough left to fill a biscuit tin let alone a bloody casket."

"My father died at Passchendaele," said Jane.

"Then he was as much a fool as my Arthur, wasn't he." The old man paused. "Help you then?"

"I'm looking for a place called Strathmere House. I think it's supposed to be close by."

"Oh, aye, the sisters," said the man obscurely. He frowned, his thick black brows knitting slightly. "But we're not supposed to talk to strangers hanging about," he added. "So says Tom Drury." The man grimaced. "Home Guard officer."

Jane laughed. "I'm not a German spy if that's what you're worrying about."

"I'm not worrying," said the man. "Just explaining." He paused. "You're a Yank then?"

"Yes."

"Not a flyer though."

"No. A war photographer. Like Lee Miller." The name didn't make the slightest impression on him.

"Enough flyers of our own hereabouts. Spits."

"I saw some of them flying over."

The man nodded. "Nineteenth Squadron out of Fowlmere. That's just down the road a little."

Jane smiled again. For a man on the lookout for Nazi spies, he was certainly giving out a lot of unasked-for intelligence. "Noisy," she offered.

The man snorted. "Scares the hens and they stop laying. Haven't had an egg since they moved out of Duxford." He paused, then took another step forward, eyeing the insignia on Jane's cap and uniform blouse. "A war correspondent is it?"

"That's right." She nodded and held out her hand.

The man nodded, wiped his right hand on his jacket and extended it. "Blundel. Howard Blundel." He shook Jane's hand. "The proprietor," he added.

"I saw the sign," Jane answered. There was a short silence. "About Strathmere?" she prompted after a moment.

"Aye," Blundel said. "Straight on down the road a mile and a bit. Biggish oak tree at the gate, can't hardly miss it."

"Thanks." Jane smiled. She looked around the room. "Is it always this quiet?"

Blundel let out a little snorting laugh. "If it was always this quiet I'd be out of business then, wouldn't I?" he said. He shook his head. "No, woman, it's teatime, that's all."

"I thought maybe that was it."

"Would you like some then?"

"Tea you mean?"

"Or summat else if you'd like. A pint perhaps?"

"I'd love to," said Jane. "But I'm expected at Strathmere House."

"Oh, aye," Blundel said. "So you said."

"I'll come back again," Jane offered. "Perhaps we can talk about the fishing around here."

"Why talk about it when you can do it then?" Blundel responded.

"Is that an offer?"

Blundel thought about it for a moment, considering the question of fishing with a woman. "Could be that it is," he said finally. "I don't suppose you brought your own tackle, did you?"

"As a matter of fact I did." She'd packed two of her favorite reels and a pair of three-piece rods, carefully slipped into their own hard leather carrying tube.

"What's your fancy then?" Blundel asked.

"Pardon?"

"What do you fish for in America?"

"Trout," Jane said. "Sometimes salmon in the spring."

"Trout in race stream by the mill," said Blundel. "Browns. Some chub." He smiled. "And then there's Old Esox in the Tay just beyond."

"A pike?" said Jane. *Esox lucius* was the Latin name for the European variety.

"Right you are!" Blundel said, pleased. "The vicar almost brought him in last year but his line broke. A yard long and forty pounds if he's an ounce, the vicar says."

Apparently fish stories were the same in England as they were back home, even when it was a man of the cloth telling them. "Sounds like fun," Jane said with a grin. "But I really should be going."

"A mile and a bit straight on and turn in at the big oak by the gate," Blundel repeated, and stood aside to let a fellow angler pass by. Jane thanked Blundel again, climbed back into the jeep and headed down the road to Strathmere.

Three

The entrance to Strathmere was like something out of Edgar Allan Poe. Massive wrought-iron gates sagged between two granite columns, gates and columns overgrown and choked with ivy and clinging pellitory, each column topped by the vine-covered stone forequarters of a rearing horse, legs kicking high, head lifted, eyes wild and mouth open in a screaming snarl. What could be seen of the columns beneath the foliage was stained and crumbling, and the gates were covered with streaks of rust.

Jane climbed out of the jeep, pushed open the gates, then drove down a long lane lined with overhanging monkey puzzle trees. The lane itself was barely a rutted track, ditches on either side overgrown with chickweed and yarrow. A quarter mile on the monkey puzzles ended and Jane reached a circular driveway that ran around in front of the house. In the center of the circle were the remains of a large marble fountain, nothing at all spurting from the penises of half a dozen cherubim or the mouths of an equal number of ornate stone dolphins.

The house itself was a two-and-a-half story slate-roofed, gray granite monster more than a hundred and fifty feet across. Slightly offset from the center of the building a stone portico jutted, and carved above it was a huge coat of arms, which included a pair of chained swans holding up a shield, topped by a crested helmet. The euphonious scrolled motto beneath the coat of arms read: *Quaesita Marte Tuenda Arte.* Digging up whatever remained of her high school Latin Jane roughly translated the motto as: *"What is captured by strength is held by skill."*

Jane climbed down out of the jeep and went up to the main door under the portico. She hammered at a brass knocker that repeated the forequarter horse motif from the gate columns, stepped back and waited. A long minute passed and she was about to use the knocker again when the door opened and Jane found herself staring at a portly, balding man in his fifties, dressed in a perfectly cut morning suit complete with bow tie, waistcoat with watchfob, and a crisp, high-collared white shirt. The man's black shoes had a gleaming, lapidary shine.

"Yes, madam."

"Jane Todd."

"My name is Bunter, madam," said the fat man. "We've been expecting you." He looked over Jane's shoulder. "The jeep is yours?"

"Well, it actually belongs to the Judge Advocate General's motor pool, but for the moment it's mine."

"I see." Bunter cleared his throat. "The bag in the back is your luggage?"

"That's right."

"I'll have one of the servants take it to your rooms."

"That won't be necessary. I can do it myself."

The butler's lips twitched briefly. "It would be best if you left that sort of thing in my hands, madam."

Jane hesitated, wondering if she'd crossed some arcane trench line of etiquette. One way or the other, Bunter didn't look like someone you wanted to argue with; he had the kind of blank, unwavering stare most often seen on lions crouched in front of libraries and museums. Finally Jane nodded. "As you wish."

"I do, madam," the butler murmured. He stepped to one side. "Please come in."

Jane stepped into a small entrance foyer guarded by a half-scale carved oak figure of a Saracen with a scimitar in his hand. The dark wooden face bore a remarkable resemblance to the dangling heads portrayed on the sign of the Journey to Jerusalem. Behind Jane the butler shut the door, then stepped in front of her.

"If you'll follow me, madam, I'll show you into the drawing room." Bunter led the way up a short flight of marble stairs into a larger vestibule fitted with fruitwood wainscoting and pale green watered silk. From there they headed across a large open area past an immense, curving stairway that led to the upper floor, finally reaching a pair of high double doors that opened into the long, high-ceilinged drawing room. "I'll fetch the ladies now, shall I?" Bunter asked rhetorically. He stepped out of the room and swung the doors closed, leaving Jane on her own.

She crossed the room, going to the floor-to-ceiling French doors, which led out to a narrow balcony. She looked out. Directly in front of her there was a tangle of what might once have been an ornamental garden, long since gone to seed, and on the right

there were several stone outbuildings, the largest
being a coach house, the smallest appearing to be
some kind of kennel. At the far end of the garden
there was a small pond, beyond which was an extensive woodlot on rising ground.

Jane turned back into the room, examining her sur-
roundings. There were ornate rugs scattered willy-
nilly across the slate floor, chairs, side tables and
couches strewn about with equal abandon, although
most were oriented toward a massive fireplace and
overmantel carved with at least a dozen different
coats of arms. The walls, wainscoted like the entrance
foyer, were hung with an astounding array of ornately framed paintings, each one lit by its own little
lamp and identified with a small brass nameplate.
The paintings were mostly religious scenes or brood-
ing seascapes with titles like *An Angel Interceding for
a Soul*, *The Entombment*, or *A Scandinavian Wooded
Landscape with a Waterfall*. Most of the painters were
Dutch, with names like van Ruisdael, Joris van Son,
and Jane's favorite, Joos de Momper the Younger.

"Bloody awful if you ask me," said a voice behind
Jane. She turned, surprised, and found herself staring
at a pretty young woman wearing a very unflattering
brown uniform with a red "Provost" shoulder flash
on her jacket and a metal badge over the left breast
pocket with the letters ATS picked out in bronze. The
uniformed girl looked to be about twenty, and even
the shapeless below-the-knee skirt couldn't completely hide the fact that she had beautiful legs. She
also had light brown curly hair, blue eyes and a
bright, wide smile. "You'll be the correspondent
then," she said. "I heard you drive up in the jeep
and came looking for you." She took a few steps into

the room and held out her hand. Jane took it in her own. It was small, smooth and warm. "I'm Lance Corporal Darling, ATS Provost Corps, assigned here."

"Corporal." Jane nodded.

Her smile broadened. "Polly," she said. "Think of me as a general dogsbody. Coffee, sandwiches, anything on the tea cart. Odd bit of typing, some filing."

"Okay, Polly it is."

"I thought I'd pop in and say hello before Billy brought down their Ladyships."

"Billy?"

"Bunter. Billy's not his real name though. At least I don't think it is. We just call him that."

"I don't understand."

"Bunter? The Fat Owl of the Remove? Greyfriars? The Famous Five?"

"You lost me back at the Billy part."

"That's right, you're a Yank, so you wouldn't know about Bunter, would you?" She turned and looked back over her shoulder. "Crikey! Here come Billy and the Potties!" She gave Jane another beaming smile. "I'll give you a little time with the old girls and then I'll come and rescue you. Must run!" She turned and left the room at a trot, closing the door behind her. Half a minute later the butler reappeared, pulling the doors open wide before bowing ceremoniously and standing to one side, pulling himself up into full attention. "Lady Annabel and Lady Alice Pottinger."

Two elderly women stepped into the room, one slightly ahead of the other. Both appeared to be in their early eighties. They were not more than five feet, five inches tall, rail-thin, white-haired, both dressed in surprisingly fashionable tweed suits and sturdy brown oxford walking shoes. They were obviously twins, although not identical.

The first of the women stepped forward, frail hand extended. "Miss Todd, how good of you to come. I'm Annabel Pottinger and this is my sister, Alice Pottinger." Jane shook the old woman's hand, and then that of her sister.

"Call me Jane, please."

Annabel Pottinger gestured in the direction of a red velvet upholstered chair. "Do sit down, Miss Todd. You must be quite tired after your journey."

Jane sat down in the offered chair and the two women arranged themselves on a small couchette across from her. "Bunter will bring us tea in a moment," said Annabel. She sat primly on the couch, tiny hands clutching her bony knees. "He informed me that you arrived in a jeep," the old woman added.

"That's right." Jane smiled.

"Noisy things," said Alice Pottinger.

"Alice doesn't like jeeps." Annabel looked toward her sister. "She's convinced Lawrence was killed in one."

"Murdered," Alice corrected. "He was murdered."

"Lawrence?" asked Jane, bewildered.

"Of Arabia," said Annabel.

"I thought that was a motorcycle."

"Alice is convinced it was a jeep."

Jane wondered if the jeep had been invented then, and if they'd had any in England when the famous man died. She didn't think so. Potties indeed; at least Alice was.

"Our husbands knew him from the Hittite dig at Carchemish."

"Carchemish?"

"In Mesopotamia," said Alice.

"Syria," Annabel corrected.

"It was on the Euphrates," Alice said, insisting on the last word. "That was just before the war. They were very knowledgeable about the area." She paused, frowning. "It's what got them killed actually, when you think about it."

"Our late husbands were in the foreign service then," said Annabel, as though that explained anything at all.

"Your husbands," said Jane, completely lost now.

Annabel smiled, lifting twenty years of time from her face. "You must think us quite mad, Miss Todd, prattling on like a pair of doddering old ladies."

"Not at all," said Jane gallantly, although it had been exactly what she was thinking.

"We *are* a pair of doddering old ladies," said Alice firmly. "People expect us to prattle on. It's what doddering old ladies do."

Jane wasn't about to argue.

Bunter appeared carrying a large silver tray loaded down with a tea service and a plate of sandwich triangles, crusts neatly shorn away. The bread was the color of pale sawdust, neither white nor brown. The butler drifted across the sitting room, bent ponderously to set the tray down on the table between the women and Jane, then stood again. "Shall I pour?" he asked.

"No thank you," said Annabel.

"As you wish." Bunter withdrew.

Annabel did the honors, pouring out a cup for each of them, putting milk and sugar into Jane's without asking if she wanted them or not. She handed over the delicate porcelain cup and saucer, which Jane took. Then Alice Pottinger suddenly darted forward, picked up the plate of sandwiches and offered it to her guest.

"Sandwich?" She smiled. "It's only the national flour now, I'm afraid. I doubt we'll see white again before the end of the war."

Jane took one of the dusty-looking little triangles just to be polite, then realized she was trapped, cup and saucer in one hand, sandwich in the other. There were no side plates so her only choice was to pop the wedge of bread into her mouth. The taste was faintly reminiscent of liver paste mixed with olives. She swallowed, trying not to think about what passed for liver paste in England after two and a half years at war.

"Good?" asked Alice.

"Mmm," said Jane, gulping her tea.

"Have another, by all means," said Alice.

"Perhaps in a little while," Jane said, putting her cup down on the table between them. She was suddenly struck by an odd, and quite startling, thought. Annabel had twice mentioned that they had both been married; "Our late husbands," she'd said, but she had also introduced both herself and her sister as being Pottingers, which could only mean that the two sisters had married two brothers, both of whom were now dead.

"You look very young to be a correspondent," said Annabel Pottinger, studying Jane over the rim of her cup.

"They say it's a young war," she answered.

Alice gave a bitter little laugh. "It's always a young man's war," she said. "That's because you don't live long enough to get old."

"Do be quiet, Alice!" chided Annabel, but she was smiling. "I think my sister wants me to get to the point."

"And what point would that be?" Jane asked, eager for some kind of enlightenment.

"Rules," said Alice.

Annabel nodded. "Quite so." She paused. "We offered Strathmere to the War Office because we wanted to do rather more during this war than we did during the last."

"We were a great deal younger then," said Alice, as if in explanation. She ate another sandwich. Jane did a quick calculation in her head. Even shaving twenty-eight years from their ages both women would have been in their middle to late fifties when the Great War began. Hardly innocent youth.

"We did have one codicil to the arrangement," said Annabel. "Regardless of what the War Office decided to do with Strathmere, we insisted on being allowed to remain here for the duration."

"I see," said Jane, not seeing at all. If she was hearing them right, she was supposed to try to work with these two old bats flapping around in the belfry.

"I hope you do," said Annabel. "This is our home and you are our guest for the duration of the war, but as I said before, there are rules for good houseguests if you see my meaning."

"What would those rules be?" Jane asked. "Although I hardly think I'll be here for the duration."

"There are twenty-five rooms in Strathmere," said

Annabel. "Thirteen rooms on the ground floor and an additional twelve rooms on the upper floor."

"Not counting the servants' quarters in the attic," put in Alice.

"And we *don't* count them, do we?"

"Well," said Alice, "they *are* empty." She turned to Jane, frowning. "Turned perfectly good house-maids into farm girls and lorry drivers. Appalling." She sighed. "All we have left is Bunter."

"As I was saying, Miss Todd, there are a total of twenty-five rooms in this house. Of those we have put twelve at your disposal, all of them on the ground floor. You will not, unless invited, come to the upper floor of the house for any reason whatso-ever. Those rooms are now our private apartments and are thus sacrosanct. Is that understood?"

"Perfectly," said Jane.

"Good," said Annabel. She waved a hand. "This room shall be common to both you and the others here from the Judge Advocate General's office, and to my sister and I on the condition that the furniture and appointments be treated with respect. The kitchen in the basement will be shared. There are two large cold storage lockers. Bunter has clearly marked the one for the use of the Judge Advocate General's staff."

"Sounds equitable enough," Jane said.

"The jeep," said Alice, nudging her sister, her face dark.

"Ah, yes," said Annabel. "The jeep." She paused. "I mentioned that my sister doesn't like them."

"So you said."

"We have several automobiles in the carriage

house," said Annabel. "You are welcome to use any of them except for the Alvis. Bunter uses that to do the shopping. You will of course have to provide your own petrol."

"Very kind of you to offer, Lady Pottinger, but I'm sure the Army will provide transportation."

Annabel Pottinger smiled knowingly. "Perhaps," she said. "But it is not a question of whether or not they will provide the transportation, Miss Todd; it is entirely a question of when. Until such time as it is, please feel free to use the vehicles in the carriage house."

"But not the jeep?"

"But not the jeep," Annabel said, "if you can avoid it."

"Anything else?" Jane asked.

"Just one thing," said Annabel primly. "We have taken it upon ourselves to billet Lance Corporal Darling, a female member of the staff, in the chauffeur's quarters above the carriage house. Our driver is now in the Signal Corps, so the rooms are empty, and we felt it would be more seemly that you be quartered there as well." She paused. "I hope you don't feel that we have been presumptuous in this matter."

"Not at all," said Jane. "I'm in complete agreement with you ladies."

"Good," said Annabel.

There was a long silence. Jane took another sip of her cooling tea. Alice Pottinger ate another wedge of liver sandwich. She chewed and swallowed, then leaned forward, an intense expression on her face. "Have you ever heard of a place called Kut-al-Amara?" she asked quietly. Her sister Annabel looked as though she was going to say something, but in the end she remained silent.

"No," said Jane, wondering if this was some kind of test. "I haven't."

"It's in Persia," Alice continued. "On the road to Baghdad."

"Oh," said Jane, not sure how she was expected to respond.

"Yes," said Alice. "In September of 1915 a very foolish young officer named Townshend decided that capturing Baghdad would be a jolly nice Christmas present to give to the British people, so he took fifteen thousand troops up the Euphrates to Kut-al-Amara in pursuit of that goal. He assembled his force and marched north to the ancient Roman ruins at Ctesiphon." Alice paused again. "I don't suppose you know them?"

"No," said Jane.

"Never mind," said Alice. She continued. "At Ctesiphon, Townshend and his men met with the forces of a man named Nur-Ud-Din, who was in league with the Turks and the Germans. He forced Townshend's column back to Kut-al-Amara and laid siege to the fort there. This was the seventh of December. A Tuesday as I recall."

"Yes, it was," murmured Annabel. "I still have the telegram."

Alice went on. "The siege lasted from December 7, 1915, to the end of April the following year. Almost exactly five months. In the end, the men were reduced to eating their horses to survive. Almost three thousand died within the walls from dysentery, malaria and cholera. The conditions must have been appalling. When Townshend finally capitulated, the remaining men were marched off to a number of Turkish prison camps. Twelve thousand of them died, our husbands among them."

"I'm very sorry," said Jane.

Alice Pottinger shook her head. "I didn't tell you about Kut-al-Amara because my sister and I want sympathy. The story has a purpose."

"Yes?"

"It has only been twenty years since the end of the Great War, Miss Todd, and not one in a hundred schoolchildren could find Ypres, or Passchendaele or the Somme on a map. I doubt that *any* could find Kut-al-Amara."

"I suppose that's true," said Jane, flushing slightly, knowing perfectly well she couldn't do it herself.

"In twenty years the memories of that war have faded for all but a very few," Alice went on. "In fifty years it will be forgotten altogether. Remember that. Our war is over, Miss Todd, while yours is just beginning, but in the end all of it is dusty history and counts for nothing."

There was a sharp knock on the door and it opened. Polly Darling popped her head into the room, smiling brightly. "Hello, all," she said pleasantly. "Jane must be getting tired after all her travels, so I thought I'd get her settled."

"Excellent idea," said Annabel Pottinger, obviously relieved that her duties as hostess had come to an end. She rose, steadying herself with her cane. "Off you go, Miss Todd. We'll talk again another day."

"Pleasure to meet you," Jane replied. She gave the ladies a polite bow, then followed Polly out of the room. She led Jane toward the front of the house, then turned into a smallish room with French doors leading out onto the side lawn. From the paintings on the wall and the scattered furniture it looked as though it had once been a sitting room, but now it had been converted into a reception area, complete with a monsterously large, battle-scarred government-issue wooden office desk kitted out with a green blotter, inkwell and pens, and a large black telephone. Off to one side was a tall pair of dark green filing cabinets.

"My little kingdom," said Polly, dropping down into the chair behind the desk. She gestured toward a door on her left. "The major's office is in there." She smiled. "You look completely ragged."

"It's been a bit of a hike," she said, yawning.

"Well, at least you survived the Potties."

"Just barely."

"Presumably they gave you the Kut-al-Amara speech," said Polly. "Alice gives it to anyone who'll listen."

"You presume right," said Jane.

"I should have warned you but there wasn't really time." She smiled at Jane. "Don't worry, they're really quite harmless."

"They married brothers?" Jane asked.

"Better than that, they married *twin* brothers." She made a little giggling noise that Jane found oddly attractive. "George and Godfrey." She giggled again. "Sets all sorts of wheels in motion doesn't it, the four of them all living under the same roof."

Jane yawned again. "I could sleep for a week. When do I get to see the mysterious Major Dundee?"

The telephone on Polly's desk gave a dissonant double rattle. Polly reached out and picked up the receiver before it could make the sound a second time. "Three-two-one-five-nine, Lance Corporal Darling speaking." She listened for a few moments without saying anything, then hung up the phone.

"Himself," she said. "He was supposed to be coming back here tonight. Now he wants you down there."

"Down where?"

"London," Polly answered. "There's been a murder. The body's being sent to Simpson, the Home Office pathologist. The major wants you there for the autopsy tomorrow morning."

"Why me?"

"Because the body is one of yours. United States Army Air Force. An officer. He thought you might be interested." She beamed. "Come along. I'll drive you to the station." She reached down beside the desk and came up with a fat leather briefcase. "Pack a few things for overnight. I'll meet you out at the coach house."

Five minutes later they were puttering down the long driveway between the monkey puzzle trees in the Pottinger sisters' ancient Austin 7. They went out between the rusting gates and turned northward. Ahead, Jane could see the overcast tearing into long ragged strips, pink-lit by the lowering sun. She felt a strange tug at the dusky sight, mentally running the clock back. Breakfast time in L.A. The hoods would be having egg and beans at the Broadway Hotel and the vice cops from Hollywood Division would be divvying up the pad from the night before. The movie stars would have been up since dawn getting into their makeup. An alien world to her now.

It took Polly less than ten minutes to drive from Strathmere up the road to the station at Leighton Buzzard and five minutes later Jane was on a local bound for London.

Four

Jane had a first-class compartment all to herself, the blackout curtains closed. Her long odyssey from Los Angeles was beginning to take its toll and she had a sinking feeling that it was far from over. From a few thousand miles, a continent and a cold ocean away, the war had seemed a clear-cut event, crisply detailed within neat paragraphs in *Time* and *Newsweek*, bleakly observed in *Life* pictorials, a chess game textured with people and places and bombs and blasted earth, but a game nevertheless, with pieces playing by strict rules of conduct—so many moves in this direction, so many moves in that, until the noble resolution of a king tipped over on the board.

She peeked out through the curtain over the window. The sky had turned purple and there was only a sharp sliver of light on the western horizon. West. The States. New York. L.A. Home. Once maybe, but not now and perhaps never again. She dropped the curtain, blotting out the last of the sunset. Maybe she'd never go back at all. Maybe the war would go on forever. Jane sighed, reaching into the briefcase Polly had handed over and pulling out the file on Major Lucas Dundee.

Son of Jack Dundee, sometimes referred to as Blackjack Dundee, a big-time L.A. land speculator, womanizer, and said to sometimes be just barely on the right side of the law. Once in a while he even made the gossip columns, especially if he was bedding a starlet, which is where Jane had heard about him. His son Lucas went to West Point, class of '29, law degree from Stanford in '32. Spent the next five years with the Los Angeles Police Department, three of them as a detective, which seemed like an odd choice of employment for a man with an honors law degree from Palo Alto.

At this point he went to work for Burton Fitts. Jane leaned back in her seat and thought about Fitts for a moment. He hardly ran what anyone would call a "clean" office. Burton Fitts had been district attorney of Los Angeles from 1928 to 1940 and it was widely rumored that he was in the pocket of California's rich and powerful, not the least of whom was Lucas Dundee's father

Jane remembered where she'd seen Dundee's name before. Someone had sent her a clipping from the *Los Angeles Times*—according to the story Blackjack Dundee had been arrested on a charge of statutory rape. The girl was the daughter of a Warner Brothers extra and was fourteen. The article said that his father was being defended by the well-known "socialite" lawyer Jerry Giesler and prosecuted by the recently elected D.A., Burton Fitts. Her friend Rusty Birdwell had called him up for a comment and his reply had been short and to the point: "If she's old enough to take my money, she's old enough to fuck. Forget about it."

Ironically, it seemed that Fitts, an assistant district attorney at twenty-four, lieutenant governor of California at thirty-one and Los Angeles district attorney two years later, had inadvertently planted the seed of Dundee's career as a policeman and a lawyer. Even though the case against Lucas's father was dropped before it came to trial—the result of a deal brokered by Giesler, Jack Warner and the girl's mother—Dundee saw Burton Fitts as the shining crusader he was made out to be by Harry Chandler, publisher of the *L.A. Times*: a West Coast version of a young Tom Dewey, at that time Assistant U.S. Attorney for the Southern District of New York.

Jane started reading between the lines of the skeletal file.

Disgusted by his father, but deeply impressed by Fitts, Dundee applied to Stanford and was accepted. On his graduation from law school he immediately joined the Los Angeles Police Department, part of some overall plan to join the D.A.'s office not just as a lawyer, but as a cop who knew the criminal justice system from both sides of the fence.

Two years in uniform and three more as a detective out of Hollywood Division seemed to have taken some of the blush off the crimestopper rose. According to the corruption reports he'd filed as a patrolman, he'd seen low-level graft and bribery at every level from cops taking free meals to evidence mysteriously missing from precinct property rooms. As a detective it became even more apparent that corruption in the force rose throughout the ranks to the very top. Hollywood suicides turned into unfortunate "accidents," rapes and assault cases like his father's were dropped for lack of evidence and the infiltration of Mob snitches on the force from one end of Los Angeles to the other was a cancer.

The Thelma Todd case in '35 was apparently the last straw for Dundee, one of the lead investigators on the case. Even the most basic investigation showed a relationship between Todd, Todd's mother, and both Meyer Lansky and Charlie Luciano, as well as a longtime relationship with Tony Carnero, owner of the *Rex* and several other L.A. and San Diego off-shore gambling barges. Thelma, a Mob hanger-on as far back as the early twenties, had been running her mouth a little too loudly and in the wrong places, and Luciano had decided to shut it once and for all. Right from the start the investigation was a botched, Keystone Kops affair and, steadfastly refusing to believe that Fitts was involved in the mishandling of the case, Dundee went to the D.A. and asked for help.

Instead of help, the district attorney offered the young detective a job, promising him that the D.A.'s office would quietly establish a secret police corruption committee to investigate his allegations. Dundee accepted the job, left the police force and became an assistant district attorney. The police corruption committee never materialized and instead the newly appointed A.D.A. found himself prosecuting an endless series of meaningless robberies, domestic assaults, suicides and other "B" crimes, relegated to a backwater of second-rate felonys where his zeal wouldn't get anyone, himself included, into any trouble.

As the train rumbled into the blacked-out suburbs of London, Jane saw where all of it was going. The young Dundee had been sidetracked, a potentially bothersome fly stuck onto a piece of gummy paper in the back rooms of the D.A.'s office.

According to the dates in the file it took almost six months for Dundee to track it all down, first running through his files from the Los Angeles Police Academy and then his police record, both in uniform and as a detective; at every step of the way he recognized the signs of his father's influence and he could see it easily in his mind's eye—a cocktail-party comment to one of the five police commissioners appointed by the mayor, all of them pals of his father, all of them more than happy to pay off a debt to their good friend Jack Dundee.

The job offer from Fitts had presumably come to him the same way, and digging back through the dusty stacks in the basement of the D.A.'s Spring Street offices Dundee saw that Fitts and his father had been doing business as far back as 1919, when the young Fitts had been first appointed as a special district attorney to bust the so-called "labor radicals" who were threatening the old man's interests.

Dundee's humiliation must have been complete; since returning to Los Angeles his career had been stage-managed by his father like that of a bit part actor in a movie. Presumably he was destined for future starring roles. By that time the war had already begun in Europe. Unlike a lot of his colleagues, Dundee was reasonably sure the United States would ultimately become involved in it. He resigned from the D.A.'s office and enlisted.

The train pulled into the booming confines of Euston Station with a chorus of whistles, steam venting and slamming doors. Jane stuffed the file back into the briefcase, crushed the unfamiliar cap over her hair and stepped down from her compartment. Surrounded by streams of people, all of whom seemed to know precisely where they were going, it suddenly occurred to Jane that no one in the world she loved or cared about had the slightest idea where she was right at that moment. It was the ultimate form of being lost—even she didn't know where she was.

She reached the gate leading out to the main concourse and found her way blocked by a tall man in uniform. She tried to sidestep him but he gently took her by the arm. He was a good six inches taller than she was, with dark, thick hair, dark brown eyes set deeply in their sockets behind wire-rimmed glasses and a pronounced stoop to his gangling walk. He looked like Ichabod Crane in uniform. He was wearing major's oak leaves on his shoulder tabs and the wreath, sword and quill of the Judge Advocate General's office on his chest.

"Lucas Dundee," he said, extending a hand. "You'll be Jane Todd."

"How did you know?"

"How many other female correspondents with a California tan are there coming in on the local from Leighton Buzzard?" He smiled. It was a nice smile, a little on the shy side. "Didn't they tell you I used to be a cop?"

"In other words, Polly called you."

"You found me out."

Jane took the offered hand and shook it. The grip was surprisingly strong.

"I've got a car outside," said Dundee. "Hungry?"

"Famished."

"I know just the place," he said.

"Music to my ears. Lead on," Jane answered. They left the terminal and climbed into a nondescript olive green Dodge parked at the curb with a serial number stenciled on the fender. Dundee got behind the wheel, managed to find his way to the Edgeware Road and headed south into the blacked-out city.

"I'll take you to the Red Cross Club after dinner," said Dundee. "Find you a billet."

"Thanks, but I've got a flat in Shepherd's Market as a matter of fact," said Jane. "Brit friend I made back home offered it to me. He's off in some out-of-the-way spot for the duration. Loads of room, I think. But I've never even seen the place and I wouldn't know how to find it." She gave Dundee an appraising look and then made up her mind. "You can stay there if you want. Save time in the morning if we're under the same roof."

Dundee thought about it and then shook his head. "Wouldn't be such a good idea," he said. "But thanks for the offer." Twenty minutes later Dundee turned into a narrow road a block away from the looming presence of Paddington Station and pulled to a stop. The ratcheting sound of the hand brake being set brought Jane out of a light sleep.

"We have arrived," said Dundee. "Mrs. Staines's Restaurant."

Jane yawned and blinked and stared out the window. They were in a mews of two-story brick townhouses, one of which had been transformed into a Continental-style bistro by the simple addition of an awning, a sign made out of plain metal letters that said RESTAURANT and a few tables scattered around the front entrance. The doorway and windows were blacked out, but through the gloom, Jane could make out the firefly glow of cigarette ends flaring around the outside tables. Jane and the major climbed out of the car and crossed the cobbled street.

"What's the menu like?" Jane asked as they stepped up onto the sidewalk.

"I think it's what's generally referred to as 'hearty fare,'" Dundee answered. "Which means lots of things made from potatoes, long rolls with a bit of ham and a lot of mustard, and the occasional pork chop if the black-market butcher's been around. Not much in the way of variety these days, I'm afraid." He pointed. "Take that table and I'll bring you out a plate of something." Jane nodded and dropped down onto one of the plain wooden chairs.

She let out a long, sighing breath and closed her eyes, half thinking about the whispering men and women at the other tables. All the voices were young; flat, slightly nasal Canadian accents and something heavily European, probably Polish. The men's voices were sly and the laughter of the women was charged with expectation and anxiety. Jane smiled to herself. It was like being at a high school dance. What was that joke the B-17 transfer pilot had told her? Overpaid, Oversexed and Over There.

According to the most recent numbers she'd heard there were more than a hundred thousand Americans in England now, with thousands more streaming in every day. If Hitler's back was going to be broken there'd eventually be a million, or maybe two or three. An invasion of smiling faces and pockets full of Hershey bars and Lucky Strikes, but an invasion nevertheless.

Dundee returned, followed by a middle-aged,

plain-faced, heavyset woman carrying a tray. "Mrs. Staines herself," said Dundee.

"Pleasure," said the woman, setting down the tray. She unloaded two plates and a pair of glass pint mugs of ale. She smiled and Jane smiled back, then she vanished into the darkness, outlined for an instant in the light from inside the restaurant as she pushed through the heavy blackout curtain. Jane examined her plate: a cold ham sandwich on a long, crusty bun that was pointed at both ends and a small pile of lukewarm French fries. The beer was room temperature, had no discernible head and tasted wonderful.

The two ate until their plates were clean, then Dundee went and fetched another two pints before the bar closed for the night. He set down the mugs, then reached into his pocket and pulled out a packet of tobacco. He deftly rolled himself a cigarette and offered it to Jane, who took it, amazed at how perfectly it had been created. He rolled himself another one and lit them both with a solid-gold Dunhill lighter; the only sign so far that he came from a wealthy background.

"Long day," said Dundee.

Jane nodded sleepily. "Too long, that's for sure." She closed her eyes for an instant and felt a sudden surge of mental vertigo; too much to think about, too much to see, an ocean and a continent away from everything she knew, every inch making her the Bible's Stranger in a Strange Land.

"You look a little overwhelmed," Dundee commented, watching her.

Jane nodded absently. "I am feeling a bit out of place."

"I used to love the thought of coming here," said Dundee wistfully. "I wanted to go to Oxford, as a matter of fact. Read in history or archaeology or something."

"So why didn't you?"

"You read my file, I'm sure," he answered, his voice sour. "Blackjack Dundee's son doesn't do anything even remotely out of step. I became a lawyer just to spite him, I think; a cop even more so."

"What about the Army?"

"To get away from him." He grinned, then shook his head. "He's got a long reach though. Nice cushy job where I'm not likely to run into too many Germans. Half the people in JAG know it, too: daddy's boy." He sucked on his cigarette, then put it down in the ashtray. "What about you?" he said after a moment. "Bit of a pariah yourself?"

"Self-made," Jane answered. "Los Angeles has good weather, but that's where any comparison to paradise ends, no matter what the postcards say." She shrugged and left it there, still not sure of Dundee or how much she should tell him about the past. Working for Donovan and his bunch wasn't the best recommendation these days. "I guess you can take the girl out of New York but not New York out of the girl. It just never felt like home."

Dundee laughed. "Never felt like home to me either and I was born there."

Jane changed the subject, bringing up the obvious. "What can you tell me about this corpse we're going to be seeing tomorrow?"

Dundee took a small notebook out of his breast pocket and flipped it open. "Two boys found him early this morning, lying beside the railway tracks near a place called Letchworth."

"Where's that?"

"North of here, about thirty miles."

The location meant nothing to Jane. "Any idea who he is?"

"The man had no wallet, but he was wearing a uniform and dog tags on a chain around his neck."

"Who was it?"

Dundee consulted his notebook, holding it up to the faint light leaking around the blackout curtain over the entrance to the restaurant. "Kelman, David J., serial number 1251893, blood type B, religion, Hebrew."

"The uniform?"

"Lieutenant, Eighth Army Air Force," said Dundee.

"What killed him?"

"Devon C.I.D. says it looks as though he was shot in the face with a large-caliber weapon and then dumped from a train."

"Who says he was on the train at all?"

"There was a ticket in his overcoat pocket," said Dundee. "Cambridge to Cardiff, the late express last night."

"Anybody see him?"

"The train crew is being interviewed. We should have their statements by tomorrow."

"Fair enough." Jane nodded. It all sounded very efficient. On the other hand, she found herself wondering why Dundee had been called in on the case at all—from what Dundee had said it was a straight-forward murder and by rights, at least to this point, it should have been a matter for the Provost Marshal's office to investigate. She looked across the table at her handsome dark-eyed companion. "There's something else, isn't there?"

"My, aren't we quick," said Dundee.

"So there is something else."

"Simpson did a preliminary once-over. They found gold dust under his fingernails. Now, what do you think of that?"

"I can't think," said Jane. "I'm too tired."

"Then I'd better take you home."

The drive took only a few minutes and Jane wasn't aware of much of it beyond Dundee's description of what it was like in daylight. Shepherd's Market was a little enclave just off Piccadilly, with Green Park to the south and Hyde Park to the west. Not quite Mayfair and la-de-da, but no slum either. He let Jane out at the right address on Hereford Street, then watched while she fumbled with the keys in the blackout darkness, and stumbled up the stairs to what had once been Morris Black's home.

Five

Jane awoke to the scents and sounds of frying bacon and percolating coffee. She blinked, sat up on the old, brown leather couch and tossed back the thin blanket that had been covering her. She was dressed in nothing but bra and panties, her uniform folded neatly on a comfortable-looking upholstered chair beside one of the room's tall windows, her jacket draped carefully over the back of it. The blackout curtains had been pulled back and the room was flooded with weak, early-morning light. For a split second she couldn't for the life of her remember where she was and then, just as suddenly, it came back to her: Morris Black's flat. She blinked, feeling a little odd about being surrounded by his things without the man himself being there.

The room was large and square, the pair of tall windows on her right, the breakfast sounds coming from beyond an alcove on her left. The couch faced a black-enameled gas fire on the far side of the room. The hardwood floor was partially covered by an oval rag rug done in a geometric design of grays and blues. There was a modern-looking black lacquer bar cabinet to the right of the gas fire and a plain wood dining table and a trio of chairs squeezed in between the windows. There were a number of framed watercolors on the off-white walls, all clearly painted by the same person, most of them depicting neighborhood scenes—a postman on his rounds, children playing in a small, fenced park, a butcher leaning against the entrance to his shop smoking his pipe. The only exception was a formal portrait of a younger Morris Black, at the age of maybe thirty or so, seated in an armchair with a wall of books behind him and a book open in his lap. The artist's touch was deft and gentle, perhaps a woman with a woman's careful eye for detail.

Jane got up and struggled back into her uniform. A few minutes later Dundee came out of the kitchen, fully dressed and wearing an apron, a black lacquer tray in his hands loaded down with breakfast. "Morning," he said brightly. He carried the tray over to the dining table and began setting out two places. "Coffee?"

"God, yes," said Jane. She yawned and stood up, stretching. "What time is it? And how the hell did you get in here?"

"Seven. And you left the downstairs door unlocked and the keys in the flat door," Dundee answered, pouring coffee from the enameled metal pot. "Simpson starts work at eight and he's a stickler for punctuality. We better get going."

Jane crossed to the table and sat down. Dundee had outdone himself. Both plates were loaded down with scrambled eggs, fried potatoes, sliced fried tomatoes and several rashers of streaky bacon each. "I thought the Brits were being rationed," Jane commented. She ate a forkful of the eggs—real, not powdered.

"They are." Dundee nodded. "Which means, of course, that there is a red-hot black market."

"Ah," said Jane, and took a sip of coffee. It was wonderful.

"Ah, indeed," Dundee replied. "The maid always told me that breakfast was the most important meal."

"The maid?"

"It was that kind of family. My old man was at work by six and the old lady was either drying out in one of those places in Santa Barbara or upstairs with a bottle of pills and a silk sleeping mask."

They waded through the breakfast, keeping conversation to a minimum. Finishing up, they loaded their plates back onto the tray and Dundee poured them each another cup of coffee.

"Nice place," said Dundee, sipping his coffee and lighting up his pipe. "I saw a commendation on the wall. He was a cop?"

"Little more than that in the recent past. Some secret wartime thing." She pointed to the portrait over the gas fire. "That's him."

"You met him Stateside?"

"We did some work together."

"Sounds interesting."

"It was."

"So, tell me about it?"

"Why?"

"Just curious."

"Don't be."

"Who's the artist?" Dundee asked, changing the subject.

"His wife," said Jane. "She died shortly before the war." She paused. "All the paintings are hers, I think."

Coffee finished, Dundee gathered up the last of the cutlery and crockery and took the tray back to the kitchen. Jane spent fifteen minutes in the bathroom trying to put herself back together, picked up her Rolleiflex twin lens reflex and by twenty to eight they were out the door and on their way.

Dundee guided the car from Hendon along Market Street to White Horse Street, then drove one short block to Piccadilly. It was still early and traffic was light, mostly double-decker buses and black cabs, so they made good time. A few minutes later they reached the confluence of Piccadilly, Shaftsbury, Regent Street and Haymarket. Turning right onto Haymarket, they were heading for the Thames.

Jane turned in her seat and stared back through the rear window of the car. The statue of Eros was shrouded with a gray-painted and sandbagged cover that had been further disguised with a papering of War Bond posters, but the gigantic Bovril sign and the Guinness clock were right out of an old *National Geographic*.

"I'll be damned," Jane said. "Piccadilly Circus. I really am in England." Since flying into Prestwick she'd been operating in a bit of a fog, disconnected from virtually everything familiar to her. Seeing the famous traffic circle triggered something in her and, for the first time in days, she had a real sense of being on solid ground. She was "here," not "there" anymore.

"I always wanted to come here," she said, rubbernecking like a tourist. "I didn't think it would be like this though."

They drove down to the Victoria Embankment and the Thames, and off to her right Jane could see Westminster and Big Ben. "I feel like a yokel," she said, turning to Dundee and smiling.

The major grimaced. "Enjoy it while you can. You're going somewhere few tourists have on their itinerary." Dundee continued on down the Embankment, ducked down into the underpass at Waterloo Bridge, then came up again, skirting Blackfriars as they turned onto Lower Thames Street.

Dundee piloted the car up to London Bridge and Jane saw the grim, bomb-blasted remains of dozens of buildings all around her. Other than the covered statue in Piccadilly, they were the first real evidence to her senses that she was actually in an active war zone. They reached the bridge itself and Jane also noted the sandbagged pillboxes on either side of the roadway.

They crossed London Bridge with Tower Bridge on their left, swept past the sooty façade of the London Bridge Railway Terminus, then continued down Borough High Street with its cramped rows of shops, offices and warehouses on the tottering floors above. Everything was brick, everything was covered with a fine layer of soot and grit, and everything was old. There was bomb damage on this side of the Thames as well, but it seemed random; single blocks of buildings smashed to bits giving the street a gap-toothed look.

Dundee turned into a narrow lane called Angel Court, slowing the car as he eased down the half-lane passage, then turned onto a wider street ancient enough to still have old-fashioned gaslights on tall, ornately worked iron lampposts. An enameled sign riveted onto a wall announced that they were on George Street. As they turned, Jane saw that the side streets and courtyards on the left had vanished in a welter of brick rubble and interconnecting craters, turning a dozen blocks into a single gigantic bomb site. Apparently oblivious to the blasted landscape, Dundee continued on down George Street, then pulled up in front of a windowless stone building guarded by a low brick wall, which was in turn topped by a tall, rusted, wrought-iron fence.

"Southwark Mortuary," said Dundee, switching off the engine and setting the hand brake. Jane nodded, feeling a slight acidic twinge deep in her stomach and regretting the size and content of her recent breakfast. She knew what was coming and wasn't looking forward to it at all. It wasn't the first time she'd attended an autopsy, but it wasn't her favorite early-morning occupation.

The reception area of the mortuary was oak-paneled, marble-floored and topped by an ornately plastered ceiling, but beyond the swinging doors at the far end of the large open area it was gruesomely familiar. A dank, wide corridor with dark green linoleum on the floor and a particularly vile shade of yellow on the walls was lined with loaded gurneys, each corpse covered with a once-white sheet now gone to gray, the heads of the bodies covered but the feet exposed, one or the other of the big toes looped with a large cardboard tag inscribed with a scribbled number and notation. At the end of the line of wheeled stretchers a squat, broad-shouldered man wearing a gray, striped suit and a waistcoat to match the walls was filling out a tag and looping the string around a subject's toe. The tag fitter had the square, broken face of a prizefighter, with a pair of jug ears to match and broad, thick-fingered hands. He looked up at the sound of Dundee's shoes on the linoleum and smiled broadly.

"Morning, West," said Dundee.

"Ah. Morning, Major. Doctor's already begun working on your fellow." West grinned, thick lips drawing back to reveal gigantic teeth. "Missed the grand opening, so to speak."

"Thank you, West," said Dundee. He led the way through another pair of doors and they entered the postmortem room itself. It was almost a match for the L.A. County morgue, right down to the white-tiled walls, the painted concrete floors sloping down to a central drain and the rows of chipped, bathtub-enameled tables and matching sinks. The room even smelled the same: camphor, ammonia and the tainted-meat smell of old death.

A slight, almost willowy man with a large, balding, egg-shaped head was standing at one of the tables peering down at the naked man laid out upon it. The man examining the corpse was wearing a white post-mortem gown to match the table, the gown in turn covered by a green-gray rubber apron. He was also wearing heavy rubber gloves, in one of which he held a large, hook-bladed knife. There were white rubber galoshes on his feet. To his left, seated at a small stenographer's table on wheels, a stunningly beautiful blond-haired woman waited with her fingers poised over the keys of a small portable type-writer. Like the balding man, the blonde was robed in a white postmortem gown. Barely visible around her long, pale neck was a single strand of gleaming, jet-black pearls.

Dundee approached the table, Jane close behind him, and the balding man waved the knife in greeting. "Morning, Dundee." He looked inquiringly at Jane.

"Morning, Doctor." Dundee turned to Jane. "Dr. Keith Simpson, Jane Todd."

"War correspondent?"

"Yes, sir. And photographer."

"Playing Watson to the major's Holmes."

"For the present I guess you could say that." They obviously weren't going to shake hands over the bare chest of the corpse, so Jane simply nodded. "Pleased to meet you, Doctor."

Simpson inclined his large head toward the stunning woman at the typewriter. "My inestimable right hand, Miss Molly Lefebure." The woman smiled and the sudden animation of her face was completely out of place in the cold, grim room. Jane smiled back. Molly Lefebure looked about eighteen years old and completely smitten by her egg-headed boss.

Simpson glanced down at the corpse in front of him. The remains of the man's head had been placed on a battered, rectangular mortuary pillow, the ruined face looking down the length of his flayed body like a man in a bathtub searching for his feet among the soap bubbles. Jane started taking pictures; it wasn't the first time she'd been in a morgue and not the first time she'd seen a body in this condition. The corpse had already been cracked open, ribs pulled back like trick doors to reveal the shining pool of glistening organs within. Simpson looked up at Dundee and Jane. "Thrown from a train you say?"

"It would appear so," Dundee said. Jane noted that the major's face was drawn and there was a faint line of perspiration on his forehead even though the room was quite cool. He liked autopsies even less than she did.

Simpson's large head bobbed in agreement. "Postmortem fractures are consistent with such an event, I suppose. One can never be absolutely sure in cases like this with so much trauma." Behind him Miss Lefebure clacked away on the typewriter, the keys clearly muted somehow as she took down everything that was said. "I can already see that he smoked and drank heavily." He used the knife to point out the little patches of exploded blood vessels growing on either side of the man's nose and the dark yellowing just inside the nostrils. He picked up one of the lungs in a pair of tongs. It looked gray and shriveled.

"Any evidence of narcotic use?" Jane asked, ignoring the grisly object as best she could.

"Why?" Simpson asked, the dome of his forehead wrinkling. "Should there be?"

"I'm not sure." Jane shrugged. "Just curious."

"Any narcotic in particular?" Simpson asked.

"Morphine. Heroin."

Simpson shook his head. "No evidence of intravenous use. No punctures on the arms or legs that I could find." His tone also made it quite clear that if there had been any punctures to find, he would have discovered them. Simpson smiled briefly, then turned away for a moment, searching the shelf behind him. He took down a wooden rack of test tubes corked with rubber stoppers and placed it on the table. He then brought up a small ceramic bowl from below the table, opened one of the test tubes and poured half its contents into the bowl.

Using his tongs and a scalpel he quickly carved a small piece of muscle tissue from the abdomen of the corpse and dropped it into the ceramic container. "Sulphuric acid and formaldehyde," said Simpson. "Turns bright magenta and then blue in the presence of morphine or heroin." Jane peeked into the bowl. No purple, no blue. "Your man was not an addict," Simpson stated flatly.

"What about the head wound?" asked Jane.

"Large caliber, two shots, probably from an automatic pistol."

"A forty-five?"

"Possible. Probable. I'll know more after I'm done."

"Anything in the clothes?"

"Packet of Players Medium, vestas, twenty pounds and some silver. Punched ticket, Cambridge to London. Also a three-day pass."

"No wallet?"

"No."

"I'd like to see the pass," said Dundee. Simpson reached down onto a shelf below the table and came up with a cardboard square protected by a small cellophane bag. He handed it across to Dundee.

"It looks genuine, but they're easy enough to forge." He handed it back. "Is that it?"

"As far as personal effects are concerned, yes."

"Anything else out of the ordinary?" Dundee inquired.

"You tell me," Simpson said with a small smile. "Considering his dog tags said he was a Jew."

Dundee and Jane scanned the corpse. Dundee saw it first. "Shit," he said quietly.

Simpson saw the direction of the American major's glance and nodded. "Quite so," he said.

"Oh, dear," said Jane. Color rose in her cheeks and she looked sidelong at Miss Lefebure, then back at the corpse. "He isn't circumcised."

"Indeed," said Simpson. "In this day and age being circumcised is no real proof of *being* a Jew, but being *uncircumcised* is proof positive that you are *not*."

"The dog tags are phony then," said Jane. "Probably stolen."

Simpson nodded again. Miss Lefebure's clacking went on without a pause. The pathologist reached out to roll the corpse half on its side and used his free hand to point to a tattoo on the upper biceps of the man's left arm. Within a crudely drawn heart there were two pairs of initials and a single word encased in a scroll:

W.B.
L
B.K.
FOREVER

"One presumes this means the victim's name is not David J. Kelman," said Simpson.

Jane looked down at the ruined face on the table. "Then who the hell was he?"

"His dental work is not American; that's really all I can tell you."

"Locating the real Kelman might give us a place to start," suggested Dundee. "I'll need a telephone."

"Just outside," said Miss Lefebure, smiling sweetly. Dundee left the room.

Jane stepped away from the table and went over to Molly Lefebure. She lifted her camera. "Where can I get these developed?" she asked.

"I could do it for you here," Molly said, "but I'm days behind. Do you normally do your own developing?"

"I prefer it."

"Take them to the Press Club then." The woman smiled. "They have the facilities. It's on Salisbury Square. Just off Fleet Street at Ludgate Circus. Any cabbie can take you there."

"Thanks," said Jane. She offered the young woman a cigarette. "You worked here long?"

"A bit more than a year now." The young woman beamed. Jane lit Molly's cigarette and she puffed contentedly, completely inured to the ambience of the mortuary. Behind her Jane could hear the sound of a bone saw.

"Like it?"

"Love it."

"Takes all kinds I guess," said Jane. She turned back to Simpson. "Major Dundee mentioned something about gold dust."

"That's right. Under the nails of both hands."

"Where would you normally expect to find that?"

"Dental technicians, pawnbrokers breaking up old

jewelry for smelting. A manufacturing jeweler himself, perhaps."

"Any military trades that handle gold?"

"None that I know of. The military uses nickel, and even civilian dentists don't use what appears to be twenty-four karat."

"Best guess?"

Simpson bent over the body again and began tapping away at the remains of the man's face with the mallet.

Molly shrugged. She puffed on her cigarette thoughtfully, her other hand fingering the string of black pearls around her long, swannish neck.

Simpson spoke. "He's not in the military at all. The uniform is a disguise."

Six

Bushy Park administrative HQ turned out to be a
ghastly conglomeration of sprawling, one-story
concrete-block buildings set on the edge of the
Hampton Court Palace grounds. One side faced the
Kingston Line embankment of the London and South
Western Railroad and the other faced the red-brick-
and-mortar townhouse suburbs of South Teddington.
The headquarters complex was still under construction, with the muddy ruts of heavy equipment, an
erratic symphony of shouted, incoherent orders, the
rumble and roar of bulldozers and the belching ex-
haust fumes from a fleet of large olive drab trucks
in constant motion completing the picture.

An MP at the main gate gave them directions.
Dundee drove the Dodge to a gravel parking lot in
front of "A" Building, a long, barrackslike structure
with four shorter wings sprouting out of each side.
Once inside, Dundee and Jane eventually tracked
down the head of Records Division, a round-faced
young captain named Singletary with an office the
size of a shoebox, crammed with filing cabinets. He
wore circular, steel-framed spectacles and he was

clearly barely old enough to shave. The silver bars on his shoulders looked as though they'd just been taken out of the presentation box that morning, and Jane was reasonably sure the West Point ring on the third finger of the man's left hand was polished with a soft cloth every night.

"I've never had to deal with this kind of request before," Singletary said cautiously, eyeing the JAG insignia on Dundee's collar.

"Always a first time," Dundee answered.

The young captain's glance slid over to Jane. "I'm not sure I'm supposed to divulge personnel information with . . . civilians present."

"Think of her as my adjutant."

"Yes, sir, but still . . . a Warco and all."

Dundee pointed to Singletary's West Point ring. "Digit still teaching Military Hygiene?" "Digit" was the nickname given to the academy surgeon, Colonel Walter DeWitt. The colonel was best known for the rigid, greased finger he used during the annual cadet physicals and his animated, graphically described lectures to the plebes in first year "Beast Barracks" on the horrors of what he referred to as "autoerotic manual personal stimulation and self-abuse."

Singletary's eye flickered to Dundee's left ring finger and found nothing. He looked across the desk, his round face flushing darkly. "You knew the colonel?"

"Intimately." Dundee smiled. "Three long years of him."

"But you don't wear . . ."

"The ring? Never felt the need to advertise."

"What class?"

"Twenty-nine," Dundee answered.

The round-faced captain went on the defensive. "Any letters?"

"Major 'A' in Baseball, Minor in Pistol and Long Distance."

Singletary's face fell slightly. "I had a Minor in Golf."

"Good for you," Dundee said with a nod.

"And I was on the staff of the *Pointer*," Singletary added.

"*Howitzer*," said Dundee, smiling pleasantly. "Editor-in-Chief."

The *Pointer* was the Academy's bi-weekly magazine and the *Howitzer* was the annual yearbook. Of the two, the *Howitzer* was far and away the more prestigious. Dundee watched as Singletary sagged slightly in his chair, beaten.

"About Second Lieutenant Kelman," Dundee prompted.

Singletary slid a file folder off the pile on his left and flipped it open. "He's attached to the Fifteenth Bomb Squadron at Polebrook," said the captain. "A bombardier."

"Where's Polebrook?"

Singletary flushed brightly. "I'll have to look it up."

"Why don't you do that."

Singletary went away and came back a minute later. "Northampton," said the round-faced man. "Not far from Kimbolton."

"Call Polebrook and ask Kelman's C.O. to have him ready for an interview in someplace reasonably private."

"He'll want to know what this is all about," said the captain, making a last stab at regaining control of the situation.

"I'll tell him when I see him." Dundee smiled and put his hand out across the desk. "You've been a great help, Captain. Thanks."

Grudgingly, Singletary shook the outstretched hand and mumbled a reply. Jane and Dundee headed back to the parking lot outside the building and climbed back into the Dodge.

"You had him thoroughly rattled," said Jane as they pulled away from the low cinder block building and headed for the main road.

"The West Point experience isn't something you forget overnight," Dundee answered, smiling. "As far as our moon-faced captain back there is concerned, he's still in first-year Beast Barracks and I'm still an upperclassman who can make him drop and give me fifty push-ups any time I have a mind to."

"Were you really the editor-in-chief of that publication you mentioned?"

"The *Howitzer*? No."

"I didn't think so," said Jane, smiling.

"I didn't letter in any sports, either," Dundee continued. "In fact, the only thing I was ever famous for was being the cadet with the most demerits overall in the history of the academy." He laughed. "I've always been quite proud of that."

"How do we get to Polebrook?" said Jane.

"There's a road atlas in the glove compartment. You can be the navigator, Watson."

"Right you are, Holmes." Jane reached for the book.

Polebrook was forty miles or so from London but there was no main route and it took them the better part of two hours to get there.

From the air, Polebrook would have looked like a giant, scruffy, off-centered X carved out of the surrounding fields of yellow rapeseed, the X circumscribed in turn by an equally scruffy perimeter track. Cradled between the shorter upper arms of the X there was a patchwork of hangars, maintenance sheds, barrack huts and a large fuel dump. Originally built in 1940 for RAF Bomber Command, the runways had been extended to accommodate B-17s several months before, and in June it had been officially handed over to the Ninty-seventh Bomber Group, making it the first operational American airbase in England with two full squadrons of Flying Fortresses calling it home.

Dundee showed his pass at the main gate and they drove along the hardstand toward the administration offices. They passed half a dozen B-17s lined up beside the runway, all of them with names and luridly colored, cartoonlike devices painted on the noses. One in particular caught Jane's eye—*Double Trouble*, the illustration being twin naked women divebombing out of a cloud with propellers whirling on the tips of their large pink breasts.

"They all have names and pictures like that?" she asked.

"A lot of them," Dundee said. "Kind of like good luck charms, I think."

They drove to a small wooden building tucked in just behind the concrete-block control tower. The driver informed Dundee and Jane that Second Lieutenant Kelman was waiting for them inside.

The building was so new it still smelled of sawdust and fresh paint. Inside it was bare bones, with a low stage, a blackboard and fifteen or twenty wooden folding chairs. It must have been a preflight briefing room. Kelman, very much alive, was dressed in his flight suit and was sitting in one of the chairs in the front row, a dark brown A2 leather flying jacket draped over the back of it. Dundee could see a large patch on the back of the A2 Jacket: *Black Dog*, with a snarling hellhound breathing fire. The bombardier was in his early twenties with sandy brown hair and the beginnings of a mustache. He stood as Dundee and Jane entered the briefing room and snapped off a smart salute to Dundee in acknowledgment of his senior rank.

"Sit down, Lieutenant."

"Yes, sir." Kelman dropped back into the wooden chair. Dundee sat down on the edge of the stage, facing Kelman, and Jane remained standing.

"Permission to smoke, sir?"

"Of course," said Dundee. Kelman brought out a package of Luckies and lit up. Dundee brought out his pipe.

Kelman took a drag on the cigarette and pushed smoke out through his nose. Unlike the corpse in Southwark Mortuary, Kelman had no yellowed nostrils or nicotine-stained fingers. "Can I ask what this is all about?"

"Sure," said Dundee. He brought out the dog tags and leaned forward, handing them to Kelman. The young man held one up, reading the information.

"Son of a bitch," he whispered. He looked up at Dundee, then over to Jane. "Sorry."

"They *are* yours then?"

"Yes." Kelman frowned. "Where did you get them?"

"From around the neck of a corpse," said Dundee bluntly. "Someone shot him twice in the face then pushed him off a train." He paused. "I don't suppose you'd know anything about that, would you, Lieutenant?"

Kelman had gone pale. He stared down at the dog tags, then back at Dundee. He shook his head. "No."

"When did you lose the tags?"

"April."

"You were over here that early?" Dundee asked.

Kelman nodded. "We were training at Swanton Morley with an RAF squadron," he explained.

"How did you lose the tags?"

There was a long silence. "I'd rather not say," Kelman mumbled.

"Why?"

"It involves a woman."

"Oh dear," said Jane quietly, with feigned consternation.

Dundee looked down at Kelman's hands. He was wearing a wedding ring. "Married?"

"Yes." The young man nodded. "Just before we left the States."

"The woman in question is not your wife then?"

"No."

"An English girl?" Jane asked.

"I don't think you could call her a girl, really."

"Prostitute?"

"I wouldn't call her that either." Kelman paused, frowning. "I don't *think* you would anyway."

"Why don't you tell me what happened," said

Dundee. "There's no reason your new wife is going to have to know."

"Do I have to?"

"You can do it now, in private, or you can do it before a board of inquiry. Up to you."

There was a pause. Kelman kept on puffing away at his cigarette. The roof of the small wooden building shuddered as a flight of bombers came in low over the airfield. "All right," said Kelman finally.

"Where?"

"A club."

"Where is the club?"

"London. I'm not sure where exactly. It was called the 43."

"Gerrard Street," said Dundee, turning to Jane who now had a small notebook out, jotting things down with a small stub of pencil. "Soho, just off Piccadilly Circus. Run by a very nasty little creature named Kate Meyrick. Club is stretching it a bit; a whorehouse with liquor is more like it. Bar downstairs, rooms up." He paused. "What was the frail's name?"

"Annie."

"Last name."

"I don't know." Kelman flushed again. "She was Irish."

"Aren't they all," said Dundee. Jane gave him a quizzical look and Dundee explained. "It's always been that way; poor girls from Cork and Limerick and Dublin who can't find any work at home. It's worse now with all the soldiers. Not enough pros to go round." He turned back to Kelman. "So you went up to one of the rooms with Annie?" Dundee asked.

Kelman nodded. "Yes."

"Had relations with her?"

"I'm not sure," said the young man. "I'd like to think that I didn't, but I can't remember. I think I passed out."

"Slip something into your drink?"

"She might have. I was pretty drunk before I got there."

"Dog tags were gone when you woke up?"

Kelman nodded again. "Everything was gone. Annie, the dog tags. Wallet."

"Did you report the theft to the police?" asked Jane.

"No," said Kelman. "The woman who owns the club asked me not to. Said she'd be in a lot of trouble if it came out." He flushed. "Said I could have one for free the next time I was on leave if I kept my mouth shut. She gave me a card."

"Have you used it?" Dundee said.

"No."

"Does your C.O. know anything about this?" Dundee asked.

"No," said Kelman.

"How did you requisition new dog tags?"

"I said I lost them at the YMCA. Happens a lot from what I hear. I've gone swimming there once or twice. Nobody questioned it."

Dundee thought for a moment, then stood. "I think that just about does it, Lieutenant."

"Are you going to talk to the C.O.?" Kelman asked nervously, also standing.

"I don't see any reason to." Dundee shrugged. "I might have a few questions later on, but for now you're in the clear."

"Thank you, sir." He snapped another salute and Dundee returned it. Kelman left the room.

"What do you think?" said Dundee.

Jane shrugged. "Pure as the driven snow," she answered finally. "An innocent abroad."

"The prostitute steals the dog tags and wallet so our murdered man can have a new identity."

"Presumably."

"Which in turn presumes a relationship between the chippy and the dead man."

Jane lifted her shoulders. "Or the club itself. Can we find out if Kelman's girl Annie is still working for her?"

"Shouldn't be too difficult," Dundee said.

"Now what?" Jane asked. "Your place or mine?"

"Let's get back to Strathmere. The Potties are doing their famous steak and kidney pie tonight, and I've had enough of this for one day. Club 43 can wait until another time. I'm not sure we'd get very far anyway."

"Maybe I could even get a bit of fishing in. I left all my gear with Polly."

"Fishing?" said Dundee.

"Fishing," Jane said.

Jane stood in the river, just upstream from the old, dark mill, and cast across toward the marshy little island a dozen yards away. She was using an eight-and-a-half-foot, three piece Wright & McGill Granger Special bamboo trout rod and a Shakespeare Russell aluminum reel. She'd threaded the reel with light line, fitting it with a silk-bodied California Coachman, one of her favorite late-afternoon and evening dry flies.

She was shooting the line in a basic roll cast, targeting a spot directly under an overhanging branch where a plump, critical kingfisher watched each shot Jane made into the fluttering pool of nymphs caught in a backwater created by an old treefall. While Jane had seen half a dozen risings, none had condescended to take the Coachman. Not that she really cared; it was enough that she was alone and she was fishing.

Not really a sport people would expect from a Brooklyn girl born into poverty at the turn of the century, but times changed and so did Jane, it seemed. Once upon a time she'd had every girl's dream of marriage and children, but here she was, a bona fide war correspondent in the middle of a bona fide war. Now who would have thunk it? The fly fishing had come from her friend Rusty Birdwell, who covered the Hollywood beat for the *Daily News*. He'd taken her to a few of his favorite trout streams just outside of L.A., but she'd long ago given up on those and had now fished from Canada to the Sea of Cortez.

Jane cast her line once again, farther upstream this time, letting the fly drift down on the current, past the dense, overhanging yew trees that stood on the edge of the marsh island. The sky had gone to twilight and the shadows under the trees were becoming deeper. Overhead, the first nighthawks and swifts were booming and screaming as they fed. The river was hushed and expectant as Jane's line lay flat upon the water, drifting slowly on the current. No trout rose to the fly, and, perhaps bored with her poor efforts, the kingfisher flew sharply away from the perch on the end of the dry limb and angled toward the dark silhouette of the village's barely visible sky-line, downstream from the mill. Jane reeled in her line and let herself think about her day with Dundee again.

The dead man wearing Kelman's dog tags had also been wearing the appropriate uniform and rank insignia and, with the forged pass found in his coat, he would have easily passed a simple "stop-and-go" inspection by the Military Police. Pretty sophisticated for a deserter on the run. If he was a deserter, and if he was on the run.

Jane felt a small thrill of excitement shiver through her, the first scent of the fox, the beginning of the chase. She tried to put the thought out of her head and walked back toward the bank. Twice before she'd become too involved with a subject she was only there to observe and document, and on both occasions it had almost gotten her killed. She was here to take pictures, nothing more, and that's exactly what she was going to do. Still, a murdered man with gold dust under his fingernails wasn't something you came across every day. As she reached the bank and began breaking down her rod and climbing out of her hip waders, the single thought turned into a string of possibilities and finally a theory. Just then Dundee stepped out of the bramble path and stood in front of her. She took a couple of steps back and drew in her breath. She could see the red flare of his cigarette end in the darkness.

"Getting dark," he said. "Thought you might need a little guidance getting back."

"I have an idea," said Jane. She gently tipped the three-piece rod into its leather carrying case and put the reel into the small wicker pocket of her fish creel.

"About what?" asked Dundee. He had his tobacco out and was rolling her a cigarette. He lit it and handed it to her. She took it gratefully and puffed away on it for a few moments, putting her thoughts in order.

"About our man with the Midas touch," she answered finally, packing away the last of her gear.

"What about him?"

"He was wearing a uniform and carrying dog tags that didn't belong to him. The assumption is he's a deserter, using the uniform to be inconspicuous. There's more Yank soldiers around these days than there are civilians."

"Interesting point."

"But he's got gold dust under his fingernails and there's no function within the U.S. military that handles gold on a regular basis, right?"

"As far as I can tell." Dundee nodded.

"So what if he's not in the military at all. What if the uniform and the dog tags are a cover for something else."

"A disguise?"

"And I'll take it one step further," said Jane. "Why dispose of his body in a town when it would have been much easier and much more inconspicuous to dump him in the countryside? It doesn't make any sense at all."

"So you're saying he was in Letchworth for a reason?"

"It's worth checking out, don't you think?"

The dingy warehouse stood at the end of Pekin Street, a foul-smelling cul-de-sac close to the West India Docks in the Limehouse district of London.

Half the businesses around it had been bombed out and most of the rest abandoned, but Chow Yun Fat Meat Products still appeared to be in business, at least in some small way. Once every few days a truck would appear, sheep, goat, pig and cow carcasses would be unloaded, and, for a few hours, the chimneys of the building would blur with an oily turbid vapor that spewed the scent of blood and death in the air. Chow Yun Fat was a meat rendering plant where meat too old, too stringy or too diseased for human consumption was supposedly broken down into its component parts and used for everything from soap to motor lubricant to the glue on the back of postage stamps. In fact, only half the building's energies were bent toward rendering; it was also the center for most of the black-market trade in meat in London. Much of the material deemed unfit for humans was mixed with government-approved product, or sold to companies manufacturing tinned products. Approximately half the output of this particular operation was used to manufacture the British version of C rations. God forbid that The Colonel should be disloyal enough to sell the stuff for use by his own men.

On this cloudy and moonless night, Limehouse was a wasteland of rubble. Nothing moved along the short length of Pekin Street except the occasional scurrying rat, usually a recent immigrant from convoy ships unloading at the docks. Most of London's native rodent residents had been burned out by the recent conflagrations in the area.

There were several dim lights on within Chow Yun Fat, illuminating four men. One was The Colonel; one was his ever-present aide, Lieutenant Menzies;

the third was an MP on The Colonel's payroll and the fourth was a young black man named Thomas Wier. They were all standing beside one of the high concrete rendering vats that were scattered around the gloomy, high ceilinged chamber. A series of chain-driven overhead conveyors fitted with gleaming meathooks formed a latticework over their heads. The warehouse stank of animal dung and fear. The black man, Wier, was dressed in a filthy army greatcoat. His G.I. boots were scuffed and untied. He looked hungry and defeated. The MP, a man named Saksamun, stood beside the black man, a long truncheon held in both hands. Above them, the rendering vat bubbled and gasped. The smell in the place was a throat-grabbing horror, and the thick wooden planks of the floor were dark and oily, soaked with a hundred generations of animal blood.

"Where do you come from, son?" asked The Colonel.

"Company C of the Twenty-seventh Quartermaster Truck Regiment, sir."

"Ah."

The MP spoke up. "He hit a superior officer, a white officer, Colonel. Court-martialed. Escaped from the glasshouse in Bristol. Been AWOL for two weeks or so. Just caught him. Due for transport to the Shepton Mallett facility tonight."

"Excellent." The Colonel smiled. He stared at the young black man. "How'd you like to avoid that, son?"

"Do just about anything, sir."

"You know who I am?"

"Heard tell. You run a lot of the angles over here."

"That's right. I can keep you out of jail."

"I'd sure appreciate that, sir."

"Take off your clothes."

"Pardon."

"You'll need new clothes, correct?"

"Oh. Yes, sir." The young black man began stripping off his clothes until he stood naked in front of the other three men. He looked embarrassed and tried to cover himself.

"Dog tags," instructed The Colonel.

The black man nodded, ducked his head and slipped the punch-pressed dog tags from around his neck. He held them out. Menzies plucked a snow-white handkerchief out of his pocket and took the tags. He wiped them down, then handed them to The Colonel, who glanced at them briefly. "What rank are you, son?"

"Corporal, sir."

The Colonel turned to the MP and nodded. Saksamun stepped forward, raised his truncheon and struck the young black man across the forehead as hard as he could. The man's face split open and blood poured down his dark body to the darker floor. He crumpled without a sound.

"Now what?" asked the MP.

The Colonel slipped the dog tags around his own neck, smiled and looked up at the bubbling vat of boiling animal fats. "You know the old Chinese saying: render unto Caesar what is Caesar's, render unto Chow Yun Fat what is Chow Yun Fat's." The Colonel shrugged. "So render him."

Seven

They left Strathmere late in the morning, shortly after a motorcycle courier brought up the photographs from Simpson's office at the morgue. Hunched behind the wheel, Dundee piloted the big American car down the A10 to the A507. They were in Hertfordshire now and every turn brought a new vista of rolling hills, oddly shaped hedgerow-divided fields and clumps of ancient forest. She'd brought her camera bag and a fully loaded Leica with her, but so far she had resisted the temptation to photograph the passing scenery, almost as though recording it would somehow destroy its enchantment.

"It's so hard to believe there's a war on," said Jane, staring out the window, breathing in the gentle, lightly scented air. She was about as far from the ash and smoke and traffic sounds of New York as you could get. "Sometimes, when I was in school when I was a little kid, they'd take us to the library. I had this special book I loved called *The Yellow Fairy Book* and all the illustrations were like this. Magic. You expect gnomes to pop out from behind trees and to find trolls under bridges."

"There's nothing magical on the other side of the Channel," said Dundee. "The gnomes are riding Panzers and the trolls don't live under bridges; they fly Heinkels and Stukas and ME 109s. Hitler's no fairy either; he's the devil in the flesh, right down to the pointy ears and the tail. It's a real war, even if I'm not allowed to fight it."

"Your boss, Hedrick, seemed to think I was too chicken for a combat battalion. You sound like you want to fight."

"Hedrick hates my guts. Thinks I'm a rich man's kid trying to get out of the war. I'm pretty sure the old man pulled some strings to keep me out of it. Hedrick doesn't like to be anybody's puppet—not that I blame him." He reached into the pocket of his dark green officer's jacket and pulled out his cigarette makings, handing them across the seat to Jane. She started rolling them up. "The truth of it is I'm too tall to be a fighter pilot, I get seasick on any boat you put me on, from a rowboat to the Queen Mary, and I'm too blind to fire a rifle and hope to hit anything. Sad to say, being a lawyer is what I'm good at."

"And Hedrick gave you his so-called 'Special Unit' as punishment? To keep you out of the way?"

"I think so," Dundee said. "It hasn't worked out that way though; I've been involved in a fair number of hush-hush situations already."

"Hush-hush?"

"There's a lot of prosecutors think any so-called intimacy between a black soldier and a white woman is rape by definition. So far I've come upon four sweet young things, one of whose father was a member of parliament, who went out on dates with one of our colored men and wound up with a whole wheat bun in the oven before they called foul."

"What happened?"

"I proved otherwise," said Dundee. "Rape in England is a capital offense. You hang for it. Serious business and these boys were just stupid, not guilty. Hedrick was embarrassed by the whole thing; said I was acting more like a defense lawyer than a prosecutor." Jane picked up a somewhat droopy cigarette, lit it and handed it to Dundee. She started working on one of her own. "Truth is," said Dundee, "I think he just wanted to use that new death house they just built at Shepton Mallett.

"Shepton Mallett?"

"Three-hundred-thirty-year-old English prison they handed over to us for the duration. Off in the middle of nowhere. They say it's worse than Alcatraz."

A few minutes later they reached the outskirts of Letchworth, a distinct greenbelt of dead flat, perfectly manicured agricultural land planted in fields as regular as squares on a checkerboard. At dinner the night before Jane had asked the Pottinger sisters if they knew anything about the place.

"One of those perfect garden cities invented by what they used to call a 'social scientist,'" said Annabel Pottinger, scowling over her portion of steaming steak and kidney pie.

"Nothing social about them, or scientific I should say," put in her sister Alice.

"The whole thing was devised by a lunatic named Ebenezer Howard," said Annabel. "For some reason they knighted him eventually. He'd visited America, you see, and come back with all these mad ideas about everyone being equal, and everyone having the same opportunities. Completely did away with the aristocracy, tradition, royalty, the lot. I mean, good heavens, what would have become of people like us?"

"I'm sure you would have managed just fine," said Jane.

"Don't be so sure, my dear," said Alice. "Ideas sometimes have a way of catching on you know. The American Revolution for instance. Look at all the damage that did!"

"Letchworth?" Dundee reminded.

"Called it a Garden City or some such," Annabel replied. "Clean streets without any curves in them, houses all looking the same, trees planted in perfect rows. Insufferably boring I should think. All that brick."

"What happened to his idea?" Jane asked.

"Well," said Alice, "it's as I said. These things catch on. They formed some sort of building society and actually created the place. From what I understand it's full of tradesmen and factory workers." She gave a little shudder. "I think they make furniture there."

"You've never been there?" asked Polly Darling, the ATS girl.

"Good lord no!" said Annabel. "Whatever for?"

They came through the greenbelt in the Dodge and the landscape abruptly changed from countryside to neatly designed built-up housing areas, regularly spaced commons and parks, recreation grounds and what could only be grammar schools, looking more like small glue factories than places of education, the only giveaway being the goal posts in the fields and boys in short pants and soccer shirts doing calisthenics in rows as neat as the trees that lined the streets.

"It sure as hell isn't New York," commented Jane. "Not even Garden City, Long Island. Bet you can't find so much as a single troll or gnome here."

"Probably banned Peter Pan years ago," agreed Dundee. They went by a large white building that advertised itself as the Letchworth Public Baths, then went over a short bridge arcing over a double set of railway tracks. There was an attractively gabled Tudoresque railway station done in ornamental brick and surrounded by narrow beds of pansies and other simple flowers, and then they were on what was obviously the town's main street. There were a score of shops, all sporting identical awnings, with flats above, and extremely broad sidewalks. Buses ran in both directions at regular intervals, young mothers pushed prams and the traffic, what there was of it, moved sedately, occasionally pulling over to park in the abundant spots available.

"Urban utopia," said Dundee.

"Boring as hell," Jane responded. "Not enough crime here to fill a thimble. Probably need a permit to rob a house."

There was a police station however, and several men inside it. The chief constable was a man named Bearisto; pudgy, short, with thinning hair and a uniform sprinkled with cake crumbs down the front. They found him behind a desk in his office, sipping a cup of tea and smoking a cigarette as he leaned back in his chair, contemplating the ceiling.

Dundee tried to read the name plate on the desk. "Chief Constable . . . Bear . . . risto?"

"You don't pronounce the '*i*' in the middle," said the man. He made no move to get out of his chair. He eyed Dundee's uniform. "You're the Yank policeman I was told to expect."

"That's right."

"Don't quite know what it is you think I can do for you."

"I'd like to see the spot where the body was found."

"Can't see what it matters where the fellow was chucked from the train, can you?"

"Nevertheless."

"And the woman here?"

"Her name is Jane Todd. She's a war correspondent."

The chief constable turned to Jane with a slightly greasy smile. He had small, rodentlike teeth and small, broken veins on his cheeks. "Shouldn't you be covering the social page, dearie? What the generals' wives are wearing?"

"I prefer dead bodies," Jane answered. The man looked vaguely like a pig, as well as acting like one, but she remembered her conversation with Hedrick, Dundee's boss, and kept her feelings to herself.

"All right." Bearisto sighed. He levered himself up from his chair and went out into the main office. He pointed to a young, carrot-haired man in uniform behind the counter. "Constable Mainz will show you."

"One more thing," said Dundee.

Bearisto sighed again. "What now?"

"I'll need a fingerprint kit."

"What would that be?" asked the chief constable. "We're not the bloody Met, you know."

"Something to dust for prints with."

"We don't keep anything like that."

"Do you have an art shop in town?"

"You mean a gallery?"

"No," said Dundee. "A shop that sells supplies to artists."

"There's a Windsor and Newton on Commerce Avenue, not that I can see why you'd possibly need such a place."

"Don't worry about it."

"Mainz," said the chief constable, raising his voice. The red-haired man looked around.

"Yes, sir."

"Accompany these two, would you please."

"Of course, sir."

The constable followed Jane and Dundee out into the sunlight. "We only have the two patrol cars," Mainz apologized. He pointed to a pair of zebra-striped spots in front of the municipal building. "They're both on duty, I'm afraid." The young man's cheeks flushed to match the color of the hair on his head, a spray of freckles standing out across his nose. "The chief constable doesn't think I have enough experience yet so he has me doing the work of a clerk." He pronounced the word "clark."

"I wonder how much experience the chief constable has," said Jane, trying not to laugh.

"He was on the council for a year or two. We had a real policeman, a retired man from Birmingham, but he's working at the War Office now."

"So Chief Constable Bearisto stepped into the breach," said Dundee.

"Yes, sir," Mainz said.

"Well," said Dundee, "I think we can get along

without him for the moment." He patted Mainz on the back. "And we can take our car. You can tell us where to go."

"Of course, sir." The young man nodded agreeably. "I've never been in a Yank car before." He flushed again. "Sorry, sir."

"For what?"

"Calling you a Yank."

"That's what he is," said Jane. "We both are. Now come on, let's get a move on."

The Windsor and Newton Store turned out to be just around the corner and a block up. Dundee sent the young constable into the shop with orders to buy some powdered lampblack, three broad sable brushes, some blank index cards if they had them, a water colorist's atomizer and a roll of Scotch tape. There was some brief confusion until Mainz realized that Scotch tape was the American term for Sellotape, but after that things went smoothly. He came out of the shop with a small paper bag in hand and then they drove another block up to Ley's Avenue, then turned left onto Station Road, which ran parallel to the railway tracks. This was clearly the industrial center of Letchworth. There were small factories left and right, including a furniture manufacturing concern, a dairy and the electrical generating station. Where necessary there were spurs off the main line that led to the sooty brick buildings.

Jane looked around as they drove. No matter how you cut it, not a nice place to die.

Eight

Mainz directed Dundee down a narrow paved road that led to the back of a looming, rust-stained gasworks, where he pulled to a stop. Twenty feet away Dundee could see the raised embankment of the railroad right of way. By the looks of it there was no spur leading to the gasworks.

"LNER," said Mainz, getting out of the Dodge, followed by Dundee and Jane.

"London North Eastern Railroad," said Dundee.

"Yes, sir." Mainz nodded. "No freight carried on this line. It's all passengers. Nonstop line for the express trains from Letchworth to London."

"How long does the ride take?" asked Jane. She took the Leica out of its case and started taking a few photographs to establish their location.

"Less than forty-five minutes," said Mainz, leading them over to the embankment. There was a small red metal flag on a stick marking the spot where the body had been found. They reached it and Dundee squatted down as Jane continued to take pictures.

"What was done here?"

"Done?" asked Mainz, his expression confused.

"Was a crime scene marked out, did anyone look

around for anything that might have belonged to the victim?"

"No, sir. The chief constable called the Home Office and they sent out a coroner's team from London."

"Jesus," muttered Dundee. He sighed. "Photographs taken?"

"No, sir."

"Has it rained since the body was found?"

"No, sir."

"Well, that's something anyway." He glanced at Jane. "Have you done this kind of thing before?" he asked.

"Taking snaps of crime scenes? Sure. It's usually got the body along with it. I used to fill in when the cop photographers were on vacation sometimes."

"I wonder if there's anything to salvage," said Dundee.

"Well, at least we've got a pretty good idea of where he impacted," said Jane. She pointed down to the embankment. It was made up of gravel and old coal clinkers. There was blood sprayed everywhere and the track itself had a large, gruesome stain. Jane began to take more photographs. Dundee remained squatting, looking over the area carefully, working it in square inches instead of feet.

"See anything?" Jane asked.

"Blood, some gray stuff that looks like it might be brains."

"Fits."

"Maybe." Dundee turned to the red-haired Letchworth constable. "The train he had a punched ticket for was going from Cambridge to London."

Mainz nodded. He pulled a small bound notebook

out of his back pocket and flipped through the pages. "Jotted it down even though Chief Constable Bearisto said it was a waste of time and I should let the Yanks investigate their own."

"What can you tell me about the train?"

"It's a daily, sir, except Sundays. Leaves Cambridge 9:40, arrives in Letchworth 10:15, arrives London 11:05."

"Fifty minutes."

"Forty-five, actually," said Mainz. "Letchworth halt is five minutes on the down train, fifteen on the up. That one anyway."

"I don't understand," said Dundee.

"Most of the trains up to the eight o'clock are for people coming 'up' from London. People who live in Letchworth but work in the city. The trains 'down' are going into London late. In fact, it's the last train down to the city for the day."

"Was his ticket up or down?"

"Down, sir. He was going to London, from Cambridge."

"Or Letchworth?"

"Yes, sir. The station's back that way." He pointed. "The line curves around the outskirts of the town and then heads south."

"When we drove past the station the track was masked by the building," said Dundee.

"Yes, sir."

"So presumably the compartment side of the train faces the station so people can get off, and the corridor side faces this way."

"Yes, sir. It's the same in both directions. They just place the engine on either end depending on whether they're going up or down."

"Which leaves us with a problem, don't you think?"

"I didn't understand a word of that," said Jane.

The constable's eyes widened. "Good lord."

"That's it, Constable."

"What's it?" said Jane.

Mainz looked toward the track and then at Jane. "On British railcars the exit doors are on each compartment. The corridor side has no exits except at the ends of each carriage and they're securely locked while the train is in motion. This is the corridor side."

"In other words, there's no way he could have been thrown out of the train and landed here," explained Dundee.

"So what happened?" Jane asked.

"Someone forced him up the embankment just as the train went by and put two bullets in his head. He fell back against the train, which did all the damage. It was a night train, so no one would have seen anything because the blackout curtains would have been drawn, and the sound of the engine would have masked the sound of the shots."

"Which means he was already in Letchworth," said Jane.

"Probably," Dundee said. "But it doesn't get us any closer to identifying him."

"What about his fingerprints?" asked Mainz. "I assumed that's what all the lamp black and brushes were about."

"Smart boy," said Dundee. "According to the Home Office coroner in London he was an American, so his prints wouldn't be on file with Scotland Yard. On the other hand, maybe the man who killed him left something behind with his prints on it. Maybe we can identify him, even if we can't identify the corpse.''

They began quartering the area directly around the blood-splashed cinders where the man with Kelman's dog tags had been shot. As Constable Mainz and Dundee carefully gathered up the detritus along the railway line Jane took several photographs of each piece. After almost an hour they had two brass shell casings from a Colt .45 automatic pistol that had been forcefully ejected and landed a dozen feet away, almost hidden in the tall weeds growing at the foot of the embankment, an empty ten packet of Darts Cigarettes, an equally empty bottle of Watney's Red Barrel ale and a book of paper matches advertising the services of J. G. D. Satchell, Surveyor, Estate Agent & Auctioneer.

Dundee spent the next thirty minutes dusting each object with the lamp black and the sable brushes, then gently applying the tape to the resulting prints, lifting them off the objects, then putting the strips of tape down firmly on the plain index cards purchased by Mainz. By the end of the half hour he'd taken prints from the cigarette packet, the beer bottle and the book of paper matches. There were several sets of prints, smudged and overlapping, on the beer bottle as though it might have been passed back and forth, but the ones on the book of matches and the packet of Darts were clear sets.

"I've never seen it done that way," said Mainz. "I thought you powdered and then took pictures with some sort of special camera."

"It's not the camera, it's the film," Jane explained. She'd used the technique more than a few times for the New York Police Department. "It's very high contrast so when you develop it the only thing that shows are the prints on a plain white background."

"I heard they were doing something like this in Czechoslovakia," Dundee answered. He shrugged. "It seems to work."

"Chief constable won't like it," said Mainz, frowning. "Doesn't like anything new." The young man cleared his throat. " 'If 'twas good enough for my da, it's good enough for me,' " he said, doing a fair imitation of his boss.

"His father probably fought in the last war and was used to Germans dropping bombs by hand," said Dundee with a sour note in his voice. "The world moves on."

"Yes, I suppose it does," said Mainz. "Sometimes I wonder where it's headed for."

"Hell," offered Jane with a grin. "But not in a handcart. In a fast car."

"Long as it's not a German one," grumbled Dundee. He nodded to Mainz. "Put all of this into the paper bag. We'll go to this estate agent's place, and then I'll deliver the prints to Scotland Yard myself."

"No need," said Mainz happily, gathering up everything and putting it into the paper bag from the art store. "We have a dactylograph back at the station. I can send them direct."

"And the chief constable?"

"He's usually on the links by this time of day," Mainz answered, smiling. "Probably with the chairman of the council. Elections this month."

"All right," said Dundee. "We'll drop you off. You send the prints to Records at Scotland Yard, and Miss Todd and I will go and see Mr. Satchell."

The estate agent was located on Eastcheap, one street west of the art supply store and directly behind the new Urban District Council building that faced onto the town square and looked like something they might build in Philadelphia, complete with a clock tower and belfry done in white. Satchell's itself was one of fifty identical storefronts on the street, in another one of the block-long connected buildings that seemed to be so popular in the town.

The green awning over the door, like the book of matches, referred to it as J. G. D. Satchell's but, as they were quickly informed, J. G. D. had been in his grave for the past twenty-five years and the office was now run by his son, W. H. Satchell, who, according to the instantly proferred business card, was also M. Inst. M. & Cy.E., whatever that meant.

He was also short, almost completely bald, sporting tortoiseshell spectacles, a pencil-thin Clark Gable mustache and several chins, one after the other. When he smiled his teeth were obviously—albeit expensively—false and clicked slightly when he talked. He was wearing a three-piece Harris tweed suit in a houndstooth check, a red-and-green-striped bow tie and what were usually referred to as "sturdy" walking shoes in brown. In other words, Jane thought, he was a near-perfect caricature of an English country gentleman; all he needed to complete the picture was a Tyrolean hat like the one the duke of Windsor was invariably photographed wearing and a knobby walking stick. If pressed, a man like Satchell could probably talk about salmon fishing, sheep shearing and cricket all in the same conversation.

The office itself was on the small side. There was a single desk behind a courtroomlike bar with a swinging gate, several waiting room chairs, half a dozen wooden filing cabinets with rows of large ring binders above them. The walls were painted a vague mustard color and covered with framed photographs and drawings of houses and commercial buildings. The floor was dark green linoleum.

"So, what can I do for our American allies?" asked Satchell after the introductions had been made. He looked almost fiercely pleasant, as though the smile on his face and the twinkle in his eye were theatrical props and had nothing at all to do with his actual feelings. Everything was bluff, hearty and irrepressibly friendly.

"I wonder if you can tell us if you've rented to another one of your allies lately?"

"An American?"

"Yes."

"As a matter of fact I did. He was from the quartermaster's division I believe. He was looking for warehouse space. I only had a very small property but he leased it immediately."

"What was his name?" asked Dundee.

Satchell got up from behind his desk and went to one of the old filing cabinets. He opened one of the drawers, pulled out a file and returned to his desk. He sat down and flipped open the file.

"Danby. Lieutenant Colonel Charles Danby. First Infantry Division, First Quartermaster's Company."

"Shit," muttered Dundee, his face falling.

"I beg your pardon?" said Satchell.

"Something wrong?" Jane asked.

"Forget it." Dundee took a deep breath and let it out slowly from blown cheeks. "Where exactly is this warehouse?"

It turned out to be a small brick building on Northway Road, right beside the railway overpass and equidistant from the station and the place where the body had been found.

"How long was the lease for?" Dundee asked as Satchell turned an enormous key in the padlock that secured the garage-style doors of the little building.

"Three months."

"What did he say he needed it for?"

"He didn't," said the dapper little man. "He simply showed me a requisition form from his office and a purchase order. That was enough for me."

"I'll bet," Jane murmured.

"I beg your pardon?"

"Nothing."

The key finally turned and Satchell swung open the doors. The square space inside was empty except for several workbenches up against the far wall.

"He's come and gone by now, of course," said Satchell. "The lease was up a few days ago."

"Were the tables here when you rented him the place?" Dundee asked, walking back into the shadows.

Jane followed him. She looked down at the floor. There was no sign that anything had been stored here. The concrete floor was clean except for a small darkened patch in one corner, close to one of the worktables.

Dundee had spotted it too, and bent down for a closer examination. There were four equidistant bolt holes drilled in the floor, as well as a corresponding, but larger, hole in the ceiling.

Satchell frowned. "He wasn't given leave to make any alterations."

"Charlie Danby never asked leave for anything," said Dundee, a sour note in his voice. He touched the dark spot on the concrete floor. Scorched. The hole in the roof might have been for a ventilation pipe or a metal chimney.

"You know him?" asked Jane.

"I had the unfortunate experience of going to the same private school with him in California. His old man and mine were in bed together."

"I beg your pardon," said Satchell, his bushy little eyebrows disappearing into his forehead.

"Just a saying," said Dundee.

"I'm assuming the Army is going to pay for the damages here," said Satchell. It wasn't a question.

Dundee shrugged. "Put in a requisition," he said. "Maybe you'll get lucky."

"Requisition to whom?"

"Don't ask me," said Dundee, shrugging again. "I'm just a lawyer." He went to the tables lined up against the back wall and ran his hand across the smooth wooden surfaces. Jane used the Leica. Dundee lifted his hand and held it palm up toward Jane. "What does that look like to you?" he asked. Jane took several photographs of the shiny grit on his hand.

"Gold," she said.

Lieutenant Colonel Charles Danby, First Infantry Division, First Quartermaster's Company, dressed in the uniform of an Army corporal, the stripes removed from the sleeves and a large white *P* for "prisoner" stitched onto his back, sat on his haunches and stared at the large vegetable patch he was tending. The patch had been laid out against the west wall of the old prison and got plenty of sun on the days when there was any sun in this godforsaken country. The carrots seemed to be doing especially well. Tending the vegetables was rated highly as far as jobs in the prison went, since it got him out into the fresh air more than the standard two hours a day, but it was also an indulgence on his part since he was officially only a corporal, and new to the place at that. It was the kind of thing that would make others at Shepton Mallet suspicious, staff and inmates alike. On the other hand, he wasn't planning on being here much longer. He fished around in the pocket of his shirt, pulled out a cigarette and a book of matches, and lit up, dragging deeply. A shadow suddenly fell across the vegetable patch. Out of the corner of his eye he noted a highly polished boot with a brilliantly whitened high-top gaiter attached. He kept smoking his cigarette and stared out at his vegetables, balancing himself lightly on the small trowel in his hand. There was a faint thudding sound as a large cast-iron key hit the ground by the trowel. Danby used the trowel to cover it.

"It's all set," said a voice. "Anytime after the shift change at midnight. The key will get you into the old women's section."

"Lot of old women in the old women's section?" Danby joked.

The voice ignored him. "People who need to be paid off have been given the word . . . sir."

"Good," said Danby. "What about transport?"

"Ready and waiting, just the way you ordered." The gaitered boot swiveled and the shadow disappeared from the vegetable patch. Danby put down the trowel and picked up a handful of the loamy soil, the key hidden within his fist. He let the soil trickle through his fingers until all that was left was the key. He climbed to his feet and slipped the key into his pocket.

Danby looked around at the bleak, stone perimeter of the prison. It had been an interesting experience but not something he'd like to repeat. He thought about having a nice glass of single malt. By this time tomorrow he'd be able to have his fill. He looked out at the rows of vegetables and thought about the Okie stoop labor he used to pick his fields back home. They might as well be prisoners here; at least that way they got to eat what they grew.

He dropped the butt of his cigarette and ground it out with the toe of his scuffed brown shoe. He turned then and walked toward the high oak door that led back into the prison. There were half a dozen MPs in the yard. All of them with polished boots and chalk white gaiters. He wondered which of them had given him the key; they all looked exactly the same. He smiled. That was one of the best things about armies and soldiers and wars. Everything and everyone looked the same; you could hide a million trees and no one would see anything but the forest.

Nine

Jane stood in the millrace stream a little down from where she'd fished before. Dundee was ten feet behind her, perched on a large boulder, smoking a cigarette. They'd been back in Swan Hill for an hour but had spoken little about the day's events. Dundee's face had been dark as a storm cloud all the way back from Letchworth, and his expression hadn't done much to encourage anything but the lightest and most inane of conversations. She was surprised when he offered to accompany her down to the fishing stream; keeping her company didn't seem as though it would be high on his list of priorities.

She was using the Granger reel again, with a light line and a small-hooked Coachman fly, not much bigger than the midge it was designed to imitate. She flicked the line with a bare twitch of her wrist and watched as it sailed out into the current and began moving downstream, the line trailing behind it almost invisible in the dusky light. Jane finally decided it was time to do some fishing in Major Lucas Dundee's thought processes.

"So who's this Danby guy?" she asked. "You went white as a sheet when Satchell mentioned his name."

She paused and looked back over her shoulder. "He a friend of yours?"

Dundee flicked the butt of his cigarette into the stream and Jane watched, astounded, as a fish rose to take it, then spit it out. It occurred to her that she could invent a wet fly and call it a Du Maurier and probably do pretty well with it.

"I'd hardly call him a friend." The major took out another cigarette and lit it. Jane reeled in the Coachman. "Do you ever actually catch anything?" he asked. "We've been here for almost an hour and you haven't had so much as a nibble."

"Fly fishing is about patience, or at least that's what my friend Birdwell says. And you're trying to change the subject." Carrying the rod and reel high she waded out of the hip-deep water and sat herself down on the boulder beside Dundee. He handed her a cigarette and lit it for her. They both stared out over the placid, quietly burbling water. In the fading light she could hear vespers chiming from the church at the edge of the village.

"Charles Danby," Jane said. "Any relation to the Danby with his name all over everything?"

Dundee nodded. "Charles Danby. Son of Cornelius Danby, owner of the Danby Trust Bank, owner of Danby Oranges, owner of Danby Cartage, owner of Danby Lines, with twelve cargo ships and god only knows how many freight cars in its fleet of vehicles. What my old man doesn't own in California, Cornelius Danby does, and Charlie is his only son and heir. Corney's wife died early on of some kind of mental disease, which everyone knew meant she drowned herself in the ornamental goldfish pool. The daughter, Grace, didn't make it much past eighteen. She drank like the fish her mother drowned with, and drove her car off a cliff an hour north of Los Angeles near a place called Castaic."

"Where the Saint Francis Dam collapsed."

"That's the place."

"So Charlie was the only one left." ˙

"One too many for Cornelius, at least if you believe Charlie. He sent him off to the Bain Academy about the same time my old man sent me to the same place. We spent four years learning how to ride horses and beat the living hell out of each other in the boxing ring."

"Who won?"

"He did, mostly. He was a couple of inches taller and he had longer arms. Not to mention the fact that he took it all seriously."

"Took what seriously?"

"Competition. He had to be the best, no matter what it was and no matter what it took."

"What does that mean?"

"Hit below the belt if the referee wasn't watching. He cheated if it suited him, which it usually did, lied all the time, blamed things on other kids, beat up kids smaller or weaker than him. Bullied."

"And he got away with it?"

"The library at Bain is called Cornelius Danby Hall."

"Ah," said Jane. She flipped her butt out into the stream, but nothing rose. Maybe it was in the flicking, not the butt itself. "Go on."

"We both went to West Point. At the end of it all he took a commission rather than go back to work for his old man. I went to Stanford Law. I was a cop and an assistant D.A. in Los Angeles for a while and then, when it looked like there was going to be a war, I enlisted and joined the Judge Advocate General's office. I guess Charlie had been in long enough to make lieutenant colonel. Either that or his old man bought the rank for him." Dundee shook his head. "Quartermaster. Jesus! That's like giving a kid the key to a candy store."

"What do you mean?"

"He's probably hip-deep in some kind of black-market deal, and that poor son of a bitch by the railway tracks got in his way."

"So what are you going to do about it?"

"He's a legitimate part of my investigation now. I'll track him down, see where all this leads."

"Sounds good to me."

"You don't have anything to do with it," Dundee said abruptly.

"I don't get you," said Jane. "It sounds as though you're brushing me off."

"That's exactly what I'm doing."

"Why? Because I fly fish?"

"Because you're a journalist. A correspondent. You take pictures and you write stories. I don't think it's the kind of thing JAG wants, and I don't think it's the kind of thing the Army wants, period."

"You think if this gets out it'll be too embarrassing for the generals?"

"Something like that."

"Look, Major, I've been involved in a couple of very sticky stories when it comes to things the big guys would like to sweep under the rug. That's why they sent me to this little bucolic backwater, complete with trout streams and moo-cows. They're trying to sweep me under the rug, or at the very least put me in a place where I can't do any damage. I think they did the same thing to you. Like you said, your old man might have had something to do with it as well."

"That doesn't have anything to do with it."

"Then you're not thinking, Major. You need me."

"How so?"

"You said this Danby owns the half of California your old man doesn't."

"So?"

"So what happens if you do track him down, and you do prove he was part of this guy getting murdered, or that he's behind some blackmail ring or gold smuggling operation or whatever it is. He has power. His old man can pull strings. He's going to get away with it unless you have someone like me to independently blow the whistle. I'm your guarantee."

Dundee looked at her for a long moment as the shadows continued to gather over the stream. Dark against the fading light of the sky overhead, a nighthawk swooped and boomed, chasing some invisible insect.

"Call me Lucas," he said.

She took another smoke out of the pack and he lit it for her. She took a long drag, then sighed. "Call me an idiot for getting involved in a crazy stunt like this."

"It could get even crazier," Dundee warned. "Danby's no angel."

Jane shrugged the warning off. "Crazy makes a good story," she said. "Better pictures too."

Together they walked up the hill to the gates of Strathmere. Jane had her hip waders half jammed into her empty fish creel and carried the leather tube holding her reel across her back like a quiver. She paused at the columns and looked up at the mad-eyed horse that capped each one.

"So I guess this is what we're fighting for," she said quietly. She shook her head and quoted the inscription over the front entrance of the main house by rote: "*Quaesita Marte Tuenda Arte.* A dying way of life lived by people like the Potties, and a dead language on top of that. I mean, who needs Latin?"

Dundee pushed open one of the squeaky, rusty old gates to give them space to pass through. "Louis B. Mayer for one." He grinned. "*Ars Gratia Artis.* Art for the sake of Art. And you'd be surprised how alive it is. The law is full of it. Habeas corpus, corpus delicti, modus operandi, ex parte. Its value is in its absolute precision. Each word has a specific and singular meaning so no one gets confused, or says they got confused at some later date."

"Thank you, Professor Dundee."

"And if it hadn't been for people like the Potties, the Germans probably would have won the First World War."

"And if it hadn't been for people like the Potties a couple of hundred years ago we wouldn't have gotten so pissed off, and we might not have started the American Revolution."

"Touché," said Dundee. They slipped through the gates and headed up the overgrown track that led to the main house. A few minutes later, after a look of extreme consternation directed toward Jane's rubber boots, Bunter the butler let them into the house.

"There is a visitor, sir," said Bunter softly as Jane took off her boots and hung her creel on the hall hat rack.

"Anybody interesting?" asked Dundee.

"He says his name is Occleshaw, sir. Roy Occleshaw. A chief inspector from Scotland Yard."

"Where have you stashed him?" Jane asked.

"He is in the drawing room, madam. The Mrs. Pottingers are giving him tea, I believe. Miss Polly is also in attendance."

"How nice," said Dundee. "Lead on, Bunter old man. Let's see this policeman of yours."

"I can assure you, sir, he is not one of my policemen," the butler responded haughtily. "In fact, I would go so far as to say that he is of the . . . lower classes."

"Jesus," Jane sighed. She winked at Dundee and muttered under her breath, "Like I said, this is the kind of thing that starts revolutions."

They followed the butler up the short set of steps to the vestibule, then across the open area with the staircase. Finally, Bunter theatrically swung open the high, ornately carved double doors, then took two steps forward and one to the left.

"Major Lucas Dundee and Miss Jane Todd," he announced, his voice booming. Everyone in the room looked up, including a thick man in a brown suit. Spotting Jane, he stood up. He was in his late forties, his dark hair slicked down with some sort of oily tonic like Wildroot. He'd been using it for so long it had stained the collar of his suit jacket as well as that of his shirt. The man was wearing a bright blue bow tie underneath a broadening chin. His mouth was small, with unfortunate, cupidlike lips, and he had a drinker's slightly bulbous nose. The small dark eyes matched the mouth and, even without looking for a ring on his finger, Jane knew he was unmarried. No man's wife would let his eyebrows, nose and ear hair go untrimmed, or sew on a brown middle button for his white shirt, and too small for the buttonhole to boot. She hated to think it, but maybe Bunter hadn't been so far off the mark after all.

"This is Chief Inspector Occleshaw of Scotland Yard," said Alice Pottinger. She flashed a brief smile at Jane and Dundee, then nodded toward the tea tray on the table in front of her.

"There's biscuits as well," said Annabel.

"Not as many as there were before the arrival of the chief inspector," Polly grumbled, seated on the far side of the room, a stenographer's notebook in her lap.

"Nothing for me thanks," said Dundee, keeping his eyes on Occleshaw. "What can I do for you, Inspector?"

"Detective Chief Inspector," Occleshaw corrected.

"Then you must know my friend Morris," said Jane, sinking into one of the drawing room armchairs. She was liking Detective Chief Inspector Occleshaw less by the minute.

"Morris?" said Occleshaw, a little sourly. "Sounds like a Jewish name."

"Black," said Jane, ignoring the aside. "Detective Chief Inspector Morris Black, Scotland Yard C.I.D. Same rank as you."

" 'Fraid I don't know him."

"Odd."

"Yard's a big place, madam. Not surprising really."

"I suppose not. He was chiefly involved with murder cases."

"I see, ma'am," Occleshaw answered, although

clearly he didn't. In fact, he was looking quite uncomfortable.

"Maybe we should see your warrant card," said Jane, a faint suspicion stirring.

"What's a Yank like you know about warrant cards?" Occleshaw asked. Alice Pottinger eased a small dark biscuit from the plate on the tea tray and bit into it.

"Hardly polite to call her a Yank, Detective," said Alice Pottinger. "Rather like calling you a split or a copper, don't you think?" She turned around in her seat and gave Jane a broad wink. "Or a Limey for that matter."

Occleshaw stared at the old woman, astonished. Alice took another bite of her biscuit and then smiled, sweeping invisible crumbs from her lap. "Dear me, Detective, my sister and I may be old, but our lives haven't been as sheltered as one might think."

"By no means," her sister Annabel put in.

"Maybe Jane's right," said Dundee. He sat down and lit a cigarette. "Maybe we should see some identification."

"Not with civilians about," Occleshaw answered.

"Why?" asked Dundee. "Are you about to divulge state secrets?"

"I need to speak with you alone."

"Well, you're not going to."

"I'm afraid I'm going to have to insist, Major. And I will have to ask that young lady to put away her notebook as well."

"Insist away then," said Dundee. "I'm a member of the United States Judge Advocate General's office. You have neither authority nor jurisdiction over anything I do. A fact you are well aware of."

"Nevertheless . . ."

"Nevertheless nothing. Spit it out or go away," said Dundee.

Alice Pottinger finished off her biscuit and went through her brief crumb-brushing routine again. She chewed and swallowed. "I believe he's telling you to bugger off," she said.

"Yes," agreed Annabel. "I believe the appropriate American colloquialism is 'piss or get off the pot.' "

"Bloody hell," said Occleshaw.

"Yes, that too," said Polly, getting into the act. Throughout the performance Bunter had said nothing and had stood statuelike by the door. Jane thought she saw a very faint smile on his lips, however.

"Look," said Dundee, sighing. "Everybody in this room has signed your Official Secrets Act, including the Pottingers, and even Miss Todd. So either get on with it or get out of it."

Occleshaw took out a small, somewhat ragged-looking notebook and the stub of a pencil. He flipped open the notebook and then licked the end of the pencil. Jane was now completely in agreement with Bunter's assessment. The man had no class at all. He also had mismatched socks, which she noticed for the first time. And the metal tips of his laces needed replacing. She shivered slightly, imagining him licking the tips to a point each morning before he put the shoes on. The shoes themselves were brown, with heavy-looking toes. Cop shoes.

"You are acquainted with one Charles Andrew Danby, a lieutenant colonel in the American First Division."

"I haven't seen him in years," Dundee answered.

"You went to school with him, I understand."

"Why?" Dundee asked.

"Just checking, Major."

"Check somewhere else."

"Lieutenant Colonel Danby is an old friend then."

"I never would have considered him a friend, no. I simply knew him."

"In what way, sir?"

"As you said, we went to school together for a few years."

"The Bain Academy."

"That's right."

"Were you aware that Lieutenant Colonel Danby had a criminal record?"

"No."

"Theft, assault, car theft, statutory rape on several occasions. Blackmail."

"Ridiculous," said Dundee. "He never would have been let into the Army with a record like that, let alone been given a commission as an officer."

"His run-ins with the law came when he was still a juvenile," Occleshaw responded. "His record was sealed."

"That wouldn't have made any difference to the Army."

"His father is a very powerful man."

"Yes."

"As is yours."

"What does this have to do with anything, Occleshaw?"

"Just getting to it, Major." He paused and cleared his throat. He glanced down at his notebook again but Jane was sure he was doing it for effect; he knew all of this from memory. "You worked at the Los

Angeles District Attorney's Office for some time, is that correct?''

"Yes."

"A Mr. Burton Fitts? A man who was eventually disgraced for his actions. Corruption?"

"Yes. That's why I quit, although I don't see that it's any business of yours."

"During your time at the district attorney's office you had access to all the files held by the criminal courts in Los Angeles, is that correct?"

"Yes."

"Juvenile files?"

Jane watched as Dundee's jaw went rigid with anger. "Yes."

"Did you know that your friend Danby's juvenile record was not only sealed, but vanished altogether?"

"No. I didn't know that."

"You're sure about that?"

"What are you implying, Occleshaw?"

The detective held the hand with the pencil stub in it palm up. "I'm not implying nothing, Major, nothing at all."

"Why are you asking these questions?"

"I'm investigating a murder then, aren't I?" he said, throwing a look Jane's way. "Just like your friend Black."

"Whose murder?" Dundee asked.

"Name's Collins. Timothy Collins. Dressed up like one of yours, dog tags and all wasn't he?"

"The man with the gold dust under his fingernails," said Jane.

"That'd be him," said Occleshaw. "Worked at Garrards, the toffs' jewelers on Bond Street."

"What does Danby have to do with that?" asked Dundee.

"It's your friend that killed him. We already had him but those prints you had sent down from Letchworth prove it beyond a shadow."

"His prints?"

"Right in one, Major."

"You didn't come all the way up from London just to tell me this."

"No," said Occleshaw. "I did not."

"So why then?"

"Because you're sniffing around the same people for one thing. Because I'm of the opinion, as my superiors are, that Lieutenant Colonel Danby had his accomplices in this black-market ring he was nabbed for, not to mention the death of Mr. Collins."

"And you think *I* might be one of his accomplices?" Dundee said, stunned at the idea.

"It crossed our minds."

"Then you're out of yours," snorted Jane. "The major's no murderer or black marketer and you know it."

"Nevertheless, I'm warning you," said Occleshaw, and here he glanced at Jane. "I'm officially warning you off, so to speak. It's a wise man or woman who'd steer clear of poor old Charlie Danby these days." The thickset policeman smiled, the expression almost reptilian. "It might not be good for the health, or the career for that matter."

"You're threatening, not warning. I wouldn't have thought that was Scotland Yard's style."

"It's not," said Jane quietly. Morris had told her about these thugs. Occleshaw was Special Branch.

England's version of Hitler's Gestapo. Stupid, pig-headed and very powerful.

"These are difficult times," said Occleshaw, trying to soften his position. "War makes strange bed-fellows."

"I wouldn't argue that," said Dundee, "but Dan-by's American, and whether you like it or not he falls under American military law."

"I'm afraid not, sir. Your friend Danby has almost certainly committed an act of treason against the king of England and I'll bloody see him hang for it when I catch the bugger."

Part Two

SHEPTON MALLET

Ten

"Occleshaw's almost definitely Special Branch," said Jane, sitting on the far side of the first-class coach. Outside, rain was streaking the window glass and the sky was a broken, scudding gray.

"Who are, exactly . . . ?" said Dundee.

"According to my friend Morris, they're the domestic wing of MI5. They're supposedly attached to Scotland Yard so they can arrest people, but that's about the only real connection. A tougher version of the FBI." She frowned. "Or the Gestapo. They've been around since the 1800s. They used to be specially trained to deal with the Irish."

Dundee smiled at her curiously. "You certainly do know a lot about spies and spy catchers for a girl photographer." He paused. "And just what does this Special Branch have to do with a U.S. military prison in the middle of the English nowhere?"

The middle of nowhere was fifteen miles south of Bath, a little west of the seaport of Bristol and nestled on the edge of the Mendip Hills in the west of Somerset. Once upon a time Shepton Mallet had been a market town, but then the duke of Monmouth decided to go to war with the king and the people in the town had felt the duke's wrath as he went around skewering people's bowels with red-hot pokers and putting their heads up on poles all around the town. The revolution over, Shepton Mallet had become a prison town, the first building built in 1610, slowly but surely growing like a stony gray cancer for the next two hundred fifty years to accommodate various thieves, rapists and murderers that seemed to crop up everywhere, especially during and after the industrial revolution. By 1939 there were a separate woman's wing, a laundry for the women to work in and more rats than prisoners. There were also rumors of ghosts, a well-documented case of four prisoners who had suffocated when placed in a cell for one, and persistent rumor about a river that flowed under the prison.

Early in 1942, anticipating the worst, the Judge Advocate General's office had begun negotiations with HM Prisons for a U.S. Army prison in England, and Shepton Mallet had been the result. The Americans built an efficient red brick death house for their gallows that the Brits grumbled wasn't made out of the proper stonework, and the first prisoners started marching in from the train station in their standard fatigue uniforms stenciled with a large white *P* on the back. They were soon up to their capacity of slightly over four hundred and showed every sign of staying there for the foreseeable future.

"What was Danby doing in the prison?" asked Jane, lighting a cigarette. The rain outside had increased to a hammering downpour, streaming down the window glass, blurring the view of the rolling hills and patchwork of fields outside.

Dundee lifted the folder in his lap. "According to this he wasn't. It was a man named Wier. Thomas Wier. Caught for desertion in London six weeks ago." He put the file down on the seat beside him and lit a cigarette of his own. "Only trouble was, Wier is a Negro, or should I say was. He turned up dead in a bombed-out lot three weeks ago with most of his face blown off. Took the police this long to identify him. Turns out Danby took Wier's place in a transfer from the stockade in London to Shepton Mallet."

"Danby *wanted* to get put in jail?"

"Looks that way." The fact that Danby had been held and had since escaped from Shepton Mallet was the only other fact revealed by Occleshaw on his visit to Swan Hill.

"But why? What could possibly be in it for him?"

"Maybe we'll find out in Shepton Mallet."

Jane tapped her cigarette into the ashtray built into the side of her seat. "Or maybe that's what Occleshaw wants you to think," she said thoughtfully.

The roundabout hundred-mile trip from Swan Hill to London, then west to Shepton Mallet, had taken the better part of half a day. When they arrived at their destination it was mid-afternoon. A jeep was waiting for them at the side of the gray stone station, complete with a blond-haired military police captain named Selkirk carrying an umbrella. Diplomatically he tried to cover both Jane and Dundee, but by the time they got under the canvas roof of the jeep, Dundee was soaked. Selkirk ratcheted the vehicle into gear. With the hard rain pounding loudly on the roof over their heads they headed off down the narrow, twisting streets of the ancient town.

"So what's this place like?" asked Jane from the backseat, leaning forward and raising her voice over the sound of the rain. All around her the buildings were crowding in, the sidewalks only wide enough for one, the buildings made of the same gray stone, the roofs slick wet slate.

"Well, ma'am, basically it stinks. Cigarettes and . . ." He paused and Jane could almost see his ears redden.

"Farts," said Dundee, turning to look back at her.

"Farts?"

"Yes, ma'am," said Selkirk.

"It's a glasshouse," said Dundee. "They're the same wherever you go. Bad food, cigarettes, and gas."

Without warning a row of houses jammed together in a jumbled row gave way to a tall gray wall pierced by a single ancient gate made of roughly sheared planks that looked almost as old as the stone. Selkirk gave three honks on the jeep's horn and a few seconds later the gate swung ponderously open. The prison seemed to be in the middle of town with nothing separating it from the surrounding population.

They drove across a cobbled yard to a small doorway. All around them were high walls with crossbarred windows looking blindly down on them. Like everywhere else in the town, the roofs of the buildings were gray slate. They climbed out of the jeep, ducked into the doorway and entered the prison.

"Major DuMuth's office is on the top floor," said Selkirk, leading the way. The major was the warden of the prison and had been from the beginning of the Americans' arrival.

Jane thought briefly of taking some pictures with

the small Leica she carried in the pocket of her trench coat, but she saw almost immediately that there wasn't nearly enough light. She was standing in a barred sally port that was manned by a fat military policeman reading *Stars and Stripes* under a weak lamp that dangled from the ceiling. The interior of the prison beyond was barely visible, but Selkirk had it right—the whole place smelled of stale cigarettes and staler farts. It was also noisy; echoing shouts, hoots of laughter and whistles mixing into a single roaring madhouse barrage that reminded Jane of the asylum her sister had lived in on Welfare Island in the East River until her blessed death the previous year.

"That being done for our benefit?" asked Dundee.

"Some maybe. They know something's up," said Selkirk. He nodded to the fat guard, who groaned and got to his feet. Pulling a heavy ring of keys away from his belt he opened the inside door of the sally port and let them through.

"This way," said Selkirk, and led them forward into the main hall of the men's wing of Shepton Mallet prison.

The men's wing was three tiers high and 140 feet long, built of the same monotonous gray stone that comprised nearly everything in the prison and the town. The floors were broad, stained planks as old as the prison, worn down in front of each cell, the doors also wood, sheathed in steel and bound in wrought iron.

As they walked beneath the cells, Jane and Dundee became aware of the booming sound above them taking on a rhythmic, chanting sound, and Jane felt a shiver run down her spine. This was no place for a woman. These were men, already trained in the savagery of professional soldiering, who had gone one step further into darkness. "What rough beast is this . . ." she whispered softly as she walked quickly over the old, heavy planks, wondering to herself how much blood they'd soaked up in the last three hundred fifty years. "You sure this is a good idea?" she muttered to Dundee, her eyes scanning the noisy tiers.

"I'm afraid it's the only way to find out what the hell is going on." Occleshaw had refused to divulge any information and had tried to block their access to the part of the prison still maintained by the British authorities, but Dundee had pressured Hedrick at JAG headquarters in Cheltenham, and eventually they'd been granted access. Even so, the access had clearly been grudging.

Eventually they reached the end of the gauntlet below the tiers and followed Selkirk through yet another barred sally port. Going through a heavy steel door they found themselves at the bottom of a circular stone staircase that looked as though it belonged in some storybook castle. Jane expected a lady in a long dress or a knight in rusty armor to come clanking into view at any second. Selkirk trotted upward and they followed.

They eventually reached the top floor, the roofline of the ancient building creating sloping walls fitted with heavy beams at least a foot thick. A grilled platform looked down on the tiers of the prison, giving anyone looking down a view of the entire prison. Opposite was an open office door. Selkirk stood aside to let them enter, then promptly disappeared.

Major Donald L. DuMuth was every inch a prison

warden; bullet head, close-shaved steel gray hair, massive shoulders and a build like a Pier Nine stevedore on the East River docks. He wore a holstered .45 caliber automatic on his hip and there was a sawed-off shotgun lying casually on one side of a worn and scratched wooden office desk. Seated off to one side was a small, round-faced man in horn-rims and a toothbrush mustache that made him look rather like Hitler as an office clerk.

"Major DuMuth." Dundee held out his hand but the warden ignored it. They were the same rank, so there was no need to salute.

Two straight chairs had been set in front of the desk. DuMuth waved them to sit. "This is Mr. Johnson from the Public Records Office."

Mr. Johnson nodded from his seat but remained silent.

"We understand Charles Danby managed to get himself into your prison," said Dundee.

"That he did," said DuMuth. "And out again for that matter."

"What we'd like to know is, why?" said Jane.

DuMuth turned his attention toward her, eyeing her uniform. "I take it you're the war correspondent, Todd?"

"Call me Jane if you'd rather."

"I'd rather not," the man said icily.

Jane shrugged lightly. "Suit yourself."

The warden made a face as though he'd just smelled something bad. "I'm given to understand by the powers that be that you have some very high security clearance. Maybe I'd like to know why."

"Friends in high places," said Jane, smiling pleasantly.

"I'll bet," the warden muttered.

"Danby," Dundee reminded.

"He came in on a forged transfer requisition. Easy enough to get for a man in his position. The man he was impersonating was in his own unit."

"Doesn't really answer the question," said Dundee.

"We're pretty sure he came in to steal something."

"What do you steal that has any value in a place like this?" Jane asked.

"Mr. Johnson?" said the warden.

Johnson released a tight little smile and sat up straight in his chair like a schoolboy reciting his lessons. "My title at the PRO is officially Keeper of Special Acquisitions. At the outbreak of hostilities it was decided to remove some of the nation's more valuable historic documents to a place of safekeeping. Shepton Mallet was empty at the time and out of range of any known German bombers, so the documents were brought here."

"A lot?" asked Jane.

"Some ten thousand boxes."

"Jesus," blurted Dundee.

"Quite," said Johnson.

"Danby came to steal documents?" asked Jane. Valuable or not, documents didn't sound like the kind of thing that would interest the man Dundee had described.

"No," said Johnson. "We think not." He paused, turning to the warden. "Perhaps we should show them."

"Let's go for a walk," said DuMuth.

They left DuMuth's office, this time with the little man from Public Records leading the way. They went down a level, veered away from the triple-tiered cell block and went down a narrow corridor into another, smaller wing of the prison. Jane was now thoroughly lost and had no idea where she was in relation to the way they'd come. Useful if you wanted to keep prisoners from escaping, but it hadn't stopped Danby.

Once again she struggled with the man's motives; a soldier of rank, obviously well connected on the civilian side, takes on the persona of a private soldier to finagle his way into a grimy English prison. Where was the sense in that? She thought about what Dundee had said about his old schoolmate. Danby didn't need money, that was clear enough, so what was it?

She remembered a boy named Teddy McSeveney in fourth grade. Teddy's father was the manager of the local bank, and there were any number of stories of how he used that power, holding it over the people who needed his help, and, more importantly if the rumors were true, how he used that power over those people's wives. Teddy had taken a page from his father's book, threatening to tell the school principal that one girl or another had stolen money from his desk unless the girl went with him into the cloakroom. It worked well enough until the young bully made the mistake of choosing Jane as a victim. Jane had gone to the cloakroom with the squat, fat-faced boy all right, and once there, proceeded to kick the shins out from under him, then sat on his chest and punched him senseless. Teddy had gone wailing to the principal, who proceeded to give Jane ten whacks with his cane, but Teddy had ceased preying on young girls from that day forth. Jane had taken away the one thing Teddy cherished most of all, just like his father: power. So if that was Charles Danby's objective, what form would power take in a place like this?

They stepped out into what had once been the women's wing of Shepton Mallet, on the second level. It was almost identical to the men's wing, but half its size. It was also deafeningly silent.

"There hasn't been anyone in these cells for almost forty years," said Johnson, trotting out over the metal walkway that circled the tier. "Fortunate for us." At the far corner of the walkway Jane saw an open caged elevator that had obviously been recently installed. The cell block was also much more brightly lit than the men's side, and there were guards at each level, armed with wire-stock machine guns.

"The guards always there?"

"Day and night."

Johnson reached a cell with a metal number plate identifying it as number 17, reached into his jacket and withdrew an old-fashioned key, and inserted it in the massive lock. He unhooked a hanging work lamp from the wall beside the door, turned it on and shone it inside the cell. Instead of a bunk and toilet the room was packed from floor to ceiling with drab cardboard boxes, each with a penciled number. The numbers ran consecutively and in order from bottom to top, showing which ones had been stored first. Jane could see that boxes numbered 1790 and 1791 had gone missing from roughly the center of the wall. The rest of the boxes had sagged in to fill the space.

"So our stolen items were in those boxes," said Jane

"Correct," said Johnson.

"Valuable?" asked Dundee.

"You could say so. Some would say *invaluable*."

"What were they?" asked Jane.

"The Crown Jewels of England."

Eleven

"I beg your pardon?" said Dundee, staring at the little man.

"Well, not all of them. Specifically the Imperial Crown, the one worn for coronations, and a sword, the Great Sword, which is the one the king would hand over should he ever cede the country."

"Cede the country?" said Jane

"Surrender in time of war, that sort of thing," the little man said blandly.

"That sort of thing," said Jane faintly.

"You're repeating yourself an awful lot, sweetheart," said DuMuth.

"It's a lot to swallow."

"Might I remind you that you're also bound by the Official Secrets Act regarding this information," said Johnson.

"We're Americans," said DuMuth belligerently. "We're not bound by anything of yours."

"He's right," said Dundee. "Regarding British state secrets we're bound by their laws." He stared into the cell, pale with the enormity of what Danby had done. "Part of the agreement when we joined forces," he added.

Johnson beamed. "Quite right," he said.

"We know how he got in," said Jane. "How did he get out with the Imperial Crown and a sword?" She looked around. "It doesn't seem possible, especially with the guards."

"Well, palpably he did," said Johnson. "Seeing that the items in question are no longer here."

"Come with me," said DuMuth. "I want to show you something."

Like any institution built over a long period of time, each era had new and different needs. In its earliest incarnation, Shepton Mallet had no heating system at all and the basement area was used for the storage of food and dry good supplies. Later, an early coal heating system was installed, requiring coal tips and areas for vents and blowers. Eventually gas lighting required fixtures and new installation of equipment, and by the 1930s the basement was a rabbit warren of overlapping and intersecting rooms and passageways underlying the prison, some of the passages ending in dead ends and others meandering one way and another with no particular rhyme or reason.

At the lowest point in the basement the main sewage line opened up into an underground river that had been the original sewage outlet when the prison was built. Over the years it had been enclosed; first with timber, then with clay tile and finally with brick. The brick had begun deteriorating in the early 1920s and eventually collapsed in several strategic spots directly under the warden's residence, necessitating serious repair work, this time with concrete.

Leaving Johnson to mourn the loss of the jewels, DuMuth led Dundee and Jane into what were literally the bowels of the prison. Stooping under a section of old staircase, they peered into a large jagged hole in a section of rotted concrete, aided by the flickering light of the warden's Zippo. The smell wafting up from the hole was easily ten times worse than the smell in the prison itself. Jane wondered if DuMuth was wise in using his lighter.

"A month before Danby showed up here there was a break-in at a local contractor's, Penby and Sons. Penby was one of the companies that bid on the job here. They didn't get the job but they filed plans with their bid."

"And the plans were stolen?" asked Dundee.

"The police didn't discover that until we made the connection. The plans were obviously used to find the spot where the underground river came up into the basement at an accessible spot."

"Where does it come out?"

"It joins another stream on the far side of town."

"That's how they got in?" asked Dundee.

DuMuth shook his head. "That's what we thought at first, but there was no sign that anyone had tampered with the grille. We kept looking and found a hole in the concrete casing fifty feet from the outlet, and a tunnel that led into the basement of a cottage on a lane next to the stream. Pretty smart really; they could come and go as they pleased and no one knew anything was going on."

"You looked through the cottage?" asked Jane.

The warden gave her a withering look. "Of course, Miss Todd. And we didn't find a damn thing."

"We'd still like to take a look if you don't mind," said Dundee.

"We went over the place thoroughly. So did Scotland Yard, and that guy Occleshaw and his bunch. Nobody came up with anything."

"We'd still like to take a look."

"Suit yourself." DuMuth shrugged. "Take the jeep if you want; just remember to bring it back when you're done." He waved them off. "Selkirk will tell you where to go."

"Not the friendliest man I've ever met," said Jane as they stepped out of the prison a few moments later. It was still raining hard and they ran to the jeep, standing in the yard a few feet away, Dundee climbing behind the wheel and Jane getting in beside him. Dundee punched the starter button and the engine coughed and caught. He crunched the gears and they drove out of the prison.

"It's all bluff and bluster," said Dundee as they followed Selkirk's directions out of town. "DuMuth is in big trouble, and he knows it. He was responsible for letting Danby into the prison as much as for his escaping from it. That's bad enough, but letting him walk out with the crown jewels is enough to get him busted back to the motorcycle corps. At best it's going to make him the butt of a whole lot of bad jokes."

"I doubt it," said Jane, shaking her head. "Everyone is going to want this kept quiet. Even the Brits. You might see DuMuth reprimanded, but that's about it." She laughed. "I just think he doesn't like seeing women in uniform."

"Foolish man." Dundee grinned.

The cottage turned out to be on the southern edge of town, only a short distance from the train station where Selkirk had picked them up. It was the only dwelling on the laneway and completely isolated, both by its location and by a tall bramble hedge of blackberries that screened it from view. As they pulled up in front of the cottage the rain stopped and the sun made a valiant attempt to break out from behind the bruised and sultry clouds. Jane took out her Leica and took a few rapid shots of the low-roofed little house. "Pretty," she said.

"I just realized, we don't have a key," said Dundee.

"Probably don't need one from the looks of it," said Jane. She stepped forward and tried the latch, and the door swung open. "This isn't New York or Los Angeles, after all."

"That's a mistake a lot of people make," answered Dundee. They ducked under the low door frame and stepped into the cottage. "This being a case in point."

"I guess you're right."

The house was made up of two small rooms and a bath. The main area inside the door was a combination kitchen-living-sitting room, furnished plainly in simple country furniture that all looked old enough to be called antique. There were several amateurish-looking landscapes in oil hung on the walls for decoration, but nothing of a personal nature at all. The fireplace mantel was bare and so was the small table by the door. The small bedroom at the rear was equally barren, and there was actually an accumulation of dust on the quilted bedcover. There were no towels, toothbrushes or anything else in the bathroom that might have belonged to the occupant. The cottage was as featureless as it was possible to make it.

"According to Selkirk it was rented over the phone

and paid for three months in advance by mail." Dundee pursed his lips thoughtfully. "Happens quite regularly, according to the estate agent who handles it. People going on holiday calling from London. That kind of thing."

"No name or mailing address I suppose."

"No."

The door to the basement was in the hallway between the main room and the rear bedroom, although, on inspection it barely qualified as a basement at all.

"More like a root cellar," said Dundee.

They peered around in the gloom, the only illumination coming from the spill of light from the stairway. They were standing in a musty, brick-lined room about ten feet on a side with an earth floor and the beams of the cottage floor less than six feet overhead, causing Dundee to stoop a little. In one corner the bricks had been smashed out of the wall, probably with the pick that was still lying beside a mound of earth piled to one side of the gaping hole torn in the wall of the cellar.

"How many do you think?" said Jane.

Dundee approached the hole in the wall, his nose wrinkling at the smell. On the floor there were dozens of cigarette butts ground into the dirt. Dundee got down on his haunches and sifted through them slowly. "Players, Senior Service and Luckies. At least three people, then."

"The Luckies. One of them American?"

"Or with access to an American Army PX," Dundee answered, standing and almost cracking his head against a beam. Jane reached out a hand to steady him and as her hand touched his shoulder she felt a jolt of something almost physical in the pit of her stomach. She backed away a little at the unexpected sensation and felt her cheeks flush.

Dundee appeared not to notice anything, which angered her as much as the sudden feeling of attraction; the last thing she needed or wanted right now was involvement with this man, no matter how good-looking he was, but the least he could do was feel attracted to her. Which was ridiculous; if anything she should be pleased that it was one-sided, but somehow that irritated her even more. In the space of a few seconds the whole thing had gone from the sublime to the ridiculous. She bit down on the inside of her lip hard and forced the whole silly thing out of her mind.

As she backed up, she glanced down and saw something poking up out of the dirt floor. She bent down and dug a little with her fingers.

"Got something?" said Dundee.

"Maybe," she responded. The object came free. A matchbook.

CURTISS & SONS
REMOVALS
Fountainbridge
Glasgow

She handed it to Dundee, this time being careful not to let her fingers brush his. He glanced down at the damp, dirt-streaked paper folder. He opened it. There were still a dozen or more unstruck matches.

"Smart crew," said Dundee. "It's a ruse." He shrugged and handed it back. There were some words scratched onto the inside of the matchbook with a pencil, almost too faint to see.

Salem/h.t. 712/12

"What do you think it means?" asked Jane.

"Nothing," said Dundee "It's been left for us to find, a feint, to send us off on a wild-goose chase. Why would you throw away a matchbook with matches still left in it?"

"Maybe one of them dropped it by accident."

"Doubtful. They're meticulous about everything else except a single matchbook? No, take my word for it; these gonifs are doing a plant. Bristol is less than a hundred miles away; that's the more likely escape route. A coastal steamer, even a fishing boat, could take you anywhere, north or south. Even across the Channel from Europe to Ireland for that matter. A neutral country. Not some obscure place in Scotland." He tossed the matchbook onto the floor again, then turned and went back up the stairs again. Jane bent down and retrieved the square of cardboard, wiping it off and slipping it into the pocket of her uniform jacket. She followed Dundee back up into the daylight.

They went over the cottage again, but there really was nothing out of the ordinary, and Jane knew the second look was really nothing more than a formality for Dundee's report to his boss at JAG headquarters in Charlton House. When he was done they went outside again.

"Well, that's that. I've done my job," said Dundee. "Maybe now I can get out of this dreary place."

"And I'm supposed to sit on the biggest story in the war so far," said Jane. "It's not fair."

They climbed back into the jeep. Dundee took a last look around. "It stinks," he said quietly.

"What?"

"The whole thing." Dundee leaned back in his seat and lit a cigarette, staring blankly out through the windshield. "Occleshaw, the visit here, that matchbook cover. The tunnel." The lawyer shook his head. "I'm being led around like a bull with a ring through his nose and I don't much like it." He paused. "And I still don't see how they got away with it; a dozen guards within sight of that room. It's impossible."

"No it's not," said Jane. "He did it." She smiled. "You're pissed off because he's smarter than you?"

"That'll be the day."

"Let's start at the beginning," said Jane. "What about Occleshaw, other than the fact that he's a horse's ass?"

"From the dates I was given, he was onto me within twenty-four hours of the robbery and Charlie's escape from Shepton Mallet. Why? How could he have found out about my relationship with Danby that quickly, and what difference would it make? It's not as though we were the best of friends or anything. Plenty of people knew him as well as I did."

"But you're here and you're a cop," said Jane. "It makes a bit of a difference."

"It still doesn't answer the question. How did Occleshaw know about me? I doubt that it's in my jacket."

"Jacket?"

"Personnel file."

He had a point. It was Jane's turn to light up. She

caught a movement out of the corner of her eye and spotted an elderly figure climbing out on the path, emerging from an almost invisible gap in the bramble hedge. He was wearing gumboots and a worn old sweater and carrying a fishing creel and a bait fishing rod. He had a face like an old tree root, a gnarled pipe sticking out of the center of it. He saw Jane, gave her a polite nod and crossed the roadway behind the jeep, then went down the path that led to the river, the same path she and Dundee had used to inspect the grille.

"Do you think he's a plant too?" Jane asked, throwing her leg over the side of the jeep.

"Why?" said Dundee.

"Because if he fishes there every day, maybe he saw something."

She went after the old man, Dundee close behind her. They found him on a stump at river's edge, about twenty yards from the prison sewer grille. His name was Gaffney and, as it turned out, he was a retired prison guard who lived in another cottage nearby. They also learned in quick order that the "fookin' sausage eaters couldn't be trusted, pardon-my-French-Miss, I fought in the first one. What does the price of butter have to do with fighting a war and it's eels I fish for; best eels in Sussex out of this stream, I thinks they're particular about shit, adds a richness to the water like."

"Know anything about the people who just rented the cottage up there?"

"The ones that let old Maggie's place?"

Jane didn't now how old Maggie had to be to qualify as old to Gaffney, but she nodded anyway.

"Aye." Gaffney bobbed his head, the pipe stuck

precariously in the corner of his mouth, almost defying gravity.

"Remember anything?" asked Dundee.

"Aye."

"Such as?"

Gaffney finally took the pipe out of his mouth. He made a thoroughly revolting sound somewhere deep under the frayed old sweater that covered his sunken chest and spat something equally ugly into the sluggishly flowing stream beside him. Then he spoke.

"There was four. One of them was in charge; you could tell that by the way he was dressed. Sharpish like, and modern, not from around here. Two of the other three were Irish, you could tell that, clear as glass."

"How?" asked Dundee.

"Because of their fookin' accents, mind?" said Gaffney, giving Dundee a withering look. Then he continued, "Like I said, two was Irish, but I don't rightly know about the third fellow. He looked English enough, or maybe American like you, but you can't tell these days and he never once opened his mouth, don't you know, to speak like."

"That's it?" asked Dundee.

"No lad, not by half." He repositioned his pipe, magically brought a kitchen match into view and struck it on the edge of one yellowed, talonlike thumbnail. He sucked, wheezing, and then tossed the match away. The pipe stayed lit for a few seconds and then went out again. Gaffney didn't seem to mind; he put it into the corner of his mouth again and continued his narrative. "Now, Maggie had a garden, lovely dafs in the spring, jonquils she called them. Always fookin' daffodils, you arsk me, but what does an old grinder like me know about such? At any rate, Maggie had a garden, so you was expectin' dirt, but those men—dirt! Shovels, picks, a wheelbarrow, and all going in the front door, mind. Made no sense at all. Wrong kind of dirt, too. Dark stuff, not the dirt you get in a garden at all, at all."

"Ever talk to any of these gentlemen?" asked Jane.

"Oncst," said Gaffney. "The fourth man as I just recounted to you. Just to say goodday and nice weather for fishing. Tried to get a look inside the cottage, see what they were doing to old Mag's place. One of the Irish stood in front though, wouldn't let me see past him, and Robbie Burns in the fancy suit—never any dirt on *his* hands, mind! He took me by the elbow, he did, all nice as you please, asking me all about the eels, and were they lampreys or were they true eels, but I knew what he was doing, he was leading me away from the cottage so I couldn't see past him."

"Robbie Burns?" said Jane.

"Sure," said Gaffney. "Did I tell you he was a Scotsman?" He paused, looked into the bowl of his pipe. He looked up again. "I forgot to tell you," he said. "Why it was he did no work, other than his fancy suit."

"Yes?" prompted Dundee.

The old man spit down into the dirt at his feet. "He only had one arm."

A little more than twenty-four hours later in London's King's Cross Station, Dennis Patterson, a baggage hauler, was waiting for customers on that evening's Robbie Burns to Glasgow and wondering if he'd get enough in tips to buy a single Guinness at McGillicuddy's pub around the corner, let alone the three or four he craved. Not likely he thought, flipping through the pages of someone's *Daily Express,* left behind on the bench outside the WC. He didn't know who to blame—the Germans for starting the war or the Brits for using it as an excuse not to pay for a poor man's beer.

"You taking bags onto the Robbie Burns?" said an American officer.

"I am, I am," said Patterson, putting on his best Irish lilt.

"Dundee, bedroom C, the Glasgow Express car. Miss Todd's bag goes in bedroom D."

Patterson nodded. "Sure enough, sir. With pleasure."

He glanced at the pair. He was handsome enough but she was a bombshell, for sure and all, all legs and hair and eyes you could drown in. Everything his sainted mother would have found dangerous in a woman. A blond Maureen O'Sullivan you might say, but one you could actually screw, not just look at like she was a painting in church, or one of the nuns too pretty for her habit but still a nun. He'd dreamed about a few of those in his youth, that was for sure. The Irishman took the luggage and stacked it on his cart, then tipped his hat. The officer handed him a pound note, smiled, and turned away, taking the woman's arm. They headed for the station restaurant.

Patterson glanced up at the ancient clock suspended from the station ceiling. A little less than an hour until departure. More than enough time for the couple to have dinner and for him to make his telephone call. He pocketed the pound and went off whistling toward the telephone kiosk close to the main doors. His unit chief would be pleased with the news that Dundee was finally on the move. Patterson jammed his hand into his pocket and grasped the pound. A good evening after all. A good evening indeed.

Anthony Blunt—art connoisseur, Cambridge graduate, ardent though discreet homosexual, MI5 agent and Communist spy in order of importance—led Colonel Charles Danby through the labyrinthine basement rooms of the Tate Gallery on the Thames Embankment while a desultory bombing raid took place overhead.

"You enjoy art, Colonel Danby?"

"Never really thought much about it."

"What *do* you think about?"

"Money, mostly, and how to get it."

"Seems like a somewhat extraordinary line of thought during a war."

"You'd be surprised."

"Nothing would surprise me anymore, Colonel." They stopped in front of an enormous painting propped up against one wall and covered with a huge tarpaulin. Blunt gripped one corner of the tarp with a long, delicate hand and pulled. The tarp slid off, revealing a giant canvas in a heavy, ornate frame. Danby stared at it in the dim light. Overhead, the ceiling shuddered as a bomb fell nearby. A faint sifting of hundred-year-old dust floated down over them. Blunt paid no attention. He stared at the painting and so did Danby.

"*The Great Day of His Wrath,*" murmured Blunt. The painting's subject, in minute detail, appeared to be the end of the world, complete with tiny freight trains careening into bottomless pits, flares of primordial lightning, boulders the size of asteroids tumbling down from a boiling sky onto unfortunate hordes of terrified people below. "This is the kind of thing you say your people are working on?"

"And yours," said Danby. "In the States they call it the Manhattan Project, even though it's no longer confined to New York, and over here they call it Tube Alloys."

"Interesting."

"You work for the Commies, Mr. Blunt." Blunt raised his eyebrows. "My people have already figured that out even though yours haven't . . . yet."

"That sounds rather like a threat."

"Not at all. Just a fact, Mr. Blunt. Why don't you cover up the crazy painting and go off to your Commie bosses or whatever you do and find out how much Stalin will be willing to pay for something that would do *that.*" He nodded at the picture, as he surreptitiously slipped a piece of paper with an outrageous sum of money written on it—the asking price. Blunt pocketed the paper without acknowledging its receipt.

"He was mad, you know," Blunt murmured. "He eventually learned how to paint this sort of thing on glass, from behind. Inside out painting. He used to tour them across America. Mad John Martin. His brother was England's foremost arsonist."

"Forget the history, Mr. Blunt. Just get me an answer, and soon. You're not the only one who's interested."

"Of course," said a nodding Blunt, never taking

his eyes off the painting. Above them another bomb exploded. "Of course."

Danby looked at the slight, fey man with his long, delicate fingers, wondering if Blunt was as crazy as the painter or if he was simply looking into some terrible future.

Twelve

At 7:10 precisely, the Robbie Burns, pride of the Glasgow and South Western Railway, "The Golfer's Line," moved off from the smoke- and steam-filled caverns of King's Cross Station and began weaving its way through the blacked-out city of London, heading for the northern suburbs and the final freedom of the English countryside, its massive wheels thundering over the rails with a satisfying, monotonous sound that was so familiar to Jane. The train was the late-night version of the much more famous Flying Scotsman and covered much the same route, traveling almost due north to York, then veering slightly west and then north again, crossing into Scotland over the seventeenth-century arches of the Tweed Bridge in the early hours of the morning, before steaming even farther north into Glasgow, arriving at eight thirty in the morning.

The exterior of the train, famous for its striking, high-gloss red-and-black color scheme, was now covered in a dull, nonreflective gray-green, the wheels and all other visible metal work coated with a black shine retardant. It was doubtful that any German bomber had either the range, the fuel or the interest in bombing a passenger train on its way to Scotland, but the G&SWR wasn't taking any chances.

The interior of the train had been dealt with in much the same way. Every window was covered with thick, jet-black felt curtains to blot out any light, and corridor illumination was dimmed by half during the hours of darkness, giving the public areas of the train a somber, almost sinister look that kept most of the sleeping car passengers in their bedrooms, or the dining car. Although the menu wasn't as varied as it had been during peacetime, it was still possible to get a half-decent late dinner and an equally decent early breakfast.

Jane sat in her bedroom, smoking a cigarette and enjoying the gentle, lurching movement of the train. She had her eyes closed, taking in the dozens of squeaks, rattles, sighs and groans that made up the background symphony of a train's motion. Her father had worked the main line between New York and Boston, and had enough seniority to bring along his kid every once in a while, and Jane had enjoyed every minute of every trip, thrilled by the gruff man's attention and by the surging power of the train itself. This was different, certainly—she'd never ridden in a sleeping car back then, but if she kept her eyes squeezed shut and breathed deeply she could almost smell the faint tobacco-whiskey scent of her father's skin, and hear the gentle rasp of his laughter. Gone for over twenty-five years now, dead on the bloody, blasted wasteland of Passchendaele but still alive and echoing in the smells and sounds of another train, three thousand miles and an ocean away.

The Robbie Burns lurched heavily over a set of points as it switched to a different line and Jane came out of her reverie. She took a puff on her cigarette and surveyed the room. A little on the old-fashioned side, but nice. It was compact and snug, paneled in wood with most of the fittings in gleaming brass. The small sink and tap fitted into one corner were porcelain, and there was actually a silk-tasseled bell-pull by the pillow of the ship-style bunk that ran along the adjoining bulkhead wall. It occurred to her briefly that Dundee's bed was only the thickness of that wooden panel away, a thought which she quickly banished; the last man to share her bed had disappeared into the never-never land of the British Secret Service, while almost getting her killed in the bombing of Pearl Harbor less than a year ago. The one before that had turned out to be a cold-blooded killer hell-bent on killing the king and queen of England and anyone else who got in his way. If this were the Brooklyn Dodgers, she would have been traded long ago with a batting average like that.

She sighed and sat back in her chair, wishing she could take off the blackout curtains and look at the passing landscape. They'd be moving out of the city by now, and the night before, in Swan Hill, she'd noticed that it was a full moon.

Bomber's Moon.

Wasn't that what they called it? So much for that idea. She didn't much care for the idea of some trainborne air-raid warden giving her hell in front of all the other passengers; not good for the American image, which was about to get a pie in the face if news of His Majesty's bijoux getting scarpered got out.

For the past twenty-four hours, virtually since leaving Shepton Mallet, she'd tried to get Dundee to discuss the theft and its implications, but he'd barely talked to her. She sighed again; for the first time since that one freezing night in the Eskimo village in Greenland she was regretting her trip to England and her decision to become a war correspondent and a part-time OSS agent for Wild Bill goddamn Donovan.

Sitting there in the swaying railway carriage, it suddenly occurred to her that it was Donovan who had put her onto Lucas Dundee in the first place. Maybe he'd known something about the possibility that the crown jewels might be in jeopardy, and, if that was the case, that Lucas Alexander Decimus Dundee might be involved. She sighed for a third time and stubbed out her cigarette in the ornate silver ashtray fitted into the arm of the chair. She hadn't heard anything directly yet, but she knew that, one way or another, Donovan was going to expect a report pretty soon. She was damned if she knew what to tell her contact, or even who her contact was for that matter.

She made a little snorting sound under her breath and lit another cigarette with her brand-new PX Zippo. She'd always thought of war as a black-and-white business with good guys and bad guys ranged against each other on opposite sides of a muddy field, the way it had been in her father's day, but times had changed since she was a little girl; war was now a modern affair of lies and secrets and subterfuge, filled with skulking soldiers of the darkness and knife-in-the-back betrayal. She ached to tell Dundee about her job for Donovan, and ached equally knowing that she couldn't. She heard a light tapping at her door over the clatter of the wheels.

"Come in." Dundee at last. Maybe she could take

him to the lounge and ply him with drink, get him to open up about the case.

The fair-haired lawyer let himself into the little room, leaving the door slightly ajar behind him and looked around for somewhere to sit. The only place was a small pull-down seat on a hinge under the window. He pulled it down, locked it in place and sat down gingerly, his hands on his knees. He kept his eye on the partially opened door.

"You're looking a little nervous," said Jane.

"I've had the feeling we've been followed since Shepton Mallet," he said bluntly.

Jane frowned. "What makes you say that?"

"Just a feeling."

"Who?"

"Occleshaw's people. Who else could it be?"

"I'm not sure. Danby?"

"Danby's long gone," said Dundee. "Anyway, why would he be trailing us?"

"To see if we're on his tail?" Jane shrugged. "You thought that matchbook was a plant; maybe he wants to see if it worked."

"Maybe," said Dundee. He took out his Luckies, tapped one out of the pack and lit up, never taking his eyes off the cracked open door.

There was a little silence, then Jane said, "What took you so long?"

"I went through the train. I wanted to see if there was anybody familiar."

"Was there?"

"No. A bunch of Army types on leave, or rotating back to the States and flying out through Prestwick. Some golfers, business people, but not many. The train's three-quarters empty."

"Maybe you're worrying for nothing."

"I don't think so," he said, shaking his head. He looked around for an ashtray, didn't find one and finally leaned over and used the one on the arm of Jane's chair. "And it wasn't one matchbook cover, it was two. There was the one for the surveyor, what was his name?"

"Satchell."

"Satchell, that's the one." Dundee nodded. "Gold under the dead man's fingernails. All very neat and tidy, pulling us along."

"So you said before. I think you're giving Charlie Danby and his pals too much credit. People do make mistakes and they do leave matchbook covers behind." She grinned. "And anyway, where would a cop be without a clue or two?"

"It doesn't really matter," said Dundee. "We've got nothing else to go on." There was another silence. The train creaked and moaned, lurching over another set of points. There was a sudden, massive shrugging sensation and Jane could feel the train begin to accelerate; she looked toward the blackout curtain, imaging the landscape beyond it—the city and its endless suburbs giving way at last to the bucolic countryside of old oaks and rolling fields, hedgerows and woodlots, all of it shrouded in inky darkness. She put out her second cigarette, half smoked, and climbed to her feet, suddenly finding the sleeping compartment claustrophobic and uncomfortable with two people in it.

"Let's go to the bar car," she said. "It's getting a little stuffy in here." Without waiting for his agreement she headed out of the bedroom and into the dimly lit corridor. Wisps of smoke from other passengers' cigarettes hung like a torn curtain of fog in the narrow walkway as they made their way toward the rear of the car, swaying like sailors to keep their balance in the train, which was now moving even faster than before. Jane turned for a moment to make sure Dundee was behind her, then turned back. She gave a startled gasp as a man appeared out of thin air in front of her, and then realized that he'd come around a sharp bend in the corridor directly ahead of them. He was slim, elegantly dressed in a black suit that was surprisingly well cut and a dark blue tie with an oddly sinister motif of tiny black doves on it. He had piercing, intelligent eyes and fair hair going gray at the temples, and for a fleeting instant Jane was sure that she'd met him somewhere else. He smiled politely as he edged past Jane and Dundee, and then he was gone.

The lounge car, located three cars back behind a pair of second class carriages, was almost empty. A civilian in a pinstripe suit with a bowler on the seat beside him was drinking from a stemmed glass and reading a newspaper, a pair of flight officers from the newly formed Eighth Army Air Force were drinking at the bar and halfway down the car a group of privates and one corporal from the First Infantry Division were playing cards, laughing loudly and drinking warm beer while the lounge car steward looked on from behind the bar, wiping out glasses with a cloth, giving each one a methodical twist of his wrist and looking terribly bored with it all. Like most of that kind of worker you saw these days, the steward was in his late fifties; anyone eligible for duty had been called up long ago.

Jane dropped down into a seat beside one of the blacked out windows closest to them and Dundee followed suit, sitting across the small polished table from her. The steward appeared a moment later, took their orders and disappeared again, moving easily with the movement of the train.

"Better now?" asked Dundee

"Much," said Jane, not meaning it at all. Their drinks appeared, a scotch and soda for each of them. Jane tasted hers. Watery, the liquor itself as rough as diesel fuel. "How's your drink?" she said.

"Awful," said Dundee, making a face. "Yours?"

"Awful." Jane laughed. "And on a train going to Scotland. Doesn't seem proper somehow."

"No," said Dundee. He twisted the small glass between his fingers, staring down into it as though looking for answers to difficult questions. He finally looked up, opened his mouth to speak, then closed it again.

"Cat got your tongue?" said Jane.

"I ran a check on you while we were in Shepton Mallet," he said flatly. "It didn't take long. I've got some friends in Scotland Yard and I mentioned this friend Morris Black, the one you told Occleshaw about. Turns out he's in the Strategic Operations Executive now in Cairo, the British version of Donovan's bunch in Washington, who, it turns out, Black was also working for. And so were you. Now you turn up in my backyard just in time for this mess." He stared at her, tiny circles of angry white appearing on the hard line of his jaw. "Anything to say? I don't much like being spied on, Jane, or the people who do the spying. Are they *your* people following us, Jane? Just what the hell is going on? Who the hell are you?" He kept his voice low, the tone harsh.

Jane stared at him, wondering at his intensity and at her own reaction: anger. "I'm exactly who I said I was, Major—nothing more, nothing less. I was assigned to you by your superior, Brigadier General Lawrence H. Hedrick, and before that I'd never even heard your name. My friendship with Morris Black is none of your goddamn business, and neither is anything else I did before we met." She got up from the table, picked up her drink and downed it in a single toss. The man with the bowler hat looked at her over the top of his newspaper, then raised it again. Jane turned on her heel and stalked out of the carriage, pulling open the door and stepping out onto the jerking plates of the adjoining platform, horrified to feel the sting of salt tears in her eyes, telling herself that it was the steam or the smoke or a bit of clinker from the engine blown up by the wind that whirled around the platform. She pushed open the door to the next car and headed down the gloomy corridor, biting her lip and praying that no one would see her in this condition.

She reached her bedroom, opened the door and went inside, the bad scotch sour in her stomach now. Her head aching with a tangle of conflicting emotions, she threw off her uniform, letting it fall in a mess on the floor, switched off the overhead light using the control panel by the sink and then stumbled into bed, pulling the covers up to her chin and reaching up to switch off the reading light over her crisply starched, pale green pillow, monogrammed with the rail line's complex and old-fashioned logo of intertwined letters.

"To hell with him!" she muttered, punching the pillow hard. "To hell with them all!"

Thirteen

She awoke sometime later in the night, heart pounding. It was pitch-dark and silent in the tiny bedroom. She had no idea where the train was. Jane brought her wrist up to her face and read the illuminated dial of the men's Hamilton that Rusty Birdwell from the *Daily News* had bought her as a going away present when she left New York. She was always complaining that ladies' watches were too small to read and were a waste of money. Birdwell had taken her at her word. The watch had caused a few raised eyebrows since, but it was worth it; at least she wasn't going to go blind trying to tell what time it was in the dark.

According to the Hamilton it was two minutes past midnight. She listened hard but heard nothing except the sighing wheeze of brake couplings and the faint creaking of expanding metal. They had stopped somewhere. Risking an unlikely fine from the air-raid warden she rolled over, leaned out of the bed and poked a finger between the glass of the window and the blackout curtain covering it. She was rewarded with a tiny sliver of window looking out onto what appeared to be the platform of a major station. She could see a man in a blue smock and a greasy old felt hat closing and shuttering a news kiosk, and a fat old woman dispensing tea in brown mugs from behind a counter farther down the platform. Stopping for passengers perhaps, or to take on new crew the way they used to at New Haven on the New York–Boston run. The ordinariness of the scene was somehow comforting, even if it was a foreign land, and Jane smiled.

She yawned, trying to recall the schedule, wondering exactly where they were. Not that it would make a lot of difference to her since her grasp of the geography of Great Britain wasn't the best. A second or two later she had the answer to her question when a baggage cart rattled by with G&SWR/YORK stenciled on the side. She couldn't remember exactly, but she seemed to recall that York was about midway between London and their destination, which made sense given the time of night and the length of the trip. She yawned again, wondering if Dundee was snugged into his bed, an inch or so away from her, or still sitting in the lounge staring moodily into his Scotch. She told herself she didn't really give a damn, closed her eyes and went back to sleep.

The second time she awoke it was three thirty in the morning and it was with the sound of what she could have sworn was a gunshot echoing dully in her ears. She sat up in bed, eyes wide in the darkness. She turned, flicked on the night-light and threw her legs over the side of the bed. She stopped there, listening, not sure now whether she'd dreamed the sound or if it had been real.

She strained, turning left and right, but heard nothing; the train was in motion, clearly going around a series of curves the way it was jolting and jerking, and there didn't seem to be anything out of the ordinary going on except the muffled sound of voices in the corridor. They moved off and there was only silence again. She flipped on the overhead light, fully awake now. She reached down, dug into her uniform jacket, still lying crumpled on the floor where she'd left it, came out with her cigarettes and lit up. She frowned. She hadn't thought to bring a dressing gown with her and she wasn't about to go into the corridor in her unmentionables.

She pulled her suitcase out from under the bed, hefted it onto the chair next to the window and undid the straps. She threw it open, rummaged around inside and came out with a pair of corduroy trousers and a roll-neck sweater she'd picked up at a Macy's sale a year ago. She slipped her feet into her favorite pair of Wigwams without bothering to put on her socks and opened the door a crack. She peered into the corridor and looked in both directions. Empty. Feeling like a bit of a fool, she slipped out into the corridor and tapped lightly on Dundee's door, wondering just what she was going to say to him; hearing a gunshot in her dreams wasn't much of an excuse for waking him up at three thirty in the morning.

After a full minute of waiting there was still no answer and for a few seconds she thought of simply turning around and going back to her own bedroom, but instead she knocked again; there were sounds heard in dreams and real ones, and this particular shot had seemed all too real. Another minute passed and she rapped again.

"Dundee?" She paused. Maybe he was a heavy

sleeper. She grimaced. She certainly hadn't had any cause to find out, one way or the other. She knocked a fourth time, firmly.

Nothing.

Taking a deep breath and holding it, she reached out, took the door handle and twisted it gently. The door opened and she stared inside. If anyone came down the corridor right now it was going to look pretty bad. It was too dark in the room to see anything. She opened the door wider, letting the dim light from outside wash into the room. The bed was empty and neatly made up. There wasn't even an impression in the top blanket as though somebody had lain there for a moment. Odder still was the fact that Dundee's luggage was nowhere to be seen.

Rather than remain in the passage, Jane stepped into the bedroom and closed the door behind her. She turned on the overhead light and looked under the bed, which was the only place big enough to conceal anything. Nothing. She sat down on the bed and took a pull on the cigarette. Where the hell was he?

She let her eyes roam over the interior of the room, apprehension growing with her confusion. At first glance she couldn't see anything suspicious; no splintered wood work, no neat little hole in the blackout curtain and corresponding hole in the window, no bloodstain on the worn green carpeting on the floor. Nothing out of place at all. This wasn't like that movie she'd seen, *The Lady Vanishes,* and she was no half-wit who'd been hit on the head with a teapot.

She got up and checked the ashtray set into the arm of his chair—empty and gleaming, looking freshly cleaned. Maybe it was *The Lady Vanishes* after all, because there sure was no sign that anyone had ever been here. What was the name of the vanished woman? Foy? Froy? That was it, Miss Froy, and her name had been written in the condensation on the inside of the window. Her eyes flickered to the blacked-out window in the bedroom, almost as though she expected to see Dundee's name. She made a little grunting sound of disgust at her foolishness and stubbed out her cigarette in Dundee's pristine ashtray. She sat down on the edge of the bed again, trying to think it out, going through the alternatives.

Dundee could have gotten off the train in York; maybe it was his leaving that woke her up the first time. He was mad enough at her to just up and leave, but it didn't seem like the kind of thing he'd do, and it was more likely that he'd tell her to get off the train, not get off himself. It was his case after all; she was just along for the ride. Then there was the question of whether they were being followed or not; if they were, and he figured out who was doing the following, he could well have turned the tables and followed them, once again getting off the train at York or some other stop between here and London. But in that case, would he have had time to collect his luggage?

Her head was beginning to hurt. The most likely solution to the mystery was that there was no mystery at all. Dundee's luggage had been misplaced in London and he hadn't bothered to mention it, and he was sitting in the lounge car right now, drunk as a skunk. She climbed to her feet and took a last look around. Still no bloodstains. She let herself out of the bedroom and headed up the corridor. It wouldn't be the first time she'd poured a colleague into bed.

She reached the lounge car without meeting another soul, passenger or crew. On every train she'd traveled on in the States there'd always been someone up and about; a porter shining shoes; one of the conductors, like her father, methodically "walking the train" as he'd called it, checking that everything was in order; or somebody drinking or playing cards in the bar car long after everyone else had gone to bed. At the earliest hours of the new day, like now, the first of the morning crew would be getting up and preparing for the early breakfast call at five thirty for the staff, and six for the first of the morning passengers.

On the Robbie Burns it was as quiet as death and Jane felt a little strange, the only thing alive on a ghost train. She shivered with the feeling; having Dundee vanish like something in a magic act was bad enough without scaring herself with superstitious nightmares like that. This was a perfectly ordinary train going through a perfectly ordered and ordinary landscape that in peacetime would be the kind of thing you saw on postcards and the pages of *Picture Post*. The kind of pictures that, in peacetime, she took to make her living.

She reached the door of the lounge car and pulled it open. The steward was still awake, seated at one of the empty tables, reading a newspaper and eating something greasy on a pale blue plate. He had a tall glass beside him full of something that sent tiny, silver bubbles up the side of the glass. He looked up as she stepped into the car.

"We're closed, miss."

She looked around. There was no sign of Dundee at the spot she'd left him in, or anywhere else for that matter.

The steward cleared his throat. "Anything I can do for you, miss?"

She moved down the car to the man's table, steadying herself as the train gave a sudden lurch and slowed. The steward gave an instinctive glance toward the window to see what the train was doing, then turned back to Jane. "Now that's a little odd," he said conversationally. "Never stopped around here before. Good rate of speed from here to the Tweed, then over we go and Scots w'a hay as they say." He stared up at Jane and smiled, showing off a gleaming set of profoundly false teeth. "Name's Pieman, miss, like as what Simple Simon met on the way to the fair, 'cept my name's Arthur, miss. Arthur Pieman."

"Do you remember the man I came in with earlier this evening, Arthur?" said Jane. She dropped down into the seat opposite the steward. The meal on his plate appeared to be some kind of pressed meat covered with a glutinous gravy that didn't look quite real. A small green blob of very wizened peas sat shoulder to shoulder with some too-orange carrots and tiny, slightly translucent canned potatoes. Thank God they weren't rationing food back home, she thought. She glanced at the man's glass and he wrapped a protective hand around it.

"Quinine," Arthur said. "Served in India between the wars. Malaria." Jane wasn't quite sure you could get malaria in India, and she didn't really care if it was quinine or whether Arthur was sipping the stock.

"A major," she said.

" 'Course I remember. Been a barman on English trains for twenty-nine years and I swear I remember everyone I've ever served. Now take you, f'rinstance; last time I seen you, you was wearing a uniform. War correspondent, wasn't it?"

"Right." The train lurched again, even more roughly this time. Jane gripped the edge of the table to keep herself from hitting it.

"Stopping," said Arthur. His hand went out to pull back the curtains a little and then withdrew. He threw a quick, guilty look at Jane.

"The major," said Jane. "What happened to him?"

"What do you mean, 'what happened to him'? Nothing happened to him. He finished his drink and then Mr. Mallinson bought him another and they had a talk like."

"Who's Mr. Mallinson?"

"Fellow sitting reading the paper." He rattled the newspaper in front of him. "This paper as a matter of fact. Had a bowler hat, if I recall correctly."

Jane vaguely remembered the man. "How long did they talk?"

"Till York or thereabouts. Midnight."

"Then what?"

"A military policeman came and fetched him away, didn't he like?" said Arthur with a long-suffering sigh. "Which I'm about to do in a minute, by your leave, miss. Must get my beauty sleep, you know."

"They left together?" asked Jane. She sat back in

her chair as the train wheels ratcheted to a slow, grinding halt.

The steward finally gave in to his curiosity and peeked out the window exactly as Jane had done in York. "Well, bugger me!" he exclaimed. "It's bleeding Selkirk! Now why on earth would we be stopping there?"

Jane followed Arthur as he climbed to his feet and headed for the exit door between the cars. The steward pushed out through the lounge car door, then turned and unbolted the top half of the Dutch door leading out to the small platform of the little station they were stopped in. Arthur looked out, peering up the train through the clouds of steam rising from under the train. It was chilly; even with her sweater on Jane could feel the cold biting at her lungs. Early morning in the Scots Border Counties apparently wasn't the most inviting of times, at least as far as the weather was concerned. Jane paused in the vestibule between the cars, wrapping her arms around herself.

"What is it?" she asked Arthur.

He turned and shrugged. "Can't tell yet, ma'am. Seems to be a bunch of coppers at the station. Arguing with Campbell, the chief trainman." The steward let out a crowing laugh. "That won't do them much good, I can tell you. Andrew Campbell would argue with God himself, given the opportunity, and win, likely." He ducked his head out the opening and checked again. "Looks like they're getting on board."

Why would the police be getting on the Glasgow express at this hour of the morning unless there was something seriously wrong? thought Jane. She paled. Something seriously wrong, like one vanished major.

She squeezed in beside the steward and looked out into the darkness, lit only by the chief trainman's shrouded lantern and the small amount of light leaking out around the roughly covered windows of the station; clearly the blackout rules applied here as well.

Three cars back, appearing and disappearing in the bursts of steam that puffed out over the narrow platform between the train and the tiny Victorian brick station, three uniformed constables stood like mute sentries around a tall, lean plainclothes officer in heated discussion with Campbell, the chief trainman. Several other constables scurried along the platform, boarding at various points along the length of the train. The steam hissed around the plainclothesman and then cleared, a sudden silence following. The man's voice came to her as though he was standing no more than a foot away, bullying and imperious.

"I'll wake up every last soul on this train if I've a mind to, Mr. Campbell, whether you care for it or not." Jane recognized the voice instantly. The last time she'd heard it had been in the Pottingers' sitting room at Strathmere in Swan Hill.

It was Occleshaw.

Fourteen

The Special Branch officer looked up suddenly, peering through the steam, almost as though he'd sensed Jane's presence. She ducked her head back inside the train and flattened herself against the side of the vestibule. What the hell was she supposed to do now?

"Something wrong, miss?" asked Arthur Pieman.

"No, nothing," said Jane hurriedly. She took a deep, ragged breath, trying to think straight. Occleshaw was boarding the train in the middle of the night, and his only possible objective was Dundee; anything else was too much of a coincidence. The trouble was, Occleshaw wasn't going to find him, and she had no plausible explanation for his disappearance. Chances were the weasel-faced gunsel would pull her off the train and hold her in custody until she told him where Dundee was, which could be a long time since she didn't have the faintest idea.

"Miss?" said Pieman, concerned now.

Without responding she turned, pulled open the door behind her and fled down the corridor. It had looked like Occleshaw was about three cars down. She tried to keep her walk slow and steady; if anyone came out of their rooms right now to investigate the reason for their unscheduled stop she wanted to be nothing but another passenger with a full bladder. There was a crashing sound from the far end of the corridor as the door burst open. Barely pausing, Jane turned, pushed down on the latch of the bedroom closest to her and let herself in, praying that the bedroom would be empty.

It wasn't. Seated in the day chair, still dressed in the same black suit and expensive-looking silk tie with its muted pattern of tiny black doves on a field of midnight blue was the man she'd run into in the corridor much earlier in the night. He was reading what appeared to be a biography of Mendelssohn and smoking a cigarette.

"You like music?" he said pleasantly, as though it was the most normal thing in the world to have women burst into his bedroom at three thirty in the morning.

"Well enough," she said. The closest she'd come to live music in the last few years was seeing the band singer Doris Day smooching with Cary Grant in the Brown Derby. The train lurched, heaved and lurched again. There was the strident, brain-rattling shriek of its whistle, and the train began to move. Jane's heart sank; any vague idea she'd had about sneaking back to her compartment, collecting her suitcase and somehow getting off the train undetected disappeared with the blowing of the whistle.

"I am reading about Fingal's Cave," said the man in the blue tie, as though that explained everything. He had an accent, but she was damned if she could place it. "It's in Scotland you see," he explained, seeing her confusion. "Mendelssohn went to Scotland, the island of Staffa in particular. He thought that the cave was a magical spot, deeply spiritual, and he created his famous overture based on his impression of the place; I tend to agree with his assessment, having been there quite often, although I do not have Mendelssohn's belief in the supernatural." He paused. "Have you been? To Staffa I mean?" His English was clear, precise and well enunciated, almost professorial, but she had the sense that the words were thought first in a different language entirely before he spoke.

"No, I haven't."

"That is most unfortunate."

He took a puff on his cigarette and smiled up at her. "If you don't mind me saying so, you seem somewhat agitated. Are you in some sort of trouble?"

"No," lied Jane. She turned from the man and cracked open the door. Directly in front of her, no more than a handspan away from the door, she could see the back of Occleshaw's overcoat as he gave orders to one of the uniformed constables.

"Find the man; he'll be in a major's uniform. Just as likely he'll be in that damn woman's bed. I want them both, and quickly."

"Yes sir," replied the constable. He gave a quick salute and took off down the corridor. Occleshaw turned slightly, looking back the way he'd come and Jane could see every detail of his features, from the bristly white hairs growing out of his overlarge ear to the large, dirt-filled pores and broken veins on his nose. His lips thinned almost into nonexistence, his jawline hardened and then he turned away, moving off in the same direction as the constable had gone, leaving a faintly sour smell behind him.

Jane turned. The man was still watching her, a

faintly amused expression on his face. "Thank you," she said quietly.

"For what?" said the man. "I did nothing out of the ordinary."

"You were awake," said Jane with a grin. "That was enough for me." She paused. "Mendelssohn was a German composer, right?" she asked, something about the man nagging at her memory.

"That's right," said the man. "He's best known for bringing Bach back into favor in the early 1800s. He conducted *St. Matthew's Passion* for the first time since Bach's death, you see. Also, of course, he is famous for his *Scottish Symphony*; 'Fingal's Cave' being the overture." The man made a strange sighing noise, then frowned and stubbed out his cigarette in the chair's ashtray. "Unfortunately, at least for the German people who are no longer permitted to listen to him, he was a Jew."

"Right," said Jane, feeling oddly embarrassed by the controlled venom in the man's voice. "Anyway, thanks again." Her memory still itched, but now was not the time to scratch it.

"The pleasure was mine, believe me, miss; I'm glad I could do you the favor of my insomnia."

Jane gave him a quick smile, turned again and opened the door a little wider. Occleshaw had disappeared and there was no sign of any of his constables; she slipped out through the half-open door, shutting it softly behind her, and headed quickly back to her room, not quite sure what her next move was going to be. She was almost at her door when the train suddenly lurched again and then rolled to a stop. From all the trips she'd made with her father, and all the questions she'd asked in that half-remembered time, she was pretty sure she knew what was going on; the train had gone up the line to its watering point. Probably taking on more coal as well. They wouldn't be here long; no more than five minutes or so at best. She'd have to hurry if she wanted to slip away in time. She turned the door latch on bedroom D and stepped inside, safe at last, at least for the moment.

The woman sitting in her chair appeared to be in her mid-thirties, dark hair done in a double-twist braid mostly hidden by a worn-looking brown felt cloche hat. She was also wearing a dark blue cardigan with one cuff unraveling, a gray blouse with a badly matched and not-very-well-fitted gray skirt that fell just below the knees, sagging off-white knee socks and an oddly youthful pair of bucko saddle shoe two-tone pumps with a low, thick heel, the kind they advertised in *Life* magazine as having "your footprint in leather." Over all of this she was wearing a wool overcoat thrown over her shoulder like a cape. Her left eye was wide open and misty blue; her right eye was missing, almost as though someone had jammed a pencil directly into the pupil and then stirred it around, destroying what was left of the eye. Liquid had dripped down her cheek like tears and congealed there, but there was almost no blood. She was very dead.

Jane came very close to screaming. Instead, she stepped into the room, turned and closed the door, throwing the latch as she did so. She looked around the room; it had been tossed—her suitcase was overturned on the bed and her clothes had been thrown around, and the little cupboard for her shoes was hanging open in the bulkhead above the sink. Not that there was anything to find. Her mind was racing and she tried desperately to slow it down; now was no time for panic, but what the hell else was she supposed to do when finding a body in her bedroom?

You're supposed to think.

Whoever the woman was, Occleshaw would turn it around and put it on her, which you really couldn't blame him for since she was in Jane's room; on the other hand, it would take her out of the game entirely. God only knew how long they'd have her in custody while all this was sorted out. There was no way she was going to explain this away easily, which was probably the reason for dumping the body here in the first place. Somehow they'd gotten to Dundee, and now her.

She wanted a smoke but there wasn't time. She stared down at the dead woman slumped in the chair. Swallowing hard she stepped forward, knelt down and went through the woman's coat pockets. Nothing to identify her and no purse, and right now she didn't have any time left to try to figure out who she was and why she was in her bedroom.

There was only one question: cut and run, or stay and face the music? If Occleshaw had ever given her cause to think that he was a reasonable human being there might have been a choice, but as it was she barely hesitated. Her own shoulder bag was lying open on the bed. Grabbing it she stuffed the contents back inside and then flipped off the overhead light at the control panel above the sink and edged in behind the shadowy lump of the woman in the chair. Using both hands she caught hold of the felt window covering and pulled hard, peeling it away from the window. She stared out into the darkness and found herself facing a low dry stone wall with a sign in front of it:

MCSEVENEY'S HALT

Behind the wall were the blank silhouettes of several small buildings huddled together. Storage sheds? Beyond that was the deeper darkness of a low hill, sweeping up and away to the right, its lower flanks thick with scrub brush and clumps of barren rock. Not very inviting.

Like the windows on most English trains, this one opened with a small push latch on its upper edge. Jane pressed it with her thumb and pulled hard, dragging the window down in the frame with an alarming squeak and letting in a blast of frigid night air. Much time wandering about in that and she'd freeze to death. She turned, swallowed hard and tugged at the coat that lay across the dead woman's shoulders. It came off easily enough and Jane shrugged into it. Outside, in the corridor, she could hear voices approaching; she was running out of time. She swung one leg up, balancing herself for a painful moment, then swung the other up just as the train ground into motion once again. Her precarious perch jerked out from under her and she found herself pitched out into the darkness, arms outstretched in a clumsy fall. She landed hard, the wind knocked out of her for a few moments, her hands lacerated and torn by the razor-sharp clinkers and sharp stones that made up the raised roadbed for the tracks. Behind her the wheels of the sleeping coach clattered over the ties as the train gathered speed and pulled away. Staggering to her feet, head spinning, she tucked her pain-lashed hands into the armpits of the dead woman's overcoat, half falling and half sliding down the side of the roadbed, making for an opening in the stone wall she could faintly see just beyond and to the right of the sign. She made her way through the opening, then dropped out of sight on the far side of the wall, her back against the rough stone as she caught her breath and the train passed on and out of sight, swallowed by the night.

Chest still heaving and barely recovered from her fall, Jane clambered to her feet and looked around cautiously, listening for the slightest clue that her presence had been noticed. Ahead of her a narrow track led down to a small yard servicing the sheds she'd seen from the train. Their doors were tightly shut, large padlocks hanging from substantial iron hasps. Turning, she saw a coal chute poking out of a windowless storage container, and a stumpy-looking water tower beside it. There didn't seem to be any human habitation anywhere; apparently the engineer and his fireman did the work themselves.

Wrapping the dead woman's coat tightly around her against the biting cold she listened again. There was nothing to hear except the moaning of the wind across the dark, distant moors. She shivered and wondered if jumping off the train had been such a good idea after all. Jane peered into the darkness beyond the little group of sheds. Beyond, there was nothing but a rolling, empty landscape of scrub brush and heather stretching into the distance like an endless, frozen sea. There was no road or any sign of civilization anywhere. Visions of Basil Rathbone and a bumbling Nigel Bruce as Watson, stumbling across the fog-wreathed burns and braes of Dartmoor chasing after phosphorescent mastiffs came uneasily to mind, and, more realistically, getting lost and falling into a bog and being trapped in quicksandlike ooze, or simply dying of cold and hunger.

Not to mention being found by the wrong people. Occleshaw was one thing; whoever had killed the woman in her bedroom was another. Being on the open moors would be much the same as being a fly crawling across a dead-flat table. Given a good pair of binoculars, or worse, a small airplane, of which there were still a few around, and she'd be a sitting duck. Bird or insect didn't matter; in the desperate dark of night the open countryside was a death trap all by itself, in broad daylight it was crazy.

Jane looked back along the railway tracks. A quarter mile away she could see the darker, regular shapes of Selkirk's train station and nearby high street, flat black against a background of purple sky. Nowhere to hide there, and no way in or out of town without a good chance of being seen, especially after all the excitement caused by Occleshaw and his men. No. The only way was forward, following the direction the train had taken. She buttoned the overcoat up to her neck, turned up the narrow collar and adjusted the strap of her bag, settling it more comfortably around her shoulder. Stuffing her hands into her coat pockets she climbed up the gravel roadbed, stepped onto the tracks and began to walk.

Fifteen

It was just about the oldest trick in the book, and like a fool, he'd fallen for it. Mallinson had kept him mesmerized with boredom all the way to York, apparently convinced that, because he'd been to California ten years back and had read his father's name in the *L.A. Times*, they were bosom buddies or something. The white-capped MP who came into the lounge car was actually a relief, so much so that he never questioned the fact that the military policeman knew where he was on the train or what he looked like, even though they'd never seen each other before.

If he'd really had his wits about him he would have wondered how the MPs, or anyone else for that matter, knew he was on the train at all, since the only person who knew was Polly Darling, his ATS secretary back at Swan Hill, and it was doubtful she would have told anyone or that anyone would have known enough to ask, with the possible exception of Occleshaw or his own boss, at Charlton House.

The clincher had come when the MP had quietly informed him that there was a driver waiting outside the station with an urgent message from Brigadier

General Hedrick. It was exactly the right thing to say; Dundee had gone along as obediently as a buck private in boot camp, never questioning the validity of any of it. The MP led him out of the station onto a blacked-out street beside the dark, hulking station. Directly in front of him on the far side of the narrow street was an ancient stone wall a good twenty feet high that was probably as old as King Arthur, and off to his left there was the sound of lapping water and a faint booming as the hollow hulls of small boats or tethered barges rapped gently together in the chill breeze blowing down from the north.

The street was deserted. With the blackout in place, it was also perfectly dark. The only car in sight was a brownish green deuce-and-a-half Dodge ambulance. For the first and only time, Dundee hesitated. The ambulance was definitely wrong. He tapped the MP on the shoulder.

"I thought you said there was a message?"

The MP smiled wearily in the darkness, one hand resting easily on the lanyarded automatic holstered on his belt. "Had to hitch a ride, sir. Only vehicle available."

Which was nonsense of course; no divisional commander would let an emergency vehicle be used to relay a JAG message, no matter how high-level, and the MP would almost surely be riding a motorcycle. The MP frowned, reading the look on Dundee's face.

"What the hell is going on, soldier?"

Suddenly the MP was standing right beside him, the muzzle of the .45 pressing into his jacket just under the rib cage. The first of a series of questions began forming in Dundee's head, such as, at what point did military cops start carrying .45 automatics and not the standard-issue S&W revolver?

"Just walk over to the back of the ambulance and open the doors, sir. It'll all be explained to you."

"If it's all going to be explained, then why the pistol?"

"Just do as you're fucking told, sir, or I'll put a pill in you that'll blow your fucking balls into the wall over there, *capice*?" There was the vague accent of the Bowery in the man's voice, or maybe it was Brooklyn. Dundee wasn't sure.

"You know what the penalty is for kidnapping?" asked Dundee, trying hard to remember if there was such a crime on the Army books. The answer was a dig into his side with the automatic.

"Shut the fuck up, Major, and maybe you'll stay alive a little longer." The MP gripped Dundee's elbow with his right hand and guided him toward the rear of the ambulance. He tensed as they approached the doors, realizing that this was his last chance; once inside the truck his expectations of escape were zero. If all of this was Charlie Danby's doing, his chances of getting out alive were equally low.

He reached up with his right hand to grab the twist handle on the rear door of the ambulance, then turned on his heel, wrenching his elbow out of the MP's grip, trying to dig it into the man's side, catching him off guard. Before he was halfway through his turn he smelled something sweet and burning cover his mouth as someone came out of the darkness beside the truck and pressed an ether-sodden surgical sponge over his mouth and nose. He strug-

gled, but it was no use; his legs wobbled and gave
out at the knee. As the ambulance doors swung open
like the mouth of a monster waiting to swallow him
up, the last conscious feeling he had was the MP's
hand between his shoulder blades pushing him forward into the black interior of the vehicle.

He woke up with smells of tar and hemp in his
nostrils, his cheek pressed against damp wood and
the sound of burbling water in his ear. He could
feel a steady thumping vibration through the wood
against his cheek. As consciousness returned he
vaguely understood that he was on a boat. He sat
up, cracking his forehead against an overhead strut.
He stretched out his hand and immediately became
aware of two things: he wasn't bound and the space
he occupied was very small and curved on both
sides, with very little room between himself and the
bulkhead above him. His knees were bent, feet pressing against a wall or a door, also wood and leaking
a faint trace of light. From the rough feeling against
his skin and the shape of the hull on either side of
him, he had been stuffed into a rope locker in the
forward end of the boat. One thing was sure: he
wasn't at sea. There was no sense of the ocean's
power around him; they were going quite slowly. A
river or a canal seemed more likely.

He sat up slowly, moving carefully to keep from
banging his head a second time. He eased himself
forward, twisting himself around until his face was
turned to the rope locker hatch. It was roughly made
from old timber, three planks wide. He shifted
around quietly until his eye was against the narrow
space between two of the slabs of wood.

The space on the far side of the door looked like

some kind of hold or storage area. There were a dozen or so barrels to the left and stacks of hundred-weight sacks on the right, leaking some kind of roughly ground wheat or barley onto the decking. All of it was lit by a clear glass, low-wattage lightbulb with a filament that glowed and faded to the rhythm of the engine in the rear.

Looking from side to side, Dundee gauged that the hull was no more than ten or twelve feet wide; carrying that kind of cargo it had to be a canal barge like the kind that used to run between Baltimore and Washington. Long out of use in the United States, there was still an active system of such canals in England that stretched the length and breadth of the country. He'd read somewhere that they'd become even more important with the coming of war, taking on a lot of the cargo that used to go by the much more vulnerable coastal steamers.

At first Dundee couldn't figure out why Danby had chosen such an odd way to transport him to whatever their destination was, but the more he thought about it the more sense it made. Just before entering York the train had rattled over a bridge, and a few seconds before being knocked out he'd heard water moving and the sounds of boats at anchor. Probably the river he was now on. If by some wild stretch of the imagination Jane had discovered that he was missing and had alerted the police, they'd hardly be looking for him in the rope locker of a canal barge. Danby's men could make their way across the countryside with nobody the wiser; if they'd already gone to this much trouble, they would have made sure they had the right travel permits and fuel coupons for the journey. Charlie might be a crook, but he was no dope. He had, after all, success-fully made off with some of the Crown Jewels of England.

Which was obviously what this whole thing was about, and that, in turn, didn't make a lot of sense to Lucas Dundee. Why steal something and then make it obvious you'd stolen it, especially when, by all the evidence, including the smelter they'd found, you'd gone to all the trouble of making copies? On top of that little conundrum, why steal something you couldn't sell in the first place? No. When Charles Danby did something there was a reason for it, no matter how twisted the logic or nasty the motive. For the life of him, Dundee couldn't figure it out this time. He put the problem out of his mind for the moment; right now he had to figure a way out of Charlie's clutches, and fast.

Dundee turned his face away from the crack in the door and pressed his ear to it instead. Nothing but the steady, lumbering stutter of the muffled engine and the gurgle and plash of water against the heavy old hull. He turned himself around and, after a few moments, managed to get his foot braced against the middle plank of the door. Of the three boards making up the door it would probably be the weakest, fas-tened only at the top and bottom without being nailed or screwed to whatever made up the door frame itself.

Dundee squirmed until his back was firmly pressed against several coils of heavy rope, then took a deep breath and held it. He straightened his leg and pushed with his foot as hard as he could, seeing if there was any give to the plank. As far as he could tell there wasn't. He tried again, feeling the first real sense of panic since getting off the train. This time he was rewarded with a faint, damp squeak as the ancient iron staples clewed hard into the top of the plank began to give way.

He tried a third time, actually kicking at the plank this time, and suddenly the entire board gave way with an ear-splitting wrench. Easing his foot back Dundee waited, expecting the sound of booted feet running across the decking over his head.

Nothing.

Moving himself around in the cupboard-sized space, he pushed the plank farther out of position, then squeezed his left hand through the space between the boards on either side. About halfway up the side of the bulkhead he felt a large bolt. Moving it slowly up and down, he managed to loosen it. Pressing his hand against the hatch he pushed it open, then crawled out into the open hold.

Ten feet or so past the gently swinging lightbulb there was a second hatchway door, and slightly to one side was a companionway ladder that had been hidden by the piled sacks of wheat. For the first time he got a strong whiff of the stuff and realized it was hops, probably destined for a brewery somewhere. Oddly, deeply buried beneath that rich scent was the smell of chocolate, so faint he thought for a moment he was imagining it.

He straightened, and from the stiffness of his neck and back he realized that he'd been in the rope locker longer than he'd first thought; several hours at least. He also had a splitting headache from the ether he'd been given. Both legs were cramped from being shoved into the locker. Dundee blinked in the half-light, looking around the hold carefully; there wasn't

anything in sight that looking even vaguely like a
weapon except for the plank he'd kicked out of the
door. He picked it up off the deck and hefted it; three
or four pounds of solid oak with a long, uneven piece
torn away from the side, giving it a shape a little bit
like a cricket bat. Dundee smiled briefly. Somebody
had once tried to explain the game to him using baseball as a point of reference, but Dundee gave up
when they got to the part about stumps and sticky
wickets.

He moved slowly down the narrow aisle between
the barrels and the sacks of hops, pausing every second step to listen. Once again he heard nothing. He
crept forward slowly, pausing at the foot of the short
companionway leading up to the open deck. He
stood there for a moment, taking in the fresh, earthy
smell of the cold river air, and the scent of new-
mown hay from the fields beyond. He tried to imagine the farmland bordering the narrow waterway and
wondered how far it would be to the nearest help.
Too far probably, but he didn't have much choice.

Dundee put one foot on the ladder and adjusted
his grip on the oak plank. He started up the ladder
and a voice stopped him.

"Major."

Dundee froze. The voice came from behind him,
and was accompanied by the sound of a hammer
being cocked. He held up both hands, figuring his
chances on getting his licks in with his cricket bat
before the faceless voice got off a round.

"Not a hope, pally. Now be a good boy and drop
the stick." He did as he was told, the slab of oak
falling to the deck at his feet. A few seconds later a
smiling face appeared at the top of the stairs. The

man on deck was easily in his sixties, a greasy cloth
cap pulled down over an unruly thatch of bristled
iron gray hair that seemed to shoot out from under
the cap like fireworks.

"Come on, laddie-buck, give it a try if you think
you've got the brass."

His face had the lined, leathery flush of a man who
spends a great deal of time outside. His small dark
eyes were like black beads set into the craggy old
face. He had the stub of an ancient, twisted briar
clenched between his teeth and he was holding a
short, steel-tipped gaff in one fist and a gigantic Webley Navy pistol that looked old enough to use black
powder and ball shot in the other. Dundee backed
down the companionway. Just being hit on the head
with the barrel of the monstrous gun in the old man's
hand would be enough to kill him. He turned
around. Behind him, a young, blond-haired man in
an Air Transport Command North Atlantic Wing
flight officer's uniform was standing to his left, holding a much more modern Smith and Wesson.

The ATC officer waved the barrel of the gun. "This
way, Major." The flight officer stood aside, revealing
a spill of light coming from the open bulkhead hatchway behind him. As Dundee edged past him, the
flight officer moved back, careful to keep clear of any
sudden moves. Dundee ducked his head and went
through the doorway.

He found himself in a remarkably neat and luxuri-
ous cabin set midships in the old barge. The decking
under his feet was clean and freshly varnished to a
honey shine, several braided rope rugs giving it a
pleasant, homey feel. The swinging lights overhead
were all brass and the bulkheads were all paneled in

a pale blond wood that might have been beech or ash. To the left there was a tidy, sensible-looking galley with a kettle sitting on an electric hob, and farther on were two bunks, beds neatly made, one on either side. Between the bunks and the galley was a waist-high divider with a built-in table, a bench and a chair. A litter of charts was spread out across the table along with a compass, a slide rule of sorts and a pair of steel dividers. The cabin was high enough to stand in, the brass portholes on either side blacked out with wooden plugs and shutters. It looked more like the cabin on an expensive sailboat than the living quarters of a river barge.

The ATC officer saw Dundee's look of surprise as he came into the cabin, shutting the door behind him. "Nice, isn't it?" he said. He used the gun again, gesturing to the bench. Dundee sat down, careful to keep his hands in plain sight, but away from the steel dividers; the last thing he wanted to do was give the man an excuse to fire the Smith and Wesson. Dundee had seen chumps like this before during his first days on the L.A. Police Force. On the surface they looked calm and at ease, but scratch the surface and you found a scared kid who was into something deeper than he knew. This one was no exception; barely twenty and his trigger finger was white-knuckle scared.

"Very nice." He paused. "You really with Air Transport Command?"

The young man sat down in the chair opposite. "Was."

"What happened?"

"How'd you get out of the locker?" The young man reached into the breast pocket of his tunic and pulled out one of the new white packs of Luckies instead of the green—something about copper dye being necessary for the war effort. He tapped one out on the table, all the while keeping the gun aimed steadily at Dundee's chest. He reached into his other pocket, pulled out a slim, almost feminine Ronson that certainly wasn't PX stock, and lit up. He drew hard on the cigarette, taking the smoke deep into his lungs, then ejecting it from his nostrils in twin dragon plumes. "Russell was pretty sure he gave you enough ether to keep Dumbo down for a month." He put the cigarette pack and the lighter down on the table.

"The MP, right?"

The young man smirked like a schoolboy. "Russell can be anything he wants to be."

"You never told me what happened between you and the ATC."

"Nothing happened," said the young man angrily. His finger tightened on the trigger.

"Charlie would be pretty angry if you killed me before he got a chance to talk to me," Dundee warned. His mouth and throat were already dry and burning from the ether, but now they'd turned to parched cotton. The kid was a firecracker.

"Charlie?"

"Your boss? Charlie Danby?"

"You know The Colonel?"

"We went to school together."

"Well, I'll be," said the young man. His finger eased off on the trigger.

Dundee realized he'd been holding his breath. He let it out slowly. "You have any idea what this is all about?"

"We just follow orders," said the young man. "Just like the Army." It was definitely the past tense, uniform or not.

"You're not in the Army any more?"

"The Colonel's army now, not Uncle Sam's. In The Colonel's army you get treated right." So, by definition then, Uncle Sam's version had treated him badly. Things were starting to fall into place.

Dundee sat back against the padded backrest of the bench. He gestured at the cigarettes, trying to buy some time to think. "Mind if I have one of those?"

"Sure. I got lots more and they don't cost me nothing anyway."

Dundee picked up the pack of Luckies and the Ronson. He lit the cigarette carefully and slowly, clicking the lighter on and off a few times. "Nice," he said. He jerked his thumb upward. "That old guy upstairs was never in Uncle Sam's army. Where does he fit into the picture?"

"Old Bob?" The young man laughed. "He goes up and down the river just like he's done for the last hundred years or so, except now instead of coal he's carrying butter and beef in one direction and liquor in the other. All thanks to The Colonel."

Dundee nodded. Black-market trade, run by deserters and young idiots like this one, AWOL from their units for petty crimes and some not so petty.

He stared at the boy, trying to figure out how someone so young could get into enough trouble to warrant running away from his unit and getting involved with Charlie Danby. Young and good-looking, blond hair, blue eyes and a build like a prize fighter. He decided to take a guess.

"It was a girl, wasn't it."

"What?" The young man's eyes narrowed. "What did you say?"

"It was a girl. You get her in trouble?" Dundee kept his eye on the boy's trigger finger. The gun shifted in the ATC man's hand as though the weight was beginning to bother him, or maybe an old memory.

"She said she was going to go to my C.O. and tell him I'd raped her unless I paid to . . . you know." The kid's neck flushed, the color creeping onto his cheeks like cold weather on a winter day.

Dundee shook his head. The young man had thrown away his life because some country girl had decided how to make him pay for her virtue. Or maybe she really did have one in the oven. It didn't really matter; rape was a capital offense over here, and he could hang for it.

"How did you find out about The Colonel?"

"There was a guy . . ." the boy mumbled. Dundee let out a plume of smoke. There was always a guy. It had even been that way back at Bain Academy; there'd always been three or four other boys circling Charlie like flies around shit, using the bigger, stronger boy as a shield against their own weaknesses, the same kind who'd be recruiting for him now.

That was Charlie, all right. Efficient, smart, and above all, organized. It all made perfect sense, especially if you knew how many deserters there really were wandering around England these days. It was top secret, but Dundee had seen the reports being sent back Stateside and knew that more than seven thousand GIs and other ranks had disappeared over the past year, a figure the brass didn't want made public. It was assumed that most of them had vanished into the larger cities, especially London, swallowed up by local British gangs of crooks, but no one ever figured them for being organized from the inside; Capone had tried something like that in Chicago twenty years ago. So had others, but no one had ever pulled it off for sure. Certainly not in England and certainly not in the middle of a war.

"Where are you from?" Dundee asked.

"You ask too many questions."

"Just making conversation, kid, calm down."

"I'm no kid," the young man growled, lifting the gun slightly as though making a point.

"Sorry. I was just interested, that's all."

"Green Bay."

"Where's that?" asked Dundee. He'd never heard of it.

"Wisconsin. On Lake Michigan." The young man in the flier's uniform made a little snorting sound under his breath. "Thought you big shot lawyers knew everything. Biggest meat-packing center in the Midwest."

"I didn't know." But the kid knew who he was, which was interesting. Dundee tucked the information away for future reference. "You ever think you're going to get back there?" It was a question he'd thought of the first time he'd heard of the enormous number of deserters in England. The place was, after all, an island. There were only two ways off, by air and by sea, both methods of transportation easy enough to monitor. It didn't take a genius to figure out that deserting was no good if you couldn't go home. On the other hand, anybody stupid enough to go AWOL in the first place wasn't first in line when the brains were being handed out, were they? It was like that old limerick about robbing banks in Nantucket; you can rob the bank, but you can't get away with it, so . . .

"Sure. We can go home." The kid paused, a smile spreading across his young face. "Anytime we want. Colonel's got that all figured out too."

Dundee was just about to ask how Charlie intended to pull off that little bit of prestidigitation when there was a dull thump that ran through the boat. The sound of the engine coughed into silence. There was a low whistle from above.

"That's our signal," said the young man. He waved the barrel of the gun stiffly. "Up you get."

Dundee got up from the bench, and the young man watched as he came around the table and headed out the door. There might have been a chance to make a break for it at the top of the ladder, but Old Bob was right there, sitting on the curved roof of the cabin a few feet from the open hatch in the deck, the huge old Webley held unwaveringly in one old hand, the hooked gaff in the other. A gangplank had been laid from the hull of the barge to the shore a few feet away. Dundee shivered in the night air. The sky was deep purple, pricked with a shimmering field of bright stars but not lit by any moon at all. The riverbank was fairly steep and the gangplank jutted up at an angle. Whatever lay beyond the top of the bank was invisible, screened by a line of willows that hung down over the water like a green veil that whispered in the faint breeze, the trees so gnarled and old that their twisted roots had long ago torn free from the rich, dark earth of the bankside like ancient bones thrown up from a grave. Dundee found himself wondering if a grave wasn't the next step, or whether Charlie had something else in mind. If so, he was going to a hell of a lot of trouble to see him planted.

Russell the MP suddenly appeared from the rear of the barge. The MP's uniform was gone and, like the young man, he was wearing an ATC uniform covered by a leather flying jacket. He smiled at Dundee but said nothing. Stepping forward he took a pair of handcuffs from the pocket of the leather jacket and snapped them over Dundee's wrists, ratcheting them down painfully. It seemed that Russell was the kind of person who liked inflicting pain; not surprising, considering who he worked for.

"How ya doin' . . . Major," said Russell. He nodded at the handcuffs. "Can't have you running away on us, now can we?"

Old Bob laughed at the comment, the laugh turning to a phlegmy gurgle. Somehow the barge pilot managed to spit over the side of the boat without taking the filthy old briar out of his mouth. Dundee noticed that the stained old life preserver hanging on a rusted iron hook next to Old Bob read MV *Bagby Park*. Another fact to be put away for later. Russell put a large hand on Dundee's shoulder and turned him toward the gangplank. "Move out, soldier boy."

Dundee climbed onto the gangplank and made his way up it to the riverbank. Russell followed and then the kid. Coming out from the enclosing cover of the willows Dundee was vaguely aware of a small meadowlike pasture set with a stone wall on one side and a high, thorny hedgerow on the other. There was a small group of sheep in one corner of the field, looking like a drift of old snow. The air was ripe with the heavy, wet odor of their wool. They moved skittishly to one side as Dundee and his companions stepped into view. A hundred yards up a gently rising slope a tree lot stood like a dark, shadowy line blotting out the stars.

"Follow the path," said Russell, gesturing to the hedgerow. At the base of it Dundee could now see a faint, dark line in the clover, leading up into the trees. He stumbled forward, guiding himself haphazardly across the uneven ground, surprised at how difficult it was to keep his balance without the free use of his hands. All thoughts of making an escape on foot vanished; the hedgerow on one side and stone wall on the other were impenetrable barriers to a man in steel bracelets.

They moved into the trees and instantly the breeze fell off and then died, and the close air was full of the smell of the brown cedar boughs that blanketed the forest floor. Peering ahead Dundee saw that the path continued through the trees in a meandering fashion that probably meant rabbits. He had a sudden memory of a trapline of snares he'd set one summer with his cousin Paulie in the hills above their summer place in Santa Barbara, and his horror at actually catching one; strangled, throat torn and eyes glazed over with a reproachful expression on its dumb, dead face, ants crawling into the mouth and out again.

No more than five minutes later the trees abruptly ended and Dundee saw there was a second meadow running along the slope of the shallow hill they'd been climbing. It was barely a meadow at all, more like a scar in the side of the hill, and Dundee could see where it had been artificially widened, the white of freshly cut tree trunks gleaming in the faint starlight. At the far end of the narrow pasture he could see the batlike shape of a small aircraft. It was a high-winged monoplane like the Fairchild-24s his father used for land surveying in California, except this one was painted olive green and fitted out with USAAF stars and a serial number on the tail. The trio walked toward the waiting plane. Upon reaching it, Dundee heard a faint tumbling sound that steadily grew in volume. A moment later the air was full of the sound of pounding, powerful engines as dozens of aircraft thundered over their heads, no more than two or three hundred feet overhead. Looking up he picked up their familiar shapes like cardboard cutouts against the carpet of stars.

"B-17s," said Russell needlessly. "Practicing night raids. Newton-Abbot airfield is only a few miles south of here. We take off and land here all the time; no one notices."

"Where did you get the plane?" Dundee asked.

"Now that would be telling," said Russell. Suddenly the air was full of the smell of ether again. Dundee felt the rag pressed over his mouth and nose and then he didn't feel anything at all.

Sixteen

She'd never been good with heights and this was no
exception. Jane Todd stood on the bridge abutment
and looked out over the valley of the Tweed, trying
not to think of how she'd gotten herself into this
mess. Here she was in a country you could fit three
or four times into the state of New York, and she
might as well be with John Carter on the sands of
Mars. She wasn't quite sure how such a small place
could look so desolate and empty.

And high.

The slope was a good seventy-five degrees; not
quite a cliff, but close enough not to make any difference to her. Her stomach flip-flopped like one of
Aunt Jemima's flapjacks when she got close enough
to look over, and she backed up, head swimming
after one brief glimpse. Even with her eyes shut she
could see the long fall of bare, stony ground and bits
of vegetation barely clinging to the earth and the
gray-black outcroppings of stone ready to smash her
skull like an eggshell if she were dumb enough to
come too close and fall over. It was still too dark to
see very well, but Jane was pretty sure she could

make out the river glinting a good three or four hundred feet below.

She bent her head into the collar of the overcoat and lit her second to last cigarette. She'd been walking steadily along the tracks for the past hour, and so far she hadn't seen a single fence, village, building or path. Except for the call of the occasional night bird and the sighing of the wind there had only been the heavy silence of the empty moor. It was as though McSeveney's Halt had been the end of the world and she'd just stepped off it. Except for the railway track unraveling in the inky dark there wasn't the slightest sign that civilization had ever *thought* of coming this way.

"Hadrian's Wall," she muttered to herself, remembering a shred of poetry from somewhere in her past. Something about a lost legion of Roman soldiers. She drew deeply on the cigarette and stepped a little closer to the edge of the concrete bridge mooring. Lost legion was right. If the Germans ever decided to invade they'd be wise to stay away from this godforsaken place, too.

The bridge itself wasn't much better than the edge of the cliff; one track, with perhaps three feet of clearance on either side and no handrail, stretching into the distance—at least five hundred yards to the other side and solid ground. In the gloom she could make out a complex web of old iron girders that looked as though they dated back to Queen Victoria's time and didn't look strong enough to support any kind of weight at all, let alone a heavily loaded passenger train. She edged a little closer and swallowed hard, her mouth gone dry. The track wasn't even on some kind of solid foundation; looking downward she could see the rust-blighted support girders making shadow patterns between the ties.

Turning away from the bridge she looked east and west. Eastward there was a faint line of lighter purple marking the arrival of dawn sometime in the immediate future, rising up out of the English Channel, announcing a new day and a renewed effort by Occleshaw. Westward, into the darkness, the cliff went on as well. Which made some sense. Why build a bridge four hundred feet in the air if there was an easier place to cross the river? Jane laughed sourly around a bitter mouthful of smoke. She had no idea where she was going, but she was taking the most direct route. She turned and looked behind her; still black as Carter's Ink. If she retraced her steps she'd make it back to Selkirk, or whatever the place was called, about sunrise—just in time for breakfast and a quick trip to the lockup.

The thought of food was almost enough to tempt her into taking her chances with jail, but then she remembered their trip to Shepton Mallet and thought again. She'd done a tour of the women's prison in Los Angeles for *Life* magazine a couple of years back and it had scared the hell out of her; there was no reason to think Occleshaw would do any better.

She flicked her cigarette into the darkness and wished she hadn't. Her eyes following the brightly glowing butt as it sailed out into the abyss and then spiraled down, disappearing finally, swallowed up by the all-consuming darkness; the same darkness she'd have to cross if she were to have any chance at all of staying out of Special Branch's clutches.

"Stop being a baby and get going, Jane, or you'll never hear the end of it back home." Which was exactly where she wanted to be right now, playing poker at the Plaza in one of the rooms "reserved" by Pelay, the diminutive senior bellman, drinking Rusty Birdwell's Old Grandad, watching Noel Busch demonstrate how to deal from the bottom of the deck without anyone noticing—except everyone else at the table—and smoking Spuds and telling dirty jokes until dawn finally put Broadway to sleep and woke up Fifth Avenue.

Putting one foot in front of the other and thanking God and anyone else she could think of that she was wearing flats and not heels, Jane stepped out onto the bridge, not quite sure where to let her eyes come to rest and finally deciding on straight ahead, peering into the dark at her invisible destination, counting each tie as her foot came down on it, resisting the terrifying impulse to look left, right or down because she knew, beyond the deepest, darkest shadow of a doubt, what would happen.

Her head would start to spin, or she'd be sick, or the worst horror of all, she'd freeze where she was, turned to stone in the middle of the bridge, unable to go forward or back, and inevitably taking the only option open to her: falling, tumbling endlessly, the last thing in her ears her own petrified scream, and her final vision the river rushing up to meet her. Far above her an early-rising curlew screeched in the last of the night and Jane quietly cursed its mindless ability to fly.

By the three hundred and twenty-eighth tie Jane was reasonably sure she'd gone about a third of the way, and with every step she was equally sure she was never going to make it to the other side; the one factor she'd failed to take into consideration was the wind, no more than a soft breeze standing on terra firma, but out here it was a blustery, tugging gale, whirling the hem of the overcoat around her legs and taking air like a sailboat, sending her into a teetering tightrope walk, arms spread to keep her balance. Twice she slipped on the dew-damp ties, and once her leg went into the space between the heavy wooden blocks and she spent a terrifying minute dragging herself upward. She crawled forward on her hands and knees for a few feet, tearing her stockings, forced to look downward into the canyonlike depths below, her breath now coming in desperate gasps as she gathered up the courage to stand again.

She finally managed to regain her feet, fighting off the urge to simply stand there for a moment, knowing that if she did she might never start again.

"One foot in front of the other," she panted, fixing her eyes on the far side of the bridge. She'd lost count of the number of ties so she simply picked up where she'd left off. "Three hundred twenty nine, three hundred thirty. . . ." She was close enough to the opposite side to make out some detail. The bridge foundation here was rock instead of concrete, the way it had been behind her; a natural cutting made by two jutting humps of rock that rose like twin stone whales surfacing on the edge of the slope leading down to the river in the depths below.

Jane was vaguely aware that the slope on the far side wasn't as steep, but that wasn't going to do her any good now. The first light leaking out of the east was painting the upper edges of the two stone hills a faint pinkish purple. While keeping her eyes glued to that strangely optimistic sight, she missed the two winking dots of red between the massive stones.

Her first warning came with a faint vibration like rolling, distant thunder announcing the coming of a storm. An instant later the wild shrieking of a steam whistle froze Jane where she stood—a bolt of mind-numbing terror running down her spine and turning her bruised and aching legs to jelly. She saw the twin signal lights now, burning like unblinking eyes in the darkness on the far side of the gorge; the Robbie Burns was coming back and she was directly in its path.

There was no time to think or even panic; she had to act in the next few seconds. Left and right there was only that rust-stained three-foot ledge of iron and cement; if she lay down there the train would either hit her a glancing blow if any part of her came too close, or its passing would shake her off her perch. Her body was too wide to fit between the ties and, unlike the subway in New York, lying down between the rails would be suicide. Her only chance was to reach one of the old inspection ladders set onto the side of the bridge every fifty yards, the rusted hooplike safety rails the only thing between her and a plunge to certain death.

She ran forward, barely keeping her footing on the slippery ties, praying that no one could see her in the lifting darkness. She reached one of the rusted old ladders and immediately saw that there was a semicircular iron fitting roughly bolted onto the topmost railing, probably intended for some kind of old-fashioned safety harness; a safety harness she didn't have. She stopped and stared, almost sure she'd seen the swinging beams of flashlights arcing out from the rear of the train. If Occleshaw or his men were on the rear platform of the coach they'd almost surely spot her crouching in the small, open well of the ladder.

She went down a step, ducking down out of view, and in the same moment her feet came out from under her as the corroded rungs pulled away from the main struts and sent her hurtling down to the foot of the ladder, her hand shooting out and gripping the last of the surrounding hoops and stopping her headlong fall into the chasm. She could feel the whole ladder giving way, wrenching out of its supports. Her right arm felt as though it was tearing out of its socket. She brought up her left hand and gripped the hoop, putting all her weight on the fragile band of weathered metal.

She pulled upward, managing to swing her leg onto the nearest beam, and then her whole body, until she was lying along its length. In the distance, on the far side of the narrow valley, the train reached the bridge and moved upward, the bridge's entire length shivering and groaning with the weight. The last of the loosened rungs of the ladder gave way and went twirling and twisting down out of sight. Even if she wanted to give herself up to Occleshaw it would be impossible now; there was no way back up onto the bridge.

She lay petrified on the beam, the erratic gusts of howling wind picking at her coat and sending her hair flying in all directions. Her fingers gripping the rough, rusted edges of the iron were stiff with cold. Every movement forced by the blustering wind brought panic closer. She knew that if she didn't make a move soon, she'd fall. The Robbie Burns was closer now, the locomotive panting and snorting with a steamy mechanical sound like some gigantic horse.

The bridge shuddered with its approach and Jane bit back a scream.

Out of the corner of her eye she could see the swinging beams of the approaching flashlights; Occleshaw's men were getting closer with each passing moment. Blindly, she began to inch down the beam on her back, using the heels of her shoes to propel herself and her hands gripping the wide flanges on each side of the beam to guide her body on a downward-sweeping arc that she knew would eventually take her to the bolted joint to one of the upright support columns.

Eventually her feet struck a metal obstruction and she managed to lift her head a few inches and get her bearings; one of the support columns stood in her way. From above the flashlight beams were almost on top of her, and she could hear the shouting voices of Occleshaw's men. They'd found some evidence of her being on the bridge and had come to a stop. She forced herself forward with her hands, now scraped and bleeding, her knees bending as she pushed along. Finally she could go no farther and she was forced to plant her feet and reach out with her hands, grabbing the upright by its outer edges and hauling herself into a standing position, hugging the vertical iron beam as though it was a long-lost friend.

Above her the flashlights were concentrated on the dilapidated remains of the inspection ladder. She clearly heard a voice saying, "Down here!" They'd found out where she'd gone and it wouldn't take them much longer to pinpoint her position; if she wanted to avoid being found she'd have to be quick about it.

She eased her body to the left, shifting her feet in a shimmying movement that allowed her to move without lifting her feet. Fixed to the left side of the vertical beam was a curving horizontal girder that arced across to another, wider beam like the one she was standing on. She could see in the lifting darkness that the pattern was repeated over and over again until the beams ran out at the end of the bridge; the whole system of vertical meeting horizontal was mirrored on the right.

Moving as quickly as she dared, and still hugging the vertical beam in front of her, Jane felt her way with her feet, biting her lip as a piece of rusted iron gave way under her prodding shoe, almost making her lose her balance. Finally, her foot reached the horizontal girder. With her eyes squeezed tightly shut and her pounding heart beating in her throat, she swung her way across. She realized she'd been holding her breath the whole time and let it out in an explosive gasp. From above, over the sound of the train, she could hear more calling voices, much closer now. Arching her neck, she stared upward into the tangle of iron. The flashlight beams were stronger, circles of bright light now cutting in and out of the girders all around her. She had no choice; she had to move.

She edged out onto the next girder and this time she scuttled forward in a crouching, headlong run, arms outstretched like a tightrope walker, keeping exactly in the middle of the narrow iron path, then grasping the next upright beam like a long-lost lover. The wind was still tearing at her clothes and hair with its invisible, clawing talons, trying to dislodge her from her precarious aerie, but she knew how to beat it now; the iron beast was tamed. She grinned in the stormy, angry air, eyes squinting, and edged quickly around the next vertical girder. Terror was still at her back and whispering in her ear, but now at least she had a chance. She repeated her rush along the steadily curving beams again and again, leaving the swinging, searching beams of the flashlights far behind her. As she made her way around each vertical, she neared the far side of the valley and her spirits soared; it was beginning to look like she might actually make it.

The bullet struck no more than six inches in front of her face as she reached the next iron upright, sending out a clanging explosion of sparks, burning her cheeks and half blinding her. She stopped, ducked and, grabbing hold of the beam at her feet, wobbling and almost falling, she finally dropped to her knees and managed to steady herself in the instant before she toppled. She whirled, searching for the bullet's origin and found it almost immediately as her assailant fired a second time, coming so close the projectile actually singed her hair. She swung around to the right this time, putting the narrow width of the vertical iron post between her and the goon with the gun. The attacker had come down one of the inspection ladders closer to the far side of the bridge, and had simply waited for her to make her appearance. He wasn't interested in capturing her either; he was aiming to kill.

But who the hell was he? Whatever else he was, Occleshaw was a British cop, and as far as she knew, British cops didn't carry guns. Come to think of it, she'd never met *any* cop who could shoot that well. Then again, maybe Special Branch was "special" that way, too. Not that it mattered; somebody was firing a goddamn great big gun at her with the clear intention of blowing her head off and it was the gun, not its owner's identity, that concerned her right now. Whoever he was though, he was smart, lying in wait the way he had; more like a hunter than a cop. She found herself thinking of John Bone, and for a brief, superstitious instant wondered if his ghost had come back to haunt her, but she cast off the idea like the bad dream it was; ghosts haunted with moans and rattling chains, not .45 automatics.

She eased forward an inch or two, just enough to see around the beam and up to what she thought was the shooter's position. If he was firing from there his aim would become more difficult the closer Jane came to the end of the bridge, more and more crossbeams getting in the way of his line of fire. The real problem, though, was the inescapable fact of the gathering daylight; another few minutes and there'd be enough to pick her off with ease—he was coming close enough as it was.

Edging outward she tried to draw his fire, once and for all establishing his position, but nothing happened. Above her head the train had moved almost entirely past and there were no signs of any flashlights from above. Maybe he'd moved, but Jane didn't think so. Clenching her teeth and trying to keep down the rising bile of fear in her throat, she forced herself to look down. The arc of the bridge's construction had taken her within a hundred feet of the water. She could now just see the brownish inshore currents swirling around the massive cut-stone footings of the bridge.

No way out, even if she was going to try to duck

out of view by going to the girder below, simply because there wasn't one; in crossing to this side of the bridge she'd moved steadily downward until there were no more support beams. The only way open to her was down the next three or four horizontal girders to one of the two massive end beams sunk into the footings, and onto one of the metal ladders she could see attached to both of them. From the ladders she could climb down to the base of the bridge with relative ease, and then make her way along beside the water, hidden from above by the screening line of willows and old beech trees at the river's edge.

Her only chance was surprise. Taking a deep breath and bending low, she came out from behind the protective ironwork in a rush, ignoring the open air beneath her feet, fixing her gaze on the next beam.

She was within a few feet of it when the first shot rang out, the bullet plucking at the hem of her coat with a sound like an angry bee. She never heard the second explosion. Toppling off the downward arcing girder, she twisted and turned in the empty air as she fell toward the dark, roiling water below.

The man crouching in the well of the inspection ladder a hundred feet away peered into the dark, massive fretwork of girders and beams, trying to see if he'd hit his target. He rarely missed, but this hadn't been the easiest of positions to shoot from. He smiled wanly to himself. He must be getting old; next he'd start blaming his eyesight or his quivering, arthritic fingers. He waited, but there was no further movement, although he was fairly sure he'd seen someone fall. It didn't really matter; one way or another his

work here was done. As long as that fool Occleshaw
didn't capture her he was happy.

He slipped his flat black pistol back into its holster.
The wind had tossed his necktie back over his shoulder and he flipped it down again with an irritated
movement of his small, long-fingered hand. He had
purchased the tie in London in the Burlington Arcade
off Bond Street the day before the entire place had
been bombed into perdition. He thought it was quite
attractive: little black doves on a dark blue ground.
He eased himself upright and began to climb the
inspection ladder to the bridge and the Robbie Burns.

Seventeen

When Lucas Dundee woke for the second time, the rope from the cramped locker of MV *Bagby Park* had been replaced by a thick, down-filled mattress, and the smell of hops by the faint scent of lavender. Opening his eyes he saw that he was covered by a heavy quilt done in rag squares, and his head was resting on a plump pillow covered in crisp, starched linen. The words "AKERGILL SANITORIUM" were stamped across it in faded blue.

Dundee sat up and blearily looked around. He was in a small room, no more than twelve feet on a side, the roof over his head sloping down to an eave. The dormer window was covered by blackout curtains, but not so well that he couldn't see a faint line of weak dawn light between them. An attic room under the roof, then. In the distance he thought he could hear the boom of the sea against rock but he wasn't completely sure.

He swung his legs out of bed and discovered that his feet were bare and he was dressed in green striped pajamas. There was a pair of plaid, well-used slippers on the bare wood floor and he slipped them on. Directly in front of him was a mirror-topped chest of drawers. On it he could see a porcelain sachet like the ones his mother had kept in every bedroom of their estate; the source of the lavender smell.

The only other furniture in the room was a plain wooden chair with a well-worn seat placed under the window. Over the back of the chair was a set of clothes suited to the country: corduroy trousers, a heavy cotton shirt and a tweed jacket. On the seat of the chair a pair of heavy lace up ankle boots, scuffed but sturdy-looking, waited side by side. There was no sign of his uniform. To the left, a few feet from the bed, was a wooden door, its top lintel cut at an angle to accommodate the slope of the roof. All very homey. He stood up and headed for the door. He'd only gone a step or two from the bed when he had to stop, one hand shooting out to grip the dresser for support. His knees almost gave out on him and he stood there, breathing deeply for a moment, head swimming and the room doing a slow dance around him. There was a dull ache in the back of his head and a sharper pain behind his eyes, a fierce headache that pounded beneath his forehead and even across his cheeks and jaw. His throat was raw and he could still smell the rich, sweet chemical reek of the ether Russell had drugged him with a second time.

The room stopped moving and Dundee managed to move away from the dresser, and reached the door without falling down. There was no lock, only an old-fashioned latch and bar. He pressed down on the handle, the bar lifted and he pushed open the door. It led into a second, larger area at the top of a narrow flight of stairs.

A man in a white jacket with "Akergill Sanitorium" stitched on the pocket was leaning back in the mated pair of the chair under his window. He was wearing white trousers to match the jacket and a white collarless shirt. On his feet he was wearing heavy-soled black shoes of the kind a policeman might have. He was reading *Rogue Male*, a penny dreadful with a garish cover by someone named Geoffery Household.

At first glance he looked like a hospital orderly, except for the bulkiness of his shoulders and neck, and the visible leather strap of a holster harness under his jacket. There was a small, plain table beside the man's chair with a blank-faced telephone on it. Seeing Dundee peering out the door, the man calmly put his book upside down in his lap, then leaned over and picked up the telephone receiver. He waited calmly, then spoke softly into the phone for a moment before hanging up. He looked at Dundee and smiled. "The doctor will be up shortly," said the man. The accent was flat, bland and Midwestern.

"Where am I?" asked Dundee

The man stared at him with an absolute lack of interest. "In a hospital, of course. You had a bad fall, don't you remember? You banged your head." He picked up his book again, wetting the end of his thumb and flipping the page.

"Like hell!" Dundee was starting to feel nauseated. His head hurt worse than ever and all he wanted to do was lie down again. "A guy named Russell knocked me out with ether. Twice."

The man in the white jacket looked up from his book. "Sure he did," he said, and went back to his reading. Dundee looked at him fiercely, his frustration rising. His head continued to pound and there was a faint ringing in his ears. He slammed the door with as much energy as he could muster, then turned around and staggered back to the comforting embrace of the down mattress and the crisp white pillow.

His eyes closed but he didn't sleep. Comfortably outfitted or not, it was definitely enemy territory. Surely Charlie hadn't gone to all this trouble just for him? It was too fantastic. But the whole charade of a convalescent hospital, complete with attendants in white jackets and attending physicians, couldn't have any other, more specifically criminal, purpose. Leaving West Point and trying to avoid both his father and his father's sometimes questionable business enterprises had seemed like a good idea. Above all, Lucas Alexander Decimus Dundee saw the civilized world as a structure based on logic and truth. His father had spent a lifetime bending both to his own pursuits, so bending them back seemed like a reasonable alternative. Now he wasn't so sure. With the exception of the regular and boringly obvious crimes of passion, every wrongdoing he'd ever investigated or prosecuted had its own rationale, at least to the perpetrator; find that rationale and follow it and everything would inevitably fall into place—method, motive and eventually the *gonif* who'd done the deed. The elegant simplicity had attracted Lucas right from the start. He liked rules, and putting away people who broke them.

Except this seemed to be doing nothing but breaking them, with no rhyme or reason. Dundee listed them again, dragging them through his tortured, ether-addled brain, kicking and screaming, trying to put squares pegs into round holes once again: *Why steal something you couldn't sell? Why make expensive duplicates of jeweled objects you didn't intend to use? Why make your trail so easy to follow? Why use ether when a bullet would have been simpler? Why go to all the trouble of a phony hospital to convince an old school-mate of . . . what?*

"Mr. Portal?"

Dundee's eye fluttered open. There was a man in a knee-length white coat sitting on the edge of the bed. He was young, no more than thirty or so, with thinning red-brown hair and a plain, roundish face with intelligent eyes and a boyish scattering of freckles across his nose. Like a lot of red-haired people he had virtually no visible eyelashes or eyebrows, giving him a chronic look of surprise. He had a stethoscope hanging from around the collar of his finely striped white shirt. A doctor. He paused and reached into the breast pocket of his white coat and brought out a pair of steel-rimmed spectacles. He put them on, fitting them over his pink ears. They made him look a little less boyish, but not much. Dundee looked past him at the window. The pale line of light between the blackout curtains didn't seem any brighter; if he'd slept it hadn't been for long.

"My name is Dundee. I am an officer in the American Army. The Judge Advocate General's office."

"Not according to the identity papers you were found with. Apparently your name is David Portal. You're a Canadian in the Merchant Marine. From what we can tell you had an accident while you were on leave. You wound up here." Dundee stared blankly at the man. He was in the looney bin and this guy was one of the inmates.

"Where is Charlie Danby? I want to talk to him right now."

"Who?"

"Charles Danby, Colonel Charles Danby, the man who runs this place." Dundee's earlier feeling of panic was returning; he struggled to sit up.

"Mr. Portal, please try to calm down. The director of this facility is not named Danby, it's Sir John Gadsby, and he is neither American nor is he a colonel. He's a doctor. So am I. My name is McNab." The man in the white coat put a hand on Dundee's shoulder. He struggled to get hold of himself; if he kept on this way they'd put him in a straitjacket and throw him into a padded room.

"Then I want to see this Gadsby guy," he said, settling back against the pillow.

"In due time," said McNab. "At present we have your health to think of." McNab fell silent and got about his business, listening to his patient's heart and taking his pulse. Dundee let him, his mind racing; there was no need to antagonize him before he knew what in God's name was going on. If Charlie wanted to continue with his elaborate charade, then let him; he'd play along for the moment. After five minutes McNab sat back and smiled down at Dundee.

"Well, Mr. Portal, you seem fit enough for someone who took a serious blow to the head."

"Where exactly am I?" asked Dundee.

"Akergill Hall," said the doctor. "It's a sanatorium."

"Private?" asked Dundee. It would have to be for Charlie's purposes.

"It was at one time," McNab answered, "but that was before the war, of course." He sighed and took off his spectacles, folding them and putting them back into his breast pocket. Dundee watched him carefully as he did so, then smiled to himself. McNab went on. "Most of our patients come from His Majesty's Government now. Air Force in the main."

Dundee sat up in bed and buttoned his pajama top. "Oh?"

"We specialize in burns and reconstructive surgery mostly. I believe you Americans call it 'plastic' surgery. We also specialize in injuries to the brain. Amnesia."

"I thought you said I was Canadian."

McNab smiled easily. "By definition a Canadian is an American, in the largest sense, since they occupy a somewhat greater portion of the North American continent than the United States." He patted Dundee's knee under the quilt. "You seem to be quite well, at least superficially. When you feel up to it you can come down to the dining hall and have some breakfast." He smiled. "I'd stay away from the kippers if I was you. Too salty for a man in your condition." His smile broadened. "Although I must say, Cook is inordinately proud of them."

The young man clapped him on the knee again and stood up. A moment later he was gone, closing the door softly behind, the latch bar clicking into place. Dundee remained where he was for a second. His headache was still there, but somehow he felt a little better for whatever small shred of sleep he'd just had. For a while there he'd thought he was going crazy—maybe he *was* a merchant seaman from Canada with some kind of head injury. That was no more crazy than chasing after the stolen crown jewels. He smiled grimly to himself, then flung aside the quilt and climbed out of bed again, crossing over to the chair.

He unbuttoned the pajama top and slipped off the bottoms, then suddenly stopped. It was the eyeglasses. People wear them either because they're near- or far-sighted, or perhaps just for reading, and when put on or taken off the wearer's eyes change, the pupils either dilating or contracting. When McNab had taken his spectacles off a few moments ago his eyes hadn't changed at all. Naked and shivering in the early-morning cold, Dundee began to put on the unfamiliar clothes.

Set dressing, just like they did at Metro. During the Thelma Todd investigation they tracked a potential lead to her killer to the set of the actress's last film, a Laurel and Hardy comedy called *The Bohemian Girl*. He'd been transfixed when Stan Laurel, once Charlie Chaplin's understudy, demonstrated his craft by transforming himself into a perfect evocation of the Little Tramp simply by changing his expression and walking with his feet splayed out. As Oliver Hardy, Laurel's fat partner, said at the time, "It's the little things that do it." This time it was a little thing that tipped off Dundee. McNab's spectacles had plain glass lenses; they were phonies. The red-haired man might know something about medicine, but Dundee was willing to bet he wasn't a doctor.

He finished dressing, lacing on the heavy boots, then made for the door. He swung it open, ducking low, and stepped into the tiny attic vestibule. There was no sign of the guard but his book was lying beside the telephone. Dundee picked it up. Something about a British big game hunter stalking Hitler and getting more than he bargained for.

"Wishful thinking," Dundee muttered under his breath. He headed down the narrow stairs.

Eighteen

Jane Todd hit the rushing surface of the Tweed River feetfirst; had she been unlucky enough to strike the water with any other part of her body she would almost certainly have been killed instantly. As it was, the force of her impact took her down almost to the bottom of the fast-flowing river, knocking the wind out of her and filling her mouth and eyes with water-borne silt, thick as mud, which quickly began to choke her. It was that and not the bullet that was now threatening to end her life, the bullet having done nothing more than singe the back of her extended right hand, startling her and sending her on her headlong fall from the bridge girder to the water below.

She struggled to the surface, tearing at the sodden wool coat, which was now dragging her under. She finally managed to peel it off, all the while being tossed and turned beneath the surface, tumbling along in the surging, invisible currents created by the underwater caissons for the immense bridge overhead. Fighting free of the coat, she pushed herself upward, lungs on fire as she stroked to the surface, blinded by the grit in the water and her own terror.

She knew that if she didn't reach the surface in the next few seconds she would almost surely drown.

And then she broke free, the dark, rushing embrace of the deadly water replaced by the cold dawn air. Coughing and retching, taking in deep, gagging breaths, she raised her bleeding hand and wiped the silt from her eyes, all the while being thrown steadily downstream, away from the bridge and her searching adversaries. She finally regained her senses enough to be able to look around. She instinctively began swimming toward the closest bank of the river, letting the current take her and not trying to fight. By the time she reached the water's edge and managed to drag herself up on the narrow bank she was freezing cold and exhausted. Unknown to him, the man who'd shot her on the bridge had almost made his kill after all.

She rolled over, her back against the stony ground, gasping for breath and staring up into the dawn sky. She gathered her strength and sat up, looking around. In the dim light she could see that she'd been carried a good mile along the river, a great sweeping bend putting her almost out of sight of the bridge. Silhouetted against the brightening sky she could see the last sweeping stone arch and the black shape of the train on top of it, smoke puffing from its locomotive as it pushed the train off the bridge. It wouldn't take long for them to reach Selkirk and begin to organize a proper search. Occleshaw was an idiot, but he was stubborn; he wouldn't take it for granted that she'd been killed until he saw her cold, dead body.

Which he was likely to do unless she found some way to dry her clothes and warm up a little. She managed to get to her feet, wobbling, and noticed that she was short one shoe. It was a miracle that she still had even one, but one shoe wasn't going to cut it if she was to have any hope of getting out of Occleshaw's clutches.

She shivered, her teeth chattering. The slope of the cliff leading back up to the desolate moor was less steep here, but not by much. She let her eyes wander over the near cliff, looking for some way up through the thick scrub brush and bramble. She finally spotted a pale line that zigzagged almost invisibly upward from the bank, appearing and disappearing through the low trees; a path, and almost as good, it seemed to lead to what she first thought was a darkly shadowed rock outcropping but, in the growing light, now saw was a hidden cave, the entrance almost perfectly screened by a dense barrier of undergrowth. She tried to imagine it in full daylight and saw that the entrance itself would probably fade away to invisibility. It also looked as though the path ran out shortly beyond it, making the cave nearly impossible to get to from above.

She stared. If she'd almost missed it then maybe Occleshaw and his men would miss it as well. If she didn't find some sort of refuge pretty quickly she was going to be too tired to care if she got caught. Impossibly, like a mirage to a man dying in the desert, she could swear that for a moment she'd seen a thin tracing of smoke marking the cave entrance. She looked again and it was gone. Limping on one shoe, shivering in her wet sweater, Jane trudged up the narrow path and began to climb.

It was almost full light by the time she reached the stone shelf that stood at the mouth of the cave. The sun was invisible behind low clouds that looked like tattered old gray shrouds; Scotland's welcome was no better in the day than it was by night. Jane stopped suddenly as she reached the line of brush that masked the cave entrance. For the first time she saw that the screening effect was far from natural; the brush and bracken had been cut and put in position artificially, the bottom branches and foliage already turning brown.

"I'll thank you to keep comin' on, lass, and dinna mistake my intention. I've got a wee gun and I'll blow those pretty tits of your'n into the river if I have to, which, after due consideration, I'd really rather not do."

The accent was definitely Scottish and Jane almost smiled, despite the menacing tone. "You're pretty long-winded for a man making threats," said Jane. The voice was given a figure as a bearded, long-haired wraith appeared from behind the screen of undergrowth. He had what appeared to be a German Luger in his hand. He was filthy and he was wearing a kilt. The kilt was filthy as well, stained with a month's worth of meals and what appeared to be blood. His upper body was clothed in what looked like a green, crushed-velvet lounge jacket. Insanely, he was wearing a deerstalker hat perched on his head, riding high on the tangle of black hair shot with wide streaks of gray, flaps down over his ears. "Long-winded *and* wearing a dress," said Jane. This time she did smile. Making fun of a lunatic Scotsman wearing a kilt would be dangerous at the best of times, but right now her sense of humor was the only weapon she had.

"Are ye insane, woman?" said the man.

"You read my mind," said Jane, smiling wearily.

"Most people would say ye were mad to insult a Cameron that way," said the man, hefting the Luger.

"Your name's Cameron?"

"Nay, woman, that's nae what I said. A Cameron. As in the Cameron Highlanders, late of Verdun, Mons and a host other even less palatable spots."

"You fought in the war then?"

"More like as to say I survived it, lass. Sixteen years old and had the shit scared out of me so far it went all the way back to fecking Carlisle and stayed there. I vowed then I'd never fight for fecking England again and so far I've kept that promise." He looked Jane up and down. "You're wet," he said, stating the obvious.

"No shit . . . uh . . . Sherlock," she said, eyeing the hat.

"It's McConnigle, but my friends all call me Angus. Ye sound like a Yank, but are ye friend or foe?"

"Right now I'd be anyone's friend for a warm fire."

"I can provide that." The mad Scot smiled. His lips were cracked and his front teeth were black stumps. "How about a cup of tea and a spot of breakfast to go along with it?" Angus asked, poking the gun into his belt. As he spoke a faint odor came wafting out from the hidden cave entrance. It smelled like bacon fat.

"God knows what I'd do for that." She grinned. "You don't happen to have a cigarette on you by any chance?"

Angus grinned back. "Aye, girl, I can provide that too." He stood aside and gestured to her to come forward. "All the comforts of home await. Come into our humble abode if you will."

"Our?"

"Aye, lass, our. I'm nae alone here, and thank the good lord for that."

She came limping forward, ducking her head under the foliage hanging down over the narrow entrance to the cave, aware of Angus close at her back. She stopped just inside the cave mouth.

The inside of the cave was much larger than she expected, widening substantially beyond the entrance. There was a front "room" containing a stone enclosure for the fire crackling warmly within it, a makeshift metal grill over the flames holding a battered and stained galvanized enamel coffeepot set off to one side and a cast-iron frying pan in the center cooking the thick strips of bacon she'd smelled outside. Another piece of metal, like a short fishing pole, had been attached to the side opposite the coffeepot, the skinned carcass of a rabbit skewered on its upper end, liquid fat running off its sinewy flanks and hissing as it struck the flames.

Beyond the fire, lost in the long, dancing shadows, was the rear section of the cave, a large, high-ceilinged space with rough sleeping platforms of cedar boughs built on rock outcroppings, the boughs covered in tattered pieces of what looked like the canvas roof of an army truck. The cave interior was warm, the chalky walls absorbing the heat from the fire and reflecting it back into the interior. At one time or another someone had taken a sharp stone and scratched rude landscapes on the walls like some latter-day caveman. The rock art was amateur but it did give the place a homey look. Better than hanging on for dear life on a bridge beam over a river and being shot at, that was for sure.

There were four other people in the cave, two sitting on basic wooden benches, two more, covered by old army blankets, leaning against the stone walls of the "kitchen" and mutely staring into the flames. They were an odd assortment, and certainly a match for Angus McConnigle in their eccentricities. One of the two seated against the wall was black as coal, with a broad face and the shoulders of a prizefighter. His head was shaved down to a military fuzz and there was a long, jagged scar like a thunderbolt that stretched down his cheek and into his lip, pulling it up slightly into a perpetual sneer. When he looked up, as Jane came into the cave, she was startled to see a pair of frighteningly intelligent eyes set into the savaged face. Underneath the old army blanket he had across his shoulders Jane could see that he wore the remains of a U.S. Army uniform. Above the left breast pocket Jane could see a dingy rainbow of service ribbons and through a hole in the blanket she could see master sergeant stripes.

Beside the black man was a boy half his size and white as the underbelly of a fish. He looked like a schoolboy, lank dark hair falling over a thin face still splotched by adolescent acne. As Jane entered the cave he showed no interest at all. Underneath his enclosing blankets she could see that he really was a schoolboy, wearing gray flannels and a stained and muddy jacket with a crest on the pocket. Beneath the jacket he was wearing the remains of a white shirt, several buttons gone and replaced with safety pins. There were badly scuffed and scraped black oxfords on his feet, the laces broken several times and held together by oddly shaped knots.

Seated on benches set close to the fire were the last two occupants of the cave. The one idly moving the bacon around in the frying pan with a stick obviously whittled for that exact purpose looked very much like the mute schoolboy's headmaster. He was very thin, wearing the remains of a tweed suit that had clearly seen better days, but somehow he'd managed to keep a thin brown mustache neatly trimmed and his steel-rimmed spectacles bright and shiny. On his head he wore a pristine Ivy League cap that would have looked more fitting if he'd been behind the wheel of a sports car with a pipe in his mouth. He had tiny pink ears and a narrow, pointed chin. As he worked the stick in the frying pan he was whistling quietly to himself. Jane was surprised at herself when she recognized the tune; it was a selection from Handel's *Messiah,* note for note and perfectly on key.

"I don't suppose you know Fingal's Cave, do you?" she said with a smile. "It's by Mendelssohn, I think." The thin man nodded and, without missing a beat, launched into her request, giving life to what the man on the train had told her about the long-dead composer.

The last of the cave's occupants was a huge man, head and shoulders taller than the whistler, with the flat face and slightly Oriental caste to his features that marked him as a Mongoloid. He leaned slightly in the direction of the man turning the bacon, his eyes closed with a beatific, almost rapturous look on his face as he listened to the music. Jane had known lots of these gentle creatures on Welfare Island, at the asylum where her sister had stayed for most of her life, and had never been able to see why they were put away; they were harmless, affectionate as puppies and in comparison to some people she'd known freely walking the streets of New York, they were far from insane.

"Go stand there beside Max if you're not too nervous," said Angus, nodding his head toward the Mongoloid. "Warm your naddled wee self before you turn into an icicle."

She went and stood beside the big man. He opened his eyes and smiled at her. "Hello there," she said, and smiled back. He nodded again and went back to the whistled Mendelssohn.

Angus came and stood across the fire from her, his hands extended to the flames, the Luger gleaming at his belt. "They've all got their stories, long and short, just like mine."

"I've got one too," said Jane, laughing. "God knows where I'd start though."

"Beginning is the usual place," said the black man from his corner. The words came in a soft Georgia lilt but with none of the backwoods cadence she might have expected. Instead the voice was clear and educated. There was more to the man than a scar and a sneer.

She saw too that telling her story and relating how she got to this place was the price of admission to their select hotel drilled into the cliff beside the river, so she told her tale, holding back details she thought had no relevance, but not withholding the desperate situation she now found herself in. They fed her from the frying pan, adding a slice of doughy, tough bread that Angus owned up to making in the little makeshift oven he'd created out of river clay. While she ate, surprised at her ravenous appetite, Angus listened and rolled her a cigarette from the fixings he stored in a small leather pouch that hung from his belt.

"So you think this Okkey fella you mentioned will come lookin' for ye, lass?" asked Angus when she was done.

"I'd bet on it." She took the cigarette from his hand. Without a word, the whistling man took a small piece of dried bracken from the small pile at his feet, lit it in the coals of the cooking fire and handed the makeshift match across to her. She lit her cigarette and took the first glorious puff, inhaling deeply, then letting the smoke out of her lungs in a slow trickle through her nostrils. "I'm sorry if I've put you and the others in any jeopardy." She looked around the front section of the cave; the four occupants didn't look terribly concerned.

"We've had others come looking for us from time to time," said a grinning Angus. "They've nae found us yet."

"I'm warning you, Occleshaw is different. He'll keep looking for me till hell freezes over. He's not the kind of man who gives up easily."

"Well," said Angus, stretching his arms and yawning, showing off the ghastly interior of his mouth again. "This Okkey may be different, but so are we. I've been 'at large,' as the magistrates say, for three years now, and they've nae come even close to fitting me up yet. I figure Hitler can't last forever, and when he's done we'll all go home." He nodded at the other people in the cave. "At least these lads can."

"Not you?"

"I'm nae sure what I'd call home now. I once had a boat and a little cottage at Brackness Hole—that's at the mouth of Loch Ryan mind, which has Stranraer at one end, the old ferry port to Ireland—but all that's gone with the war; submarines and such. The wife died while I was off playing the fool in the previous altercation and, sadly, we had no bairns. This is as much home as anywhere else to me."

"What about the others?" she said, tilting her head toward the giant beside her, now happily listening to *Madame Butterfly*. "Him for instance."

"Solomon you mean?"

"That's his name, Solomon?"

"None of us ken what his real name is, lass, but that's what we call him. It's a name he keeps on saying. We know he's a Jew, so it makes some wee bit of sense."

"How do you know he's a Jew?"

Angus laughed. "The tilt of his kilt, lass."

"What?"

"His *membrum virile*, girlie. His dickerie doo." Angus guffawed. "Yon enormous sausage is missing its last inch. He's circumcised."

"Oh," said Jane.

"Aye," said Angus.

"That's all you know about him?"

"I can make a guess. We've picked up bits and pieces over time."

"We think he's a recent immigrant," the black man said from the far side of the cave. "Polish, maybe even Russian. He speaks a little of both languages. Yiddish as well."

"You can tell what languages he speaks?" Jane

tried to keep the surprise out of her voice but she found it a little hard to believe.

"I was a cook on a tramp steamer for almost fifteen years before I joined the Army. I got around some."

Angus spoke. "It's likely he came with his parents; they've made the regulations a wee bit stronger in the last years before the war. A lot of people they sent to internment camps on the Isle of Man and such like. A lad like Solomon, here, they'd simply refuse. No mental defectives wanted, you might say. It was that or a camp. Solomon probably just ran off and somehow wound up here."

"He sure loves his music," said Jane.

"Aye, that he does," said Angus. "You never know, maybe his father was a musician."

"He's also an idiot savant," said the black man.

"A what?" asked Jane.

"Show him, Potter," said the black man. The scholarly-looking man beside the Mongoloid dished another few strips of bacon into the frying pan with his makeshift spatula, then rested the wooden instrument carefully on the edge of the fireplace. He turned to Solomon and spoke quietly, putting one smooth, small hand on the man's enormous shoulder.

"Solomon . . ."

The giant opened his eyes and stared down at his friend. "Yes, Peter Potter?" he asked. The voice was soft, almost girlish.

"Can you sing for us, Solomon?"

"Of course, Peter Potter." Solomon smiled happily. "What would you like to hear?"

Potter cleared his throat, wet his lips and whistled a few bars of Beethoven's Fifth, then stopped. The boy closed his eyes and a few seconds later the enormous head began to move from side to side and one hand, fingers huge and powerful, began to move with the grace and elegance of a symphony conductor. Then he began to sing the chorus from the famous music, the voice ringing powerfully, in perfect pitch, turning the interior of the cave into a concert hall, every sound ringing true and glorious. Jane sat back on her heels, entranced. Potter reached up and put his hand on the boy's shoulder again, and the music stopped abruptly.

"My God," Jane whispered.

"Doesn't matter what music you give him," said the black man. "It's like he's got God's jukebox in his head. Everything from Mahler to Eddie Cantor in *Ali Baba Goes to Town*." He paused, shaking his head. "I said the name Paul Robeson once and he gave me a perfect 'Old Man River' from *Showboat*."

Jane dragged on her cigarette, looking at the people in the cave and wondered what a photo feature in *Life* would be like. "Rural Britain Soldiers On" or something; except Angus wouldn't like being deemed British—he was on the Scotland side of the river after all.

"What about you, Sergeant?" she said to the black man. "What's your story?"

"What every Negro in America's story is, ma'am," he answered. "I did what my old daddy told me and followed God's word—right into hell and damnation."

"You sound a little bitter."

"No, ma'am, a lot bitter. You see before you the final remains of a ruined man." He laughed—bitterly.

"You were a soldier, obviously. What happened?"

"I was a soldier, and before that I was a merchant

seaman, seeing the world and sowing my youthful wild oats. Before that I was a preacher's son from Athens, Georgia, with an itch to see the world. Read too many books, dreamed too many dreams."

"You mind me asking how you got that scar?" Jane asked.

"No ma'am. I got that scar by sliding on my mother's wet kitchen floor after she'd cleaned it, cutting myself open with the glass of water I was drinking." He smiled, the left side of his mouth barely moving. "Not all scars come from violent acts, ma'am. Some of them are downright silly. Makes me look like I'm some fierce, bloodthirsty nigger, which has been useful from time to time."

"You still haven't said anything about how you wound up here."

"How I actually got to this cave is a long story, ma'am, and probably not worth telling. Why I started on my journey here is another barrel of catfish, as we used to say in Athens."

"Why, then?"

"I joined the Army because I wanted to fight Germans. I was already in the Army before I discovered that's not what they wanted us for. What they really wanted the nigger to do was haul and lift and fetch just like usual. I didn't think it was right that we'd have to do the same old peckerwood nigger shit we'd always done on top of maybe getting killed."

"You deserted."

"No, ma'am, wrong again. I talked about it. Loudly. Some people didn't like it. The Klan for instance."

"The Klan, as in Ku Klux Klan? You've got to be kidding. There's no Klan in the U.S. Army."

"Afraid you're wrong about that too, ma'am. There most certainly is. Lots of members too, I'm afraid. Anyway, they have this game where they come into your unit, kidnap you and take you twenty or so miles from your home base. In my case it was in Northern Ireland, just after we shipped out. They let you go and tell you the rules. If you can make it back to your unit alive you get to stay that way; if they catch you, they kill you. Simple. What they don't tell you is that they strip you, beat you sense-less, and cut you up a little before you start."

"You got away?"

"No, ma'am, I did not, not for too long anyway, but I took three of the sons of bitches with me on the run. I got caught by the military police and thrown in the glasshouse for murder. They were transporting me over here for trial when I managed to get away."

"That's crazy. Didn't you tell them what hap-pened?"

"Why bother?" said the sergeant. "They wouldn't have believed me."

"Jesus," said Jane.

"Now maybe *he* would have believed me." The sergeant smiled again and wrapped the blanket a lit-tle tighter around his shoulders, old memories chill-ing him.

"We're all the same here; the musician at the fire is Peter Potter, although I doubt that's his real name. A schoolteacher. Some accused him of being a homo-sexual, and that was the end for him. Lost his job and all. Even the Army wouldn't take him. The boy there just turned up at the cave a month ago. He's either a deaf mutie or he's scared out of his wits. Likely both. We're all the same, one way or the other;

we just have a different face on it. Some people even war doesn't want. We're flotsam and jetsam you might say, tossed on the tide of events." Angus clapped his hands suddenly, rising out of his crouch. "Come along now, you've sat about in those wet things for too long. We'll get some dry clothes on you and then we'll have a wee palaver about what to do about you and yon Okkey."

Nineteen

Dundee made his way carefully downward. The stairs were dark and narrow and had probably once been used by the servants who had undoubtedly occupied the attic room he'd just left. He made his way down for a long time in almost complete darkness, when suddenly the flight of steps ended in a heavy, paneled door. Dundee turned the knob and found himself standing in an immense hallway tiled in a somber gray-green marble. The walls were wainscoted in some heavy wood that was probably oak, and above that they were covered in a pale green moiré silk that matched the floors.

To the right was an archway leading to a narrow hall, and to the left the main hall widened to include a grand staircase that swept in an elegant curve up to a banistered mezzanine and doorways leading off in all directions. What had to be the front entrance to the house was made up of a pair of massive carved doors set into a vestibule guarded by a marble urn on one side and another white-jacketed guard on the other.

This one was seated, chair tilted back against the wall, snoring. Dundee looked up. The centerpiece of the entrance hall was a gigantic and obviously very old cast-iron chandelier, ratcheted up on a heavy-linked chain under the colossal, churchlike hammer beams of the ceiling at least thirty feet above his head.

At the base of the staircase stood a life-size statue in Carrera marble, the stone white as death and depicting a classically robed maiden on a plinth of withered roses. The maiden was young, barely a woman by her figure, left hand extended above her head like a dancer, long hair flowing as if being blown by the wind, right hand held up in a strange gesture—one finger extended like the holy mother giving her benediction before the advent of her child, eyes blind as justice, unaware of who might be coming in the door. In sinister contrast to the young girl's innocence, at the foot of the stairs a few feet away there was a tapestry depicting what had to be the Rape of the Sabines. Below the tapestry there was a stone bench, again in white Carrera, its bases depicting seated rams, horns sharp and twisted, mouths and teeth in terrible twin grimaces; the rams in turn supporting leering Pan figures enclosing a hellish back piece depicting a savage, unrepentant bacchanalia of coupling women and men, devils and animals.

The whole thing was more like some mad dream of a baronial hunting lodge than a hospital. The only things missing were the severed heads of a cross section of African wildlife staring down at him from the walls with glazed, dead eyes. Except for the sleeping guard there was no one around but he was aware of a steady drone of murmuring voices from behind one of the closed doors nearest the main entrance.

He could also smell the overwhelming aroma of

freshly brewed coffee and it suddenly occurred to him that he hadn't had anything to eat since the station restaurant at King's Cross. He thought of Jane suddenly and felt a tug of anxiety; if she was lucky the Robbie Burns would be coming into Glasgow just about now and she'd be waking up in time for the Scots version of bacon and eggs. Somehow he doubted it. She had lied to him about who or at least what she really was, but he'd never forgive himself if he'd drawn her into a trap prepared by Charlie Danby.

He crossed the floor, his sturdy boots booming on the marble, one eye on the guard at the front entrance. Either he was dead to the world or he simply didn't care. Dundee reached the dining room door, turned the knob and entered.

What now passed for the dining room in the Akergill Sanitorium had once been two rooms, perhaps an adjoining library and sitting room. The first room had a long and heavy side table loaded down with covered sterling silver salvers. What appeared to be a huge pheasant, head still attached and plumage arranged neatly around its dripping, roasted flesh, lay in the center of a tray devoted to various types of bacon and other fried meats. There was another table off to one side for coffee and tea, and a third table for crockery and cutlery.

From the serving table he was apparently supposed to take his food into the next room, which held a long refectory-style table set in front of a row of tall windows, all of them still covered with heavy damask curtains in the same green color as the silk walls in the hall outside. The walls in both rooms were originally paneled wood, now painted a creamy white. The ceilings were done in French plaster ovals and the light was given by dangling chandeliers in gleaming, delicate crystal.

There were half a dozen men and one woman seated at the table. The men were dressed informally, as though for a weekend in the country. The woman was in her fifties, wore a tweed suit and had her hair drawn up in a bun. She wore glasses and had the pinched look of a schoolteacher who had been doing the job for longer than she intended.

Pausing just inside the door, Dundee listened to their animated conversation. Somehow it sounded brittle and practiced, as though he was watching a bad play in a West End theater in London. The man at the head of the table looked up from his plate and spotted Dundee watching them. He was a little portly, in his early sixties, gray-haired and pleasant-looking, his eyes pale blue and curious. He was wearing a three-piece worsted suit with a heavy gold watch chain arcing from one side to the other of his substantial pot belly.

"Mr. Portal!" he boomed. "How good of you to join us." He waved Dundee into the room. "Dr. McNab said you might partake of breakfast. My name is Sir John Gadsby. I'm the director of this fine institution."

"Where is the good doctor?" asked Dundee. He drew himself a cup of coffee from a tall, spigoted urn and stepped into the dining room, trying to keep the tension out of his voice.

"Attending to another patient, I believe," said Gadsby.

Dundee brought his coffee into the room and sat at the far end of the table, as far as possible from everyone else. He took a tentative sip from the delicate cup. It was excellent. He put the cup down carefully in its saucer.

"Tell me, Sir John, what exactly is the point of all this? Surely it's not entirely for my benefit. Even Charlie wouldn't go that far. You know perfectly well who I am, and it's not David Portal, Canadian merchant marine swabbie."

Gadsby smiled. "Who are any of us really, Mr. Portal, when you get right down to it?" He took a tiny, almost feminine sip from his own cup, his small tongue flicking lightly out of his mouth as though to test the liquid before he committed himself. His eyes never left Dundee's. "My specialty is psychiatry, you see. I'm afraid you're asking a rather fundamental question which haunts us all."

"Very nicely put, Sir John, but it doesn't answer the real question." Dundee smiled. "And don't ask me what the real question is." Everyone else at the table was watching the two men silently. No one had said anything since Dundee walked into the room, their own little stage play suspended for the moment.

The portly man sighed. "This could become irksome with time."

"It already is."

"Then why don't we stop it?" said Gadsby. "You know who you are although I wouldn't be surprised if you weren't quite sure how you got here." A small smile flashed across the man's face and the blue eyes were suddenly several shades darker. "It is a fundamental of my trade, Mr. Portal, that we are the arbiters of who is who and what is what. That is our function actually—to tell people who is sane and who is not. You are not what *you* say you are, but what *we* say you are." The smile became smaller. "It's very democratic actually. It's a question of majority rule when you get right down to it."

"You're telling me I'm crazy?"

"Perhaps, although it's not a word I like to use. Let's just say I have the ability to do that." The smile was now completely gone. "And be taken at my word."

Dundee climbed to his feet, the taste of the coffee suddenly bitter as ashes in his mouth. "This is a pretty fancy mental institution. I don't think I like it here."

"Then feel free to go, Mr. Portal. This is not a mental institution, no matter what you think. It is a place of healing. The sooner you come to realize that, the better."

"So I can just leave?"

"By all means, if that is what you want. We certainly don't want to hold anyone here by force." The smile was back. "After all, this is not Mr. Stalin's Russia."

"Or Nazi Germany."

"No," said Gadsby, "not that either."

Without another word Dundee turned on his heel and left the room. He went back through the serving room, pausing just long enough to cram half a dozen strips of bacon between two thick slices of bread, and then he was back in the front hall. If he was going to get any distance he'd need something to sustain him.

Cramming the roughly made sandwich into the pocket of his newly acquired tweed jacket, he marched across the broad space to the front door. Ignoring the guard completely he threw open the door and stepped outside. Instantly he understood

Gadsby's ease at giving him leave to go anytime he wanted.

Dundee had rarely seen such a desolate spot in his life. From the light it couldn't be much more than six thirty or seven in the morning, but a torn sky of low, scudding clouds, gray as shrouds, made telling the sun's position impossible. He could be anywhere—north, east, south or west.

All he could tell for sure was that the ancient old building was located at the end of a curving, rocky headland topped by a scattering of twisted, wind-blown trees. A long gravel lane ran out from the main road, itself no more than a bare track winding through the empty, rolling landscape of some un-named moor that stretched in every direction with-out any sign of human habitation.

Beyond Akergill Hall itself was the sea, pounding at the base of low, rotted cliffs, lines of broken waves rolling in monotonously, their tops bearded with spinning foam wrenched from the top of each angry breaker by the gusting wind. Trying to orient him-self, Dundee found that it was impossible; he could be staring out at the English Channel as well as he could be looking toward the North Sea or the Scottish Hebrides. Suddenly Dundee was ten years old again, lost in the woods on a camping trip in the Santa Ynez Mountains with his father, realizing that he hadn't told anyone he was going off by himself, real-izing that right now nobody in the world had any idea where he was and that he'd have to get out of his predicament all by himself.

He turned and looked back the way he'd come. The front of the house was enormous, the main floor stone and half-timbered stucco, the stucco's original

chalky whitewash long since stained and weathered
to a sickly yellow, spiderwebs of mold and mildew
creeping over the surface like broken veins on the
cheeks of an old woman.

It went out in two huge wings from the central
hall, each at least four stories tall, ending in towers
and turrets like broken brick teeth against the hurtling sky above, rushing in from the sea. More than
anything it looked like an old resort hotel, long since
gone to seed, but why anyone would have wanted
to build a hotel in this godforsaken place was beyond him.

He turned away from the house finally, following
a barely visible path that ran out to the edge of the
cliff and a set of wide stone stairs that looked as
though they'd been blasted out of the spray-riven
stone, smoothed by years of storm and the simple
passage of time on this lonely coastline.

He finally found a clue to his location. At the foot
of the stairs there was an old concrete fortification, a
two-storied monstrosity built half into the rock, circular, flat-roofed with a wide slit in the front, a single
rectangular eye looking out over the gray-brown ex-
panse of heaving water. Built before the last war,
there would have once been a three- or four-inch
naval gun poking out of that slit, pointing toward
the enemy and her great fleet of battleships and
dreadnought-prowed cruisers. Times had changed
and no ship would cruise so close to an enemies'
coastline; today it would be a U-boat, but the enemy
was still Germany, as it had been twenty-five years
ago; not so long really as the distances between
wars go.

Dundee stared out over the water, able to see in

his mind's eye the sleek black submarines coming out into open water from Bremerhaven and the dangerous, shifting sands of the Frisian Islands; this was the North Sea, which put him somewhere on England's thinly populated northeast coast. Something flashing caught his eye from the interior of the old gun tower; a flash of light reflecting off the lens of a pair of binoculars, or maybe the scrape and glow of a match.

He took the bacon sandwich out of his pocket, eating it hungrily and keeping his eyes on the gun tower. The light didn't come again. He wiped his fingers on the jacket and headed down the stairway to the stony beach below.

He counted the steps as he went, wondering if there'd be thirty-nine like the book by John Buchan of the same name. There'd been an English boy at Bain with the deadly first name of Evelyn who'd had a collection of the Richard Hannay novels. Dundee had read them all, including *The Thirty-nine Steps*, wondering as he did how the bland and sickly Buchan could write such thrilling stories.

He reached the bottom of the stairs at a count of twenty-eight and stepped down onto the rocks, slipping and sliding as he moved across the shiny, wet stones that made up what passed for a beach here. Once again he wondered what could have possessed someone to build Akergill Hall in such a spot; it certainly hadn't been with seaside holidays in mind. Wading in that boiling water would be courting disaster, and no spade had ever cut into these stones in hopes of making a sand castle. There were no rock pools to investigate, no sand dunes to climb and no handy spot to sun yourself either, just the odd piece of seaweed-festooned driftwood and the rusting spikes of more aging fortifications that clearly dated back to the gun tower's time.

The entrance to the gun tower was toward the rear of the building, a simple metal door, studded with rivets and fitted with a welded pull ring instead of a latch. Dundee tugged on it and the door opened easily on recently oiled hinges. Somebody was using the gun tower on a reasonably regular basis. There was a flight of metal steps leading up to the second level of the tower. Dundee began to climb, his booted feet ringing on each step.

The top level was empty, the roof above Dundee's head rusted iron. There was a large semicircular mechanism with a central ratchet hub in the center, rusty as the roof, that had once let the old naval gun traverse from left to right through the wide observation slit. The gun itself was long gone. A man in a long trench coat belted tightly at the waist was standing at the slit, a pair of binoculars in his hand and a cigarette dangling from his mouth. Hearing Dundee, the man lowered the glasses and turned. He smiled a greeting.

"Hello, Ten Spot," the man said. Dundee nodded. He'd known who it was going to be from the moment he entered the tower.

"Hello, Charlie."

Twenty

Charles Danby dropped the binoculars, letting them dangle from the leather strap around his neck. He took a step or two toward Dundee, hand extended, and then stopped, the hand slowly falling to his side. He stepped back. He still had the good looks of a much younger man but there were telltale lines on his face now marking years of hard living.

"You don't look too happy to see me, Ten Spot." Somehow, years ago at Bain Academy, Danby had found out Dundee's middle name was Decimus and had never let him forget it, nicknaming him "Ten Spot" and calling him that ever since. Dundee loathed the name.

"I can think of people I'd rather spend the morning with."

"What? Can't spend a few pleasant minutes with an old schoolmate?"

"Can it, Charlie. You're no schoolmate, you're a thief."

Danby laughed. "And *you're* the thief catcher? Not doing such a good job, are we?" Danby turned around and went back to his observation post at the gun slit. He looked out to sea, dragging on his cigarette. "You really don't get it, do you, Lucas?"

"Get what?"

Danby reached into the pocket of his trench coat and took out a package of Old Golds and a Zippo engraved with his initials. He laid them on the pitted concrete of the slit and gestured to Dundee. "Take one if you want."

Dundee stepped forward, shook out a cigarette from the pack and lit it, the familiar smell of the lighter filling his nostrils. Danby was staring out at the troubled waters crashing in on the stone beach, each wave presenting a fat green underbelly before it broke over the shore with a pounding crash. "Get what?" Dundee repeated

"This," Danby answered, waving a hand vaguely. "You, me, the war, all of it."

"I think that's a little bit beyond me," said Dundee with a shrug, wondering what Danby was getting at. "I'd prefer to leave that kind of thing to the Bible thumpers."

It was Danby's turn to shrug. "Call it what you want—God, fate, destiny. Every civilization has had a word for it."

"Get to the point, Charlie." Dundee sighed. It was something Charles Danby had always had a hard time doing.

Danby flicked the butt end of his cigarette out the observation slit. He turned away from Dundee and disappeared into the dark shadows at the back of the gun platform, reappearing a moment later with a ribbed steel flier's Thermos and two tin mugs. He poured coffee from the Thermos for both of them, the rich aroma filling the cold air. Silently, Dundee took the offered mug. He tasted the coffee; it was the same as the stuff he'd had in the dining room with the Honorable Sir John Gadsby. Black, rich and expensive, especially with rationing in place; not that it would prove a major obstacle to Charlie.

"Let me tell you a story, Lucas."

"Go ahead," said Dundee, rolling his eyes. "It doesn't look as though I'll be going anywhere soon."

Danby looked at him speculatively. "You know my father, right?"

"I've met him," answered Dundee warily. He'd never known Charlie to be the loquacious type and he found the sudden talkativeness intriguing. At a guess he'd almost say that Charlie sounded lonely.

"A bastard," said Charlie flatly. It wasn't anything but a statement of fact. "But a smart bastard." He paused. "Did you know we come from German stock?"

"I never really thought about it."

"Me neither," said Danby. "Then, a few years back, my father tells me we're going to Germany, on a fact-finding mission, like Lindy or the fucking duke of Windsor."

"Interesting?" asked Dundee.

"What's interesting is finding out that my sainted grandfather's real name was Kurt Von Danboch and he was some rich fuddy-duddy in Hamburg who came out to California because he got some girl knocked up and didn't want to marry her." Danby laughed. "I guess it runs in the family." Charlie Danby's arrival at Bain Academy had coincided with one of his female cousin's extended visit to friends in the east.

"The Von Danboch family was in the fruit importing business so it didn't take too much imagination. He got rich pretty quick." Danby lit another cigarette. "Anyway, my old man and I did the tour; we even had a visit with Hitler at that place of his in the alps."

"Berchtesgaden," supplied Dundee.

"That's it," said Danby. "But he spent most of his time with business types, the heads of Agfa-Gevaert, Krupp, Farben, that kind."

"I still don't see where this is heading," said Dundee

"I'm getting there," said Danby. He grinned. "This is my story, so let me tell it."

"I just can't figure out how it gets around to you having one of your bully boys stuff an ether-soaked rag down my throat."

Danby ignored the comment and went on with his narrative. "Anyway, after a while I started to see the light, which was maybe why the old man had taken me along. He told me about the family history before we changed the name. I talked to him about it one night after we went to a whorehouse in Berlin together."

"Nice to see a father and son who can still do things together," said Dundee a little sourly.

Danby caught the acid in his tone. "Your father's been to a fair number of cathouses himself, Ten Spot, so don't play holier than thou with me."

"My father's no puritan, Charlie, but he never *took* me to a whorehouse."

"Maybe he should have."

"Forget it," said Dundee. "Go on."

"Like I was saying. I asked him and he told me what the trip was really all about."

"Which was?"

"Business. Money. Power." The handsome man looked at Dundee earnestly. "Numbers, Ten Spot. What the war would be fought about when it came."

"I thought the invasion of Poland had something to do with it."

"Poland was part of Prussia during the last war—they fought against us. In the next war they could be the enemy again. It's not about treaties and loyalties, it's about one business owing a favor to another, one hand washing the other. It's about vested interests."

"I also heard Pearl Harbor might have had something to do with it as well," said Dundee.

"Pearl Harbor was an excuse to get us into the war. Roosevelt pressured the Japanese until they had no choice. You know as well as I do that the Japs are no threat to us. Can you imagine a hundred thousand little Nips landing on Huntington Beach when the surf was up?" he snorted. "How far inland do you think they'd get? Hollywood? Palm Desert maybe?"

"I don't think that's the point, Charlie. And that's not the war we're fighting here."

"The point is, Ten Spot, enemies change and borders get moved but the money keeps on getting made. Krupp makes bombs and Ford makes tanks. The same oil makes both of them go; it's just that they buy from the Venezuelans and we get ours from Texas. But the company's the same. And big business knows it."

"Hitler isn't a factor, or Hirohito or Mussolini?"

"Who do you think runs Germany?" said Danby flatly.

"Why don't you tell me?" said Dundee, sure that Danby would do just that.

"It's not Adolf fucking Hitler, believe me. Hitler's like any little tin pot dictator. All that flag waving and all those rallies cost money and he's not getting it from the German *Volk*, that's for sure. He's getting it from the Swiss banks, who are getting it from big business, businesses like Standard Oil and International Telephone for instance."

"There are laws about that kind of thing," said Dundee, suddenly weary of Charlie's rant. "It's called the Trading with the Enemy Act."

Danby smiled shrewdly. "But don't you think that's defined by who your enemies are?" He laughed. "Up until we got into the war Standard Oil tankers were openly refueling German U-boats at sea."

"How does that get us to this?" said Dundee, making a sweeping gesture around the gun platform. "How does it get to you being a crook and maybe a traitor and me being the man who's supposed to hunt you down? Explain that to me, Charlie."

"That's easy enough," said Danby, his tone almost gentle. "My father knew there was a war coming in 1934—so did anyone else with a brain in his head. The world was going to hell in a handcart, especially Europe. Big Business knew that someone like Hitler was necessary to shock us all out of our shoes. Don't you understand, Dundee—we *needed* this war; it was a godsend. It maybe put Hitler in the headlines, but it took us out of the Black Monday fiasco and the Depression."

"That still doesn't explain any of this," said Dundee wearily. He was getting tired of Charlie's glib explanations of a world gone mad and a war that wasn't doing anybody any good.

"When the war is over, Hitler will be over with it. The big boys know that; they've always known that. They put him into power; they'll take him out."

"They've already tried a few times. They may not find it as easy as they think."

"Don't worry, when the time comes they'll make it happen. Someone like Hitler is useless in a peacetime world, so they'll get rid of him."

"And then I suppose it's back to business as usual," said Dundee.

"Exactly!" Danby nodded.

"That still doesn't explain why you got yourself into Shepton Mallet prison and helped yourself to the Imperial Crown."

"Pretty good, huh, Ten Spot?"

"Pretty crazy, Charlie," responded Dundee.

"Not really. The crown is just a symbol, but it's an important one. Without it you can't have a king."

"A king isn't the crown, Charlie. He's the sum total of the people he represents. It's like the president. It's an idea, not a person."

"Tell that to the little man they're going to crown after we invade this crappy little island. He's got some idea that being the king of England is like being King Arthur and the Round Table or something; he thinks he's a legend and he wants his Excalibur. Frankly, nobody cares what the stupid shitbird thinks, Ten Spot, but he's a necessary evil as they say and we've got to keep him happy."

Danby was obviously talking about the duke of Windsor but the whole thing was fantastic; except for the fact that Danby was right, at least on the surface. If Germany won the war, England would need a new king, and a basically stupid and naive person like the ex-king Edward would be a handy pawn, especially with him married to an American. Fantastic maybe, but not impossible, and Hitler's own attraction to symbolic mythology was well-known; the swastika and the rallys at Nuremberg were evidence enough of that. Presented in the right way, he'd buy the idea. Even if it didn't work in any real sense, the theft of the Crown would be a terrible blow to morale for England's present war effort.

"How does all that tie in to this place?"

"Akergill is a staging base; it has been since before the war. It really is a sanitorium, just like Gadsby is really a doctor, but it's also a way of getting a steady stream of agents into England without getting anyone's nose out of joint."

"Gadsby's secretly a Nazi?"

"He doesn't make much of a secret about it," laughed Danby. "He's convinced that he's going to be made prime minister after the war. Our friend Sir John, fifth earl of Hawksmoor, isn't the only Englishman in the House of Lords who agrees with the *Führer*." He laughed bleakly. "It's all a façade, Dundee. Gadsby bought his earldom just the way my old man bought me a commission as a colonel. Money, Dundee. That's all it takes, just the folding green."

All of a sudden Dundee saw the truth. Charlie was the same bullying sixteen-year-old he'd known all those years ago; nothing had changed at all. On the surface he was a charming rogue with a twinkle in his eye, but you didn't have to dig very deep to

find the bullying confidence man behind that glinting
look. Any end justified any means and manipulating
anyone was fair game as long as Charlie Danby got
what he wanted.

"You really are a son of a bitch, aren't you,
Charlie?"

"It's the sons of bitches who run the world, I'm
afraid, Ten Spot," Danby answered softly.

It was Dundee's turn to stare out the observation
slit. The gray sky had lowered and a light rain was
falling now, dropping visibility to less than a hundred yards. The sea was a cipher; a German E-boat
or a small fishing trawler could get in under the
coastal radar with none the wiser. Rumor had it that
the Nazis hadn't successfully landed one agent on
British soil but that could just be propaganda; maybe
Charlie was right after all—the forces of big business
conspiring even before the war, ultimately the puppet masters of Adolf Hitler and everyone else, a hidden power structure beneath a veneer of honor,
loyalty and patriotism.

"Where's the nearest town?" asked Dundee.

"Wondering if it would work? Believe me, Ten
Spot, it's been working on this coast for the past four
hundred years. They used to smuggle cheese from
Denmark and Flemish lace from Belgium, crates of
perfume from Cologne and hams from Hamburg.
The closest town is Lacburn, ten miles across Kracken
Moor, and no road of any consequence between.
Most of them think we're a commando training
school and steer well clear. One or two of the overly
curious have wound up disappearing; bogs on the
moor are dangerous."

"How long have you been part of all this?"

"Since that night in the Adlon with the old man, after our trip to the Kit Kat. I was an instant convert."

"You always do what your father tells you, Charlie?"

Color flared on Danby's cheeks. "It had nothing to do with my old man!" Danby jammed his hands into the pockets of his trench coat and hunched his shoulders as though feeling a sudden chill. He regained his temper and a smile twitched on his face. "I was a convert because it made good sense."

"Was being in the Army always part of it?"

"As soon as it became clear we were going to *be* in the war." Danby nodded. "Looked better if you enlisted, and made it easier to pick and choose. Anybody with sense knew there were going to be deserters, English and American both. I just made use of them, that's all."

"Your own private army?"

"Something like that." He smiled. "Malcontents into 'madcontents' as I like to say. As long as they're useful, I want 'em."

"And what happens when they aren't useful any more?"

"That's easy," said Danby. "I just send them home."

Dundee shivered. Sending deserters home where they could potentially rat on their boss to the wrong people? Not likely. In a pine box, maybe. It wasn't just the overly curious who got sent on a one-way trip across the moor.

"Where do I fit into all of this, Charlie? You didn't

keep me alive just to meet with me and gloat about being some kind of criminal mastermind. You never did anything without a reason."

"You got that right, Ten Spot, and unlike Ming the Merciless I really don't have any intention of telling you what that reason is." He smiled again. "Let's just say I'm taking you for a ride."

Twenty-one

Jane stepped out of the back part of the cave and paraded herself for the other fugitives, all of whom had studiously kept their eyes averted, with the exception of Solomon who had taken a peek or two as she changed. The clothes she'd had to choose from hadn't been much but she'd managed to put together something warm and generally clean.

She now wore a garish blue-and-white-checked shirt, a pair of darkly stained dungarees rolled up at the cuffs covering old, black, lace-up boots done up with twine, trousers held up by leather suspenders, all topped off by a filthy, old shapeless hat, which she'd tucked her blond hair into, and a patch-pocket jacket in loden green. The shirt was too large and so were the pants, but everything else fit well enough. The only thing she'd kept of her own was her wallet.

"What do you think, guys?" she asked. She'd tried scrubbing the worst of the muck off her face with the sleeve of the jacket, but looking at herself in the little fragment of mirror Angus had given her she realized all she'd done was spread the dirt in great angry streaks across her face.

Angus howled with laughter when he saw her, and

even the silent boy in the school uniform had the trace of a smile on his pale, drawn face.

"Now, ain't you the Billy!" Angus laughed. "You look like a wild man who's spent too much time hairding goats in the hills." He nodded happily to himself as he checked on the state of her wet clothing, now hanging around the fire. "That's it, lass— or should I call you laddie now? A goat hairder you are!"

Jane dropped the old-fashioned carpet bag she'd found on the floor of the cave and glanced at her fellow fugitives. The longer she stayed here the more she put these people at risk. It was an hour past dawn now and Occleshaw was sure to be on his way back to the bridge, sweeping across the moor with his men, and probably dogs as well now. It was time to be going on her own way, although God only knew how she was going to get there.

Angus squeezed by her and went into the rear of the cave himself, reappearing a few minutes later, transformed. The kilt was gone, replaced by a dirty but serviceable pair of canvas pants that might have once belonged to a sailor. His long, unruly hair was tucked up into a gigantic plaid tam that flopped down over either side of his head. A heavy workman's waistcoat now covered his shirt, the pockets bulging with an assortment of treasures. As he strode into the front of the cave he was trimming his beard with a small pair of rusty pruning shears.

"I thought I should freshen myself, seeing that we're now in the company of a woman."

It was Jane's turn to laugh. She found herself surprised and even a little enchanted that she'd fallen in with this strange lot so easily. "You look very elegant, Angus."

"As a McConnigle should look," he said proudly. He cleared his throat, standing erect so that the bobble top of his ridiculous tam brushed the ceiling of the cave. He tucked his thumbs into the wide belt he'd transferred to the canvas trousers and put a stern expression on his face. "A pairfect picture of sartorial grace and favor," he intoned.

"Angus, have you ever heard of a place called Salem?" she said, mentioning the name she'd seen on the inside of the matchbook cover in Shepton Mallet. She'd tried to locate it on an Ordnance Survey map of Scotland—assuming that it wasn't a ruse as Dundee thought—but she hadn't been able to find it. With the exception of the name of the garage in Glasgow on the cover of the matches it was the only lead they had.

"Aye, lass, it's that place in America where they burned the witches."

"I don't mean the States; I mean here, in Scotland."

"There's no Salem in Scotland, girl, at least I don't think there is." He shrugged. "God only knows, lass, I could be wrong; education was never my strong suit."

"I don't mean to interrupt," said Potter, the whistling schoolteacher, in his soft, gentle voice. "But could you mean Salen? With an 'n' instead of an 'm'?"

She dug out her wallet and took out the still-damp matchbook cover, peering at it in the flickering light thrown up by the cooking fire. "It's possible," she said, slipping the cover back in place and putting the wallet back in her pocket.

"Well, that could be it then," he said, flushing for no apparent reason except his proximity to the fire. "Angus is quite right, you see, there is no Salem in Scotland. I'm fairly sure at any rate." The flush deepened. "I taught geography as well as music, you see. There is no Salem but there is a Salen. It's on the Isle of Mull, actually."

"You mean Kintyre, or Mull?" said Angus. He laughed. "There's plenty of Mulls but no Salems."

"Mull," said Potter. "The Mull of Kintyre is altogether different."

"Well, that's settled then," said Angus. "Is that where we're going?"

"We?" said Jane.

"Aye, lass. You were no thinking of going on alone, were you?"

"That's what I thought."

"Nae, it won't do, lass, they'd be on you in a minute," he said emphatically. "You might get by on how you look, but open your mouth to natter and you're doomed." He nodded toward the schoolboy. "You can be a mutie like him, and a bit slow like our friend Solomon there; that ought to do us for the while."

"What about the others?" asked Jane.

"Take them to our winter quarters, Sergeant," said Angus, turning toward the black man. "I'll meet you there when I've done with the girlie." He turned toward the mouth of the cave and sniffed the air thoughtfully. "You've got an hour or so to be in the wind, Sergeant, if my senses are correct." He turned back to Jane. "Come along now, Geordie boy, we'd best be going."

He stripped her half-dried clothing off the sticks it

had been suspended from around the fire, crammed it into the carpet bag and pushed her toward the mouth of the cave. She turned once and raised her hand to the others but they were too busy packing up to notice, with the exception of Solomon, who lifted his hand in a little wave and smiled. She turned away and followed Angus out into the light and down to the river.

"Are you sure they'll be all right?" she asked, easing her way slowly down the treacherous slope behind Angus.

"Aye," said the Scotsman without turning around. He was moving quickly and she had to hurry to keep up, the rocky scree sliding out from under her feet. "There's an old Roman silver mine on the edge of Seven Sisters Moor about ten miles from here. The mine goes into an old barrow and there's plenty of room. Lots of rabbits and other game on the moor."

They reached the bottom of the near cliff and turned along the riverbank. A few moments later they reached the spot where Jane had come ashore.

"Is that where you washed up, lass?" said Angus, pausing briefly.

"Yes."

"You're lucky to be alive, girl. You realize that, don't you?"

"It's not the first time I've had a close call," she answered.

"No doubt," said Angus, looking at her speculatively. "Cats and kittens I suppose, except you've gone and used most of your nine lives by now." He stared upriver. "I've seen these currents take a full-grown elk and drown her in a minute," he said. He smiled. "As you're no doubt aware, lass, the Scottish side of the river is a treacherous place." He turned away and moved off down the riverbank, keeping up a steady pace for the next ten minutes. He stopped at a small backwater and moved nimbly among the rocks, almost falling into the inky pool of still water. Jane followed as best she could.

"You mind telling me where we're going, Angus?"

"Here we are then," he said, and pointed. There, tucked away between two large rocks and perfectly camouflaged from the river by an immense, over-hanging willow tree was a long, narrow, lapstraked rowboat, twin oars neatly shipped, and fitted with a wooden rudder in the beautifully curved stern. Neatly painted on the transom was her name:

FOUR WINDS

"Where did this come from?" Jane asked, eyeing the pretty little craft appreciatively; she didn't know stem from stern or abaft from abeam, but she had a photographer's eye for beauty and knew good lines when she saw them.

"She floated down the river one day and I rescued her," said Angus blithely, not meeting Jane's eyes. He handed her into the back of the boat, then let go the forward painter, which had been looped around the stump of an old tree, and climbed in himself, settling down on the middle thwart and unshipping the two long oars. He lifted the left oar out of its lock and used it to push them out into the open stream, then dropped the well-oiled spindle back into place. Arching his wide back slightly he began to row, easing them out into the main current of the broad, fast-flowing river.

"Why is it I don't believe you?" said Jane.

"A lack of judgment regarding the human condition, I expect," Angus replied, his large nose lifting delicately into the air. "Fer it's God's own truth ahm telling you."

"Did you know your Scots accent gets more and more heather in it when you lie?" said Jane, laughing.

"Now is that a fact?" said Angus, grinning broadly and showing off his impoverished dental work. "And by the bye, dearie-me-love, what would you know about the heather?"

"You're not the country bumpkin you make yourself out to be, are you?" asked Jane, the water burbling in noisy little vortexes around the transom. The clifflike banks of the river rose dramatically on either side, sparsely treed and dangerous-looking, jutting outcrops of dark rock poking out here and there like giant old teeth heaving angrily out of the hard-packed earth.

"I'm nae a bumpkin and I'm nae from the country, girlie; ah told you I was a sailor, didn't I?"

"That you did," agreed Jane. She found herself wondering what Angus McConnigle's real story was and whether she'd ever hear it. Twelve hours ago the world had been a straightforward place of black and white, good and evil, truth and lies. Now that world had been turned upside down, and her along with it. Dundee had vanished into thin air and then she'd been confronted with a dead woman in her bedroom and a killer lying in wait for her, slung under a bridge. Occleshaw the cop was the enemy bent on tracking her down come hell or high water, and her knight on a white charger was a self-admitted criminal with bad teeth, rowing her off to God knows where down the river she'd almost drowned in.

"Where exactly are we going, Angus?" she asked. The sun was breaking through the scudding clouds here and there, giving the promise of a slightly better day. In front of her Angus laid off the oars for a moment, letting the river's swirling current do the work.

"If you take Mr. Potter at his word, we're going to Salen, which, as he told you, is on the Isle of Mull. We're a fair ways from there at the moment I'm afraid. A hundrit and fifty miles or theareabouts." He frowned, thinking hard. "I'd say our best chance lies in getting away from this area as quickly as possible. The main line of the railroad is behind us, as you know, but there's a number of local trains we can take."

"Heading where?"

"Glasgow for the wa', then on to Oban. There'll be steamers to Mull." He paused. "I seriously doubt yon Okkie would be looking for you so far afield."

"I'm afraid he's not the only one we've got to worry about."

"Aye." Angus nodded. "You've said as much. But I only said there were steamers at Oban that could take us across the water to Mull." He smiled. "I did nae say we had to take one."

"How long?"

"Across the water to Mull? A few hours, I'd guess. Been a time since I've been to Mull."

"To get there. From here."

"Depends," said Angus.

"On what?" asked Jane.

"Oh, well, as thy saying goes: many a mickle mak's a muckle." He smiled and picked up the oars in his large strong hands, and started to row again.

They slid down the river quickly, the cliffs lowering on either side until Jane could see low, rolling hills and cols both north and south; great lonely moors broken here and there by small brushstrokes of wood and the occasional fell, rising like a stone spike out of the boggy earth. There were long twists of chalky road that wound through the moorland, but not many, and no signs of civilization beyond the odd line of a stone wall or a spill of smoke from a peat fire.

Eventually the river began to slow and widen, small islands appearing within the stream. Jane could swear she smelled salt in the air and said so to Angus. In reply he nodded briefly and, as they reached a low valley crossing the river at right angles, he began guiding *Four Winds* toward the northern shore.

"The North Sea," he said as he took the boat up onto the pebbled beach and shipped the oars. "Still a fair bit off yet, but we're as close to Berwick on Twa' as we dare be." He gestured. "Oot the boat, girl. We've a fair bit of walking to do before the day is done if we want to avoid thy Okkie."

"He's not *my* Okkie," said Jane, stepping over the thwarts gingerly and hopping out of the boat. Angus pulled *Four Winds* higher up the scree, then tied the painter to a log that had washed up on shore. Then he set off up the beach. Their river road had come to an end.

Twenty-two

"Is it safe to leave it like that?" asked Jane, scrambling after him. In New York it would be like leaving a brand-new Packard Clipper by the curb with its doors unlocked and the keys in the ignition.

"Well," said Angus, turning back to look at the boat and scratching his head. "We could post a guard, I suppose. On the other hand, the only person who'd steal her is someone who needed her, and who am I to deprive a man of transportation when he sore requires it?"

They crossed the beach and found a pathway leading up onto the moor. It was still cold but Jane's assortment of borrowed clothing was warm enough. She was surprised to find that she felt almost lighthearted as she matched Angus's stride. All in all, she decided, it could have been a lot worse—the shadowy figure under the bridge could have been a better shot, for instance.

They walked for an hour, heading upland through the narrow valley, the sun climbing in the sky and the air warming somewhat. They reached the top of the valley and paused beside a small, tinkling stream that seemed to spring almost magically from a knot of stone some yards away. Cupping her hands, Jane drank some of the crisp, ice-cold water, then splashed some on her face. She thought about the color of the water that came out of the tap in her Greenwich Village kitchen and smiled to herself. She checked her Hamilton and was astounded to see that it was barely eight in the morning.

"I'd hide that wee trinket away," said Angus, looking at the watch. "Nae mutie hairdsman's boy aught sich a thing in these parts."

Jane nodded. She undid the strap of the watch, then shoved it into the pocket of her jacket. She had another drink of water from the stream and sat back on her heels, taking in the view ahead.

In front of her, stretching out for at least a mile, was a long, sloping section of moor, boggy and spotted with tussocks of sparse grass. Beyond that she could see a winding stretch of road heading away to the north, bracketed by grazing pockets of sheep held behind low wire fences, broken here and there by stiles and the odd rough gate. The road itself was bare of any traffic. On the road's far side she could see a strange feather of wood that crept up the side of the hill and then topped it.

To the left and right of the road were low, sloping hills, broken by stone outcroppings as they had been in the valley they had just passed through. Beyond that, farther distant and misty even at midday, were low, heathery mountains. There was no sound intruding into all of this except the tinkling of the stream and the distant calls of plovers, winking and darting from side to side, high in the morning sky.

"It's beautiful," she said quietly.

"It's bloody dangerous," muttered Angus, squatting down beside her and looking out over the barren countryside. "Land's as bald as a babies arse and there's nae enough cover for a tom-tit in all that fooking grass." He stood. "We'd best be getting across all that to the railway before they send out beaters."

"Beaters?"

"Aye, girl," Angus said, scanning the horizon. "It's how they hunt for pheasant . . . or escaping prisoners. They set out a line of men to beat the grass and flush yon prey." His lips thinned. "And then, like as not, they fire their great bloody guns. Whisht! Sometimes they have bloodhounds as well, d'ye ken?"

"I think so," said Jane. "Let's get going." They both trudged over the crest of the valley and began working their way around the shallow patches of bog. The air smelled sweetly of peat, and the death of small things, and grass. It was, thought Jane, the exact opposite of living in a city where every odor came from either man or machine. For all Angus's dire predictions about the dangers of such a place, Jane found herself thinking once again about the stories about England and Scotland she'd read when she was a girl, and almost believing them once again.

"When you were young did you ever read *Kidnapped* by Robert Louis Stevenson? Or *The Master of Ballantrae*? I used to get copies out of the library with these great illustrations, as good as any comic, and . . ."

"Hush!" said Angus, stopping and leaning his ear into the wind.

"What is it?"

"Quiet, lass!" Angus hissed, listening hard. Then Jane caught the sound as well, rising out of the distance to the south like a little mechanical gnat.

Airplane.

"Where?" asked Jane.

Angus pointed. "There," he said. Jane followed his raised arm to the western horizon, more or less in the direction of the cave, far upriver from the little, toylike valley they'd just left. At first she saw nothing but the rolling hills and moor and the ragged, magic shadows of the clouds passing overhead, but then it appeared, a small shape growing larger with each passing second.

"Shit," said Angus flatly.

"Maybe they're not looking for me at all," said Jane. "There's got to be some other reason for a plane to be flying around up here." She paused. "There is a war on, you know."

"What kind of war would that be?" asked Angus. "One with sheep and wee Scots bunnies for the enemy? Armed to the teeth, presumably?" He shook his head. "Nae, girl, they're looking for us, there's little doubt of that; and they'll catch us soon enough, you can be sure. Naw doubt they're having radios and all, talking to their people on the ground." He gave a long heartfelt sigh. "It's nae like it used to be when a runner at least had a bare chance of getting away from the flatties and flouders."

"Who?"

"Police, lass."

"I don't think so, Angus," said Jane, watching the sky. It was a high-winged monoplane, small, with a spidery, awkward-looking undercarriage. The Army called them Grasshoppers, small inspection and courier aircraft that could hop easily from one military installation to another, carrying personnel and mail. It wasn't the kind of thing the cops would have access to in an out-of-the-way place like this, and somehow she didn't think Occleshaw would want to call attention to himself by asking for military aid.

She bit her lip; this was something even more dangerous than the man from Special Branch. These were the people who'd taken Lucas and killed the woman in her bedroom on the train. They didn't play by anyone's rules except their own.

Watching, they saw that the plane was traveling in wide circles about three hundred feet off the moor, making a slow pattern in the air. Searching. With their backs against the sun and keeping to the shaded side of the hill it was doubtful they'd been spotted yet, but it was only a matter of time. Directly ahead, with nothing but open moor between, was a dense wood on the far side of a narrow road that was barely more than a track twisting and turning through the small glens and hills that made up the landscape.

"The woods!" yelled Angus. "Run!"

He grabbed her and they began pelting down the hill, cutting around the tussocks of grass and the treacherous areas of slippery bog waiting to entrap them. With one eye on the approaching aircraft and the other eye on the ground at their feet, they raced down the slope, heading for the road and the dark patch of trees just beyond.

"Christ, look!" said Angus, pointing up the road. A mile or so distant, separated from them by a string of small cols and glens, Jane saw a plume of dust coming out of the north; a car or some other vehicle that stood between them and the safety of the forest. Angus grabbed Jane by the arm and they began to run again. Jane knew it was no use; the car would get there before them; they were trapped out in the open. She caught a flashing glint of reflected light out of the corner of her eye. Someone in the Grasshopper had a pair of binoculars.

Angus suddenly pulled up short and dragged her to the left. They were fifty yards from the road and the car had disappeared into a small valley to the left. Directly in front of them now was a flock of fifty or so sheep scattered about the hillside, calmly grazing at the low, rough grass. Angus began to wave his arms and hoot loudly. The startled sheep suddenly clumped together skittishly and headed down toward the road. Angus stopped his flailing and clapped his hands once or twice, making little yipping noises in the back of his throat and sounding remarkably like a dog.

"What the hell are you doing?" asked Jane, looking toward the road. The car was still on the far side of the hill and out of sight.

"Hairding," he said. "It's what a sheep hairder does, and I'd advise ye to do it as well if you value your freedom." He continued making the yipping noises, the sheep now flowing around him, content to be herded along toward the road. Jane did the same, following Angus's lead, making sure her gestures weren't too broad and always keeping one eye on the road.

Reaching it, Angus opened the simple gate and the sheep began to flow out onto the rutted track, completely blocking it within seconds. The car appeared at the top of the hill and began coming down. It was an old Alvis with a flat windshield, black and covered with the gray, chalky lime dust that covered the road.

"Now what?" Jane whispered.

"Keep your yap shut and act like a mutie. Leave the talking to me."

Once the sheep were all into the road Angus calmly closed the gate behind him and began guiding the benign, flat-faced animals directly toward the car, making a huge wooly roadblock of gently moving sheep. The car pulled to a stop and two men climbed out. One was tall and heavyset under a dark brown belted coat and an old-fashioned soft derby that threw most of his face into shadow. The driver was much slimmer, hatless and wore small, steel-framed spectacles, the lenses tinted a pale green.

The driver spoke, his voice calm and without accent. The only thing Jane could be sure of was that he wasn't a Scot. "Your sheep are in our way," he said, smiling.

"Aye," replied Angus. "And your automobile is in mine."

"I suppose that is the case." The man paused, his smile widening. He had false teeth and the ones in the back gleamed. Steel, or white gold perhaps. Not the kind of thing you saw in England. Whoever this man was, he wasn't one of Occleshaw's boys.

"Perhaps you can tell me if you are from this area."

"Why should you want to know that?" asked Angus. Jane wished he'd just get on with it and move the sheep out of the man's way.

"Idle curiosity," said the man. Jane could see a distinct bulge on the left side of the man's heavy winter coat. He was carrying a gun.

Angus satisfied it. "Well, a bash on your curiosity. Here I am tethered to yon dumb lad with sair 'een and a back like a suckle. My heid burstint too, for sure. I am nae sober, you see, in cause my young dochter Merran was waddit and they danced till foyer in the byre. Me and some other chiels sa' down to the drinkin' and here I am. Peety I een looked at the wine when it was raid." Angus smiled and Jane simply stared, dumbfounded. She'd barely understood a word he'd said. The driver of the Alvis looked blankly at him, the wide smile frozen on his face.

"Can you tell me if you've seen anyone here-abouts today?"

"Only yourself and your friend," said Angus.

"Other than that."

"Nae. The sheep."

"I see."

"Not many of the tourist kind get to the likes of this place," mused Angus. "They're nae much to do except watch sheep fookin'." He smiled back at the driver, waving a broad flat hand over the flock that stood between them and which had already begun to absorb the car into its midst. "Which, as you can plainly see, they've been doing with a might." For the first time Jane actually took a good look at the animals surrounding her. They either had a patch of pale pink coloring on their bellies or their backs, and it didn't take her long to figure out why. By putting some sort of red dye on the rams bellies it was possi-ble to tell if an ewe had been mounted, and was likely to be lambing in the spring, if there was a mark on her back. Whoever really did own this flock appeared likely to be dining on lamb chops in March or April of next year.

Above them, the airplane had come down for a closer look and Jane saw that she'd been right; it was a Grasshopper, painted in the colors of the Eighth Army Air Force, with a serial number on the tail. It flew directly over them a hundred feet or so in the air, engine roaring, scattering the sheep in all directions. Ignoring the Alvis driver and his companion, Angus started rounding them up, making the yipping noise in the back of his throat again. Jane joined him, watching the two men out of the corner of her eye. They stood in the roadway for a moment, and the driver seemed to be paying particular attention to her, but eventually he turned and said something under his breath to his friend and they both climbed back in the car. A few moments later the last of the sheep trotted out of their way and the car drove off slowly. A minute later it was gone, hidden by the crest of the next hill.

"Now what?" asked Jane.

"Keep at it," said Angus.

"What?"

"Listen," said Angus. Jane did. All she could hear was the distant drone of the plane as it headed across the hilly moor.

"I don't hear anything."

"Exactly," said Angus. "Watch the road on yon rise over there." Jane turned slightly. She suddenly saw the two men from the Alvis come over the hill and simply stand there, watching them. "The laddies are nae fools. Catch us running pell mell into yon woods and they'd have had us." The two men stood peering down at them for a long moment, then turned and disappeared. Angus turned to Jane and looked at her strangely. "They weren't the police, Janey girl."

"I know," she said. "Maybe it's time I told you the whole story."

"Aye, maybe it is," he answered. "Since I appear to be one of the characters in it now."

It took Jane and Angus ten minutes to round up their plump, wooly charges and set them back to foraging in the upland pasture they had been briefly released from. When the gate was firmly latched behind them, the two crossed the road and entered the woods they'd seen from the top of the long burn that led up from the river. They found an old deer trail and began to make good time, safely out of sight of both road and air. They stayed in the woods for most of the morning and Jane told her tale. For his part, Angus simply listened, nodding now and then or making a small grunting noise when something interested or surprised him. He didn't show the slightest surprise at the crown jewels being involved, or the fact that Jane and Dundee had stumbled on a rat's nest of organized deserters. He showed even less surprise that their leader was a well-heeled officer in the same army.

"It was ever so," he said. "During the last war it wasn't just the big industrialists who turned a farthing or two at the expense of the lads in the trenches. It was bad enough that bullets had half the powder they should have had and one out of three barrage shells was a dud, but the food was rotten in its wee casks and the boot soles were sometimes made of cardboard. A lot of senior officers made a fair wage out of shortchanging their own lads." He scowled.

"You sound as though you're talking from personal experience," said Jane, trudging along beside him.

"Aye," spat Angus, "along with four brothers and a lot of mates who died for no good reason. I came back from yon bonnie war with a bone in my craw for a lot of little men in the Department of Supply and Services, of that you can be sure." He laughed, his voice booming hollowly over the broad, dreary landscape they'd come to after leaving the trees. "And to make it worse, when I came home I found the tax man had taken my boat for want of payment owing for two years; they said that fighting for 'my' country was no excuse for not making the proper quarterly payments to the fookin' Inland Revenue."

They tramped on through the morning, cutting across Cold Law and Collyburn Hoy, then moving across the Cheviot, Comb Fell to Crookedsike Head and Standrop Rigg, always heading north and west, heading for someplace called Tom Tallens, where Angus said there was a proper local train to be had.

Three times on the journey they had to take shelter from the Grasshopper, and three times they managed to find cover before they were spotted. Finally, just after twelve, their luck ran out.

They had just reached the crest of yet another hill among a frozen sea of them that seemed to stretch on forever. Jane was famished, and for the last hour or so they had been walking across the hills and moorland silently, lost in their own thoughts. At this point most of Jane's were about food, and so far she'd come to the conclusion that for overall volume and weight, Beefsteak Charlie's on West Fiftieth was the best deal in New York. There were sawdust on the floor, waiters with their hair parted down the middle and aprons down to their shoe-caps, great fat-dripping beefsteak sandwiches, baked potatoes that you could hide behind and lamb chops three inches thick. The only decorations were rows of photographs of racetrack accidents on the walls, as though seeing jockeys trampled in the mud and thoroughbreds cracking their ankles as they fell head over heels, crushing their riders, was some kind of aid to digestion, like chewing your way through a roll of Jests as she'd done more than once after an evening at Charlie's. She was also beginning to seriously crave a cigarette. Twice now she'd vainly gone through the empty pockets of her jacket on the off chance a pack of Spuds or Pall Malls might have mysteriously appeared. They hadn't.

"Down," said Angus, spotting them first. He put a large hand on Jane's shoulder and pushed her down into the heather.

"Where?"

"Behind a bit . . . there," said Angus, pointing, but keeping himself below the crest of the hill. Jane looked back down into the valley they had just climbed out of and saw them. There were half a dozen men, spread out like a fan, slowly making their way down the hillside, coming through the heather slowly, scanning back and forth, poking into bits of brush or stone hollows with walking sticks or wooden staves they carried. At the top of the far hill, overseeing this, was a figure in a lightweight hacking jacket. He had something dangling around his neck that Jane assumed was a pair of binoculars. At first Jane thought the man was one of the two in the Alvis earlier that morning but then he was joined by a second figure, this one in a dark constable's uniform, complete with bobby's helmet, looking a little formal and out of place on the wild moor terrain.

"Cops," she said.

"Aye," said Angus.

"Can we get away from them?" Jane asked, looking anxiously forward at the immense sea of hills rising to the north, breaking down here and there in broad ridges of ancient stone that separated various wide and shallow dales.

"Perhaps," said Angus.

There was virtually no cover at all. If Occleshaw had enlisted the aid of local folk who knew the land well, which seemed to be the case, they didn't stand a chance. She was beginning to think that Occleshaw was the lesser of two evils; at least the son of a bitch wouldn't begrudge them a meal.

"Maybe I should give myself up, Angus; give you a chance to get away." She stared down into the valley at the approaching men. "I'm only slowing you down."

"Tommyrot," said the Scotsman angrily. "Come, you; follow me."

He led them forward, crawling along the ridge on his belly until they found a shallow trench that led farther up the steep hill; probably a dried-up spring. This, in turn, led to a narrow gully, widening into a burn that took them up to the crest of the hill and over it, leading them safely out of sight. Behind them the beaters were patiently quartering their way down the slope of the far hill. By Jane's estimation they were about twenty minutes to half an hour behind.

"Faster," said Angus tersely. Keeping below the skyline, they ran along the crest for almost half a mile, until Jane judged they'd reached the uppermost end of the glen occupied by the beaters. Reaching it, Angus stopped and then, to Jane's horror, he stood up, outlining himself against the sky, yelling a loud halloo and waving his arms.

"Jesus, Angus! What are you doing?!"

"Divairshon," answered the Scot briefly. One of the men in the valley had spotted Angus and was passing the word along to the others. They began to yell back and forth to each other and Jane saw that the direction of their search was drifting broadly in their direction. "This way now, Janey," said Angus, grabbing her hand. They ducked down behind the crest of the hill again and ran back the way they had come. In ten minutes they were back where they'd started, but their searchers were now moving off, hopelessly on the wrong scent.

"That'll give us some time," said Angus, breathing hard now. The sky overhead was a clear, cold blue; thankfully there was no sign of the Grasshopper. There was a choice of routes across the moor and Angus chose one that soon put a deep, wooded glen between them and their pursuers. In ten more minutes they were into the woods, which smelled sweetly of pine and old, rotted boughs dropped to the dark, rich earth. In another twenty minutes or so, panting with exertion, they were high on the next rise.

"It's nae working," muttered Angus, looking back. The beaters were cresting the far hill and the binoculars carried by the man in the hacking jacket, presumably Occleshaw, glinted in the sunlight. There seemed to be fewer people after them now, which meant that some of them at least had been drawn off by Angus's previous ruse. Either that or they were coming around from the right, flanking them and intending to cut them off.

"We'll have to make a good run for it, lass; the only thing for it is to put distance between us now. We must get across yon Common to Newton Tors if we're to get clean away."

"Whatever you say," wheezed Jane.

"Come on, then."

They began to run, stumbling down the hillside to the broad sweep of heather that lay between them and the craggy, deeply cut glens and valleys of Newton Tors that lay a mile or so to the north. Jane could see the faint line of a road in the distance, leading into the dales beyond, winding its way obscurely north. It was empty, like everything else in this damned country. Another hour took them to the wilder country beyond the narrow moor and, looking back, they could see no sign of pursuit. Yet.

"Maybe we've lost them."

"Don't bank on it. They know the countryside and we don't, at least not as well as they do."

They kept on, their breath coming in ragged gasps now, the terrain deceptively tiring. The last of the moorland tilted at a slight angle, making all progress almost imperceptibly uphill. They reached a large field of heather, blowing gently in the breeze, the direction of the grass pointing the way forward, up the side of the hill, its crest topped by a thick stand of pines like the fur on the back of an angry dog. The road Jane had seen before wound around the base of the hill, then up it, cutting through the pines. There were a fence and a gate at that point, but no sign of anyone's sheep. Angus pulled open the gate.

They went through and he closed it behind him. They kept to the top of the ridge, safely hidden by the trees, following a narrow track through the trees. Coming out on the far side of the pines, the track turned into a respectable road that ran down into a narrow glen, crossed over a racing trout stream on a stone bridge and disappeared into another stand of trees that covered the bottom of the valley.

Angus paused. "There'll be a crofter's cottage there. Maybe better. There's trees anyway, cover enough for us to bide a moment."

They tramped down the narrow, rutted road and crossed the bridge. Jane paused for a moment, watching the flitting shapes of fish in the sparkling, trilling water below. Brown trout, lots of them, swimming with their perfectly hydrodynamic snouts pointed upstream, into the current, biding their time in the shaded water beneath the bridge until the sun faded from view and it was safe to come out to eat. You might be able to tempt them with a Yellow Peril or a Rose of New England but nothing less at this time of year; with the water as cold as it was, their hunger would be dulled anyway. Size and color would be the only thing to get them to come away from the safety of the bridge.

"Ah could do with one or two of those in a skillet," mused Angus, looking over the bridge himself.

"If I had my Granger reel and a nice little Hardy eight-footer, I could catch one of them for you."

"You fish then, lass?" said Angus.

"Ah doo," she said, smiling and imitating his accent, enjoying her first moment of the day since they'd first sighted the people on their trail.

"You're a girl of many parts, lass," said Angus. "You're a good partner to have in this little escapade."

"If it wasn't for me there'd be no escapade." She laughed. "You'd be back in your cave with a nice warm fire and your friends around you."

"Aye," he said, smiling back at her. "But if truth be told, my friends aren't half as exciting as you. A man gets in a rut from time to time. It's good to get out and see the world once een a while."

They crossed the bridge and hurried into the cover of the trees on the far side. Jane looked over her shoulder just as they slipped into the shadows and once again saw the distant form of the man with the binoculars.

"We have to hide somewhere," said Jane, pointing out the figure to Angus. "Maybe if we let them get beyond us we can figure out some other way to get out of this."

"That's an idea, Janey. We'll gi' it some thought." They kept on walking and a few minutes later came out of the woods and spotted a decrepit old cottage, its thatched roof rotted and collapsed, a sagging pile of peat leaning against one wall like a hunchbacked old woman. They passed in front of the cottage's overgrown garden and stepped into a small field of young hay. Beyond that was a plantation of wind-blown firs and Jane spotted a wisp of smoke rising up from the far side of it. People.

Food.

Coming through the head-high firs they reached a narrow ditch full of stagnant water and, jumping across it, found themselves on a rough lawn, tilted slightly like the moor behind them. The lawn was very rough, cut with a scythe by the looks of it, and planted with haphazard beds of scrubby rhododendrons. A brace of some kind of moor bird or pheasant leapt up at their approach, screeching loudly and flying off with a great flapping of wings.

"If he didn't know we were coming before, he knows it now," Angus grunted.

Twenty-three

The house before them was an ordinary thatch-roofed moorland farm building with a larger, newer, whitewashed addition, its roof sheathed in slate. Attached to the wing was a glassed-in solarium or veranda. Through the glass Jane saw a small, pale-faced man looking curiously out at them. The old building had a garage attached to it, and the remains of an old mill appended to one side, where a gurgling spring coursed around a small, rock out-cropping. Beside the mill was an old stone dovecote at least twenty feet high, with a flat wooden roof that had partially collapsed with age. The last pigeons had clearly flown from the old building many years before.

They crossed the last of the lawn under his gaze and went through a narrow gate. On the gate, written neatly on an old slab of wood, was the name: Standfast. As they approached the door into the house the small man came forward to greet them. Over his shoulder Jane could see into a pleasant room beyond, one side glass, the other books—thousands of them. On the floor, instead of tables or chairs, there were glassed-in display tables of the kind she expected to see in a museum.

"Hello," said the man pleasantly. He was in his late fifties or early sixties, oval-faced, with a narrow chin and a patrician nose. He had dark eyes and hair fanning back in a widow's peak that showed a large, intelligent forehead. The hair was black as pitch without a hint of gray. He was wearing a dark three-piece suit and a shirt with an old-fashioned detachable collar. An odd choice of clothes to be wearing in the middle of a desolate Scottish moor. When he spoke it was with a faint Scots burr, overlaid with a much more pronounced upper-class English accent. "My name's Tweedsmuir. How can I help you?" He sounded reasonably sincere, so Jane decided to reply in kind.

"Well," she began, "we haven't eaten in a while, and we're being chased by the police if you want to know the truth."

"Good Lord," said Tweedsmuir. "Perhaps you'd better come inside then." He stepped aside and waved them through the doorway. As she passed him Jane caught the faint smell of cigarette tobacco on his clothes.

He led them through the room full of books into a small study or sitting room beyond and gestured toward a pair of club chairs flanking a small hearth with a bright coal fire burning in the grate. Over the mantel there was a black-lacquer-framed watercolor of a large fish.

"*Archoplites interruptus.* Otherwise known as the Sacramento Perch," said Jane, looking up at the painting before she sat down. "Its habitats are the Sacramento and San Joaquin Rivers in California. I've caught it there." She turned to their host. "How come you've got a picture of it here?"

"I've fished for it there myself."

"In California?" asked Jane, somehow a little shocked that the small, almost delicate little man had traveled anywhere.

"It's the only place one *can* catch it," the man said with a gentle smile. He remained standing. "Can I get you anything? A drink perhaps."

"Och, now that would be fine!" breathed Angus.

"A fellow countryman, I see," commented Tweedsmuir, heading for a small bar set up on a rolling drinks trolley on the far side of the pleasant, wood-paneled room. He turned to Angus. "Will The Macallan do? I'm afraid I'm a single-malt drinker, although I've got some Kentucky bourbon here if you'd prefer. Old Crow."

"Oh no," said Angus loftily. "The Macallan will do, thank you. Neat if you've a mind."

"There's no other way I'd serve it," said Tweedsmuir, and poured two tall glasses, a good three inches in each. "For you . . . madam?" he said.

"A cigarette if you've got it."

"I do," said Tweedsmuir. He handed Angus his drink, then brought down a tin of Du Maurier from the mantel and set it on a little table beside Jane's chair, along with a box of Swan Vestas. Jane opened the tin, eased a cigarette out and almost reverently put a match to it. She took a deep drag, then sighed contentedly. She looked back over her shoulder at the painting over the mantel. "Pretty," she said, "but not quite what I expected to see in the middle of a Scottish moor."

"You're an American, I take it?"

"That's right."

"New York from the accent."

"Right again."

"So is the artist, although for the past number of years he's been living in California."

"It looks Japanese."

"You have a good eye." Tweedsmuir nodded. "His name is Hashima Murayama. He used to be a staff artist at *National Geographic* magazine. He's in an internment camp now."

"Aye," said Angus. "Like the one on the Isle of Man for Jews and such like."

"Yes," said Tweedsmuir sadly. "I'm afraid we can't profess to taking any higher moral ground on that score. The Americans seem to have gone at it a little more enthusiastically however." He smiled benignly in Jane's direction. "What I can't understand is why they weren't as enthusiastic at rounding up Germans and Italians."

"That's simple enough," said Jane. "If they did that all the restaurants in New York would close and we'd starve."

"I suppose that's true," Tweedsmuir answered with a soft smile. Jane watched him; he was very pale, almost ghostly, and his occasional smile had a too-calm, ethereal quality that was almost frightening. Somehow she knew that behind that aristocratic forehead was a brain full of memories and experiences she could never hope to match. He took a thoughtful sip of his drink. "Have you ever eaten at Barbetta's on Forty-eighth Street?"

"The best zabaglione in the city," Jane said. "You really do get around."

"I've been here and there in my time. Unfortunately I was in England when war broke out. I thought perhaps I could be of some use in this war, but they won't have me you see, and there's only so much fishing that can be done on the River Test."

"You've fished the Test?" said Jane, astounded. It was every fly fisherman's dream, British, American or any other nationality. It was, in fact, the very place that the first brown trout had been carefully transplanted from to the Delaware River in Pennsylvania almost a hundred years before. A simple chalk-bed stream, cold spring fed and "clear as gin" as the saying went. Expensive too; the rights to fish the river were all privately held and a license to catch so much as one brown trout cost a month's wages for most.

Tweedsmuir nodded. "Most of it. From the village of Ashe in Hampshire, where it begins, to Laverstroke and Whitechurch, then on to Stockbridge and Broadlands, my friend Louis's place."

"I thought that was just for high-mucky-mucks, lords and knights and that kind of thing." She sighed again. "It was one of the things I wanted to do while I was here," she said.

"Drop a line in the Test?" asked Tweedsmuir.

"Um," said Jane. "That would be a dream come true."

"Come back here after your troubles are over and perhaps I can arrange something. I think Louis would enjoy meeting both of you."

"Louis?" said Jane. "That's twice you've mentioned him. Can he sneak us onto the river?"

"I should think so," said Tweedsmuir, smiling. "He's one of those high-mucky-muck knights and lords you mentioned." Tweedsmuir took another sip of whiskey, obviously relishing it even though he was drinking very slowly, almost as though the drink was medicine. He smiled. "His full name is Lord Louis Mountbatten."

Jane vaguely recognized the name from news reports. "Who *are* you?" she asked. "And why do I think I should know you?"

"There's no reason why you should, my dear. I'm afraid my day, and indeed my war, is done. Let's just say I'm a retired publisher and man of letters, in my own small way, and leave it at that, shall we?" He put his unfinished drink down on the small table beside his chair and rose to his feet. For the first time Jane realized how dark the man's eyes were: dark enough to put you to sleep forever. She shivered slightly. Tweedsmuir noticed. "Come along, then. You said you were hungry and you're obviously chilled. Let's get on to the kitchen and I'll fix you a flitch of bacon and half a hundred eggs or so. When that's done we'll put you in hot baths and fix you up with new clothes."

"What's wrong with the clothes we've got, then?" argued Angus, swallowing the last of his drink.

"Oh, nothing, nothing," Tweedsmuir murmured diplomatically. "A little travel-worn and in need of a wash after your journey perhaps, that's all."

"What about the police?" said Jane a little more urgently.

Tweedsmuir offered his dark, fathomless eyes and that soft, secret smile again. "I'll handle the police," he said. "I'm rather good at it, actually."

They adjourned to the kitchen—a large, low-ceilinged and cozy room at the rear of the house, overlooking a small vegetable garden and the hills and dales they'd just traversed. So far there was still no sign of the police.

Tweedsmuir went to a surprisingly modern bottled gas Servel Electrolux refrigerator on the far side of the room and took out a large, brown paper-wrapped package of sliced bacon and a small basket of brown speckled eggs. He took out a pound of butter as well, laid everything out neatly on the yellow tiled counter next to a huge old Dutch oven, and then took a fine, black, permanently oily cast-iron frying pan from a cupboard underneath the counter and set it on top of the stove. He found a plain white apron hanging on a hook behind the door and tied it on over his suit, then gently laid a dozen strips of bacon across the frying pan and began to cook. Angus and Jane sat down in a pair of slat-back, cane-seated country chairs arranged around a square table the color of honey that stood in the middle of the bright, sunny room.

"Now then," said Tweedsmuir, continuing to cook, easing the strips of bacon around in the pan. "Perhaps you'll be so kind as to tell me your story."

For the second time that day Jane told her tale, leaving nothing out, from the body in the London mortuary and the bloody railroad junction in Letchworth to her discussions with Dundee about Charles Danby's involvement. She told him about the revelations in Shepton Mallet prison, the missing Imperial Crown and the Great Sword and, finally, Dundee's disappearance and the corpse of the woman in her bedroom. Tweedsmuir stopped her only twice, first to ask her about the actual items that were stolen and then about the odd man she'd met on the train.

"Mendelssohn?" he asked.

"That's right," she said as he placed a plate of bacon and scrambled eggs in front of her along with, to Jane's surprise, the first bottle of Heinz, or any other, ketchup she'd seen since setting foot in England.

"And he mentioned Fingal's Cave? What was your reaction?" asked Tweedsmuir.

"I'd never heard of it."

"Interesting," murmured Tweedsmuir, putting some freshly sliced brown bread into a shiny Toastmaster.

"Why?" asked Jane.

"Don't you find it strange that, once stolen, your Mr. Danby would transport the jewels so far north? He must have a purpose. I'm assuming it's because he has to wait for something, transportation presumably."

"Transportation?" asked Jane.

Swallowing the last piece of egg on his plate, Angus leaned back in his chair, put a demure hand over his mouth and belched quietly.

"He's right, lass," said the Scotsman. "It's the only thing that makes any sense, ya see. He's got to get yon jewelry off England and into the hands of the Germans if your theory is correct about their final destination. For that he's going to need some privacy to make the exchange. There's no way a German submarine or one of their fancy E-boats is going to come sailing into Bristol, bells and whistle doing a hornpipe."

"Your friend has hit the nail on the head," said Tweedsmuir.

"What's that got to do with Fingal's Cave?"

"At the best of times the cave is relatively isolated. Staffa, the island it's located on, is only about a mile long and half as wide. These days, with no tourist trade and ten miles out in the Irish Sea from the nearest land, it's a perfect spot for such an exchange. The cave can only be approached by boat from Mull. Once inside the cave they'd be completely hidden."

"How big is this cave?" asked Jane.

"Two hundred and forty feet long, forty wide and sixty-five feet tall at high tide," said Tweedsmuir. Almost the length of a football field and about as wide, thought Jane. Easy enough for a rubber boat launched from a submarine, or more likely one of their fast attack patrol boats. She dug into her jacket and took out the old, worn Lady Amity wallet she'd carried for years. She carefully withdrew the matchbook cover she'd found in the basement of the cottage in Shepton Mallet and handed it across the table to Tweedsmuir. "Any idea what this means?" she asked.

The small man looked at it carefully.

On the outside:

CURTISS & SONS
REMOVALS
Fountainbridge
Glasgow

And then, on the inside:

Salem/h.t. 712/12

"I have no idea about Mr. Curtiss and his sons, but I'd say the inside is telling you the mean high tide for Salen in Mull for the seventh of the month is midnight." He turned and looked over his shoulder at a calendar hanging from the wall. "Two days from now."

"Christ!" breathed Jane. "We're running out of time."

"You certainly are," said Tweedsmuir, looking over her shoulder and out the window. Jane turned and followed his gaze. A line of men had appeared on the crest of the farthest hill and were coming quickly down into the valley. The man in the hacking jacket remained on the summit, the flashing lenses of his binoculars almost certainly focused on the farmhouse.

Jane pushed back her chair and stood up. So did Angus.

"Sorry to eat and run, Mr. Tweedsmuir, but its back to playing hare and hounds for us."

"No," said the small man firmly. "Wait here."

Tweedsmuir turned on his heel and left the room. A moment later they could hear his footsteps on the stairs. Jane stared anxiously out the window. The men were getting closer by the second.

"We've got to go."

"Wait, lass," said Angus. "I think the man is on our side."

"Christ! I hope so."

"I'd refrain from taking the Lord's name in vain if I was you, Janey. He has the look of a minister's son. Wearing all that black and yon upright collar; Free Kirk if I'm guessing correctly."

"You are, sir," said Tweedsmuir, smiling as he came back into the room. He was carrying a mound of clothes over one arm and a pistol in the other, a familiar-looking Smith and Wesson hammerless .38 Police Special, much like the one her cop friend Hennessey carried. "Follow me," he added as he strode across the kitchen, pushing the pistol into the pocket of his jacket and lifting the latch on a plain wood door on the far side of the room. He disappeared, and Jane and Angus followed.

They found themselves in a dark, musty storeroom with an uneven dirt floor that was obviously part of the original farmhouse. It was dark, the windows heavily shuttered, the walls lined with boxes and barrels and lumpy sacks of coal.

"Change clothes. I'll deal with the police; I know the local constable and he'll believe me if I tell him I haven't seen you." He smiled. "Or tell them I have seen you, and you've gone in a completely different direction." He handed Angus the pistol. "Take this; you're bound to need it more than I am."

"Why are you doing this?" asked Jane, her arms full of clothes.

"Because I want to have one last adventure, I suppose," he answered, with that dark, secret smile. "My friend Hannay and myself."

"Hannay?" asked Jane.

"Never mind," said Tweedsmuir with a small laugh. "A little joke." He paused, then snapped his fingers, a strangely modern gesture for a man who seemed to have stepped out of the past. "I almost forgot." He reached into his jacket pocket and pulled out a flat, gunmetal gray cigarette case and handed it to Jane. The initials J. B. were scrolled ornately on the front. "I thought you might like these." With that he turned and left the room, the latch clicking loudly as he closed the door, leaving them in the dark. Jane shared out the clothes, and, turning their backs to each other, she and Angus began to take off their old clothes and put on the new.

Lieutenant Colonel Charles Danby, back in his proper uniform after his brief stint as a corporal in Shepton Mallet, smoked a Lucky and looked out over the River Cam. Directly across the narrow river a huge weeping willow hung down, reflected perfectly in the steely water, the reflection briefly blurred as some mufflered and wooly-hatted scullers slid up the river on their narrow craft like a giant water bug. A little way along to the right stood a huge oak that was probably an acorn in Henry VIII's time, partially obscuring the castellated towers of St. John's College. To his left, the Trinity Bridge led across the river to the well-ordered and neatly trimmed fields known only as "The Backs." A fairy tale, which was appropriate, all things considered.

Danby spotted his quarry coming along the path leading down from Trinity Cloisters Library and watched him approach. The severe-looking man, hair swept back on a wide, almost arrogantly bulbous forehead that probably meant he had more brains than he needed, had a long nose with a face like a basset hound. He was tall, limp-wristed and wearing a dark blue Trinity blazer, a white shirt with an old-fashioned pin-on collar, a College tie, and a worn-looking academic gown thrown over his shoulders against the chill of the early evening. Below the blazer billowed a pair of old gray flannels, his extremely large feet fitted into oversized brown shoes. Danby knew just about everything about the man, which was more than most people could say. He was a fellow of Trinity College, and, according to Danby's information, he'd been a Red since he was a student here but was never so foolish as to join the party.

"Well, Colonel, we meet again," said Blunt, seating himself on the bench beside Danby. He reached into his blazer pocket and took out a silver cigarette case with his monogram etched into it and a slim, solid-gold Dunhill lighter. Danby remembered that Blunt was vaguely related to the royal family somehow, a cousin of somebody's brother-in-law or something. Blunt popped open the cigarette case and removed one of his foul-smelling yellow-papered Broyard cigarettes and lit it, placing the fat, dark tobacco tube in the exact center of his rather feminine mouth.

"The day turned out rather well, I think," he murmured.

"We're not here to talk about the weather," said Danby. Even sitting beside the guy made him nervous.

"No, we're here to talk about Tube Alloys and our friend here at the Cavendish Laboratory."

"That's right." Danby knew both the Nazis and the Russians wanted the information so badly their teeth were aching, and he had it, all bundled up in a skinny little German Jew named Fuchs whom he had a couple of things on. Klaus Fuchs was working on the Tube Alloys thing in Birmingham but, by the sounds of it, they were about to send him to the States to join the big boys on the Manhattan Project. Fuchs was worth his weight in gold. He smiled at that. It was pretty funny when you knew the people involved. Danby looked straight ahead as he spoke to Blunt. "You and your people still interested?"

"Yes."

"At the price I suggested?"

"I believe so, yes.

"Good, then we'll go ahead. I can have what you need in Geneva pretty soon."

"Let me know the dates and I'll have a representative there."

"Good man," said Danby. He held out his hand to seal the deal. Blunt looked at it like it was a dead fish being offered. He stood.

"I have a graduate lesson in fifteen minutes," Blunt said, standing without shaking hands. "Poussin. I really shouldn't be late."

"Then you better toddle off, then, shouldn't you Tony old fellow?" Blunt winced. Danby smiled; he liked playing the American oaf without any culture. He wondered what the manicured little prick would think if he knew the old man had a Poussin in the dining room back home. *Landscape with Polyphemus*, picked up from the Russians by Armand Hammer, years ago, then laid off on the old man. A bunch of naked Greeks standing around a volcano. Probably give Blunt a hard-on in his gray flannels. To hell with it. Why make the faggy jerk jealous? He waved to Blunt as he went back up toward the College gates, wondering how long somebody like that was going to last in the spy business. He looked at his watch and stood up himself. He had a plane to catch.

Twenty-four

Twenty minutes later the first of the beaters arrived at Tweedsmuir's door, and a few minutes after that the local constable appeared. Jane and Angus saw them arrive, watching through a broken slat in one of the jalousie-style shutters and the grime-encrusted window it covered.

"This is crazy," Jane whispered. "We're trapped in here. We should have run when we had the chance."

Angus peeked out through their small spy hole. He nodded. "I'm afraid you're right, lass; there's a dozen men out there and they don't appear to be taking no for an answer."

Angus began moving about the dark, dank room, looking for some other exit. He found a ladder against the back wall, fixed in place on metal brackets. He began to climb. Jane went to the door leading into the kitchen and put her ear to it. She could hear the raised voice of one man and she knew it in an instant. Occleshaw, like some vindictive ghost haunting her footsteps, refusing to give up. Tweedsmuir's calm voice answered the man carefully, refusing to be led into an argument with the perpetually angry man from Special Branch. A third voice joined in, Scots, and from the countryside by the sound of it; probably the chief constable for the district.

"Come now, Mr. Occleshaw," said the chief constable. "This is no ordinary man you're speaking to. A little respect is in order."

"I don't give a bloody fuck who he is, man; he's getting in the way of an official investigation by Special Branch and if he continues to interfere I'll fucking have the little Jew-lover thrown in the fucking Tower. Do. You. Understand?" He spaced the last three words out, enunciating carefully.

"I'm simply asking for an explanation of why you want to ransack my house," said Tweedsmuir evenly.

"And I want an explanation as to why, your Lordship or whatever you are, has two plates drying in your dish rack, and why there's enough eggshells in your trash tip to feed an army."

"I had breakfast with my friend Richard," said Tweedsmuir. "He'd been out for an early-morning stroll about the moors."

"Richard?"

"Richard Hannay." Tweedsmuir's mysterious friend again.

"Who is he?" asked Occleshaw. Jane thought she could hear the sound of the policeman's pencil scratching. Behind her Angus continued climbing the ladder.

"As I said, a friend. From Rhodesia."

"A colonial," said Occleshaw.

"I was born in Scotland; by your standards I assume that makes me a colonial too."

"Christ," muttered Occleshaw under his breath. "More fucking Scottish Independents."

"Mind your tongue in my house, sir; I'll take your

insolence but I'm damned if I'll take your blasphemy."

"Janey, lass! Here!" hissed Angus behind her. She turned and looked up the ladder. A bright square of sunlight was cascading into the storeroom. At the top of the ladder Angus had found a trapdoor that led up to the roof. Realizing that whatever Tweedsmuir did, Occleshaw would eventually win the day over the small man's protests, she scurried across the dirt floor and began climbing the ladder. Angus boosted himself out onto the roof and Jane followed a moment or so later. Angus eased the trapdoor shut. They were on the back side of the old slate roof, no more than three or four feet from the peak, barely out of sight of the beaters and uniformed police below. They weren't much better off than they had been in the storeroom.

Angus gestured silently and began to edge along the slope of the roof, taking care to keep his head below the peak. On this side of the roof Jane could see down to the little stream that gurgled along beside the mill, and the broad trough that took the water over the mill wheel to the race beyond. She quickly saw what Angus intended: the trough ran directly beside the back of the house, blocking the view from the rough lawn and the vegetable garden on the other side—the view from the kitchen window and the place where all the cops seemed to be congregated. There was a lead downpipe visible at the corner of the house, and if they could climb down that they could get into the water trough and travel across the opening between it and the mill. Dangerous, but just barely possible.

Jane followed Angus's every move, careful not to

put too much weight on the slippery roof slates.
Knock one down and it would all be over. Finally
Angus reached the corner of the roof, took one look
back over his shoulder at Jane and then eased himself
over the edge and made his way down the old lead
downspout. She reached the corner of the roof herself
and looked over; Angus had made it to the water
trough and was just turning himself into it. Jane
peeked around the corner and saw several of the
beaters talking together and lighting each other's cigarettes. There was a lot of laughter going on, as
though the whole thing was no more than a game.
Perhaps it was just that for them, a day's outing on
the moor and perhaps a sovereign to boot, but they
hadn't seen the woman on the train with her eye
poked out. Jane frowned, thinking of the dowdy
young woman in the crushed cloth cap and the sagging knee stockings. Who was she, and why had she
been in Jane's bedroom in the first place? It hadn't
made any sense then and it made even less sense
now. She shook her head; this whole escapade had
been like that: none of the puzzle pieces seemed to
fit.

  She turned away, lay flat on the roof and let her
legs slide over and down, wrapping her ankles
around the drainpipe. It was remarkably firm and
she had no trouble reaching down to grip it in both
hands and shinny down to the mill trough. Following
Angus's lead she rolled herself into the trough and
began to crawl along it, keeping flat on her belly.
Thankfully the trough hadn't seen used in years and
was dry, its interior nothing more than a catchall for
wind-blown leaves. After a few minutes she was in
the lee of the mill wall and scuttled forward more

openly. She reached the end of the trough and found her way to the mill wheel's axle hole and wriggled through it, tumbling into a bed of old and dusty chaff inside.

"This way," hissed Angus. She followed him across the floor to a door that hung half off its hinges. She peered outside and saw the dovecote. "Come on," said Angus and began to ease out through the gap in the doorway.

Jane gripped him by the arm. "Wait." Looking back the way they'd come she saw a scuffed line of footprints through the chaff leading from the axle hole to the doorway. They might as well have painted a sign. Jane took a moment, went back to the axle and the huge old stone, then came back to the door, scattering more chaff over their footsteps as she came. When she was done there was no sign they'd been there at all. This time, when Angus went out the door she went with him.

The ground outside the mill and leading to the old dovecote was cobbled stone, where no footprints would show. It was also screened from the house and the garden by the bulk of the mill. Quickly, Angus sprinted across the small section of open ground between the two buildings, making his way to the rear of the dovecote. The rear wall was made of broken old stones and covered with vines. It took no more than a minute or so to scramble up to the roof, where they collapsed behind a narrow parapet. Looking around, Jane spotted a trapdoor in the floor. She'd seen enough of her friends flying pigeons in New York to know what it was for; the pigeons would be kept below the roof in protected wire cages and brought up here to be flown. She prayed that

Tweedsmuir had a lock on the downstairs door; if he didn't, and Occleshaw decided to search, they would be trapped as surely as they'd been in the storeroom.

It was the middle of the afternoon before Occleshaw's men finished their search. At one point Jane was sure that they were going to search the dovecote roof, but apparently the inside of the old construction was so decrepit they only gave it a cursory look. Eventually, with the chief constable making effusive apologies, they left, cutting back through the small woods near the bridge and making their way across the open moorland again. Another half hour passed and then Jane heard a shrill whistle from below. She looked cautiously over the narrow parapet of the dovecote and saw Tweedsmuir standing on the rough lawn, his fingers on either side of his mouth as he whistled a second time. Once again Jane found the modern, almost youthful gesture didn't fit in with the man's aristocratic, slightly antiquated personality.

"Halloo!" he called, shading his eyes with one hand and glancing up at the dovecote. "Are you up there?"

Jane stood up and waved.

Tweedsmuir smiled. "Good show," he said. "I knew you'd find a way up."

"Can we get down through the trapdoor?" she called.

"You'll get filthy, I'm afraid; there's a great deal of birdlime and detritus from the days when it was in use."

"We'll come down as we came up," said Angus, climbing to his feet. He waved at Tweedsmuir and then turned to the rear wall. A few minutes later they were standing beside the small man on his lawn, brushing off their clothes. Jane took out the cigarette case Tweedsmuir had given her and gratefully lit one with one of the Swan Vestas; she'd craved a smoke more than once while they were up on the roof but hadn't dared light one.

"You're sure he's gone?" asked Angus, looking around anxiously.

"I gave the pompous ass enough time," said Tweedsmuir, his face darkening as he thought of Occleshaw. "If he was going to double back he would have done it by now." He took a packet of twenty Senior Service out of the pocket of his jacket and lit one with a small gold lighter he took out of his waistcoat. He inhaled, then coughed lightly.

"I'm sorry if I didn't give you much time, but I never thought he'd inspect the house itself. A very modern policeman, I'm afraid." Tweedsmuir smiled tautly and took another draw on the cigarette. "There was a time when a gentleman's word would have been enough."

"Occleshaw's no gentleman and he wouldn't recognize one in a million years," said Jane. "And we should be the ones to say we're sorry. We've interrupted your day, I'm afraid."

"A welcome interruption it's been," said Tweedsmuir. "When one is writing one's dreary old memoirs, one looks for the slightest diversion, I'm afraid."

"I'm pretty sure they're not dreary," said Jane, smiling.

Tweedsmuir shrugged. "Time will tell, Miss Todd." He smiled sadly. "My friend Mr. Wells decries the fact that he will apparently be remembered for little amusements like his *Time Machine* and *War*

of the Worlds more than for his *Outline of History.*"
The little man laughed. "I venture to say that the
Roman scholar Pliny the Elder is better remembered
for his love of trout fishing in Lake Como than for
his studies of Herodotus." He shrugged again. "It's
all a matter of accident, you see; I've come to believe
that much of life is like that. One's birth and death
and everything in between all hinge on the flip of a
coin, I'm afraid." He glanced speculatively at Angus.
"Although I suppose that's no way for the son of a
Free Kirk minister to speak."

"Och," said Angus, and left it at that.

Tweedsmuir field-stripped his cigarette and threw
a few bits of tobacco into the air, judging the wind.
"The breeze has dropped," he said pleasantly. "I
think I'll take my rod and see what our old friend
Salmo trutta is up to this evening." He glanced up at
the sky. Jane knew it would be dusk in an hour or
so; the brown trout would be coming up to feed at
the bridge a few hundred yards away. "I shall be
gone for at least an hour or so, perhaps a little more
if I remain by the water enjoying a cigarette or two
before I go back to my work. If my automobile,
which is in the garage with the key in the ignition,
were to be stolen I'd have no one to blame but myself, would I?"

"No, I suppose not," said Jane.

"Good then, that's settled," he said. He shook each
of their hands in turn and then went back into the
house. He appeared again a moment later with a
fishing creel slung at his waist and a nine-foot bamboo rod in his hand. On his head he was wearing an
old and battered Tyrolean hat pin-cushioned with a
score of trout flies. Jane thought she could make out

the flashy colors of a Wizard and a Silver Doctor. Tweedsmuir paused, gave them a brief smile and a wave, and then he was gone, disappearing down the narrow path through the stand of trees between the house and the stream, slipping into the shadows like a ghost.

"What a strange man," said Jane, watching him go.

"Aye," said Angus. "But a good man for all that. He did'na have to take us in and he could have handed us over to yon Okkey if he wanted, easy as pie."

"Maybe he really did want one last adventure," said Jane, looking toward the woods. "Him and his friend Hannay, whoever he is."

"Well, Janey girl, we're still in the midst of our own wee adventure, and we've had the offer of transportation if I'm not mistaken. We can put a lot of miles between ourselves and Mr. Occleshaw if we hurry."

"All right," said Jane, and they headed for the garage.

Tweedsmuir's car turned out to be a huge old canvas-topped McLaughlin Buick in robin's egg blue and equipped with American-style left-hand drive. The top was down and Jane had no idea how to put it up. She got behind the big, polished wood wheel and quickly scanned the dashboard. Angus climbed in beside her.

He gave Jane a nervous look. "You sure you know how to drive this great boat?" he asked.

"Stick to your oars, Angus." She turned the key in the ignition and the engine roared into life. She tapped experimentally on the gas a few times, put her foot on the clutch and manhandled the column shifter into reverse. "Hang on," she said, and eased the big car out of the garage and into the daylight.

She turned the car around in the little yard behind the house, put the big Dayton balloon tires into the ruts of the road and gave the car a little gas. They moved forward easily, the tires absorbing the uneven surface, and a moment later they were crossing the bridge over the stream they'd passed on their way to the farmhouse several hours before. There was no sign of Tweedsmuir either up- or downstream.

"He must be fishing in some other spot," said Jane, raising her voice over the heavy rumbling of the Buick's powerful engine. "I wanted to give him a last wave good-bye."

"Drive," said Angus. "Before Occleshaw decides to come back." Jane put her foot on the gas.

They drove for hours, heading directly north as far as it was possible on the winding, back-country roads. Angus found a Gall and Inglis Safety Map of Scotland in the room-sized glove compartment, showing all roads in different colors, rated for their drivability. Also in the glove compartment was a wax-paper-wrapped packet of cheese-and-onion sandwiches, a large chased-silver flask of The Macallen's single malt and a small, flat, ornately scrolled, silver-plated automatic pistol with mother-of-pearl handgrips.

"Well armed for a retired publisher and man of letters, wouldn't you say, Janey?" Angus asked. Jane just nodded and kept on driving. Angus handed the gun to Jane. "You should have this, Janey," he said. "It's a wee lady's gun." Tweedsmuir, bless his dark and fathomless little heart, had meant them to be well fed and well armed. She took the weapon with one hand and stuffed it into the deep pocket of her oversized jacket.

They continued north as night fell, up out of the moor country and into the region of coal pits and small industrial towns that ringed the dark smudge of Glasgow like remora around the teeth of a shark. They ran beside great craggy fells and lochs that were miles long. Full darkness came and Jane turned on the blackout-shuttered headlamps, faint slits of illumination barely lighting up the road ahead. They drove this way steadily, wondering how soon they'd come to a roadblock resulting from the necessity of Tweedsmuir reporting his car as "stolen." She smiled as she drove, wondering whether Occleshaw would believe him or not, secretly hoping that he wouldn't.

The names of towns flew by as they crawled steadily north and now slightly west across the map. Carluke, Newmain, Kilern, Glen Fallon and Glenorchy, Loch Broom and Loch Mayne. Occasionally they'd see the stark remains of a castle silhouetted by the moon or reflected in the still black waters of a loch, but mostly they saw dark hills and villages sleeping through the soundless night.

They pulled over and slept for an hour in the shoulder of a mountain called Ben Lomond that lay beside the loch of the same name. They woke, ate the last of their sandwiches and then drove on into the dawn, the new day bringing banks of fog that lay thick and heavy across the glens and moors.

With the first real light came trouble: entering a sleepy village huddled on the edge of a small loch, somewhere west of Tyndrum on the last long stretch of road down to the coast and the seaport town of Oban. The high street in the town was also the main road, with shops on one side and a few docks and small outbuildings and boathouses on the other. A constable wearing a rain cape stood beside a white globe and pillar box that marked the post office. The roadblock took the form of an oil drum set on the verge of the road with a large hand-painted sign in red letters that said: STOP.

"Shit," said Jane. Her foot automatically slid over to the brake and they began to slow.

"Bloody hell," said Angus. "Go, woman!"

Jane dropped her foot onto the accelerator just as the policeman made a clawing motion at the hood and then dropped away as they shot past and roared out of the town.

Craning his neck Angus turned and looked back down the road. "He's done a prat, but I think he's all right." Angus turned in his seat again and looked out the windshield. "We've got to get off the main roads," said the Scotsman. He pointed off to the right. A narrow gravel road led into a deep glen between two broad-shouldered hills. "There's a chance we'll wind up on somebody's farm road or in a duck pond, but it's a risk we'll have to take," he said. "They've obviously broadcast some sort of description; this bonny bit of transport is clearly a liability to us now." Jane nodded and swept the big car off the main road and onto the gravel byway. They continued on through the thickening fog, their lights almost completely useless now. Somewhere off to the left they could see occasional glimpses of a narrow, rushing river, thick stands of trees obscuring the view. The river ran out through a steep glen with hills all around, the road corkscrewing, forcing Jane to fight the heavy wheel. They slewed east, then west again, running between trees on both sides now, moving up the hill and away from the river. They reached the top of the hill and then moved down the other side, thumping across a main rail line, then following beside it down a broad valley that held the fog in its grasp.

Soon they were in another deep-cut glen, wooded on either side. The woods ended, opening into a meadow. Directly ahead Jane saw a narrow bridge exactly like the one across Tweedsmuir's trout stream. She was halfway across the bridge when she suddenly saw the back end of a small black car backing slowly out onto the road. She put her palm down on the horn ring and slammed on the brakes, but she knew it was no use. The car was fully out onto the road now and had come to a full stop, its lights flashing.

"Son of a bitch!" Jane yelled. She dragged the wheel around and closed her eyes as the big Buick rocketed off the road and briefly took to the air before it blasted through a section of hedgerow as though it were tissue paper, then plunged downward with a sickening lurch. A limb from an old, brittle hawthorn rising beside the road clipped the front end of the car, crushing it. Bucking and pitching, the car dropped headfirst into the shallow stream below.

There was a long moment of silence: the only sounds were the hissing of the crumpled radiator and the harsh ticking of an engine cooling before its time. Jane and Angus struggled with the doors and finally managed to get out of the car and climb up the stream bank to the road. The owner of the small black car, an old, matchbox-shaped Morris, was waiting for them. He was small, like Tweedsmuir, but considerably younger. He was a little on the plump side, dressed in rough tweeds, a tartan cravat and a fat tweed cap to match his suit. He wore owlish-looking round steel eyeglasses and he had a small pair of binoculars around his neck. For a moment Jane froze, remembering the twinkling of lenses she'd seen from the Grasshopper. Then she relaxed; this man looked incapable of harming a ladybug. He looked like Mole from *The Wind in the Willows*.

"I'm terribly sorry!" said the round little man. "I'm tracking a particular family of young Mallards you see; they forage down by the loch and I thought if I got there early enough . . . Oh dear, pardon me; I suppose I really should introduce myself." The man in tweeds gave them a bright, eager smile and extended his hand, fog condensing on his eyeglass lenses like dew. "Bond," he said. "James Bond."

Twenty-five

The ruins of Dunstaffnage Castle lay some eight miles from the seaside town of Oban on the shores of Loch Linne, and were virtually inaccessible except by water from the little village of Donollie on the road to Connel, a mile or so to the east. There was a rough track that led to the castle from the village, but it was only suitable for sportsmen wishing to test the waters or agile walkers willing to risk a turned ankle or even a broken leg on the upland crags leading to the ruins.

There were signs indicating that anybody chancing the path were doing so at their own risk, part of that risk being the likelihood of being summarily arrested, since the entire southern side of the loch was private property.

The castle ruins themselves lay on a rocky promontory that extended out into the loch like the great, rough claw of some ancient dinosaur. The castle itself looked like a huge, ominous broken tooth jutting up out of some monstrous stony jaw. The main building was square and dated from the thirteenth century, and at one time had a tower at each corner. The entrance to this was by a precarious ruined staircase that faced the loch. The walls were nine feet thick, and on the foremost tower were two guns, which formed part of the armament of the Spanish Armada and had been raised from Tobermory Bay on the Island of Mull. Both guns were inscribed with the maker's name: *Auseurus Koster, Amsterdamm me fecit*. Two hundred yards from the castle were the remains of a small chapel where some of the early Scottish kings were believed to be buried. In modern times it became the burial place of the Campbells of Dunstaffnage, the hereditary captains of the castle, whose mansion, a great, dark tomb of a place, lay another hundred yards distant, occupying the top of the stone outcropping, its back protected by a jutting cliff, its front door only reached by a long climb up a flight of stone steps leading from the landing place on the loch. The mansion was old, brick and stone covered in a gray, cracked stucco sometime in the past, its windows heavily mullioned and unattractive, the roof flat and sprouting chimneys like old warts on a haggard face. A house built for time and the weather.

Staring out of his third-floor bedroom window in the mansion, Lucas Dundee could see the castle ruins like a black shade obscuring the moonlit waters of the loch. Dundee had arrived by air, landing on a small, private strip above the house. On their way here Danby had informed him that Loch Linne was used by elements of the RAF to perfect night bombing over Holland and to not be disturbed by low-flying bombers, occasionally making runs up the twenty-mile stretch of peat-colored water. He also advised Dundee not to try to escape; there were guards on the footpath and the loch was close to seven miles wide; possible for an excellent swimmer like Dundee, but not when the water was forty-five degrees. Even so, even an attempt to escape would result in extremely serious consequences. On the other hand, however, there were some kind of festivities taking place tonight and, if he was willing to dress for the occasion, he was welcome to attend. Danby had smiled then.

"With a name like yours it seems appropriate, Ten Spot, don't you think?" He paused. "In fact, old friend, I insist on it."

They'd flown in to the airstrip behind the house in the early hours of the morning and it had been too dark for Dundee to see much of anything at all. The mansion seemed empty with the exception of a few properly dressed servants, all male, and a few men in navy pullovers and jackets who had the faceless look of armed guards. Since then he hadn't left the enormous room he'd been summarily taken to; there was an adjoining bathroom if he needed the facilities, and so far he'd been brought three adequate meals.

The room he occupied was enormous, completely at odds with the claustrophobic garret at the Akergill Sanitorium. The ceiling, box-beamed and dark, was at least a dozen feet over his head. There was a massive fireplace on the far side of the room, the mantel arching up almost over his head, held up on either side by two life-size caryatid figures, suitably clothed in nothing but a few delicately placed stone leaves on the vines that entwined their bodies. Over the mantel, was a large gilt-framed oil painting of an unidentified, hard-faced man wearing a kilt and leaning on a broadsword that in real life would be almost impossible to lift. A scroll on the sword said simply 1603. On the ground at his feet, the point of the sword pierced the center of a gold circlet ornamented with Maltese crosses and fleur-de-lys next to a large rectangular stone.

The rugs on the floor were thick and warm with some sort of worn heraldic theme; the floors themselves were waxed oak planks at least ten inches wide and so dark they were almost black. Dundee had no problem imagining the man over the mantel treading these same boards three hundred plus years ago.

The furniture suited the room: a giant old four-poster bed as dark as the floors, with dark green velvet curtains and a bedspread the same color. The washstand, bureau and a pair of heavy chests were of even darker wood than the floors and looked faintly Spanish, deeply carved and obviously very old, perhaps liberated from the same ship of the armada as the pair of cannon on the ruined castle walls.

The door into the room was lighter oak, spanned with a heavy pair of strap hinges and securely locked. When Dundee tried to open the window shutters he found behind the drapery, he discovered that they, too, were locked, and further covered with blackout curtains. He was as securely caged as he would have been in Shepton Mallet prison.

He went to the bed and sat down, staring across the room into the cold hearth of the giant fireplace. Danby had let him keep his Zippo and had given him a pack of Luckies: "The only free thing you're going to get from this army, Ten Spot." Dundee lit one, took a deep drag and settled back against the large, green velvet bolster that stood against the headboard of the four-poster, thinking.

He went over the facts again carefully, trying to weave them together into a coherent whole. If Danby was in league with the Germans he supposed most of it now made some kind of sense, but he still wasn't sure he entirely bought the idea. Charlie Danby wasn't anybody's patriot and, in all the time Dundee had known him, he'd never done anything for anyone except himself. It was barely possible that somewhere along the line Danby might have become an ardent Nazi, but somehow he doubted it. Power, cash and maybe his father's real estate holdings, but not strict discipline, jackboots and an oath of loyalty to a madman; that wasn't Charlie's way. Besides, back at the sanitorium he'd referred to Hitler as "just another tin pot dictator." That didn't rate as loyalty in his book.

Then there was the question of his own kidnapping; he seriously doubted that Charlie had done it just to show off to his old schoolmate that he could; bully, liar, cheat and maybe a little bit crazy, but always, above all else, Charlie was smart. There was a reason for everything he did, and there was a reason for this. But what? How did kidnapping a lawyer and investigator from the Judge Advocate General's fit in with a plan to steal the Crown Jewels of England and sell them to the Germans?

Dundee stubbed out his cigarette into the ashtray that sat on the night table beside the bed.

Occleshaw.

The Special Branch cop had been on top of Charlie right from the start; had, in fact, known that Charlie

had somehow managed to get inside Shepton Mallet
and then out again, and had known about the theft
of the jewels. He'd appeared out of the blue and
done everything he could to wave a flag and point
a finger in Charlie's direction. Why?

Bait.

The word stood in Dundee's mind like a blinking
sign. Bait, just like the dead body of a man from
Garrard's Jewelers with gold dust under his fingernails. Bait, like a matchbook cover from J. G. D.
Satchell, Surveyor, Estate Agent & Auctioneer. A
lease taken out in Charlie's name and more gold dust
at the place he rented. The idiotic matchbook that
Jane had found at the tunnel entrance in the basement of the cottage. A trail of bread crumbs that
inevitably led to Shepton Mallet, the Akergill Sanitorium, and finally to this place, by the shores of a loch
in the Scottish Highlands that apparently had nothing to do with any of it. Inch by inch and clue by
glaring clue Charlie had reeled him in like a trout on
the end of one of Jane's fly-fishing lines, but to what
end? Not to convince him of Charlie's divine purpose
in selling out the English crown, and certainly not to
convince him that crime actually paid in the end.

Bait. Occleshaw.

Bait for Occleshaw to nibble on perhaps.

But even if that were true it begged the question
of "Why?" Occleshaw was a cop, and this wasn't a
game of Hare and Hounds, like a dime thriller. Why
give Occleshaw any help along the way?

Frustrated, Dundee threw his legs over the side of
the bed and stood up. Once again he stared at the
man in the painting, wondering who he was and
what momentous occasion had resulted in him pos-

ing for a portrait in full clan regalia in 1603. Some
battle fought and won no doubt, important then but
long since forgotten by everyone, with the possible
exception of the kilted man's descendants.

Dundee glanced at his watch. Almost eight. He
wasn't finding any answers alone in this drafty room.
He went to the immense cupboard beside the bed
and opened the door. There was a light on a chain.
He pulled it and the interior of the cupboard lit up.
A suit of evening clothes was arrayed on several
wooden hangers before him. On the floor there was
a pair of expensive-looking soft leather quarter Wel-
lingtons that looked about his size. Charlie didn't
miss a trick. Dundee took the clothes out of the cupboard and began to dress.

He knocked on the door when he was done and
one of the beefy-looking guards opened it for him.
The man looked him up and down, then turned to
the left and pointed to a staircase at the end of a
wide, paneled hall.

"That way . . . sir." They'd obviously been told to
be polite, but they left no confusion about who was
in charge. Feeling slightly ridiculous in the evening
clothes, Dundee adjusted his black tie and nodded.
He noticed that the guard's place in the hall was
directly across from his door. There was no table and
no book this time; the guard didn't look like the liter-
ary type anyway.

Dundee went down the stairs. The second floor
seemed to be more rooms off a narrow main hall.
Peeking around the banister, he couldn't see any
guards so he walked quickly down the hall and tried
the first door he came to. It was locked, and so were
the next three he tried. Either he was the only guest

at the moment or Charlie was being extremely careful. Dundee abandoned his search and went back to the stairs. He went down to the ground floor.

The old house was substantial, although much less ornate than Akergill Hall had been. The main entrance was small, lit by several pale electric lights in sconces set around the low stone walls. The stone floors were covered with a scattering of dark Axminster rugs of no particular pedigree. If anything, the foyer of the house was a little cramped and not half as grand as Dundee's own room, with the exception of a massive suit of armor clutching some kind of hooked lance in its gauntlet that had been placed at the foot of the stairs against the wall. The ceilings were low; the box beams dark, oppressive oak.

Underneath the front door, manned by another guard, Dundee could hear the soft moaning of the wind blowing up from the loch. Akergill Hall had been built partly as an expression of wealth; this place had been built to guard against the elements. The guard at the door nodded to the right and Dundee could hear voices and laughter from behind a closed pair of pocket doors.

Following the guard's nod, he went and slid open the doors. The room was large, well lit, and paneled in wood, with a fire glowing in a good-sized hearth. A pair of crossed broadswords over a blank shield graced the area over the mantel. Dirks, halberds and axes were displayed on one wall while swords and lances were arranged on the other. It was a room given over to instruments and appliances of violence, all of them gleaming and glittering in the firelight. There wasn't a woman to be seen.

There were a scattering of carpets on an old oak

floor like the one in his room and a number of comfortable upholstered chairs. Against one wall there was a well-stocked bar from which a number of people were serving themselves. A slightly portly man rose from one of the chairs, a glass of brandy in his hand, the flames in the hearth catching the light and turning the amber fluid to fire in his glass.

"Ah, Major Dundee." It was Sir John Gadsby; Dundee wasn't surprised. There were a dozen more people in the room, most wearing evening clothes like Dundee himself and a few in formal kilts. There was no sign of Danby anywhere.

"Where's Charlie?"

"Not here, I'm afraid," said Gadsby. "Pressing business elsewhere. He sends his regrets."

"I see you're not keeping up your little charade any more," said Dundee.

"Charade?" asked Gadsby. Then he smiled, taking a sip from his glass and nodding. "You mean the names."

"David Portal, I think it was. I was supposed to be a Canadian merchant seaman."

"You have a good memory . . . Mr. Portal." Gadsby smiled again. "Can I fetch you a drink?"

"No, thank you," said Dundee.

"Prefer to keep your wits about you, young man?" A scarecrow-thin man wearing a kilt and a ribboned and tartan-edged Glengarry bonnet suddenly appeared beside him. He had a pencil-thin mustache and thin, almost invisible lips. He smelled of Scotch but didn't seem to be feeling its effects the way Gadsby was feeling his brandy. The man had the deep, rolling Scots accent of a born Glaswegian.

"Something like that."

"Mr. William Wier Gilmour," said Gadsby, introducing the skinny man. "The man who founded the Scottish Fascist Party."

"Oh," said Dundee.

"The man standing by the fireplace is William Chambers-Hunter. He was a planter in Ceylon before he returned to join the cause." Dundee turned to look. The man in question was wearing an expensively tailored Saville Row suit with the left arm pinned up. The one-armed man in the "fancy suit" from the cottage in Shepton-Mallet. He tried not to act surprised.

"Cause?" asked Dundee.

"Independence," the psychiatrist said, an animated, excited gleam in his eye. Dundee couldn't tell if he was just drunk or if this was the beginning of some extended joke.

"You don't mean for Scotland, do you?"

"That's exactly what he means, lad," said Gilmour. "Four hundred years living under London's law, four hundred years of bending our back for London's wealth. This war is going to stop it, believe me. Before we succumbed we'd had our own parliament for a thousand years, and our own laws even before that. We'll not offer up our backsides anymore."

"I don't understand," said Dundee, trying not to smile. Was this Charlie's idea of some grand joke, or was he serious? "I always thought Scotland was part of England."

"Even the Romans knew better than that, young man." It was Chambers-Hunter, the one-armed man. He was red-faced, either from drink or standing too close to the fire. His eyes were dark, set above deep pouches, and the flesh hung slackly around his mouth and jawline. His hair was white and thin, and he had a scar running along his cheek from the top of one thick, slightly purplish lip, to his ear. He'd lived a hard life and it showed. His voice when he spoke was surprisingly light and cultured; he sounded like a lecturer in history Dundee had had at West Point. "Hadrian's Wall is more than just a pile of earth and stone, it's a way of thinking; a country is laws, culture, language, arts and industry, all of which are markedly different in Scotland than they are in England. In fact, you prove that yourself; you refer to the English as English and the Scots as Scots." He smiled broadly, showing off a solid-gold molar in the back of his mouth. "I dare say you'll have the Cornishmen in the same position in a few years; you've already got the Welsh talking about their independence. The Irish are already halfway there."

"And it took a revolution to get them on their way," said Gilmour.

"True enough," mused Gadsby, nodding.

Chambers-Hunter gave the psychiatrist a sideways glance and raised a weary eyebrow. He turned back to Dundee. "Look," he said. "We build ships on the Clyde, the best ships in the world mind you, and we build them for everyone, not just the English. That's because the entire world knows that a Scottish ship is the best. Why shouldn't we be allowed some benefit from that? We're not asking for separation from England, just Independence, and it's not the same thing." He smiled again. "The Royal Navy and the Cunard Line will still be able to buy our ships— they'll just have to pay a little more."

"Quite so, quite so," murmured Gadsby. Chambers-Hunter gave him another look. The one-armed man continued his speech, eloquently outlining Scotland's equality, and sometimes its superiority, in subjects such as medicine and various other scholarly pursuits, but Dundee was no longer listening; he'd suddenly seen the elaborate structure of Charlie Danby's plan fall into place and he was mentally kicking himself for not seeing it sooner. It was, in fact, the only explanation for the events of the past few weeks. He'd said it himself when he entered the room; it was all a charade.

A black-garbed servant entered the room and announced that dinner was served. Dinner itself was a set piece of everything from jugged hare and steak and kidney pie to game hen and a bona fide roast suckling pig with an apple in its mouth. For the purists there was a bloated, white haggis, which Gadsby very properly and ceremoniously cut with a sword. Through it all the lecture by Chambers-Hunter and several other guests continued. Dundee heard it all and remembered virtually nothing. He was too intent on what he'd finally figured out about Charles Danby's intentions, particularly as they applied to him.

As he'd suddenly realized just before dinner, the operative word was charade, or maybe more properly it was illusion. Like any magician, Charlie's main objective was to divert attention from what his left hand was doing by making all sorts of fancy motions with his right.

Even before coming to Swan Hill, Occleshaw had clearly already formed an opinion about Dundee, probably due to conversations with other inmates of Shepton Mallet or captured members of Danby's merry little band of deserters; conversations that included Dundee's name either often enough, or in

such a way as to make him and Danby sound like
they were partners in crime. Enough for seeds of
doubt and suspicion to be planted in the Special
Branch cop's head, and enough for him to have managed to collect enough information about him to as-
semble a dossier.

Presumably Occleshaw's intention had been to put
a fire under Dundee so that he'd go running off to
Danby, and on the surface that's exactly what he'd
done. In any court, if it ever got that far—which Dundee strongly doubted—it would look as though he'd
slipped off the train in York, abandoning Jane and
hightailing it off to join his partner. If Occleshaw ever
managed to follow the trail as far as Akergill Hall
and Gadsby's group of mental misfits, all the better,
because Danby was clearly willing to sacrifice the
plump psychiatrist and all his Scottish Nazi friends
for his cause: the cause of Charles Danby. Dundee
had been seen at Akergill Hall, free and unencum-
bered, and he'd been seen here, dressed for dinner
and partaking in debates about Scottish Nationalism.

Enough examination and interrogation in the after-
math and that would come out. Dundee's job, as it
had been from the beginning, was to take the fall. If
Dundee had it figured correctly he wouldn't be
around to defend himself; the best illusion after all,
was a dead one. Sometime soon, after his usefulness
had come to an end, Lucas Alexander Decimus Dundee was going to disappear—permanently.

What wasn't clear in all of this was what Danby
was getting out of the operation. The only thing Dundee knew was that it had to be valuable enough for
Danby to see his whole black-market ring of deserters disappear, not to mention Danby's own vanishing

act; he certainly wasn't going to be able to remain in England, or even the States when all this came out. What single thing was worth giving up your past, your present, your very identity for? Certainly not a sword and a crown.

"Even the sovereign's crown is Scottish," said Gilmour from the far end of the table, popping an olive into his mouth almost triumphantly.

"Quite so," said Gadsby, seated directly across the table from Dundee. "Quite so." It was perfectly clear that he didn't have the slightest idea what the Scottish Fascist was talking about.

"What?" said Dundee, startled as he came out of his long epiphany.

"I believe you have a painting in your room that tells the tale. This very location has a great deal to do with it," said Chambers-Hunter.

"Yes?" said Dundee.

"Yes. In 1603, King James the Fourth ascended the throne of Scotland and of England, where he was known as King James the First. He was in effect a Scottish king who conquered England." He flashed a quick smile. "There's even an ancient prophecy about it."

Gilmour cleared his throat and intoned: "If fates go right, where e'er this stone is found, the Scots as monarchs of that realm be crowned."

"Stone?" said Dundee. It was becoming remarkably like his conversation with Danby in the gun tower about Hitler's love of superstition and legend.

"You may know it as the Stone of Scone, if you know it at all," said Chambers-Hunter. "It was originally supposed to have been Jacob's Pillow on the plains of Luz in Genesis. It was transported from

Ireland to this castle, where it was used in the coronation of Scottish kings until it was taken to Scone in 850. While it was here it was known as the Stone of Destiny. In 1296 Edward the First had it removed to Westminster Abbey, where it remains to this day. The crown that James wore at his coronation remains the personal emblem of the sovereign himself."

"Interesting," murmured Dundee.

They all should be in straitjackets. Stone of Destiny my ass.

Stones and swords and crowns, bundles of wood wrapped around a double-bladed ax, lightning bolts and crooked crosses. Simple, strong symbols for people to grasp. Maybe not so crazy after all. And maybe Charlie was even smarter than I realized, thought Dundee.

Something scratched on the edge of memory, but he couldn't quite find the itch. Instead, he begged to be excused, citing fatigue. No one seemed to care one way or the other. Conversation was moving around to golf as he left the table; Dundee had more important things on his mind, like getting out of Dunstaffnage with his life.

Twenty-six

He went back to his room, his keeper locking the door securely behind him. A cigarette and a few moments of pacing and running through the facts again made him positive that his theory was correct. One, Charlie would never be fool enough to commit himself or anything else to the likes of Sir John Gadsby, supposedly a Scots Nationalist but vain enough to allow himself to kneel before a British king for the sake of a knighthood. Two, Charlie wouldn't risk his neck and his freedom inside Shepton Mallet Prison for the sake of a few anachronistic old pieces of jewelry, no matter what kind of price Hitler or any of his minions put on them. Three, above all he simply wouldn't have gone to so much trouble; the easy way was Charlie's way, and this little escapade was nothing short of what his grumpy old history teacher at West Point would have called Byzantine: plots within plots within plots. Something else was going on here and Dundee was in a position where he could do something about it, if he could get out of here alive. And that, of course, led directly to: Four. Dundee's appearance in Akergill and at this place was for show; he was meant to be seen and remembered, and then he was meant to disappear. There might even be informers among the staff, reporting what was going on to someone like Occleshaw. He had to get out of here before it was too late.

Which wasn't going to happen in evening clothes; the days when spies wore tuxedos, smoked cigarettes in long ivory holders and wore monocles was long gone. He stripped off his formal wear, slipped into his "David Portal, merchant-mariner" outfit and went to the cupboard. The mental itch he'd been trying to scratch presented itself again, this time taking the shape of a name: Evelyn, the English boy he'd befriended long ago at school. A book. Not an adventure, something a little more girlish than that, something that could get the boy in such terribly deep dung that he'd gone so far as to bury it in a tin box in the woods behind the stables. A gift from his parents in India, off on some Foreign Office assignment. What the hell was its name and why was he thinking of it now of all times? The author's name was there, surprisingly enough: P. L. Travers.

Mary Poppins.

A nanny in Victorian London who flew around with the aid of a magic umbrella. Chimney sweeps. Somehow Charlie had found little Evelyn's hiding place and any hopes the kid had of surviving within the school vanished. Even kids smaller than he was began to taunt him. Within a month he was sent to some relative living in Canada.

Dundee hung the tuxedo jacket up. What did the shameful expulsion of a little boy from a school in California have to do with his situation in Scotland today? He looked up and found the chain for the light switch and paused. Above the glare from the light he could see the faint outline of a plank trap-door in the ceiling.

It wasn't something you saw much of in places like Santa Barbara or L.A., but it was common enough in Northern California and Oregon: the trapdoor led to an attic or a crawl space, usually with peat moss or some other insulator packed between the roof beams. The kind of place where he and his cousin from Seattle used to go to smoke cigarettes.

Chimney sweeps.

Jacob's Pillow on the Plains of Luz in Genesis.

Jacob's Ladder.

And then he had it.

He went to the door and listened. No sound at all from the guard on the opposite side of the hall. What did he think about sitting there? Memories, women, food, drink, money? Did he do arithmetic problems in his head, count sheep, make lists of things to do and places to go when he won big at the track? Or nothing? Probably nothing, thought Dundee. He didn't really care, as long as he stayed on the other side of the door. Turning away he looked around the room for what he needed. He picked up a chair that stood by a small writing table on the far side of the room, placing it underneath the trapdoor in the cupboard. He climbed up on it and reached. Not quite high enough; his fingers only brushed the ceiling of the enclosure. He went back out into the room and looked again. Nothing. He went into the bathroom and saw the answer immediately. There was a small utilitarian footstool beside an enormous tin bathtub that had its own built-in coal fire to heat the water. No wonder they called the Scots a hardy breed.

Dundee picked up the footstool, took it back to the

cupboard and put it on top of the chair. Without stopping to think too long about what he was doing, he clambered onto the chair and then up to a precarious perch on the footstool. Trying to make as little noise as possible he lifted up the underside of the trapdoor with his fingertips, then pushed it to one side. His nostrils suddenly filled with musty, age-old dust and he strained with the effort of not letting out an enormous sneeze. Obviously, no one had been up there in a very long time. When the feeling passed he gripped the sides of the trap and boosted himself up.

He looked back down into the cupboard. The chair and the footstool made it obvious where he had gone and for a minute he thought of going back down, closing the door and switching off the light before going through the ordeal again, but finally decided against it; doing so would probably save him no more than a minute or two in any thorough search. That wasn't enough.

He stood up and looked around. The attic was enormous, running the length and breadth of the house. Twenty feet or so behind his room Dundee could see a narrow flight of steps that probably led to a small storeroom or vestibule at the far end of the hall. Other than that there didn't seem to be any other access to the attic except through a chain of trapdoors, one for each of the rooms leading off the hallway and marked by narrow plank gangways that ran across the beams.

He'd been right about the insulation; the area between the massive, hand-adzed oak beams was filled with peat moss or something like it, and the area between the struts holding up the roof had been jammed with straw and then lathed and plastered over. In dozens of places the plaster had crumbled and straw oozed out of the holes in great, tumbling masses. The only light came from the open trapdoor at his feet.

Dundee looked around, pleased with what he saw. The place was a firetrap for anyone of a mind to take advantage of conditions that looked as though they hadn't changed perceptibly in the last two or three hundred years. In half a dozen islands on either side of a central walkway, planks had been laid over the joists and beams and all sorts of junk had been placed on these platforms in no particular order. Old luggage, chairs, tables, glass-chimneyed hurricane lamps, old rope, bundles of musty clothing, paper-wrapped framed objects tied up with string. Oddly, though, there was something missing—no matter where he looked there was nothing that indicated that a child had ever occupied the house. No old rocking chair, no broken high chair, no crib, no old doll, eyeless and abandoned. It was as though this had always been a place for adults, even though that didn't quite seem possible.

Dundee carefully made his way down the central plank walkway, moving slowly, taking care not to make any noise. If he was figuring it right the plank walkway mimicked the hallway underneath, which meant that he was walking directly over the guard's head. Eventually he made it to the end of the attic and the massive stone-and-brick construction of the central fireplace.

He put out his hand and laid it flat on the brick flue; it was hot, which meant that it was probably directing heat and smoke from the main fireplace in the sitting room. Bending down, he looked around at the base of the flue but it was too dark to see anything at all. He went back to the first of the junk-filled islands, carefully rummaging through it until he found what he wanted. Sitting on a trunk he found a hurricane lamp with an inch or so of kerosene left in its glass reservoir. He took off the chimney, tipped the glass slightly to put kerosene onto the dangling wick and lit it with his Zippo. Trimming the wick with the little wheel on the side of the neck, he replaced the chimney and carried the bright light back to the fireplace. Suddenly everything sprung into sharp relief. Dundee found what he'd hoped and prayed for ever since he'd thought of the fanciful governess with the magic umbrella and her chimney sweep friends.

The average house with a fireplace in the States didn't really need the services of a chimney sweep, but it was easy enough to hire a man to come and clean the bird's nests and old leaves out of the chimney proper and then use a long-handled wire brush to get out as much of the soot as possible. A large house with more than one fireplace, and burning coal rather than wood, like his cousin's house in the wealthy Schmitz Park area of Seattle, might make use of a sweep from time to time. Dundee thought back to the day when he and his cousin had been enjoying a couple of ersatz smokes made out of rolled pages of a Bible they'd found in the attic and some Briggs Mixture they'd filched from his old man's study. Suddenly a Negro's head had popped out of nowhere a foot or so away, at the base of the chimney that stood against the attic wall. The black man was carrying an assortment of flue-cleaning tools and climbing what he referred to as "Jacob's Ladder," a

series of U-shaped bolts built into the side of the
chimney that went from the basement to the roof
within a narrow chamber that allowed the man to
clamber through the house without disturbing the
occupants while he worked. More importantly, it en-
sured that the only person who got covered with soot
was himself. The chimney sweep, after explaining his
magical appearance, took a few drags on their foul-
smelling cigarettes, thanked them and disappeared
again.

Dundee and his cousin then spent the rest of the
day crawling around in the flues, getting themselves
absolutely filthy with soot and eventually incurring
the good-natured wrath of his uncle who was far
angrier about the missing Briggs Mixture than he was
about the state of the boys' clothes.

Dundee stared down into the dark maw of the narrow chamber beside the main structure of the chimney, remembering. He grinned in the hot, steady
light from the hurricane lantern; who'd have thought
someone named Mary Poppins would come to his
rescue? He turned and gave one last look down the
length of the attic, muttered a brief curse directed at
Charles Danby and tossed the hurricane lantern into
the nearest pile of junk. The glass chimney smashed
and the reservoir of kerosene rolled under a pile of
carpets bundled in one corner, spilling dribbles of
fuel as it went. There was a brief pause and then a
huge sound like the breathless cough of some huge
beast. A wall of fire leapt up to the beams and plaster
overhead, instantly igniting the old, rotten hay.
Within a few seconds the entire bone-dry, dusty attic
was engulfed in flames.

A great howling sheet of fire came racing simultaneously along the floor and ceiling of the attic in Dundee's direction, absorbing everything in its path. He ducked down the iron ladder and disappeared; a minute or so later, covered in soot and smelling of creosote the same way he had that long-ago day in Seattle, he tumbled out of the Jacob's Ladder and into the cavernous basement of Dunstaffnage House. It took him another minute or so to locate the old coal chute, crawling across an ancient pile of old clinkers and bags of coal delivered by boat from the village.

With the first muffled shouts of "fire" coming from the floor above, Dundee crawled up the chute and ducked out of the basement, coal dust clotting his lungs and making him fight for breath in the cool night air. He stumbled away from the house and looked back. He could see gouts of smoke coming out of the upper-floor windows and flames shooting up out of gaping holes in the slate roof, tiles exploding like stony grenades as the flames ignited pockets of ancient air trapped in the slates. The fire had obviously reached down into the top floor as well; draperies had burst into flames and now the old mullioned windows were exploding as well, blasting shards of glass in all directions. Out of the corner of his eye Dundee could see the first people beginning to stumble out of the front door, followed by clouds and billows of smoke spilling out of the house and into the night air. He ran.

Stumbling down the narrow path he suddenly realized he didn't have the slightest idea where he was going; when he'd come in with Danby they came down a narrow flight of stairs from the landing strip, which had been carved out of the stone outcrop the house rested on. His senses told him that he was now moving away at right angles, the rocks visible like a black wall on his right, the loch on his left, its riffled waters a dozen yards away, separated from him by a steep, rocky beach. Directly ahead, vaguely seen in the distance through a scraggly patch of weather-beaten Scotch pine, he could see the lights of the village, Connel.

He stumbled as the ground began to rise and nearly lost his footing on a scree of loose stone at the base of a huge old tree, long dead, its main trunk almost touching the ground, its broad upper limbs naked and skeletal in the moonlight. A figure loomed up, rising behind the tree. Whoever it was, he had a gun and it was pointed at Dundee's midriff. Dundee groaned. He'd walked right into one of Danby's guards, probably stealing a minute to relieve himself.

"Bloody hell, Ian! You've stepped on my hand!" A second figure rose from behind the tree, taller than the first and bigger all around. He certainly didn't sound like any kind of guard, but he, too, had a gun. "Bugger!" he said. The hand without the gun was waving in the air.

"Jesus!" said the slighter of the two men, staring open-mouthed at Dundee. "Gangway foah de Lawd Jehovah!" he said in broad Negro dialect with an overtone of English Public School. Definitely not a guard.

"What are you going on about, Ian?" said the second man.

"Rex Ingram, you twit. *Green Pastures.*"

"That was about Welsh choir boys or something," grumbled the second man. The first man stepped over the tree trunk and approached Dundee.

"You really should go to the pictures more often Peter. That was *How Green was My Valley*. Five Academy Awards."

Earlier in the evening he'd found himself wondering about the sanity of the guests at dinner; now he was wondering about his own. It was like one of those farces that the BBC put on. The first man stopped in front of Dundee and shook his head, looking him up and down. "You are a sight." Dundee looked down at himself. Like his twelve-year-old self he was black with soot. Now he understood the reference to *Green Pastures*.

The second, larger man eased himself over the tree trunk and crunched across the wet stone, one eye keeping a lookout over Dundee's shoulder at the burning house. "I'm not the Americaphile, Ian. I don't collect these little facts and I don't particularly like American films." He joined his companion. In the moonlight Dundee could see that the men were both carrying large .45 automatics.

"You're Lucas Dundee, the American major, aren't you?" He paused. "Underneath the blackface, I mean."

"That's right. Who the hell are you?"

"Oh, I'm terribly sorry," said the man, extending his free hand. "Fleming, Ian Fleming." He nodded to the man beside him. "This is my brother Peter." He smiled pleasantly. "I'm a friend of Jane's, by the way, in case you were wondering." He pointed toward the water. "We've got a boat down there; follow us and you can make your escape."

The boat turned out to be a tiny dinghy barely large enough for two, let alone three, powered by an equally tiny "Swift" Electric outboard motor powered by an automobile battery. It was, however, almost completely silent, and they puttered up the loch to the village of Connel without a sound, leaving the burning mansion behind them. Once in the village they found Fleming's car, a massive, open touring, three liter, supercharged Bentley. Within half an hour of boosting himself into the attic of Dunstaffnage House, Lucas Dundee found himself in a room at an inn called The Sword and The Crown in the town of Oban, changing into a pair of Ian Fleming's corduroy shooting trousers and pulling one of the slim man's Navy-issue roll-neck sweaters over his head.

Face and hands washed and wearing clean clothes, Dundee left Fleming's room at the inn and went down to the ground floor. The inn was a plain, two-story affair on Shore Street, across the road from a spread of a dozen or so railroad tracks that abutted the railway station and Railroad Quay, Oban's main pier. Looming over everything close to the pier, including the inn, were three squat coastal steamers from Scottish Trader Lines, *Hebrides Trader*, *Oban Trader* and the largest of the three, *Inverary Trader*. Mist was beginning to roll off the bay, wrapping the stout vessels in heavy gray shrouds. Somewhere a foghorn started to boom out its mournful call.

Dundee crossed the small, low-ceilinged foyer and went into the public room off to the left. It was past eleven and, by rights, the bar and the kitchen should have been closed, but somehow Fleming had managed to convince the innkeeper otherwise. The naval intelligence officer and his brother were seated in a narrow, high-backed booth beside a window that overlooked the railway tracks, working their way through a pint of Courage each, and huge servings of warmed-over steak and kidney pie. Fleming waved his fork in the air and Dundee crossed the room to join them. They appeared to be the only people in the place with the exception of the inn-keeper, swabbing out pint mugs with a rag and whis-tling tunelessly to himself. Dundee sat down, sliding into the booth beside the older Fleming. The inn-keeper threw the rag across his shoulder, flipped open a pass-through in the bar and approached them. He asked what Dundee wanted. Dundee looked down at the Flemings' heavily burdened plates, thought about the dinner he'd had earlier in the eve-ning and settled for coffee. The innkeeper nodded silently and went away. He came back a moment later with something the color of mud.

"Last o' the cream and there's nae sugar," said the man, then went away. Dundee sipped. It tasted like hot iron filings in a cup.

"What exactly were you doing out there by the lake?" asked Dundee.

"Loch," said Fleming. "We were waiting to see what would happen. We knew you were in there; we just didn't know what to do about it."

"You knew?"

"Of course," said Peter Fleming. He looked to be seven or eight years older than his brother. From the lines and crow's feet on his face he'd apparently led a harder life. "We've been on your trail since York."

Dundee stared. "You knew I'd been kidnapped?"

"Certainly," said Ian Fleming. His face clouded. "Unfortunately, one of Danby's people appeared to get wind of it. The woman we had following you went back on the train to inform Miss Todd, and they killed her. Penny, that is, not Miss Todd."

"Penny?" said Dundee.

"She was one of our best," said Peter Fleming. "Her code name was Monet."

"You've lost me," said Dundee. "Who is *we* and why do you need code names?"

"Peter works for our Special Operations Executive, rather like your OSS. Monet was one of his people. She called herself Monet but the rest of the staff on Baker Street called her Money—uneducated clods. Her real name was Penny so that's what I called her—Moneypenny." His face darkened again. "Dying on a mission somewhere in a war zone is one thing—being murdered on a train in your own country is something else again."

"Back up," said Dundee. He took another sip of the ghastly coffee, then pushed it away. "Why were you tailing me and Jane?"

"Because we were, and still are, in a rather tricky political situation," said Peter Fleming. "An American like Danby involved in an atrocious crime and our own Special Branch convinced that you were in league with him? Two bad apples."

"So you thought I'd lead you to Charlie, one way or the other?"

"Something of the sort, yes. We already knew most of what we needed to know about the man, of course, we just rather wanted to roll up the whole business, your friend Charlie included. Bit of a rogue so to speak, gotten away from his own people as well from what we can gather. We almost had him when he flew in with you earlier, but we were a little too late because he flew right out again. He's been sighted on Mull."

"Mull?"

"A rather large island eight miles across the sound.

There's an airstrip on the isthmus between Salen and Loch na Keal. The Loch of Cliffs," he added, translating.

Dundee looked at him curiously. "Did you say Salen, or Salem?"

"Salen," said Ian Fleming. "Why? Do you know it?"

Dundee didn't answer. He looked beyond the younger Fleming to the old fireplace next to the bar. A poor copy of the painting over the fireplace in his room at Dunstaffnage House hung over the mantel, complete with the Crown and Sword from which the inn took its name. Dundee shook his head. It was all getting far too complex for him to take in. Ian Fleming finished his meal. He took an ornately enameled cigarette tin out of his jacket pocket. There was a picture of a vaguely oriental woman staring out of a window on the top. Fleming popped off the lid and offered Dundee one of the slightly oval cigarettes inside, lighting it for him with a gold Dunhill.

"They're Russian," said the younger Fleming airily. "Samokish of Moscow. My tobacconist in Burlington Arcade keeps them for me." He smiled. "God knows where he gets them these days." His brother threw him a withering look but Ian appeared not to notice.

Dundee took a puff. It was awful. Coffee like iron filings and tobacco like camel shit. He took a deep drag anyway. "I'm not sure I really get it," he said. "I'm helping to track down the guy who's stolen some of your crown jewels and that makes it a 'tricky political situation'?"

"Winston would seem to think so," said Peter Fleming.

"Winston?"

"Churchill. Prime Minister," the older brother said blandly.

"We're talking about crown jewels, not state secrets. And what in God's name does it have to do with Bill Donovan?" Dundee laughed.

"I'm afraid this has never been about the crown jewels," said Peter Fleming, "and I'm afraid it has everything to do with Donovan and state secrets, ours and yours."

"Donovan? How do you figure that?" scoffed Dundee.

"Didn't you know?" said Ian Fleming, obviously surprised. "Charles Danby worked for him."

Twenty-seven

Mull is an island of mountains and rough moorland, of forested glens and headland cliffs, of bare peninsulas and rocky coves measuring twenty-five miles by twenty between its farthest points, with a population of approximately fifteen hundred, most of them fishermen and sheep farmers, all of them cut from the same hardy Hebridean cloth that must clothe anyone intending to live in such a lonely and unappetizing place. All of its sheltered ports lie on its east coast. To the northeast lie the Morvern Hills, a mile or so across the Sound of Mull. To the west there is only the open sea. Looming over everything in the center of the island is the great black shape of Ben More, the island's tallest point.

The wooded village of Salen lies on the bay of the same name, facing the Morvern Hills and the Sound, situated on the isthmus of low, heavily forested land in birch and ash and oak that divides Mull's northern head from its mountainous body. On the other side of the isthmus is Loch na Keal, the Loch of Cliffs, a deep indentation that comes in from the sea to the west, thousand-foot sheer cliffs coming off Ben More and knifing directly into the dark, deep and forbidding water.

Small steamers call at Salen on their regular runs but mostly it is a fishing village, a recent addition to the island, having been developed in the early 1800s by Lachlan McQuarrie, the so-called Father of Australia, who bought an estate there on retiring. The village has a single road that also serves as High Street, a post office and a small hotel of ten rooms, the oddly named Tangle of the Islands. Just beyond the village a single-lane dirt track leads through the woods and across the isthmus to the abandoned hamlet of Killichroman, its half-dozen tumbledown huts and cottages sitting just above a span of pebbled beach that leads down to the waters of Loch na Keal. To the left of the settlement are the towering cliffs of Gribun, and above, the heavily wooded slopes of Ben More.

Jane Todd sat in the small, overheated dining room of the Tangle as the locals called it, smoking another cigarette, wondering what to do next. With the funny little ornithologist's help they had apparently slipped through Occleshaw's net and eventually made their way here. It was incredible luck more than anything else. Bond, the ornithologist, was on his way to Mull, intent on completing his latest field guide, *Birds of the Western Highlands*, and he was more than happy to take them there. He seemed very enthusiastic about a new edition of his birds of the West Indies, particularly Jamaica, which he intended to complete as soon as the present political situation allowed.

His intention was to make his way around Mull

in a boat he'd hired for the purpose, something he called a Thorneycroft, which seemed to surprise Angus because of its size. Apparently the boat in question was a forty-two-foot motor cruiser whose design had been used to produce the Royal Navy's MTB, or Motor Torpedo Boat. Somehow he'd managed to get the fuel coupons for it, or knew who to bribe to get them.

The owl-eyed bird-watcher quickly allayed any of Angus's fears by telling him he had much the same kind of boat at his home on the Beaulieu River in Hampshire and that he had, in fact, taken part in the rescue at Dunkirk. He would circumnavigate the island taking pictures and making his sketches, and if Angus and Jane were still there when he returned he'd be glad to take them back to the mainland. In the meantime they were welcome to use his automobile, considering all the trouble he'd caused them on the road to Oban. Bond had left from Tobermory early the previous morning, waving from the cabin of his boat, *Lady Beryl II*, as he slipped out of the harbor and headed into the sound. Taking his car they'd driven down the ten-mile stretch of country road to Salen.

She finished her third cup of weak, milky-sweet tea and her fourth cigarette since finishing breakfast, then checked her watch. It was past nine and Angus was still using the large clawfoot tub in his room. They'd been in the hotel for less than a day and he'd already had at least three baths. She lit another cigarette and stared out the window overlooking Salen Bay. In the distance, on the far point of the bay, she could see the ruins of an old castle, stark against the steel gray, overcast sky. They were almost out of time and she was running out of ideas.

"I'm not goddamn Nancy Drew," she muttered to herself, sipping cold tea, then inhaling deeply on her cigarette.

"It's not right," said a voice in a broad, rolling brogue. She looked up, startled. It was Tommy, the innkeeper's nephew, a young boy from Edinburgh. He was twelve or thirteen, big for his age, with heavily muscled wrists and a broad chest. The wrists came from his previous job of milkman's assistant and the chest was apparently the result of a mail-order bodybuilding course. He had a very adult-looking and expensive tattoo of a leaping tiger on his right forearm and, according to his uncle, he preferred to be called "Shane" after the Jack Schaeffer novel, which the boy was rarely seen without. His handsome young face, with intense hazel eyes and dark, bushy eyebrows, was set in a perpetual scowl, either as a result of his age or the fact that he'd been shipped off to his uncle's hotel in Salen for the duration of the war, or perhaps both.

"What's not right . . . Shane?" she said, remembering the nickname.

"I heard you asking my uncle about the tides and he didn't know. So I found out."

"And?"

"It's not right, like I said . . . Jane." His eyes got that smoldering look she'd seen before and she was startled to realize that this big, muscle-bound boy was actually flirting with her. Well, good for him, she thought. And good luck. Not that he'd need it with his looks, but he certainly wasn't going to find many targets for Cupid's bow on the Isle of Mull.

"I telephoned Mr. Gorman in the fisheries office. He said no one's asked him for the tide tables for

Staffa since the war. Doubts any one's been there in that long except the odd torpedoed Nazi. Ka-pow!" he added, pointing his index finger at her like a cocked gun. "Anyway, high tide on Staffa is at 4:00 A.M. and 2:00 P.M."

"That'll be enough of that, Tommy Connery," said the innkeeper's wife, bustling up and changing Jane's overflowing ashtray for a fresh one. She turned to Jane and smiled. "If he gives you any trouble, Miss Todd, you just give him a good swat on the fundament and send him packing." She turned to the boy. "Didn't I tell you to bring in those kegs?!"

"Yes, Auntie," said the boy.

"He's got some information I've been looking for. It's all right, Mrs. Maclean."

"Well, that's all right, then." But she didn't looked convinced. "More tea then, Miss Todd?"

"Sure, why not," said Jane. The woman nodded, wiped her hands on her snow-white apron, and headed back into the kitchen.

"It's not the tides around here, either," said the boy. "I checked that too. Nothing even close to midnight for high tides on Mull. Eight or nine in the morning this time of the year, depending on where you are. Seven or eight in the evening. That's when the excursion steamers go back to Oban."

"Shit," said Jane and she stubbed out her cigarette.

The boy looked startled at her use of a swear word. "Beg pardon, miss?"

"Nothing. Thanks for the information."

"Right-oh," said the boy. He flexed his forearm so that the tiger seemed to jump out at her, then winked. He turned and sauntered away, the paper-bound Western peeking out of the back pocket of his trousers.

"Now what?" said Jane. Tweedsmuir had seemed so sure, and his explanation fit all the facts: the exchange would be made at Fingal's Cave on the Island of Staffa at midnight tonight. But somehow either the facts or the explanation were wrong. *Something* was going to happen today at midnight, *somewhere*. On top of that was the fact that Dundee was still missing. She knew in her heart that he was probably either dead, or he'd been part of the whole plot, right from the beginning, just like Occleshaw thought.

She frowned into her empty teacup and lit yet another cigarette. Outside the weather was closing in, the leaden skies meeting the equally gray horizon, snatches of rain gusting icily against the window glass. In the distance the shadow of the ruined castle on the point had almost disappeared.

It was all wrong; her instincts about people were usually good and the only thing she'd picked up from Dundee was an irritating case of lust. She seriously doubted that there was a devious bone in his body: *Mr. Smith Goes to Washington* in a uniform. On the other hand, he seemed to have a pretty low opinion of her, assuming that she was spying on him for Donovan. Then he disappears into the blue, or actually into the dead of night, presumably at Charles Danby's request. Why would Danby want him dead, and more importantly, how did Charles Danby know that Dundee was on that train? She might have put it all down to a nightmare if it hadn't been for the dead woman in her bedroom. Where did she fit into all of this? She sighed, clambered into the old belted-tweed coat Tweedsmuir had given her and went out into the stinging rain. Putting up the collar of the coat, she headed down the high street to the crossroads by the beach.

A big Harley-Davidson WLA was at the corner, its goggled and uniformed driver checking the signs. There were a rifle bucket and siren in front of the windscreen and heavy-duty box-style courier panniers over the rear wheel. The words Military Police were stenciled in white on the windscreen. As he turned to glance at her, Jane saw the letters MP on his helmet. The man looked away, kicked the big bike into gear and turned down the narrow track to Killichroman.

She wondered what an American Military Policeman was doing in an out-of-the-way spot like Mull; probably looking for one of Danby's deserters, or some love-struck kid who'd gone AWOL for the affections of some equally love-struck young Highland girl. Jane turned in the opposite direction, toward the pier and the beach, putting it out of her mind; she had bigger problems, not the least of which was figuring out who she should tell about her situation before it was too late. In a few hours the crown jewels would be gone and she had to do something to stop that from happening. She walked out onto the pier, where there were half a dozen fishing boats tied up, taking off boxes of flounder and curved traps full of dark-shelled lobster. They'd been out since dawn and they were already back, eager to get out of the rain. Jane noticed that the majority of the men were in their forties, fifties or even older, the war was taking its toll, even here. She stood and watched them for a minute as they unloaded the catch. Then she made up her mind. She and Angus couldn't do any more alone, and the only person left was Occleshaw. She'd go back to the hotel, find out where the local cops were and give herself up. The local constabulary could call Scotland Yard and they in turn could get to Special Branch; it was the only way, no matter what kind of trouble it got her into.

She turned around and ran directly into Commander Ian Fleming, Royal Navy Volunteer Reserve. He was wearing a navy pea jacket and an able seaman's knit cap. He looked quite roguish, which, if Jane knew her man, was the desired effect, especially on women.

"Hallo, Jane." He grinned. He nodded to his left. "I think this is the man you want to be bumping into." She turned and looked; he was wearing rubber boots, a navy sweater and baggy pants. He looked as though he hadn't slept in ages, and he appeared to have soot under his fingernails. He looked ridiculous.

"Lucas!" she breathed. Laughing, she threw her arms around the man and kissed him, hard.

Twenty-eight

The three had come in out of the rain and were sitting beside the fire in the pub at the Tangle. Tommy Connery had descended into the basement through a trapdoor and could be heard wrestling the heavy kegs of ale into position under the brass plumbing that ran down from the ivory taps. Fleming was drinking gin against the chill and Jane had convinced Tommy's aunt to make coffee for her and Dundee. She sat beside the major, her leg pressed up against his from ankle to thigh underneath the small table. He didn't make the slightest attempt to do anything about it. A few feet away a bay window looked out onto the high street. The misting rain was still blowing in from the sea, turning the panes to slow-running tears that carved weeping paths down to the bottom of the glass.

"We figured most of this out last night in Oban after I burned down Danby's mansion by the loch," said Dundee. "The rest of it fell into place while we were on the ferry coming over here this morning."

"Burning down a mansion? You've been busy."

"I've had quite a time, that's for sure. How about you?" Dundee smiled.

"Remind me to tell you sometime. Tell me if you want to start with the woman getting the pencil stuck in her eye, or the man shooting at me while I was hanging under a bridge about five hundred feet in the air." At the mention of Moneypenny's brutal murder Fleming frowned and the line of his jaw hardened. Jane sensed that at one time or another the woman on the train had been more to him than just an acquaintance.

He took a long swallow of gin and put his glass down on the table firmly. "I really think we should be getting on. We're going to have serious problems unless we figure out this last bit."

"You're right. Shoot," said Dundee.

Fleming turned his attention to Jane. "Have you ever heard of a man named Alan Turing?"

"No."

"Bletchley Park?"

"No."

"Tube Alloys?"

"No," said Jane, and she laughed. "What are you talking about, Commander?"

Fleming rubbed his thumb across the side of his glass and stared into the clear contents as though he somehow expected to find answers in the gin. "Alan Turing has invented rather a special kind of machine," he said, collecting his thoughts. "It's given us a leg up on the German military codes. Several legs up, actually. Several years ago, right at the start of the war, your friend Morris Black was investigating a series of murders. A German spy named The Doctor became involved; it all gets rather complicated after that. The point is, Hitler almost found out we'd cracked his bloody codes, and it was really only blind luck and your friend Morris who saved Britain's bacon, so to speak." He paused, letting out a long breath, then took another belt of gin. "I could probably be sacked for telling you all this, but it's too late for that now."

"I promise not to say a thing," said Jane.

Fleming snorted. "The word of a journalist!"

"Go on," snapped Dundee. "We both know she's more than that."

"All right." Fleming cleared his throat. "Part of the problem then, one of the key problems, was that all of Turing's activities, and the work done by the people at Bletchley Park who were actually breaking the codes, was put on file at the PRO, the Public Records Office. We have the same problem again, except now it's Tube Alloys as well."

"*What* are Tube Alloys?" said Jane, a little perplexed.

Fleming shrugged his narrow shoulders. "I'm not entirely sure, but it seems to be something even more important than Mr. Turing's invention. I've been advised that one or the other, or both, are capable of winning the war for us, or losing it if word gets out. Unfortunately, that's what's happened."

"What about the Crown and the Sword? I thought we were chasing after the crown jewels?"

"Quite." Fleming nodded. "Which was exactly what Danby wanted all of us to think. Meanwhile he was sneaking Turing's code-breaking information and Tube Alloys out the back door. Or front door as it turns out." Fleming finished his gin. "One doesn't bother closing the stable door after the prize stallion has run off, so it makes it all the easier to steal the mare, if you see what I mean."

"A diversion?"

"I'm afraid so. There's some evidence he was going to try to pawn off a copy of the jewels to Schellenberg and the rest of Hitler's louts, but the secret materiel was going to be auctioned off in Switzerland.

"It turns out that Charlie was working for Donovan, almost from the start. After a trip to Germany he tried to turn his own father in to the FBI, and when they weren't interested he went to Wild Bill. When the opportunity came up they asked him to infiltrate the fascist organizations in England that were busy helping the Germans. He jumped at the chance, but in the end the idea of making money out of it was too much temptation for the son of a bitch. He knew the files on the code-breaking activities would be worth millions to the Nazis, and even more if he sold them back to the British. The same's true with this Tube Alloys thing, but apparently we're the buyers for that one. The way it looks, the States is way ahead on this kind of research and we want to keep it to ourselves; we certainly don't want Hitler getting his hands on it."

"So where is Danby?" asked Jane.

"He's here, on Salen, but nobody knows where," said Fleming. "We found the landing strip a mile or so up the road; a field by the ruins of some place called Aros Castle. I've left my brother Peter there to question the locals."

Dundee turned to Jane, smiling. "You were right about that matchbook cover you found in the old woman's cottage. Chambers-Hunter probably used it as a reminder and then lost it."

"Chambers-Hunter?" said Jane.

"The one-armed Scotsman. He seems to have been the one leading that end of things. They weren't like Charlie—the people are amateurs, zealots to boot. They make mistakes. I think Charlie was even counting on it."

Jane took out her wallet and slipped the match-book cover out of it. She stared down at it, then pushed it into the middle of the table. "Well," she said, "one thing's for sure—we've only got until midnight before Charles Danby disappears for good."

Fleming reached out and picked up the small, grimy clue. He flipped it open, then paled. "That's not midnight," he said quietly. "That's noon." He dropped it back on the table. Dundee's hand jerked forward and he picked it up, staring at it.

"Christ! He's right."

Fleming checked his watch, a complicated-looking RAF Rolex with a mesh cage arching over the crystal like a fencing helmet. "That means we've only got an hour or so."

Tommy came up out of the basement, a huge, empty metal ale barrel on his shoulder. He was whistling and panting simultaneously. He pushed out from behind the bar and dropped the barrel with a thump.

"Bloody hell," he groaned, looking around casually to see if anyone was watching. He flexed his arms, the tiger leaping.

"Now what do we do?" said Jane. "Tommy checked for me. H. T. doesn't mean high tide; the times are all wrong."

Dundee kept staring down at the matchbook cover. He looked up and glanced at the overgrown boy struggling with the barrel, then back at the match-book. "H. T." he muttered. He looked at young Con-nery again. "Tommy?"

"Yes, sir?"

"When the coastal steamers come in to Salen, where do they anchor?"

"They don't," the boy said promptly. "Too shal-low, at least for the bigger ones." He shrugged his broad shoulders and sat down on top of the upended barrel to rest for a moment. "You'll get the odd ex-cursion boat, but they're wee."

"What about the ships from Scottish Trader Lines?"

"Too big, by half," said Tommy, shaking his head.

"The ships berthed by the pier in Oban last night?" asked Fleming, suddenly interested. Dundee nodded.

"They don't come here at all?" said Dundee.

"No, sir," said Connery. "There's a great bloody drop off you see; at least according to my uncle, who used to be a fisherman. A cliff underwater, like. Goes from a hundred fathoms to ten, all in a blink. So the big ships anchor in the loch and any cargo gets brought in by truck."

"The loch?" said Jane

Tommy nodded, jerking a thumb over his shoul-der. "Aye. Loch na Keal. You just turn at the cross-roads and go down the road for about two miles. Dead easy. It's plenty deep enough for them to get in close and there's the old landing place there." He grinned. "I go out to the old village on me bike to play sometimes, there's no one about and . . ." He stopped abruptly, suddenly realizing he'd used the word "play," which certainly wasn't in Shane's vocabulary. He picked up the empty barrel and slung it over his shoulder, then marched out of the room, the scowl back on his face.

"H. T." Dundee murmured. "*Hebrides Trader.* I saw her last night in Oban," he said quietly, looking at the matchbook cover. "He's meeting the ship in the loch at noon."

"You were right," said Jane, remembering. "It was the safest way; put the Crown and the Sword on a coastal steamer from Bristol to an out-of-the-way spot up here."

"No, that's not it," said Dundee obscurely. "But the ship will be there at noon, I'm sure of it."

"And Danby?" asked Fleming "What about him?"

Jane glanced out the window beside her, staring out into the rain, suddenly understanding. "I can tell you that," she said flatly. "I saw him about an hour ago."

The innkeeper's battered and sea-salt-rusted old estate wagon hurtled down the narrow road that cut across the isthmus that separated the Sound of Mull from Loch na Keal. Beyond the forest that lay directly behind the village, the narrow neck of land was more like some of the moors that Jane had recently found herself on; the land was barren, a few shrubs and hedgerows here and there but not even enough grass for a few sheep to forage on.

"You're sure?" said Fleming urgently from behind the wheel.

"Who the hell else would be driving a Harley and wearing an MP's uniform?" asked Jane in the seat behind him. In the cargo space behind her an assortment of tools and old junk rattled and banged as the old car smashed into one pothole after another; obviously the road wasn't used very often. Fleming gave the wheel a sudden jerk to avoid a large boulder in the road and they slewed into the shallow ditch for a moment. He corrected, jamming the wheel around and gearing down and suddenly they were back on the road again. Beside him Dundee was checking to see if the magazine in the automatic Peter Fleming had given him was full. "I want him alive if possible," he said. "But dead if necessary. He can't be allowed to get away with those secrets."

Fleming said nothing, simply nodding and gripping the wheel tightly. On their right, barely a quarter of a mile away, the steep slopes of Craeg Moihr and Tom Chrochaire rose up out of the dead ground, bare of trees or brush or grass; cold, wet stone leaping straight up to the high pastures five hundred feet away. To their left loomed the gaunt cliffs of Ben More and above that the heavily forested slopes of the mountain itself, the trees combing great shreds of mist, most of the higher reaches of the great dark mound lost in the rain.

Ahead they could see where the road curved around a rise in the heath and wound its way up the farther cliffs that dropped right down into the sea. According to Tommy Connery's uncle, the road serviced half a dozen tiny outposts on the way to the landing place for the boats to the Island of Iona, an ancient holy place that lay at the entrance to the loch. They weren't about to try it; the road looked like no more than a goat track disappearing up into the mist.

In front of them, now, they could see where the road divided, one branch continuing up along the cliff edge, the other meandering off to the right between a row of sand dunes that shielded their view of the water. Fleming slowed, then pulled over to the side of the road. He switched off the engine. Suddenly there was only silence.

"Listen," said Dundee, straining to hear. Jane leaned forward in her seat. Faintly, in the middle distance, she could hear the sound of a foghorn. A few seconds later its moaning, ghostly response came eerily back from the enclosing cliffs.

"It's her," whispered Fleming. "The *Hebrides Trader*. She's here."

"Come on," said Dundee, climbing out of the car and jamming the automatic into the waistband of his trousers. Fleming followed and Jane clambered out of the backseat. The mist and rain were like a wet towel wrapped around her, soaking through her cloths and making it somehow difficult to breath. She knew that if she screamed right now the sound would be swallowed up and smothered. She couldn't see much more than a few yards ahead.

They moved away from the road, angling themselves in the direction of the dunes. According to the innkeeper there had once been a settlement of peat-cutters and crofters who came in seasonally and had their small, rude houses by the shore, but they had vanished long ago, simply leaving one autumn when the leaves turned and there was frost on the hills, never returning. A northern mystery there was no explanation for.

A moment or two more and they came to a narrow stream that seemed to leap down through the rocks and cols of the steep slopes of Ben More before it quieted on its course in front of them. There was a low stone bridge and beside it a tiny chapel, the only thing indicating its purpose an ancient Celtic cross. Other than that it looked like some sort of old stone shelter, open on one side, the arch in front sagging, the stone roof half collapsed into the interior.

For an instant Jane was sure she spotted a small, lone figure dressed all in black, wearing hip waders and casting his line into the narrow, bubbling stream on the far side of the bridge. He seemed to smile and wave and then the mist swallowed him up again. She almost waved back but she didn't think anyone would understand. Instead she followed Dundee and Fleming across the bridge to the sand dunes beyond.

"Look," said Fleming as they reached the top of the nearest dune. He dropped down to the ground and the other two followed suit. They could see down to a narrow foreshore between the stream and a beach of stone and slate. Built close to the stream just before it raced down to the sea, half a dozen decrepit old sod-roofed cottages huddled against the cold and the mist coming in from the water. The glass in their windows was gone, if it had ever been there at all, and their doors were empty holes in the stone. Far out in the loch they could now hear the heavy pulse of engines and the squeaking sound of davits being swung out; they heard the muffled sounds of seamen calling back and forth to each other.

"They're lowering a boat," Fleming whispered. He dug into the pocket of his pea jacket and pulled out a compact pair of Zeiss Featherweight binoculars. He handed them to Jane. "Got these in San Francisco, remember?" he said. Jane didn't bother answering; instead, she took the binoculars from him and focused on the little clutch of dwellings beside the sea.

It took her a while but eventually she found what she was looking for; a single rutted track in the ground, running up to the furthermost cottage. She wasn't sure but she thought she saw the curl of the Harley's front mudguard peeping out from the rear of the building.

"Last hut on the right," she said. "Farthest from the stream." She handed the binoculars back to Fleming.

"The boat's coming in," said Dundee.

Fleming turned and looked out at the slate-colored water, refocusing the binoculars. A few seconds later a small boat appeared out of the fog, chugging toward shore. It was some kind of ship's launch, sixteen or eighteen feet long with an inboard motor and no cabin. There was one person in it, standing at the controls.

"I don't recognize him," said Fleming. He handed the binoculars to Dundee. He took them and swung his attention toward the launch.

"I do," said Dundee. He handed the glasses to Jane. She looked.

"Selkirk," she breathed. "I'll be damned."

"It fits," said Dundee. "It had to be someone like that."

"Who, pray, is Selkirk?" asked Fleming politely.

"He worked at Shepton Mallet Prison. Obviously one of Charlie's boys."

"What are we going to do now?" said Jane.

"Arrest them both," said Dundee.

"Wait," said Fleming. "Let's see if your man Selkirk has the goods."

They watched as the launch moved warily into shore. Twenty yards out, Selkirk leaned down and they saw him fiddling with something below the narrow windscreen. A moment later they heard the sound of a bell ringing. Once, twice, three times, then silence, then two more rings. Some kind of signal. A few seconds later a figure appeared in the doorway of the last crofter's cottage by the stream. It was Charles Danby, dressed in casual country clothes, including an Ivy League cap. He was carrying a ship's lantern, which he raised and lowered twice in response to Selkirk's signal. The engine on the launch burbled more loudly and the small boat approached the shore. Selkirk jumped out of the boat with a line and anchor in his hand. He thrashed his way through the last foot or so of water, getting his trousers soaking wet, then tossed the anchor onto the beach. He walked up the slippery stone beach, his hand outstretched and a broad grin on his face as Danby came down toward him. In place of the lantern Danby now carried an automatic exactly like the one clasped in Dundee's fist.

"Damn and blast!" muttered Fleming. "The bugger's going to shoot him!"

The two men met on the beach and Danby put away the gun and warmly shook Selkirk's hand, then clapped him on the back. They turned and went back up the beach toward the crofter's cottage, faint sounds of laughter crossing to the three people watching from the shelter of the dune. A few seconds later they reached the cottage and went inside.

"What's he doing?" said Jane.

"Reporting in," said Dundee. "They're congratulating each other."

Another few minutes passed and then the two men appeared again. Selkirk was now wearing the MP's uniform and leather motorcycle leggings. As Dundee watched, the younger man went behind the cottage and dragged out the heavy Harley-Davidson. Selkirk threw one leg across the pillion and settled himself into the saddle. The two men stood talking.

"Bugger me!" said Fleming suddenly, realizing what was about to happen. "They're trading places! He'll see the car when he goes up the road!" Down by the cottage Selkirk lifted himself off the saddle and pounded his booted foot down on the starter pedal. The big engine roared into life.

"Stop him!" Dundee hissed angrily. Fleming slithered back down the backside of the dune, then clambered to his feet and began to run, dragging his own weapon out of the pocket of his pea jacket. Jane and Dundee looked back to the cottage. There was no sign of Danby; he'd completely vanished.

"Where the hell did he go?" asked Jane.

"Back into the hut," said Dundee. "Now's our chance." He paused and gave her a quick look. "You stay here." He got to his feet and sidestepped down the seaward side of the dune in a crouch, heading quickly down the beach to the abandoned buildings.

"I don't think so, pal," muttered Jane. "I lost you once. I'm not going to let you sneak out on me again." She stood up and followed him, running hard.

She caught up with him just in front of the dark entrance to the cottage. Dundee put up a warning hand. He lifted the automatic, peering into the dark recesses of the little building.

"Come on out, Charlie."

"What?" said a laughing voice from behind them. "You've got me surrounded, Ten Spot?"

Jane whirled. Danby was three feet from her back, his automatic pointed halfway between her shoulders and her waist. In his other hand was a bulging leather briefcase. He looked perfectly at ease except for a hot, almost maniacal gleam in his eye. He'd won the prize, and she and Dundee were just a last, irritating detail to be dealt with.

"I could see you out there by the dunes." He grinned. "Selkirk couldn't see it but I could." He paused. "Drop your weapon."

"There's MPs everywhere, Charlie," said Dundee. "You can't get out of this one."

"You're lying. Selkirk is the only MP within a hundred miles of this place, and he's *mine*," said Danby. "And I can get out. I *am* out as a matter of fact. You being here makes it perfect."

"How's that, Charlie?"

"Why don't we discuss it in the boat?" said Danby. "I'm on a bit of a tight schedule here."

"What if I say no?"

"Don't be stupid, Lucas," said his old schoolmate. He lifted the pistol in his hand slightly. "You know exactly what this thing will do to your lady friend's insides. You really want her to go out like that, Ten Spot?" A small note of anger was creeping into his voice. She caught Dundee's eye but he ignored her, concentrating on Danby. "Now get into the boat, both of you."

Dundee gave her an almost imperceptible nod and she did the same in reply. She moved carefully and Dundee stepped out of the doorway to the cottage. Danby backed up, staying well out of Dundee's grasp, even though he was unarmed. They moved down the beach, feet crunching on the pieces of water-worn slate and small, smooth stones. Danby followed, the gun in his hand never wavering. Out in the loch, the foghorn on the *Hebrides Trader* moaned loudly.

"Sounds like your friends are anxious to leave," said Dundee.

"You let me worry about that, Ten Spot; you start figuring out what kind of story you and your friend here are going to tell St. Peter when you get to the Pearly Gates."

"You sound like George Raft," said Jane, and laughed.

"Shut up and get into the boat," said Danby, flushing slightly at her quip. Jane had met Raft a few times at the Stork and she'd been surprised to discover that the actor was exactly the same off-screen as on. One of his favorite dinner guests at Billingsly's club was Eddie Florio, the scar-faced head of the New York Longshoreman's Union.

Dundee and Jane waded out into the freezing water, then boosted themselves over the gunwales. "In the stern," said Danby. They did as they were told, seating themselves on the rear transom. Jane's hands were plunged deeply into her pockets against the cold. She wondered briefly what Tweedsmuir would do under the circumstances. She could almost hear the man's soft, educated voice.

Don't give away all your secrets yet. Always hold something in reserve.

Danby dropped the briefcase into the boat and then tossed in the line and anchor. He climbed into the boat, keeping his eyes on the pair as he swung his legs over the side. Still watching them he pressed the starter button on the launch's polished wood dashboard, then engaged the small gear lever on the port-side coaming, putting the inboard engine into reverse, sending them slowly out into deeper water.

Jane noticed two boxes at his feet, both sheet metal and carefully made, one large and square with a leather strap riveted to the top, the other long and narrow. A hat box and a case for a treasured pool cue. The missing jewels. There were no identification numbers on the boxes. She nudged Dundee and pointed with her chin. He nodded briefly. Beside the two boxes was the plain, soft-sided leather briefcase, bulging with documents. Turing's codes and Tube Alloys, and according to Fleming the larger treasure by far.

Danby hit the shift lever with the ball of his thumb and spun the wheel to starboard, sending them around in a tight circle and pointing them out into the loch. Directly ahead of them now, the high, black side of the *Hebrides Trader* rose like a cliff. Bending down again briefly, Danby took a pair of handcuffs out of his pocket, snapped one bracelet around the briefcase handle and left the other dangling. He threw the briefcase down the length of the launch, where it landed at Dundee's feet.

"Put it on," he ordered.

Dundee picked up the briefcase and looked at it. "Why?"

"Because I'll shoot your girlfriend in the belly and then throw her overboard so you can watch her drown if you don't."

Dundee put the second bracelet around his wrist and closed it.

"There's enough real documentation in there to make them believe you were part of it from the beginning . . . if it survives your watery grave. A nice bit of stage dressing, though; give Wild Bill something to wonder about," he said. "The rest of it's in here along with his Majestey's ancestral head-dress." He kicked the square box, laughing. "I can just see Adolf prancing around Berchtesgaden with the stupid thing on his head. Mad King Ludwig rides again; just his kind of thing don't you think?"

"You don't care about being a traitor?" said Dundee.

"I only care about making sure I'm a *rich* traitor," said Danby. "Rich enough so that I don't need the old man's money any more." He laughed again. "Or maybe I'll just buy Switzerland and settle down."

"You're crazy," said Dundee flatly.

Jane stared at the boxes at Danby's feet, thinking hard. She'd been watching from the dunes the whole time, and neither Danby nor Selkirk had come out to the boat. Ergo, the two boxes had already been here. Why?

Why would Selkirk bring him the boxes when Danby was just going to take them right back to the Hebrides Trader?

The answer was obvious.

He wouldn't.

There had to be another boat, one big enough and fast enough to take him across to Ireland and the safety of a neutral country.

There was the sudden, unnaturally hollow echo of a much larger engine starting up nearby. Jane looked around in the fog. Nothing

Danby, grinning broadly, reached out with his left hand and threw the gear lever into idle. The boat slowed and they began to drift toward the stark cliffs of Ben More, a hundred yards or so away. According to Tommy's uncle, one of Mull's most interesting and macabre tourist attractions was up there somewhere, lost in the fog; in the late 1800s, in the tiny village of Gribun, perched between the cliffs and the wooded slopes above Loch na Keal, a newlywed couple came for their honeymoon, having rented a cottage at the point where the waters from Loch Ba on Ben More's heights became the river that eventually wound its way down to the sea. On their wedding night a great storm rose, dislodging a boulder from the heights, supposedly weighing more than ten thousand tons. The boulder fell directly on the love-bird's cottage, crushing them instantly.

The boulder could still be seen, surrounded by the cottage's garden wall. Directly below that at the base of the cliffs was McKinnon's Cave. According to the stories, the ghosts of the newlyweds could still be heard on stormy nights, howling like banshees with unresolved desire. The cave was so large that, according to legend, it went right through the island, easily twice the size of Fingal's Cave on Staffa and more than large enough to hide a good-sized boat at high tide.

The powerful, twin screw Thorneycroft came barreling out of the entrance to the cave at a good twenty knots, piling up huge bow waves as she plowed through the dark, freezing water of the loch. Jane had a brief glimpse of the rotund figure with his owlish spectacles, standing grimly behind the wheel, and the name on her bow: *Lady Beryl II*.

"Bond!" she whispered. The boat, five times the size of their small launch, didn't seem to be slowing down at all. She caught a movement out of the corner

of her eye and turned, just in time to see Danby
aiming his weapon at Dundee. There was no time to
wait for the proper moment; it was now or never.
She fired first, squeezing the trigger of the little pearl-
handled automatic from Tweedsmuir's glove compartment, blowing a smoking hole in her jacket
pocket and then in Danby's thigh, spinning him
around and flipping him out of the boat just as he
fired at Dundee, striking him in the shoulder.

An instant later the *Lady Beryl II* was on top of
them, her welded-steel stem cutting through the ash-
and-fir skin of the launch like paper. She heard the
stuttering of an automatic weapon and had a brief,
unlikely vision of the plump little ornithologist rak-
ing the remains of the launch with a lethal-looking
machine pistol. Then she was thrown into the loch,
swallowed up by the dark waters.

The passage of the *Lady Beryl II* forced Jane even
deeper under. For a moment she didn't know which
way was up. Aware only of the freezing cold and
the searing heat of her exploding lungs she pushed
herself to the surface, clawing off the heavy tweed
jacket as she did so. She caught hold of the broken
transom of the launch as it drifted by and searched
around frantically for Dundee. She coughed, retching
sea water and dragged her arm across the transom.
In the distance she saw Bond's Thorneycroft charging
west into the fog, the only sign that she'd ever been
there the widening *V* of her vanishing wake.

"Lucas!" she yelled, and then choked as small
waves crashed into her face. She coughed and
retched and called again. "Lucas!"

Dundee rose out of the water, clutching Danby
with a strangulating elbow wrapped under his chin.

They struggled wildly and then Dundee managed to get his hand up, the open manacle between his thumb and forefinger. He snapped it around Danby's wrist, then heaved himself backward, out of the way of the man's windmilling arms. Danby's head went underwater and then he came up again, one hand smacking at the water. He was screaming, eyes wide with terror. In the distance, the sound of *Lady Beryl II* was finally lost, overwhelmed by the sudden, deep-throated sound of the *Hebrides Trader* as her engines throbbed into life again. Her funnel whistle shrieked.

"Dundee!" Danby's head went under again, chin tilted back, horrified eyes looking up at the rain. Jane watched, but he didn't come up again. She looked everywhere, but there was no sign of the Crown and the Sword either.

"He couldn't swim," coughed Dundee, paddling toward her. "It was one thing I always did better than him."

Twenty-nine

"I'm still not quite sure I understand all the fine points," said Dundee, walking ahead of Jane and Fleming. "Tell it to me again: who was Bond?"

Their footsteps rang on the metal steps leading to the upper level of the Women's Wing at Shepton Mallet. Mr. Johnson, the Keeper of Special Acquisitions at the Public Records Office was leading the way, his feet making an odd little *pitter-pat* like a scuttling mouse. Dundee was back in uniform, still wearing a sling from Danby's parting shot.

"An assassin," said Fleming. "We've known about him for some time, or at least his existence. The James Bond identity is new, though. There is one, and he is an ornithologist; he just doesn't look anything like your fellow. We've known him by the name of Charles Calthrop, but even that name may be wrong."

"Why an assassin?"

"To kill Danby and relieve him of his treasures, presumably."

"You're saying that the assassin was hired by the Nazis, as some sort of double cross?"

"No. We know exactly who hired him, as a matter

of fact. A man named Anatoli Borisovich Gorsky. He works for a branch of the Soviet Service called SMERSH. 'Death to Spies' or something appropriately melodramatic. Gorsky was your man on the train, according to your description. He used to be called 'The Pianist' by the way: his father was a piano tuner in St. Petersburg before the revolution, hence his love of Mendelssohn. He killed Moneypenny and saved you from Occleshaw. He had to give Danby enough time to get the papers out of here. He had to keep interest focused on you and Lucas."

"Are you saying Danby was Communist?" asked Jane.

"We think Danby was working for anyone who'd hire him, playing one off against the other. The Soviets found out about Turing and Tube Alloys through a man MI5 has been watching named Cairncross, who works at the Foreign Office. He and a little group of Cambridge poofs are all involved with the plight of the working man, apparently, although God knows what a bunch of upper-class fops like that would know about it; at any rate, the Reds decided they wanted first crack. Presumably Bond was supposed to pick him up, carry him out into the Irish Sea, then, when he wasn't looking, blow his bloody brains out, saving everybody else the trouble."

"So now nobody gets the information," said Dundee.

"Too bad we had to lose the crown jewels in the process," said Fleming

"Don't be so sure of that," said Dundee. "That's one piece of the puzzle that never really fit."

They reached the door to cell 17 and Johnson silently turned his key in the lock. He swung the door open and flipped on the light. Everything was exactly as it had been before. The room was still packed from floor to ceiling with cardboard boxes, each with a penciled number on the side. 1790 and 1791 were still missing, the rest of the boxes sagging around the hole.

"I hope there's some point to all of this," said Johnson, a note of petulance in his voice.

"There's a point," said Dundee. He stepped forward and, using one hand, manhandled box 1789 until he'd turned it back to front. On the rear of the box was the penciled number 1790.

"Good lord," said Johnson. He blinked, not understanding. Neither did Jane.

"Open it," said Dundee.

The small man from the PRO did just that, taking a small penknife out of his vest pocket and carefully slitting open the top. He tipped the box forward and peered inside.

"Dear God," he whispered. Inside was a black leather box with a brass handle on the top and a hinged door on the side. Johnson rested the container on one of the surrounding boxes and pulled open the small door. Inside, encased in white satin, was an immense crown of pearls, rubies, emeralds and sapphires. In the center was the famous 317.4 carat stone cut from the Cullinan diamond.

"Look around," said Dundee. "You'll find the sword somewhere in here too. I guarantee it." At that, Johnson began to scuttle among the boxes, muttering to himself.

"I don't get it," said Jane, her fingers itching for a camera. Her eyes stayed glued to the Imperial Crown.

"I said it at the time." Dundee smiled. "Danby couldn't have done it, not with all the guards and everything else. So if he couldn't have done it, that meant he'd done something else. He only needed to make it *look* as though they were gone anyway, to distract us. All these cardboard boxes look alike; he just switched them back to front. He needed a way in and out, so he gave us a tunnel." Dundee paused. "It never really made sense; you only make a copy if you mean to put it in place of the thing it's copying; he never made the slightest attempt to make it look as though the jewels *hadn't* been stolen, because that's exactly what he meant us to think. The real purpose of the copy was to impress Hitler and various other people along the way, I suppose, like Chambers-Hunter and his Scottish Fascist friends. Striking a blow against England sounds a lot better than stealing secret papers and auctioning them off to the highest bidder."

Jane straightened, looking away from the crown. She rubbed the surface of the silver cigarette case in her pocket. The inscription inside had been revealed when she smoked the last cigarette, and now she knew who Tweedsmuir really was:

**To Governor General, Baron Lord Tweedsmuir
of Elsfield
"John Buchan"
From a Grateful Nation
February, 1940**

She turned to Dundee. "I think," she said quietly, "that it's time to go fishing and think about absent friends."

Author's Note

An American Spy is, in terms of factual detail and description, a true story. During WWII, the Crown Jewels of England were removed from the Jewel House of the Tower of London and distributed to various hiding places for safekeeping early in the war. The Imperial Crown and the Sword of State, among other pieces, were sent to Shepton Mallet Prison along with a number of valuable and important documents including the Domesday Book and Magna Carta. Also included among the documents were all the transcripts of Alan Turing's work on the Ultra code-breaking equipment used to decrypt the German Military Codes at Bletchley Park, as well as all information on file in the Public Records Office concerning Tube Alloys, the code name for the British development of the atomic bomb, which began in 1940 in cooperation with the Manhattan Project. The joint aspects of Tube Alloys were broken off in 1943, due to what the United States felt were glaring security problems with the British effort. The Imperial Crown and the Sword of State were mysteriously "misplaced" for several weeks during 1942 and then just as mysteriously reappeared. No official explanation was ever given for this.

Shepton Mallet Prison existed, and in fact exists today, as and where it is described. Shepton Mallet was the prison on which *The Dirty Dozen* is based. Every American GI executed in the European Theater of Operations was hung there, with the exception of Private Eddie Slovik, executed by firing squad in France for desertion.

All the information regarding Lord Tweedsmuir is accurate, including the description of his "shooting box" and fishing lodge in Scotland. It is much the same as his description of the bald archaelogist's farmhouse in his novel, *The Thirty-Nine Steps.* Some facts about Tweedsmuir-Buchan have been altered slightly to suit the plot of *An American Spy,* particularly Tweedsmuir's death: he died suddenly and unexpectedly in Montreal, Canada, in February of 1940, at which time he was Governor General of that country. He was sixty-five years old. The pearl-handled automatic is accurate and was generally kept in the glove compartment of his car.

The Scottish Fascist Party existed, and was investigated by MI5 on several occasions during the war as a possible source of sabotage and espionage. William Wier Gilmour and William Chambers-Hunter (the one-armed man) were real people. In addition to being an ardent Nazi, Chambers-Hunter also owned the Scottish Trader shipping company, including the *Hebrides Trader*.

The Isle of Mull, Salen, the Tangle of the Islands and Loch na Keal are accurately described.

Tommy Connery is Sean Connery's real name and

he was inordinately fond of both the novel, and later the film version of *Shane*. He was very large for his age, worked for a dairy in Edinburgh as a milkman's assistant and has a tattoo of a leaping tiger on his right forearm. As far as I know he had no uncle on Mull, but the chance of having the real Sean Connery meet the real Ian Fleming, not to mention the real James Bond, was simply too good to pass up!

Fleming really was a naval commander and Intelligence officer during the war, and his older and (then) more famous brother Peter, a well-known travel writer, actually did work for SOE, and at one time was head of a strange, and short-lived organization that was to act as a British Resistance in the event that Germany invaded.

James Bond really was an ornithologist and he really did inspire Fleming, at least in the use of his name. The two met in the late fifties. Interestingly, there may be considerably more to the story, especially when you consider what perfect cover being a birdwatcher is. Of the six major political assassinations from 1939 to 1961, including various attempts on Charles De Gaulle, the successful assassination of General Sikorski, head of the Polish Government in Exile during the war and the successful killing of Dominican dictator Rafael Leonidas Trujillo, James Bond the ornithologist was always nearby. Frederick Forsyth, the well-known thriller writer and one-time spy in his own right, tips his hat to this odd coincidence on two occasions: his assassin, the Jackal (Charles Calthrop) is described as being a birdwatcher and is also credited with the killing of Trujillo. In his later book *The Dogs of War*, when his unnamed mercenary character goes to the small African country in question, the cover he uses is an ornithologist.

Anatoli Borisovich Gorsky, the KGB chief of station in London at the time the book is written, really did have a weakness for ties with birds on them, particularly the silk Hardie-Amies brand, which he purchased (once again coincidentally) at a shop in London's Burlington Arcade directly beside Morlands, the tobbaconist where Ian Fleming purchased his Russian Samokish cigarettes.

You never know. . . .

Acknowledgments

First and foremost I would like to gratefully acknowledge the help and understanding of my editor, Doug Grad, who helped me through an extremely difficult time. My apologies for the lack of apostrophes. I'd also like to thank the long, nameless list of librarians in England, Scotland and Canada who helped with detailed information about the life and times of Governor General John Buchan, Lord Tweedsmuir. I would also like to thank Michael Feeney Callan for his excellent biography of Sean Connery, John Cork of the Ian Fleming Foundation, John Pearson for his biography *The Life of Ian Fleming* and the Reverend Alfred Weston, Bungay, Suffolk, for digging through the parish records to discover what he could about the mysterious author of *Birds of the West Indies*, James Bond. Bond's book, by the way, is now in its fifth edition. Last, but not least, I would like to thank Mariea—wife, nurse, mother and unheralded saint.

**If you like danger, international
intrigue, and secrets
that stretch back hundreds of years . . .**

. . . you're sure to love
Paul Christopher's

MICHELANGELO'S
NOTEBOOK

*Read on
for a special preview
of Paul Christopher's
new novel.*

*Available in June 2005
from Onyx*

Her hair was the color of copper, polished and shining, hanging straight from the top of her head for the first few inches before turning into a mass of wild natural curls that flowed down around her pale shoulders, long enough to partially cover her breasts. The breasts themselves were perfectly shaped and not too large, round and smooth-skinned with only a small scattering of freckles on the upper surface of each mound, the nipples a pale translucent shade of pink usually seen only on the hidden inner surfaces of some exotic seashells. Her arms were long and stronger-looking than you might expect from a woman who was barely five foot six. Her hands were delicate, the fingers thin as a child's, the nails neatly clipped and short.

Her rib cage was high and arched beneath the breasts, the stomach flat, pierced by a teardrop-shaped navel above her pubis. The hair delicately covering her there was an even brighter shade of hot copper, and in the way of most redheaded women, it grew in a naturally trimmed and finely shaped wedge that only just sheltered the soft secret flesh between her thighs.

Her back was smooth, sweeping down from the long neck that was hidden beneath the flowing hair. At the base of her spine there was a single pale red dime-sized birthmark in the shape of a horn, resting just above the cleft of the small, muscular buttocks. Her legs were long, the calves strong, her well-shaped ankles turning down into a pair of small, high-arched and delicate feet.

The face framed by the cascading copper hair was almost as perfect as the body. The forehead was broad and clear, the cheekbones high, the mouth full without any artificial puffiness, the chin curving a little widely to give a trace of strength to the overall sense of innocence that seemed to radiate from her. Her nose, topped by a sprinkling of a dozen freckles across the bridge, was a little too long and narrow for true classical beauty. The eyes were stunning: large and almost frighteningly intelligent.

"All right, time's up, ladies and gentlemen." Dennis, the life drawing instructor at the New York Studio School, clapped his hands sharply and smiled up at the slightly raised posing dais. "Thanks, Finn. That's it for today." He smiled at her pleasantly and she smiled back. The dozen others in the studio put down an assortment of drawing instruments on the ledges of their easels and the room began to fill with chatter.

The young woman bent down to retrieve the old black-and-white flowered kimono she always brought to her sessions. She slipped it on, knotted the belt around her narrow waist, then stepped down off the little platform and ducked behind the high Chinese screen standing at the far side of the room. Her name was Fiona Katherine Ryan, called Finn by her friends.

She was twenty-four years old. She'd lived most of her life in Columbus, Ohio, but she'd been going to school and working in New York for the past year and a half, and she was loving every minute of it.

Finn started taking her clothes off the folding chair behind the screen and changed quickly, tossing the kimono into her backpack. A few minutes later, dressed in her worn Levi's, her favorite sneakers and a neon yellow T-shirt to warn the drivers as she headed through Midtown, she waved a general good-bye to the life drawing class, who waved a general good-bye back. She picked up a check from Dennis on her way out, and then she was in the bright noon sun, unchaining the old fat-tired Schwinn Lightweight delivery bike from its lamppost.

She dumped her backpack into the big tube steel basket with its Chiquita banana box insert, then pushed the chain and the lock into one of the side pockets of the pack. She gathered her hair into a frizzy ponytail, captured it with a black nylon scrunchie, then pulled a crushed, no-name green baseball cap out of the pack and slipped it onto her head, pulling the ponytail through the opening at the back. She stepped over the bike frame, grabbed the handlebars and pulled out onto Eighth Street. She rode a block, then turned onto Sixth Avenue, heading north.

The Parker-Hale Museum of Art was located on Fifth Avenue between Sixty-fourth and Sixty-fifth Streets, facing the Central Park Zoo. Originally designed as a mansion for Jonas Parker—who made his money in Old Mother's Liver Tablets and died of an unidentified respiratory problem before he could take up residence—it was converted into a museum by his business partner, William Whitehead Hale. After seeing to the livers of the nation, both men had spent a great time in Europe indulging their passion for art. The result was the Parker-Hale, heavily endowed so that both men would be remembered for their art collection rather than as the inventors of Old Mother's. The paintings were an eclectic mix from Braque and Constable to Goya and Monet.

Run as a trust, the museum had a board that was gold-plated, from the mayor and the police commissioner through to the secretary to the cardinal of New York. It wasn't the largest museum in New York but it was definitely one of the most prestigious. For Finn to get a job interning in their prints and drawings department was an unquestionable coup. It was the kind of thing that got you a slightly better curatorial job at a museum than the next person in line with his master's in art history. It was also a help in overcoming whatever stigma there was in having your first degree from someplace like Ohio State.

Not that she'd had any choice: her mom was on the Ohio State archaeology faculty, so she had attended free of charge. On the other hand she wasn't living in New York for free and she had to do anything and everything she could to supplement her meager college fund and her scholarship, which was why she worked as an artist's model, did hand and foot modeling for catalogs whenever the agency called, taught English as a second language to an assortment of new immigrants and even babysat faculty kids, house-sat, plant- and pet-sat to boot. Sometimes it seemed as though the hectic pace of her life was never going to settle down into anything like normalcy.

Half an hour after leaving the life-drawing class, she pulled up in front of the Parker-Hale, chained her bike to another lamppost and ran up the steps to the immense doorway capped by a classical relief of a modestly draped reclining nude. Just before she pulled open the brass-bound door, Finn winked up at the relief, one nude model to another. She pulled off her hat, slipped off the scrunchie and shook her hair free, stuffing hat and scrunchie into her pack. She gave a smile to old Willie, the gray-haired security guard, then went running up the wide pink marble staircase, pausing on the landing to briefly stare at the Renoir there, *Bathers in the Forest*.

She drank in the rich, graceful lines and the cool blue-greens of the forest scene that gave the painting its extraordinary, almost secretive atmosphere and wondered, not for the first time, if this had been one of Renoir's recurring fantasies or dreams: to accidentally come upon a languorous, beautiful group of women in some out-of-the-way place. It was the kind of thing you could write an entire thesis about, but no matter what she thought about it, it was simply a beautiful painting.

Finn gave the painting a full five minutes, then turned and jogged up the second flight. She went through the small Braque gallery, then down a short corridor to an unmarked door and inside. As in most galleries and museums, the paintings or artifacts were shown within an inset core of artificial rooms while the work of the museum actually took place behind those walls. The "hidden" area she had just entered contained the Parker-Hale's prints and drawings department. P&D was really a single long room running along the north side of the building, the cramped curators' offices getting the windows, the outer collections areas lit artificially with full-spectrum overheads.

The collections were held in a seemingly endless number of acid-free paper storage drawers ranged along the inner wall. In between the shoulder-high storage cabinets were niches fitted with desks, chairs and large flat light tables for examining individual items. The light tables were made of a sheet of opaque white glass lit from beneath and held in a strong wooden frame. Each table was fitted with a photographer's copy stand for taking inventory slides of each print or drawing, and every second niche contained a computer terminal with the entire inventory of the collection entered on its database, complete with a photographic image, documents relating to the acquisition of the object and a record of the works' origins or provenance.

Finn's job for the entire summer consisted of checking that the inventory number, slide number and provenance number all matched. Grunt work certainly, but the kind of thing a twenty-five-year-old wet-behind-the-ears junior curator would have to get used to. What was it her mother was always saying? "You're a scientist dear, even if the science is art, and everything is grist for your mill."

Grist for your mill. She grinned at that, picked up a stenographer's notebook and a pencil from the stationery cupboard and went down the row of paper storage units to where she'd been working yesterday. After getting her degree, she'd spent a year in Florence, studying in Michelangelo's birthplace, walking where he'd walked and learning the language as well. Now *that* was grist for her mill, even if it did involve getting her butt pinched black-and-blue by everyone from the guy in the archives office to the goofy old priest in the library at Santo Spirito.

She wouldn't be mounting seminal shows of the works of Renaissance Florentine painters her first day on the job. Besides, she'd been promised that if she did well as an intern she'd be given a paid position next year. She wanted to be able to live in New York while getting her master's, but it was expensive, even when renting an Alphabet City dump like she did.

Willie appeared again, going on his rounds, fitting his key into the watchman's box and moving on. Other than that, the whole department seemed empty, which was just the way she liked it. She found the drawer she'd been working on yesterday, slipped on a pair of regulation white cotton gloves and started to work, jotting down numbers from the acetate covers on the drawings and then taking the numbers and sometimes the drawing itself to the niche to be compared to the information on the computer database.

After two hours she was yawning and seeing double but she kept at it. She finished one drawer and then started on the next, this one so low she had to drop down into a squat to get the drawer open. From that angle she saw that one of the drawings had slipped into a small crack at the back of the drawer and was almost invisible. Unless the drawer was completely open, the drawing would be easy to overlook.

Finn carefully pulled open the drawer as far as she could, then reached in blindly, feeling for the small edge of acetate she'd seen. It took a while, but she finally got her thumb and forefinger on it and gently pulled. Eventually it came free and Finn brought it into the light. She lifted it up to the top of the paper storer and used her toe to push the drawer closed while she took a closer look at the drawing. She almost fainted.

The drawing was approximately six inches by eight inches, rough cut at the left side or perhaps torn. Even through the acetate cover she could see that the paper was in fact high-quality parchment, probably lambskin, rubbed with chalk and pumice. At one time or another it had been part of a notebook, because at the bottom corner she could see evidence of stitching.

The illustration was done in a sepia ink, so old the lines had faded to spidery near-invisibility. The quality of the work was masterful, clearly dating from the Renaissance. It was a woman; the large breasts were clearly visible. She was wide hipped, almost fat. The head was not in the drawing, nor were the lower limbs or the arms.

What was extraordinary was the fact that the woman's body appeared to have been sliced open straight up the midline and the flesh and rib cage completely removed. The neck had been opened as well, revealing both the light tube of the jugular vein and the thicker and much more prominent carotid artery running up to and behind the ear. The lungs were bared as were the kidney and heart.

The liver was prominent and neatly drawn but the stomach appeared to have been removed to give a better view of the uterus and the opened vaginal barrel leading down from it. The cervix was carefully drawn in as were the labia at the other end. Ligaments and muscles supporting the uterus and the other organs were carefully included as were all the major veins and arteries of the circulatory system.

It was a beautifully rendered anatomical autopsy drawing of what appeared to be a middle-aged woman. There was only one thing wrong. Autopsies were not done in the Renaissance; it was called vivisection and the penalty for doing it was death. Leonardo da Vinci had been accused and tried for it although the charges had been dropped. Michelangelo, da Vinci's contemporary, had been accused but never brought to trial.

Over the years the memoirs of other artists and intellectuals stated that Michelangelo had, with the collusion of the church's prior, used the dead room at the Santo Spirito infirmary in Florence to do his drawings of bodies, but since Michelangelo's mythical notebook had never come to light there was no proof.

Finn continued to stare at the drawing. She had spent a year in Florence and most of that time was spent studying the work and times of Michelangelo. Even the writing running down the left and right sides of the drawing looked like examples she'd seen of his small, angular script. Without even pausing to think about it, she went to her pack and took out her little Minolta digital. She knew she'd catch hell if she was caught but she also knew she had to have an image of this to study at her leisure. It would be a perfect illustration for her thesis. Alex Crawley, the director of the Parker-Hale, was a stickler for policy, and there would be an endless stream of documentation, permissions and just plain paperwork before he allowed her to even so much as think of taking pictures. She took a dozen quick shots, then put the camera back in her pack, relieved that no one had seen her.

She carefully picked up the drawing, carried it to the light table and examined it more carefully, using a jeweler's loupe from the desk drawer. The handwriting was too faded to make out the words but she presumed it was notations made on the dissection of the woman's body.

According to existing documentation, when someone died at the Santo Spirito infirmary they would be placed in the dead room, wrapped in a sheet overnight, then sewn into a shroud and placed in a coffin the following day. Given a copy of the iron key to the dead room, Michelangelo would sneak in at night, dissect the corpse to examine whatever section of the body he was interested in at the time and sneak out again before morning.

He was supposed to have used some strange metal device to hold a candle at his forehead to light his way but Finn wasn't sure she believed it. She'd been given a tour of Santo Spirito, including the dead room. From what she'd read of the economics of the time she was reasonably sure money had changed hands between the artist and the prior. She was also fairly sure that the rumors and stories were true.

Now she was positive—the drawing she was looking at had not been drawn from memory but from life, or rather death. It slowly dawned on her what she had discovered: this was an actual page from the near mythical Michelangelo's notebook. Finn even knew who had done the binding: Salvatore del Sarto, the binder friend of Michelangelo's who regularly bound together the sheets of cartoons he used to apply his frescoes. But why was it shoved in the back of a drawer in the Parker-Hale and how did it get here?

She checked the inventory number on the acetate covering and jotted it down in the stenographer's notebook. Taking the notebook down to the next niche with a computer in it, she logged on, typed in the number and requested the scanned slide representation. Oddly there was none, just a blank white screen and the notation "Not Filed." She went back to the main menu and asked for any documentation relating to the inventory number and was given the name of a minor Venetian artist she vaguely remembered reading about named Santiago Urbino and a second number that took her back to the main menu and the provenance documentation files. The cross-index of image, artist and provenance all matched.

According to the computer file the drawing was by Urbino, had been purchased from a private collection by the Swiss branch of the Hoffman Gallery in 1924, sold again to Etienne Bignou Gallerie in Paris in 1930, to the Rosenberg Gallery in 1937 and finally from the Hoffman Gallery gallery again, sold to William Whitehead Hale on his last trip to Europe before the war in 1939. It had been part of the permanent collection of the museum ever since.

Finn went back to the main menu yet again and accessed the museum's biographical file on Santiago Urbino. A contemporary of both Michelangelo and da Vinci, Urbino was arrested for vivisection of animals for immoral purposes, excommunicated and eventually executed. Finn stared at the screen, pulling her hair back and holding it thoughtfully. It made sense historically, but she knew that a minor painter like Urbino simply could not have executed that drawing.

"May I ask what it is you think you're doing, Miss Ryan?"

Finn jumped and turned in her seat. Alexander Crawley, the director, was standing directly behind her, the Michelangelo drawing in his hand and a furious expression on his face.